PRAISE FOR FOG & FIREFLIES

"A mesmerizing and thought-provoking fantasy. In this remarkably imagined fantasy world where vulnerability is flipped, there is endless space for thematic exploration about responsibility and maturity, and Lehnen builds an intricate premise on this original narrative conceit. The novel overflows with creativity and offers some of the most unique world-building you'll find in a genre that can feel like everything has already been done. Lehnen is a masterful storyteller, and his realm of fear and fireflies practically glitters on the page."

— SELF-PUBLISHING REVIEW

"...a magical world that combines darkness and whimsy, old gods and mundane dangers, mythical backdrops and grounded descriptions.

[...] I have no doubt Lehnen has imagination enough to populate galaxies."

— MANHATTAN BOOK REVIEW

"Dark atmosphere with Pan's Labyrinth vibes. [...] The description is right: there is a noticeable similarity with the art of Hayao Miyazaki."

— FÉLSZIPÓKÁS ŐSMOLY

"Ogma is such a fun central character. She's tough and confident. At the same time, she has so much love to give, loyalty, and a strong sense of adventure.

[...] If you like found family, fantastical world building, and coming of age stories, you will enjoy this book. It is a YA novel, but I loved it as an adult, and would recommend it to those of all ages!"

— ADRIENNE ROZELLS, AUTHOR OF
CARYATID HEART (ALIEN BUDDHA
PRESS 2022) AND EDITOR-IN-CHIEF OF
CATCHWATER MAGAZINE

"An intriguing and engrossing novel, with characters— particularly Ogma—who readers will want to root for."

— KAREN COHN

"Master storyteller T.H. Lehnen's debut novel [...] Fog & Fireflies is a truly unique and enjoyable piece of fantasy fiction."

"Fog & Fireflies is a beautifully written dark fantasy YA novel about innocence, bravery, and the magic of found family that harkens towards the imaginative and wonderful world-building and storytelling of Hayao Miyazaki. T.H Lehnen's prose weaves together an incredibly vivid world full of magic and delight that leaves readers wishing for more.

[...] I loved Ogma as a strong female lead character as well as the other fantastical cast of characters we meet along the way."

"Lehnen's lyrical English intensifies the magical feel of his splendid fantasy tale. [...] I really hope there's a sequel to this gem."

"Reminiscent of folk tales whispered over a campfire[...]a world that is absolutely glowing with magic. [...] a book that you need to have on your shelf."

— JADEN J.

"The comparison to Hayao Miyazaki is absolutely spot on. The themes and story in Fog and Fireflies fit the Studio Ghibli vibe and you find yourself instantly warming to these characters. The setting as well is so vivid and I truly felt like I was there on the wall with those kids watching out for the fog.

[...] Ogma is definitely a new favorite character!"

— SHELBY KATE

"Lehnen's prose is captivating and his characters are a delight to read. The darker theme of the story kept me hooked and I found I was soon at a place where I couldn't put it down."

— MEG I.

FOG & FIREFLIES

T.H. LEHNEN

Aspen Thorn

AUDIENCE

This is a work of young adult fantasy, but whatever your age, if childlike wonder still lives in your heart, you will enjoy it.

SUBJECT MATTER

A primary theme of this work is parentification—the role reversal where children become the caretakers of their parents or siblings.

CONTENT WARNINGS

blood (minor), bones (animal), child labor, death, forced captivity, kidnapping, parentification, serious injury, violence

CREDITS

Producer - Bryan Walsh - hellabryan.com
Editor - Laura Burge - literarylaura.com
Cover Illustrator - Nic Ferrari - bramastudios.com

CONTENTS

Fantasy is escapist, and that is its glory. If a soldier is imprisoned by the enemy, don't we consider it his duty to escape? The moneylenders, the knownothings, the authoritarians have us all in prison; if we value the freedom of the mind and soul, if we're partisans of liberty, then it's our plain duty to escape, and to take as many people with us as we can.

— URSULA K. LE GUIN

CHAPTER 1
SHADOW PUPPETS

A sobbing, guttural moan drifted over the rampart. Ogma froze and, despite herself, she shivered. At fourteen seasons old, after eight walking the wall, she still had to remind herself not to heed the voices in the fog.

Ogma had made up her mind seasons ago that it was better to be angry than afraid. But on nights like this, the butterflies in her stomach had their own ideas.

She took a steadying breath and pushed the fear away.

The night was crisp and clear, and her breath hung in the air. Her cheeks were flushed and pinched in the cold. The stars shone brightly over the roofs of the sleeping village, wheeling and dancing, winking in and out as they always did when the fog was high. She studied the gray bank as shapes gently coalesced within its form and, just as gently and silently, dispersed. The moon had just risen and hung low and large, bright enough to cast shadows. Ogma searched the sky for the moon's smaller sister, but tonight she did not join the dance. The glow of the fog under the moonlight was beautiful.

Beautiful and cold, Ogma thought, and wrapped herself more tightly in her coat.

She glanced back at the town as Enki and Enoch tolled their quarter-night chime. She held her breath for a beat and listened. A moment later, Ogma heard the cheerful chords of the twins' bells from the rampart ahead of her, and the clear basso note of Cole's single bell more distantly behind.

Ogma sighed with relief and added the sorrowful minor chord of her own two bells.

The younger children had remembered—only the bells could be trusted. Ogma rang hers in the pattern that meant: *I'm here! I'm okay. Don't worry. Keep to your post.* The other children on the wall acknowledged her with their chimes again.

Most nights were better than this. Most nights the fog rolled in gentle drifts much further from the walls, quiescent. Most nights the ground was visible and voices could be trusted. On those nights, the growls and mutters beyond the wall were as likely to be beasts of flesh and blood as they were to be fog phantoms.

But even when voices couldn't be trusted, Ogma worried a cry for help might still be real.

She bit her lip, braced her hands against the stone rampart, and leaned out. The fog billowed back, away from her. Phantom shapes chittered and cajoled, egging her on to leave the walls, to come out to open ground where the fog could envelop her. Eyes straining against the gloom, she peered at the ground.

No one would be stupid enough to be out on a night like this anyway. No other towns had drifted close in weeks.

Trying to sort out shape from shadow in the fog was making her eyes cross. Ogma pushed herself back from the rampart and continued her patrol. The gently creaking frame of one of the village's great windmills silhouetted itself against the stars. At each of the eight corners of the wall, windmills turned, powered by heavy counterweights that teams of the village men cranked up during breaks in the fog when it was safe.

Though the blades moved ponderously slow to Ogma's eyes, she could feel the breeze. With each mill angled toward the next, they created a current that redirected the fog to flow around the walls to keep it from crashing over them.

Not for lack of trying. Phantom tendrils caressed the windmill blades.

Ogma grit her teeth and glared at the roiling bank. For just a moment it billowed back, retreated, and then the phantom voices laughed at her.

The mellifluous pealing of two sets of small bells in harmony brought Ogma back to attention.

It was the twins, Mae and Maya. Their patrol crossed hers as they went the opposite way around the wall. Ogma chimed her chord in response.

She turned once again to the walkway, peering into the night for the two approaching girls. At the midway point between this mill and the next, the fog sent gently probing tendrils out over the stones. The foremost of these were just curling over the wall's inner edge.

Berating herself under her breath, Ogma hurried her steps, glaring at the misty coils and shooing them with her gloved hands. The tendrils reared up, a hooded shape hissing and spitting, winding menacingly around her before dissolving as the coils tightened.

Ogma crossed her arms, staring down the bank—summoning anger to banish fear. Yet small shapes still seemed to dart beneath its surface, and rude and laughing faces briefly coalesced just out of sight.

Ogma tapped her foot.

The petulant fog gradually quieted into a placid sea once more.

The gentle harmony chimed closer, and Mae and Maya stepped up beside her. The twin girls were holding hands and bundled warmly against the cold, eyes shining with excitement even as they looked anxiously up at her. Ogma realized she was still glaring. She put on a smile instead.

"Ogma! *Ogma-aa*! Have you *ever* seen the fog so *thick*?" Maya piped, wide-eyed and bubbling.

Mae was too excited to let Ogma respond. "Did you know? Did you know? We saw the fog make horses! And a cat!"

Both girls were breathlessly cheerful, and Ogma's smile widened, though she kept her voice stern.

"Mae. Maya. It may be your first season on patrol, but you know why the fog makes those shapes."

They shuffled their feet, ruefully studying their shoes.

"Wheeler says it's playing tricks to lure us away from our posts," Maya droned in the voice of a child reciting an oft-repeated lesson.

Mae puffed out her small chest and adopted a serious expression, deepening her voice to try to match that of the older boy. "You must be ever watchful!" she intoned pompously, wagging her finger.

Ogma tried very hard not to laugh as the young girl put both hands on her hips and swept the fog with an imperious stare. Maya giggled behind her mittens.

"That's right," Ogma said seriously. "And you should listen to him. You know what would happen if the fog got over the wall. *I* remember if you don't."

The two girls' smiles faded, serious faces now genuine. "We remember," they said in unison.

Ogma's heart softened.

Mae shuffled her feet hesitantly. "D-did you hear the voice?"

The tight feeling in the pit of Ogma's stomach returned. She and Cole had both heard several voices out in the fog these past few nights. That was to be expected. *But that voice? It's the same every night.*

"Yes, I did," Ogma warned them, "and that just means the fog is trying extra hard to get you, so be careful, and don't listen to anything but the bells."

She saw the fear on their faces, but the excitement shone through as well.

They still think of it as a game. Was I ever that young? She wished she still was.

"You two get going to the next mill. Jory should be coming soon to replace you." Ogma shooed them with her bells, and the girls clasped hands and skipped on, chattering as they went.

Ogma went on her own way, to the mill the girls had come from, and settled in to wait for Brigid to spell her for the next shift. The windmill blades turned slowly, stirring whitecaps on the fog. She pulled off her gloves to warm her fingers with her breath.

Grumbling, she kept one 'ever watchful' eye on the fog and thought longingly of hot cider and a warm bed.

It was still deep night outside when Ogma woke, the echo of a moaning cry fading in her dream. Only a few hours before, Ogma had finished her patrol, stumbled into the watch house, and climbed into her favorite bunk. This upper bunk was hidden away in the back of the watchtower's great room. The bed and blankets were warm, and for a moment she did nothing more than burrow further into them, sliding her legs beneath the soft sheets and snuggling her face against her pillow. It was no use. She couldn't close her eyes without thinking of that voice. She frowned, and rolled onto her back.

She could hear the patter of rain on the roof, and she breathed in its clean scent on the gentle draft from the shuttered windows. The rain was good; a respite. It would tamp down the fog.

The warm, flickering glow of firelight played across the wooden logs of the ceiling. A charcoal drawing was dancing on the rafters. Ogma hadn't noticed it when she'd climbed wearily into bed after returning from her patrol on the wall. Some enterprising child had teetered on tiptoes atop the bunk to draw the strange-looking bird. Ogma tilted her head. *Or is it a mule?* Probably the work of the acrobatic and determined Ambrose.

The murmur of the children in the watch house, most of them younger, was a reassuring noise. Because the children did everything in shifts—patrol, chores, lessons—some of them were always awake. From their giggling across the room, she could tell Mae and Maya hadn't even tried to go to sleep yet. They were clearly still wound up from their patrol. From another cot she heard more children whining over the claim to favorite blankets, but they were hushed a moment later. The older children, those who hadn't been on patrol that evening, were always there to calm and care for the younger ones, and to put to bed those tired enough to fuss.

After so many seasons spent living together, they were all used to the tantrums and shrieks of the smallest children. It was tiring, and irritating, and loud, and sticky, and sometimes smelly, but also comforting. Mae and Maya might be giggling, but many of the older children had been quiet and withdrawn recently. The extended duration and malevolence of this fog bank worried them.

For Ogma, that worry never left. The pit in her stomach while on patrol became a tightness between her shoulders whenever off. She sighed and rolled over again, resting her cheek against the cool, polished wooden rail of the bunk as she looked down at the common room.

One of the youngest children was tugging on the sleeve of

the eldest, nearly in his seventeenth season, draped as he usually was across one of the low bunks nearest the fire.

"Wheeler? Are you awake?" she asked in a small voice. Wheeler was face down on the child-sized bunk and, having grown almost to his adult height, his feet dangled off the edge and his arms hung down either side.

He'll have to leave us soon, Ogma thought with sudden anxiety. She shoved that icy bolt of fear away to deal with later.

"Wheeler! Are—you—awake?!" the little girl whined.

Ogma smiled, propping herself up on one elbow to watch the familiar scene unfold. If he wasn't already awake, he soon would be.

"Can we have shadow puppets?" Emma was only five seasons old, but she was a seasoned expert at wheedling what she wanted out of the older children, especially Wheeler. Once they heard her ask, the other children—even those who should have been sleeping, or at least trying to, after long shifts on the wall—started to sit up and add their voices.

"Shadow puppets!"

"Shadow puppets!"

Wheeler didn't even roll over.

"Yeah, c'mon Wheeler! Do the shadow puppets." Cole, about Ogma's age, was one of the older boys and styled himself Wheeler's lieutenant. A beat later he added, self-consciously, "You know how much the younger kids like it." Ogma snorted and gave him a look.

The youngest children were beginning to gather by the fire, laughing and hooting, while the older ones sat up in their bunks.

Wheeler, for his part, was still stoically pretending to be asleep, despite the ruckus.

Emma tugged insistently at his blanket. He opened one eye in a mock glare, and swept it around the room, then closed it again, rolled over, and gave a terrific snore. The younger children groaned in frustration. The older ones chucked their pillows at him.

"Wheeler, wake up! Shadow puppets!" Emma's voice increased in pitch with that slight edge of a child about to get very frustrated and very loud. There was a breath of silence while the children waited for Wheeler's reaction.

He burst up from the bed, firing off pillows of his own and pawing back his unruly bedhead. He tossed little Emma over his shoulder, the little girl now giggling madly, and grinned at the cheering faces.

"All right you rascals! But you'd better not wake up anyone who's been on the wall tonight." And with that, he shot a look up at Ogma's bunk and gave her a wink—

—just in time to be hit in the face by her pillow.

"Just get on with it, you big lump!" She grinned. The other children back from patrol, all wide awake and bright-eyed, whistled their agreement.

"Phah. And in my own house." He put Emma down gently, turning up his nose and stalking over to the fireplace. The hubbub of children devolved into the sound of them loudly shushing each other.

Wheeler carefully pulled an old carven fireplace screen in front of the hearth, dimming the glow in the room until Ogma could see only silhouettes. He lit the end of a stick of kindling from the fire, and used it to light a dark lantern, sliding the metal hood around to focus a single square of light on the wall. Cracking his knuckles and narrowing his eyes in concentration, he grasped at the narrow beam of light with his hands, molding the shadows to his design like so much clay. He warmed up with a few basic shapes while the children looked on: first a bird in flight, then a dog barking, and then a goose. Each successive shadow cast on the wall looked more natural and lifelike.

Wheeler's talent with shadow puppets was magical.

Ogma had never been quite sure how he managed some of those shapes with only two hands. She was fairly confident, from careful observation, that some of the ones he could make had more legs than he had fingers. But then, her own experiments had only extended so far as making some very convincing shadow puppets in the shape of—well, her own hands. Though, to be fair, he did sometimes conscript one of the other children for the more complicated scenes.

Having limbered up, Wheeler made a horse gallop across the wall and leap into the air to become an eagle. The children gasped in delight. He gave a grunt of satisfaction, and a nod to little Emma who stood solemnly by his side, eyes shining, his ready assistant for the evening's storytelling.

He put a small wooden frame in front of the dark lantern, one that he had carved himself in seasons past, casting the silhouette of a rampart onto the wall. He'd carved several others: freestanding silhouettes of castles and towers, of trees and fantastic mountains, of caravan wagons and beasts—some on sticks he could hold between his fingers, or short poles he could prop against his knee. A few were on the ends of string so he could hang them from the rafters. His props in hand, he then reached behind the fireplace screen with the tongs and took up a smoldering coal, which he then carefully dropped into a tin bowl below the lantern. The children were finally, truly silent now—in rapt attention. A couple drops of water from his mug and a cloud of steam billowed from the bowl, casting a formless, shifting shadow that drifted across the silhouette of the rampart, laying siege.

Ogma shivered as Wheeler, whispering, began. The beginning of every story was the same.

"This is why we watch the fog."

. . .

"There once was a town where every house planted their grain on their roof, and the wall was built of red stone." Wheeler paused as the children closed their eyes, trying to imagine the foreign town. "This town wasn't like ours. In this town they had no windmills, and they had no bells."

Every child's hand went to the bells around their neck. Some gasped, and others just gave Wheeler a skeptical look.

Wheeler smiled and wrapped a kerchief around one thumb. His hand fluttered and the shadow of a child in a hooded cloak walked atop the wall.

"In this town was a young boy, and like all the children of the village, it was his duty to patrol the wall and keep his village safe."

"But Wheeler!" Emma interjected. "Wheeler, how do they keep it safe without the—"

"Shh..." Wheeler chuckled, tousling her hair. "Just hold on and I'll tell you."

Emma subsided, wide eyes intent on his face.

"It was the boy's first season patrolling by himself, and it's true, the town had no bells, and no windmills. The fog couldn't touch the children, of course, but it could slip between them— and if someone were lost, they had no way to find them again."

Ogma watched the faces of the other children. The youngest were frightened, the older shook their heads at the foolishness of these shadow villagers.

"But this village had something else." Wheeler picked up several puppet sticks between his fingers. At the end of each dangled a few pieces of rounded yellow glass, glued to strings. He paused to pour a trickle of water from his mug onto the hot coal.

Steam billowed with a hiss and the shadow mist boiled up to the edge of the wall where the hooded boy stood silhouetted. Little golden lights shimmered in the fog.

There were fireflies in the boy's eyes. He watched them dancing in the fog below. Wherever they went, the fog rolled back, swirling away and disappearing. The boy's chest swelled with pride. It was only his first season on wall patrol, but he was already the village's best firefly catcher. He pulled his hood back over his head and skipped over to one of the large leaded glass lanterns spaced evenly around the wall.

The lanterns were enormous. The boy could—and had—fit easily inside one without his head even brushing the top. This one was filled with a cloud of yellow-green lights, winking and dancing sedately. He pressed his eye to one of the leaded glass panes, liking the way the blurry glass distorted the lights and shapes within.

He opened the door carefully and slipped inside. He knew the glass was rare and expensive. If they broke even a small pane, it would be very hard to replace. They could patch the lanterns with rice paper, but the boy knew that wasn't as good.

His glowing friends landed on his hood and shoulders and buzzed their little greetings. He grinned and buzzed back at them, crouching to check their food.

The dish at the bottom of the lantern was still half full, he noted happily, but he topped it up from the jars on his belt anyway.

The villagers used to use sugar water or even beer to feed the fireflies, but the boy used milk and honey and his fireflies lasted twice as long as anyone else's.

The boy kept up his rounds, happily feeding the dancing fireflies while the stars danced above. He was halfway around the wall when he came across a lantern that was dark.

Crying out in dismay, he ran up to the lantern only to find that the door was hanging open and a small pane of glass had broken, smashed on the walkway of the red stone wall. The little plate of milk and honey was completely full.

The boy wrung his hands, not sure what to do. The wall was his responsibility. This was his first season—what if he was put back with the younger children? Even one empty lantern was a danger, especially if the fog got thicker.

He ran back and forth atop the wall, worrying his lip. The glimmer of yellow-green lights caught his eye. The fireflies he'd been watching before were still dancing just outside the wall. Even as he watched, the blinking lights seemed to grow in number until it seemed hundreds of the fog-banishing creatures lit the forest below.

The boy glanced over his shoulder at the town slumbering peacefully behind him. All those grown-ups asleep, counting on him to keep them safe. The night was clear, and with that many fireflies around... he made a decision. He rushed down the steps, scrambling down to the nearest gatehouse. He rummaged briefly for a firefly net and then dashed out through the wicket gate.

The gate was some distance down the wall from where he had seen the fireflies. Glancing up, he could see the darkened lantern standing forlorn and empty. He ran.

The fireflies had started to drift away. There were so many of them, and the boy had never seen them moving so purposefully into the trees. The trees were glowing green and yellow, winking in and out, but each time farther away.

He ran after them, through the trees, faster and farther away than he'd ever been from the town before. The fireflies were outpacing him. He almost cried in frustration. They'd always liked him! They'd always come to him and sat on his shoulders and buzzed happily in his ear.

Somewhere behind him, the fog rolled slowly in and the landscape shifted.

He tried to catch them up. He tried to follow them through the trees, but he wasn't as fast as some of the other children. Maybe if he'd been older. He ran on and on but before too long, he had to stop. He couldn't even catch his breath. At first, he was panting too hard to really notice where he was. Or more importantly, where he wasn't. He couldn't see the fireflies any longer.

Dread started creeping up his spine. He didn't want to look up from his feet. He didn't want to look around because he knew that if he looked behind him, the red stone walls of home would be gone. He sniffled and rubbed his nose in the dark.

Finally, he forced himself to turn around, and when he did, he couldn't see the lanterns of the town wall, no matter which direction he looked and no matter how well he could see them when he closed his eyes.

He was lost, and he knew it.

After he had cried for a while and no one came, he decided that nothing much would come of staying put, so he might as well keep going. He stood up, pulled his hood closer around him and started walking.

The world in the fog was strange. He might see a clearing through the trees ahead, but then the fog would roll through, and by the time he got there, all he would find was a thicket of brambles and a pile of old stones. He'd start to feel like he was walking uphill, only to roll his ankle as the fog shifted his path into a ravine or the bed of a small stream.

The fog didn't harry at his heels—but it stuck close, weaving sinuously across the ground ahead. Sometimes the landscape changed so fast it seemed the trees were walking; silhouettes marching across the sky. But the fog couldn't touch him directly and so, even though it threatened, it made no phantoms. The boy knew they could have done little more than gnash their teeth—he was much too young—but even so, he was glad they did not appear. They frightened him.

Eventually the boy found himself climbing a loose scree slope, tripping over small stones and sending larger ones tumbling down the hill.

Cresting the rise, the boy found himself looking down on a valley. His heart skipped a beat as he saw, deep in the furthest part of the valley, the glow of hundreds, even thousands of fireflies. He was so eager in his excitement that he scrambled down the slope, sending a cascade of stones and dust down the hill.

He didn't see the strange figure until he'd nearly bumped into it.

It was tall and slender, and covered in what were either dirty feathers or tattered rags. It had the beak of an enormous bird and its eyes were dark chasms in a polished white skull.

Fear transfixed him to the spot.

Eyes wide, he could only watch as the creature slowly approached. It seemed to find him as strange as he found it. It cocked its head to the side quizzically.

The boy held his breath.

And then it spoke, its voice a croak. "How old are you?"

The sound startled the boy out of his paralysis and he ran, brushing right past the creature and running flat out down the slope towards the distant yellow-green lights. He stumbled over the loose rocks, tumbling in the sandy soil and picking himself up to run again. The lights were fading. The drifts of fireflies were disappearing out of the far end of the valley. The boy was afraid again, but he kept running.

At the edge of the valley the landscape changed—back to woods—the trees unfamiliar but comforting after the stony, barren slope. The boy rushed on frantically between the boles of trees, trying to keep sight of the disappearing points of light.

He was about to give up hope again when a sudden noise stopped him dead in his tracks.

The sound was clear and pure and more beautiful than anything he'd ever heard before. It was a bell, pealing in the night.

He changed direction and headed for the sound. Wearily clambering over fallen trees, he suddenly found the fireflies all around him.

The tree line broke, and he found himself staring at a town. He nearly broke down for joy, but as he ran closer, he realized the walls were not his own. The walls were brown stone, not red, and there were no great lanterns keeping watch over slumbering inhabitants.

But there were villagers.

The boy hid himself behind the trunk of an old oak and watched anxiously.

These villagers were trying to catch the fireflies. They didn't have the big glass lanterns that were the pride of his own village, but it looked like they had some wicker and rice paper ones, and they were trying ineffectually to entice the bright insects with sugar water and sweep them into the lanterns.

Even as these proceedings went on, every once in a while a villager would ring a bell, and then all of the others would ring their bells back.

A girl, about the same age as the boy, had wandered further out from the rest, paper lantern in hand, trying to sweep the fireflies inside. Each time she swung the lantern at them, the fireflies drifted further away. She seemed frustrated and was chasing the small batch of fireflies closer and closer to the tree line.

The boy made up his mind.

He stepped out from behind the tree, holding his net shyly.

"You can't do it that way," he said. "All the air's trapped in the lantern. It pushes the fireflies right away." The girl looked at him in surprise.

"You need to use a net." The boy crept closer to the milling cloud of blinking lights. He made a friendly buzzing sound through his teeth. He swung his net slowly, gently through the air and turned back to the girl.

It was full of little lights, each one sitting calmly on the inner surface of the net. The girl looked at him for a moment, eyeing him skeptically. But the boy smiled hopefully and eventually the girl grinned in return. She began to ring her bell.

Events were a whirlwind after that, but the boy was happy and he'd made a friend. The villagers were friendly too, and he caught fireflies for them and did his part to protect the town. More than that, he felt this place could be his new home.

A few months later, as he and the girl were helping to fix a paper lantern on the wall, a great bell started ringing.

"Fog break!" a voice called out. It was a loud voice: a grown-up's voice. "Trade day!"

The village bustled into activity. As even the boy knew, fog breaks were a rare thing. Though sometimes the fog could settle down and leave a village quite safe for even days at a time, they didn't call it a trade day unless the landscape had brought another town in sight of the walls.

The boy ran with the others across the town, the stream of people becoming a spontaneous parade. Even the adults had come, carrying goods for trade and barter. Young men and women, probably only a few seasons off the wall, were stepping out into the cobbled streets. They were laughing and crying and gathering bundles of their belongings. The boy didn't understand that.

"Why's she crying?" he asked, gesturing to a young woman

who was smiling and hugging everyone around her, while tears stood in her eyes.

"She has to leave now," the girl explained, her own eyes shining.

"But why?"

"She's old now. When you're old, you have to go to a new town and find a trade."

The boy remembered this same rule from his home village. When children left the wall they had to prepare themselves to trade villages.

"But can't she find a trade here?"

"No. It's tradition. Half of us must go, and half may stay."

The boy found this hard to accept. He began to worry that one day he'd have to leave this new home he'd found, too.

"Come on!" The girl pulled him into the rush of people and he quickly forgot his worry.

The adults crowded onto the wall, while the children left by the wicket gate to check that the fog had indeed broken and that it was safe to make the crossing.

The girl tugged the boy out through the gate with the rest of the children, and they fanned out into the woods. The fog was nowhere in sight, but the night was dark. It was difficult to see the walls of the other town at first. They seemed just an ominous shadow against the dark, especially with the glare of their own lanterns.

Something about that dark silhouette was familiar.

The boy's heart sank. His steps faltered but the girl was eagerly pulling him on.

"Come on—it's a town! Another town!"

He dragged his feet and she turned to look back at him with concern. "What's the matter?"

He shook his head mutely.

The girl turned and looked.

"Why aren't there any lights?"

She raised her lantern.

The boy could just barely make out red stone walls with shapes atop that just might be giant glass lanterns—but all dark.

The boy began to cry. The girl looked back at him and up at the red stone walls in the distance. She cried with him.

"This story's too sad!" Emma objected. "It's too sad for the babies." She gestured in the direction of the bunk where the very few children younger than she were asleep under the watchful eye of the older ones.

Wheeler paused in his tale, handing her one of the firefly props—the crude glass wings at the end of the stick glimmering in the lantern light.

"True stories are often sad," Wheeler told the little girl, knuckling her on the cheek.

Something in the way he said it made Ogma want to cry. She didn't understand it. Sure, it was a sad story, but she'd heard sadder stories before and had seen worse things with her own eyes. But there was something about it. She'd even told Wheeler once, when she was the young one 'helping' with the shadow puppets, that she liked the sad stories. Something in the heartache of a sad story or a sad song helped her to sleep.

Wheeler was looking at Emma kindly. "Too sad then? Shall I stop here?" There were some grumblings of protest and mutinous whispers from the other children, but Wheeler silenced them with a look, and turned back to Emma for an answer.

Emma rubbed one eye, considering the glass firefly with the other. "No..."

"Okay then." Wheeler clapped his hands and took up the tale again.

The boy grew up, and so did the girl with the bell, and gradually the shock and sadness of the lost town faded. They were now among the oldest who still walked the brown stone wall in the brown stone village that was once so strange but had become the boy's home.

They were inseparable. They traded shifts so they could patrol together. They ate together. They watched the dancing stars together. Some of the adults gave them looks, and whispered behind their backs. But the boy had already come from another village, as the girl would loudly point out if any of the elders complained, and so for the most part the village was happy for them.

Eventually, they were the oldest children who still walked the wall. And then, the oldest that anyone could ever remember doing it. But the boy kept catching his fireflies, and he liked the way they looked in her hair, and the fog never seemed to bother them.

One day they were out walking together, looking for fireflies. They were older, and they thought themselves wise, and together they were unafraid of anything the fog could offer.

But as they laughed together, holding hands and resting on an old fallen log, the fog stole up around them.

The boy saw it first. It was drifting slowly between them and the wall.

He leapt to his feet and rushed forward, waving his arms to send the sneaking tendrils swirling back. He could feel something wrong in the fog that night. It danced away from him mockingly. He rushed towards the wall.

"Come on!"

He turned back. The girl stood stock still, quaking in fear as the fog whispered and swirled around her. An insubstantial hand caressed her cheek.

The boy sprinted back and grabbed her by the arm, pulling her away from the swirling mist. They ran—dropping their nets and lanterns, heads down, as fast as they could towards the wall.

The boy burst through a bank that had curled up behind them, crashing into the wall headfirst. Lip split, the taste of blood filled his mouth. He staggered, disoriented, trying to remember where he was, what he was running from... and then he realized that the girl was no longer holding his hand.

It took her. It had snatched her away, disappeared her—like she was a grown-up.

The boy shouted and called out for her and rang the bell she'd given him, but her bell didn't ring back. The boy got angry and desperate. He tried to make the fog take him, too. He waited outside the walls, tried to let it touch him, tried to touch it, but it kept fading away from him. As if he were still a child. Though he was no more a child than she.

His throat was hoarse, his heart ached. But he had no tears left to cry. The boy straightened his back and walked into the fog.

He wandered in the fog for many seasons. But no matter where he wandered—no matter how old he got—the fog never touched him, never took him. He was always a child to the fog, and though it changed the landscape, it never changed him.

One day he was taking shelter from the rain in a small cave in the side of a scree slope. In the cave he found rags, old bones, and the skull of a great bird. He recognized these things—recognized the hollowness that matched his own—and dressed himself in them.

As he was leaving the cave and climbing the hill, a small boy stumbled into him, panting with exertion, but rigid with fright. He cocked his head to the side, puzzled, and asked the boy, "How old are you?" But the boy ran on, brushing past him down the slope.

The man walked into the night, thinking about the boy with fireflies in his eyes.

~

Emma was sitting in rapt attention, mouth hanging open. "But, but—Wheeler? What happened?" She tugged at his clothing insistently, her voice lilting up to that dangerous pitch again. "What happened to them?"

Ogma could hear sniffles around the room and wiped her own eyes on the sleeve of her nightgown. It was her favorite story—the sadness it left behind was like the peace after a good cry.

Wheeler scooped Emma up and sat her on his knee. He handed her a pinwheel and showed her how to hold it in front of the lantern to cast the shadow of a creaking windmill on the wall. Cocking an arm around her, he laced his fingers together into another shape. A figure dressed in rags with the head of a bird tilted up to look at the turning windmill.

Ogma sat up straighter. In all the times that Wheeler had told the story before, she'd never heard him keep going. She'd thought that was the end.

"The man who wore the bones, who was the boy, who caught the fireflies..." Wheeler took a breath. "The story of how he came to wander the fog is sad, true enough, but he left his fear behind. Out in the fog, he became a traveler. Some say—"

A scream burst into the room on a cold gust of wind and the children fell silent in shock. Wheeler sat stunned, the story forgotten, the shadows falling back into lifeless shapes cast by the lantern. Emma looked startled, as if unsure whether the scream was real or something from the story.

Firelight reflected on frightened faces as the children turned as one toward the shuttered windows that overlooked the wall.

Close, Ogma thought. *It must be very close.*

The watchtower that was the children's home was on the first terrace and only a short distance from the wall. She glanced at Cole. Even in the dim light of the dark lantern, she could see that he was looking back at her. *He knows it, too. The same voice. It's the same voice.* The room was still, frozen in the dark, with Wheeler's shadow puppets forgotten as the room held its breath. Ogma could see the pained looks play across their faces. *Could it really just be a phantom cry?*

And then they heard Jory's bell echoing from atop the wall. He rang a frantic, clangorous cadence—too sloppy for them to make out what alarm it really was. Ogma's eyes met Wheeler's as they cocked their heads to listen. *Someone's lost.* Emma started crying. The noise shocked the room into motion. Wheeler was on his feet, removing the shutters from the dark lantern. Ogma squinted against the bright light, blue and purple spots swimming in her vision like phantoms in her eyes. *The girl with phantoms in her eyes.* The thought brought her up short as she shook dozy remnants of Wheeler's story from her attention and clambered out of the bunk.

"Cole! The watch bell!"

Cole sprang to his feet, running for the door so that he could ring the watch bell that was meant to warn the villagers. The watch bell was too small to wake the whole village, but the bell tower in the central square could be heard for miles.

Wheeler stood, comforting Emma with a quick word and handing her to one of the older children. He started barking orders, "Brigid, Daniel—watch the little ones. Mae, Maya, and

Bowen with me. The rest of you, gather blankets, warm some cider, and stay here."

Ogma bounced anxiously on the balls of her feet awaiting instructions.

"Ogma! Get to Jory! If this is a rescue—"

"I know!" she called back over her shoulder, as she ran for the door. Cole started ringing the alarm.

Enki! Enoch! the bell called. *Awake! Alarm!*

As she pounded towards the wall, she could just make out Wheeler's continued orders as he too left the watch house. "Cole, once the village answers, I need you to take some of the others to the south wa—"

"The south wall? But Wheeler, Jory's in the north," Cole argued.

"I know, Cole, but it may be a trick. The fog might be luring us north, while it tries to slip phantoms over somewhere else." Ogma's heart skipped a beat, and Cole froze in surprise, the bell falling silent. "It's tried that before." Ogma heard an edge of pain in Wheeler's voice.

She turned her attention back to running as she rounded the corner of the wide verandah that circled the common room on the top floor of the watch house. From there, an elevated stone walkway arched directly to a landing halfway up the wall.

Too slow. What are they doing? Ogma growled in frustration as her bare feet slapped the stone. No one could remember why the old bells in the central square were called Enki and Enoch, but they were supposed to be attended day and night, so that any alarm sent from the children on watch would be echoed throughout the village right away.

Just as Ogma's feet hit the stairs, the deep clear peal of Enki rang through the night, making the stones hum. A beat later the deep resonant boom of Enoch followed, rebounding off the wall and echoing up the terraces.

Finally. She panted up the steps, the cold numbing her toes and fingers. On the penultimate step, her bare feet slid on the rain-slick stone and she barked her shins painfully.

Well done, she berated herself, panting for a moment on the top step. *Nightdress and no boots, what a rescue. I'll be forgetting my bells next.* She sighed and stood, listening for the sound of Jory's bell between beats of Enki and Enoch's general alarm.

Someone lost! Alarm! Alarm! Jory's bell was ringing frantically from somewhere midway along the northwest span.

Ogma raised her hand to the two bells on the cord that never left her neck. *I'm here! It's Ogma. I'm close,* they sang. She limped up and saw Jory leaning out over the wall, hanging with one arm on the rail while he rang his bell frantically with the other. He seemed to be struggling to keep sight of something in the fog.

Ogma came up beside him, steadying herself with one hand, and leaning out to peer into the swirling fog. The rain had tamped down the mist, at least. It was thinner than it had been on her patrol earlier that night, and lower and further from the walls.

"Jory! That scream—is someone really out there?" Ogma panted.

"It's that voice! The one that you and Cole have been hearing. It's not a fog phantom!" He was looking back at her, wild-eyed. She grabbed his belt, worried that he might slip. "There's someone out there. Look! Look!" He leaned out over the wall, bracing himself against the outer wooden railing, and pointing at something on the ground. Standing, as they were, in the shadow of one of the great windmills, it was difficult to see anything at first. The mill was still churning the fog into patches and swirls that drifted through the trees and across the ground. "It was just here, I swear!" Jory exclaimed in frustration. "Wait —the fog's moved it a bit. Yes! There it is!"

Ogma looked as the fog shifted, clearing an area that an instant ago was completely obscured. The moon was bright enough to be casting harsh, strange shadows that made the shapes below seem alien and abstract.

"I don't see anyone... wait! Yes, there!"

A figure lay in the mud, legs protruding from under a tangle of thorny brush. The hair on Ogma's neck prickled. "We have to get down there," she breathed.

She watched Jory's jaw clench as he struggled to be brave, but there was a quaver in his voice. "Do *we* have to go down there?"

Ogma's look was grim. *It's nothing we haven't done before, just... not on a night like this.*

Wheeler's bell sounded his arrival behind them, with Bowen, Mae, and Maya in tow. Relief was writ plain on Jory's face. "Wheeler! What do we do now?" he asked, turning to the older boy.

You know what we have to do, Ogma thought irritably, keeping watch on the figure below. She was losing patience with Jory's helpless attitude.

"There's someone down there, Wheeler." Her voice was completely steady. "Probably hurt."

Wheeler was standing away from the lip of the wall, eyeing it nervously. *What's gotten into him?* The older boy was always so steady. He was their rock.

"Come on, I'll show you."

Wheeler took a deep breath and stepped up next to her. While he leaned out over the rampart, Ogma studied his face. *He's terrified.* The realization shook Ogma to her core. *How did I not see it before?*

"I can't see anything. Where was it, Ogma?"

She pointed the way.

"Right." Wheeler nodded. "Here." He handed her a coat,

then glanced disapprovingly at her bare feet. Ogma felt the heat rising in her cheeks.

"No time to waste," she said defiantly.

Wheeler let out a breath between his teeth. "All right. Bowen, bring me two harnesses, Ogma's and one—" he looked out over the edge, trying to gauge the size of the figure trapped on the ground "—one about my size. Mae, Maya, I need you two to keep careful watch. You call out as soon as you see any banks of fog rolling in, or any phantom shapes, okay?"

"Right!" the two girls chimed cheerfully.

At least they're still having fun, Ogma thought, the ghost of a smile returning to her face.

"Don't forget your bells. Don't trust a voice if you can't see the person it belongs to."

The fog seemed to be holding steady and the figure on the ground was still visible. With Mae and Maya keeping track of both, Ogma turned to face Wheeler. His expression was grim. She tried to put as much determination and bravado into her own expression as she could. He must have noticed because he smiled at her. *That's the Wheeler I know. Don't go anywhere on me.*

Bowen came running back to them, arms full of leather straps and rope. A cold splash on her collar warned her that the rain was starting again. She held her arms out to her sides as Wheeler helped strap the harness over her coat and nightdress. She tried to suppress a shiver as an icy drop of water trickled down her back. Once she was securely strapped in, she picked up the other harness and waited for Wheeler to raise his arms.

"Woah—it's not for me," he said, stepping back. Wheeler dropped his eyes apologetically. "It's for—whoever that is, down there. You need me to belay."

Ogma stared at him for a moment. *Bowen and the others could do it. It'd be slow, but—he really doesn't want to go.* Bowen was setting belay pins into slots drilled into the stone. Wheeler leaned in to clip one end of the tether to her.

"It's okay," Ogma whispered in his ear. "I can do it."

Wheeler leaned back, shamefaced.

Ogma caught his gaze. *Fog knows you've cared for all of us for so long.* She couldn't bring herself to say it out loud.

He took another deep breath and put his lips to her forehead. "I'm sorry." He looked down, laced the other rope to the empty harness in her grip. She felt a warm droplet on her hand. Wheeler turned away and tied off both tethers to the wooden railing on the outer edge of the wall.

"Right." Ogma spoke aloud, giving herself a shake and turning to the wall. "Are we ready, then?" She gave Wheeler a defiantly unconcerned look.

"You used to love this part," he reminded her apologetically. "You said it was just like flying."

She clambered to the top of the parapet and looked up, watching the stars dance. *You used to like it, too.* And then she stepped off the wall.

The wind rushed through her hair and whipped at the edge of her nightdress. She felt a rush of vertigo and weightlessness. And then the rope pulled taut and she came to a halt standing perfectly straight, ninety degrees out from the wall, bare feet flat against the rough stones. Her heart pounded, but after a slow, deep breath, Ogma felt an old confidence returning to her limbs. She started to swing to the left and right, like a pendulum on a gradually lengthening chain. She kept herself moving by running in short bursts across the stones, as easily as if she were jogging back and forth along the ground.

With each swing, Wheeler paid out more rope and Ogma's jogging arcs carried her further and further back and forth across the face of the wall, and closer and closer to the ground. She kept her eyes trained on the figure lying some distance from the wall. They were definitely not just pinned under some brush, unless the brush had grown claws. Whatever it was, neither the brush nor the figure pinned beneath it were moving. It wasn't a phantom either. The phantoms were made of and by the fog itself, and though they could be solid enough, they still looked like fog, and rarely stayed the same shape for very long. This must have been a beast that lived within the fog.

"Ogma-a!" Maya's voice called down from above, her bell chiming with it. "The fog is getting thicker!"

Ogma glanced around as she started another downward swing. She was about three quarters of the way down the wall, but the fog seemed to be building in a rough semicircle at the edges of the clearing. "It's all right," she called back up, "keep going!"

At last, she made her final swing, pushing gently off from the wall and letting gravity pivot her on the end of the tether, jogging to a stop in the mud. She deliberately set herself down some distance from the fallen figure. She stood, watching the two shapes warily for any sign of movement. The ground around the two figures was torn up. Beyond them, Ogma could see furrows in the mud and broken branches. A puddle around the still forms reflected a red moon. *At least one of them is dead*, thought Ogma. She began to approach cautiously, circling closer to get a better view.

The beast was enormous. Standing, it would probably have been taller at the shoulder than Ogma's full height. It had a coat of long, deadly-looking quills, some of which were scattered on the ground. Its front claws were long and broad, as if for digging.

Ogma stepped closer, gingerly, mud oozing between her toes. She suppressed a yelp of alarm as the creature's head came into view. Two armored ridges ran from snout to shoulder blades across its head and back. It had two sets of enormous nostrils set in the front of its snout-like gills. Four eyes, milky white, stared out at her from under the ridges on the creature's skull. *There must be four eyes on the other side as well,* Ogma shuddered, *and none facing forward. It must burrow; some kind of tunneler?* She suddenly found herself wondering how deep underground the wall's foundations went. *I'll ask Wheeler when I get back.*

She stood for a moment, out of excuses, but not quite able to convince her feet to cooperate with what she knew she had to do.

A weak cry startled her into motion, and she ran to the other side of the carcass.

It was a boy, lying cheek to jowl with the beast, rows of teeth inches from his skin. He'd been crushed into the mud under its bulk. He looked to be about Wheeler's age. The rain had washed the mud from his face. Given the size of the creature's teeth, she'd been expecting something... messier. His face was locked in a grimace of pain or exhaustion, lips colorless, eyes tightly closed. He didn't cry out again. She knelt in the mud next to him and tried to find the injury. He had no wounds on his face and the beast had not managed to tear out his throat. *It might just have crushed him. It's certainly big enough.*

The boy coughed weakly and specks of blood spattered on his lips.

Wheeler's bell tolled on the wall above her. "Ogma! Have you found someone?"

Ogma chimed her bells in response and called up, "Yes! There's a boy! He's been crushed under this—thing! I'll try to get it off him."

"Well, get moving! The fog's getting thicker. And if he's too badly hurt—" Wheeler didn't finish the warning, but Ogma didn't need him to. She glanced around. The fog was pressing closer, trees around her fading into nothing. And closer to the wall, the fog was beginning to curl inward. Before much longer, they'd be cut off. If that happened, the tether would be her only hope of getting back.

The beast's body was strangely hunched above the boy, as if its weight wasn't resting fully atop him. She grabbed one of the great claws with both hands and heaved, dragging its massive paw out of the way. A putrid smell turned her stomach. There was a gap between the bodies. The boy's hands were clenched around the wooden shaft of a spear buried deep in the animal's chest. It looked like he'd tried to brace the shaft against the ground, but it had broken under the creature's weight. The jagged end had punched a hole through the boy's armor and into his stomach. It was hard to tell how much of the blood was his and how much was the beast's.

Ogma stepped back and started casting about in the mud for a branch that might be big enough to use as a lever. A stand of saplings had been dislodged in the ragged earth. *That should do.* She dragged the bole of one through the mud and knelt beside the bodies so she could slide it into the gap between them. There was no place for it to rest except the boy himself. She laid it gently across his strange armor.

"Sorry about this," she said with an apologetic glance. "I expect it's going to hurt." His eyelids trembled briefly but he didn't stir. She braced the lever against her shoulder and pulled her legs into a crouch, hoping her feet wouldn't slide out from under her in the mud when she tried to stand up. "Here we go," she breathed. She counted in her head as she braced herself for the big push. She wasn't sure the boy would survive it if she dropped the thing back on top of him. *One... two... three!*

Ogma surged to her feet with a groan, heaving against the improvised lever with all her strength. It bent frighteningly and shuddered in her grip, but did not break. The carcass of the beast lifted and began to lurch to one side. She could see the boy's hands clenching and unclenching around the spear shaft in his belly. Ogma's knee began to shake under the strain. She took some quick, shallow breaths. *One... two... three!* She pushed the bole of the sapling as high above her head as she could manage. The boy screamed as the carcass rolled off him, the spear shaft that bound them together snapping off as the great weight fell to the side.

"Au! Det svir!" he screamed out. "Vondt..." And went still.

Above, Mae and Maya's bells started ringing. Jory and Bowen were both shouting down to her.

"The fog! Ogma! The fog!"

Ever so quietly, the fog had stolen up around her. Curling tendrils were now between her and the wall and closing on every side. She hastily dropped to the boy's side and began strapping him into the second harness. Now that he was out from under the shadow of the beast, she could see that the strange armor he wore glittered with a blue iridescence beneath the mud and ichor. *Fat lot of good it did you.*

There wasn't time to fasten the harness properly, and with his wound, Ogma wasn't sure it would be safe to try, so she fastened a single strap under his arms. She gave the line two hard jerks and then ran beside him as he slid through the mud at the end of the tether. The fog dispersed around her as she ran towards the wall, but already too much of it had filled the gap between her and the familiar stones. Even as she ran, it seemed like the wall was getting more distant, rather than closer, and she had the terrible sense that her tether was stretching and unraveling. She put her head down and ran faster, lungs burning, stumbling in the mud, and the fog retreated before her.

She burst suddenly from the fog and hit the wall—hard. She cut her brow painfully and stars swam in her vision. Ringing her bells frantically in the alarm cadence, Ogma tried to keep the boy's head from knocking against the stones as he jerked into the air. His tether was being pulled up more quickly than hers.

Wheeler must be pulling him up. Bowen's not big enough to do much more than brace me. She took the tether in her hands, put her feet on the wall, and started pulling herself up to match Wheeler's pace.

She heard the fog chittering and whistling behind her. Phantom shapes seemed to rush towards her in the corners of her vision. Her irritation smoldered into frustration and burst into anger in her chest. The fear that'd been a tight ball in her stomach was missing; she'd left it lying somewhere in the mud below. She growled at the fog as she made her way up.

"You listen to me. I'm tired, and I'm cold, and I am *angry*." Her shout echoed off the stone. She took a deep breath. "I've found the wall. You can't take me, I'm not old enough. And I won't let you have *him*." The wounded boy spun on the end of his tether, head bumping on her hip as she tried to steady him. "So you may as well go away."

The fog subsided in sullen whispers and drifted back into a placid silver sea below her. When she finally reached the top of the wall, she helped Wheeler and Bowen lift the boy over the edge of the rail and then climbed over herself. Mae and Maya stared at her open-mouthed.

"You're really—um..." Mae started.

"Muddy!" Maya broke in. "Really, really muddy."

Mae nodded vigorously.

Ogma was too tired to care, too tired to notice the shame-faced look Wheeler was giving her. She was too tired to stop herself shivering. It was so cold. She sank down on the rain-slick rampart beside the boy as Wheeler sent Bowen to get a stretcher and help.

The boy was muttering something. "Jassike... ikke forlat meg..."

CHAPTER 2

THE WINDMILL TOWN

Wheeler dropped to his knees to catch Ogma before her head hit the stones. Maya raised one hand to her mouth and Mae tugged at Wheeler's shoulder. "Is she...?"

"Unconscious. Looks like she hit her head." Wheeler wiped Ogma's hair back from her brow, a bruised lump rising where she'd run into the wall. He unbuckled Ogma from the harness and tether, the buckles slick with mud and his hands fumbling in the cold. Once she was free, he wrapped her in his coat and lifted her into his arms. Ogma's mud-plastered hair dripped icy trickles of water down the front of his shirt as she shivered violently.

Bowen's bell rang out, *I'm here! Brought help! I'm here!* He came sprinting back up the cobbled steps with two stout men from the village puffing behind him. It was

Ulfred, the baker, and his brother Oscar, carrying a stretcher between them. They kept casting nervous glances at the edge of the wall. The way the fog had been, Wheeler couldn't blame them.

Without being told, Mae and Maya took up watch positions

33

between the men and the wall's edge. Wheeler nodded with approval. The fog had died down after its final surge, but it was still lapping against the wall, maybe twenty feet below the rampart's edge. Far from comforting for the adults.

The two men grimly set down the stretcher, Ulfred pointedly ignoring the roiling fog, while Oscar was transfixed by a slavering phantom maw taunting them from the bank below. With a shudder, he turned back to the boy's wound.

"It's a damn waste," he muttered, shaking his head. "Having us up here for this? Look at 'em." Ulfred shot Oscar a quelling look but didn't contradict him. "I jus' mean—it could come right over—an' we already did our watchin' when we were of age, didn' we? Tha's all." He'd clearly been drinking his courage. Ulfred gave Wheeler an apologetic look.

They crouched beside the wounded boy and lifted him carefully onto the stretcher. Even so, Wheeler winced as the spear haft in the boy's stomach jostled. The two men took up positions at each end of the stretcher and the baker gave a quick count—"One... two... three...*hup!*"—as they lifted it. Ulfred paused for a moment to nod at Ogma in Wheeler's arms, while his brother swayed slightly with his end of the stretcher. "She the one who brought this boy up? In that?"

Wheeler nodded.

"Brave girl."

Wheeler nodded again.

Ulfred's voice was gruff. "You're doin' good, boy." Wasting no more time, he and his brother clattered across the rampart towards the stairs.

"Bowen, go with them, just in case..."

Bowen understood: just in case the fog broke through. Bowen turned and ran after the stretcher, heels slapping on stone. Wheeler turned to Jory, who was still watching everything with a blank expression of shock. "Jory—hey, snap out of it!"

Jory started and met Wheeler's eyes.

"Stay here and finish out your shift. Can you do that?"

Jory nodded.

"I'll make sure someone relieves you soon."

Ogma had stopped shivering. That was bad. "We've got to get Ogma warmed up." He hurried across the cobbled rampart in the direction of the watch house. Mae trailed behind with Maya, biting her lip—both girls quiet for once. The sky was beginning to lighten, dancing stars fading to a deep blue.

When they arrived back at the watch house, it was buzzing with murmurs and worried speculation. The din died down as Wheeler carried Ogma inside. The children's faces tracked him across the room, the older with worry in their eyes, the younger with barely contained excitement. Mercifully, all were quiet. He gently set Ogma down on his bunk, mud and all.

"Daniel? Daniel—she's cold. Too cold. She's not shivering anymore." Daniel dropped the muddied clothes he was collecting from the children who'd just come off their shifts on the wall.

"Blankets, as many as you can find, and get her out of those wet clothes. Brigid, can you—?"

Brigid had been pacing the great room in her patrol leathers, waiting to call out after them if they'd signaled another alarm. She nodded and jogged over to Ogma, shooing the boys away and shucking Ogma out of her wet nightclothes and tucking her under the pile of blankets Daniel had collected. When she was finished, Daniel knelt at Ogma's side, a hand to her forehead. Wheeler hovered over them anxiously.

Ogma began shivering again, violently. Brigid turned to Daniel in dismay.

"Don't worry. That's good. It means she's warming up. She's going to be okay."

"What can we do?" Wheeler asked.

"You can stop fretting for a start. She just needs to warm up and rest. We should throw some more logs on the fire." Daniel's voice was soothing but his brow was knitted. As Wheeler turned to the wood pile, Daniel caught his eye. "Hey." He jerked his chin to the crowd of anxious faces looking out from the ring of bunks. "You worry about them. They need to know we're safe."

Wheeler hesitated a moment, then nodded and turned to the other children.

"It's all right. Ogma forgot her coat again," his voice caught and the younger children who didn't grasp the danger of the cold tittered. "She just needs to warm up. And no one was lost at the wall. We found someone, in fact." As he told the tale, excited whispers raced around the common room. "Ogma rescued him. He's... well he's pretty badly wounded, so they've taken him to the village."

"Will he...?" Brigid's question trailed off.

Wheeler shook his head. "We won't know until they've seen to him. We did our part. It was good work. You should all get some sleep."

He turned back to Ogma and went to sit on the edge of the bunk. The suggestion of bedtime went utterly ignored, and excited gossip spread around the bunks. Behind him, Mae and Maya launched into an expansive recounting of the evening's events, standing atop one of the bunks and gesturing dramatically. At the rate at which they were interrupting each other and finishing each other's sentences, they'd be at it till noon and no one would get any sleep. Wheeler fought back a yawn.

"You should get some sleep too, you know." Brigid touched

his shoulder and handed him a steaming mug of cider. She turned to Daniel, "Is she warming up?"

"She's getting there. Would you bring a washcloth? As warm as you can find."

"Sure," Brigid replied, and returned a moment later with two steaming towels borrowed from the washing. She went to work wiping the mud from Ogma's feet while Daniel worked on her hands, and they worked warmth into her icy extremities.

Gradually, Ogma's shivering slowed. She sighed contentedly and snuggled into Wheeler's pillow, smearing mud from her hair all over it. Wheeler clucked in irritation and Brigid stifled a laugh.

"She'll be just fine."

Bowen jogged to keep up as Ulfred and Oscar rattled across the cobbled avenues of the town with their in. The pre-dawn twilight had just begun to shade pale colors back into the world.

"Where will you take him?" Bowen asked.

"Goodie Hazel's," Ulfred grunted. "She'll be expecting us with the alarm an' all."

"Hope she don't have that crazy old man there again," his brother grumbled.

"He's not crazy, he just don't speak."

"Whatever he is, he ain't natural." Oscar raised his voice. "Remember? Came in with the Caravaners! Calm as you please through a bank of fog thicker than Moll's pea soup. Way he was dressed, I thought he was one of 'em!"

"He came from outside?" Bowen was stunned by this. He'd thought the mute old man who lived all by himself under the south wall had always lived there. Some of the other children told stories about him, but Wheeler always hushed them.

"Oh yes- and he was older than—"

"Hush your trap, Oscar," his brother wheezed. "Save your breath for runnin'."

Bowen hoped the baker's brother would keep complaining so he could hear more. But the baker had picked up the pace as they came up the terrace and his brother was red-faced and puffing.

They turned into a small building at the edge of the town, bearing the stretcher between them into the low, dark room. The old man *was* there, just lifting strips of steaming white cloth from a pot of boiling water and laying them down to cool, while a plump middle-aged woman laid out a row of glinting metal tools. She motioned for them to set the stretcher down on the table in the center of the room. They heaved it into place with a grunt and stepped back to the doorway.

Bowen stood between them, shuffling from foot to foot nervously. The boy on the stretcher looked very pale.

"Goodie Hazel?" he asked tentatively.

The woman turned from her tray of tools.

"Is he going to...?" Bowen gestured uncertainly at the boy, who was shivering violently

Goodie Hazel sighed and padded over to the table. "Just cold? Or fever..." she muttered to herself. His hair was plastered to his face by sweat and rain. She held his wrist in one hand and laid the other to his forehead, pursing her lips. Bowen watched anxiously, wondering if he should ask again. A moment passed in silence.

Goodie Hazel shook her head. "It's hard to say. We'll know more once..." She gestured to the spear shaft protruding from the boy's stomach.

"Damn waste," the baker's brother muttered. Goodie Hazel turned and raised an eyebrow.

The baker turned and whispered furiously, "Shut yer mouth, Oscar. You been drinkin'." He took off his cap and flushed with embarrassment by proxy. They both wilted under Goodie Hazel's stare and fell quiet. The silent old man standing behind her smiled placidly.

Goodie Hazel turned back to her patient. His breathing was shallow and his hands were clenching and unclenching on the table. She clucked her tongue and started cutting away the straps that held his iridescent armor in place. The boy started tossed his head and a weak moan escaped his lips. The old man bent over him, mopping his brow with a warm cloth. Goodie Hazel began carefully lifting the armor, trying to lift it over the spear shaft without jostling his wound—but suddenly he cried out, spasming violently.

To Bowen's eyes, everything in the room seemed to slow down. The boy's arm swung up from the table in some strange reflex and he snapped his fingers. At the same time, he pounded the tabletop with his right foot—two rapid, staccato beats. A rush of air filled the room in a sudden burst, and his whole body jerked upward, a good foot off the table, before thumping heavily back down. An earthenware jug fell from its shelf, smashing to pieces on the floor. Time returned to normal.

Bowen watched wide-eyed as the baker swore loudly and he and his brother moved to restrain the boy, holding down his arms and legs as he spasmed and shivered. Blood was dripping on the edge of the table.

He cried out again, "Vi vil slåss! For veiviseren datter!" Another gust of wind filled the room with a *whoomp* and another basin toppled.

The old man stepped forward, murmuring nonsense sounds quietly into the boy's ear. He'd stopped struggling but his face was still screwed up in pain. The old man brought a ladle of warm tea to the boy's lips. He coughed and sputtered at first, but gradually subsided again to fitful sleep.

Goodie Hazel considered the earthenware fragments

littering the floor. She complained to the air. "Traded those from the Caravaners when I was girl, I did." She shook her head. "That's what we call a *waste*," she said with a pointed glare Oscar.

With Ulfred and his brother keeping the boy pinned firmly to the table, Goodie Hazel and the old man tried again to remove the boy's armor. They moved more slowly this time, lifting it delicately over the broken shaft of the spear without knocking against it. This time, the boy did not cry out. They set it carefully aside.

The old man began slowly pouring steaming hot water over the site of the wound, washing away the gore while the woman carefully picked out slivers of wood and large fragments of the blue armor. She gave a grunt of mild surprise, knocking the piece against the table where it clunked hollowly, and then raising it to her noset. "Not iron. Lacquered wood, maybe?" With a shrug, she dropped them in a bowl and turned back to her patient.

Bowen stepped closer to the operating table and peeked into the bowl. The small fragments still shimmered with blue-green iridescence. He picked one up and retreated to a corner of the room.

It looks like beetle shell to me, Bowen thought.

The work of healing was close and difficult and slow. The boy on the table slept fitfully.

Dunkirk dreamed.

He dreamed of a green hill with blue sky above and white clouds drifting gently across the sun. He dreamed of dappled light on emerald grass. The world in shadow and sun.

"Can't you just pull it out?" Bowen asked timidly, peering over the edge of the table for a better look.

Goodie Hazel wiped a bead of sweat from her forehead and leaned in close. The boy's wound was now clear of mud and gore and splinters, but the broken spear shaft was still in the boy's belly. She pressed her fingers against the heated flesh of his stomach around the wound, probing for further signs of internal injury.

"That depends. If he's very lucky, we may be able to do just that and then stitch him up. Then again..." She paused and nodded to the old man. He pressed clean bandages around the wound and she took the spear shaft firmly in both hands. "Might be we pull it out and set him gushing."

Bowen paled. The baker and his brother pressed the boy's shoulders more firmly to the board.

Goodie Hazel pulled.

Dunkirk was lost. He couldn't remember how he'd gotten here or where all the trees had come from. *Where are the other soldiers? Where are my friends?* He crashed through the undergrowth frantically—brushing through the thicket, ducking under fallen trees—searching for any sign of the battlefield he was on just moments ago: the emerald grass, his company, the Blue Legion... or even the enemy. He knew he needed to calm down —just stop for a minute and get his bearings—but the panic was overwhelming. His breath was coming in ragged gasps.

He'd been running for a very long time. He was good at running. He could run for days. He was quick on his feet, and agile too.

But he had a terrible stitch in his side.

How did I get here? he wondered again, as he fought with brambles that tangled around his arms and legs.

He remembered the hill and his brothers of the company beside him, and the whole host of the Blue Legion below them. He remembered the enemy, standing in their companies across the emerald-green field, under a clear blue sky. The air was warm and still. The calm before the battle.

And then we... why can't I remember? Something happened. They must have hexed us. I'm lost! Dunkirk crashed through the trees, cursing himself. He was cold and thirsty. He couldn't see anything through this fog.

What were our orders? He tried to remember. *We were supposed to slip down the hill ahead of the others. Disappear into the trees.*

Before a battle had even been joined, they were meant to be behind the enemy's lines. He was one of the trilsk: the sappers company. They carried the curse staves of the Blue Wizard. He could remember he and his brothers, moving like shadows in the dappled light of the trees, carefully planting the staves in the ground according to the Wizard's instructions.

In his first battle, they planted a staff to weaken their enemies' limbs. Dunkirk met them in battle later, some so ener-vated they'd fallen to the ground under the weight of their own armor, unable to rise. The prisoners that day had wasted muscles and pinched cheeks. In another battle they planted staves to dull to their opponents' weapons and rust their armor. The metal leached through the ground, the armor rusting to dust as they wore it, while steel saplings grew up where they'd planted the staves.

The worst were the staves they'd used with no stealth at all. No deceit. For once he and his brother trilsk stood in the front line, facing the enemy across a broad field. They planted their staves and stood still as the enemy charged. At first, it seemed ineffective. The ground churned to mud under the enemy's feet, but so it would have even without the staves. But then turbid water bubbled from the mud. The front ranks stumbled as the mud sucked at their boots, but the back ranks pushed them on. The field became a stinking mire, and the soldiers panicked. First they tried to pull each other free, but found the mud sucking each of them deeper. They tried abandoning the armor dragging them down, but too late.

At the end, men were screaming and crying—climbing each other's shoulders, pushing each other deeper in the fen, yet always sinking. Dunkirk watched as the last young man—a boy really, no older than he—disappeared into the mud, his eyes pleading.

Dunkirk shivered, rebuking himself for the unbidden tears in his eyes, and stiffened his back. He was proud to be trilsk. Proud to turn the tide in the Legion's favor. They would win the day for the Wizard of the Blue Legion, and his daughter would give them blessing.

"Jassike," Dunkirk whispered.

Bowen worried at the beetle shell fragment in his hands. The boy on the table was breathing fast and shallow. He tossed and turned against the grip of the burly village men while Goodie Hazel and the old man sewed him up inside. Bowen wanted to ask more questions, but with the grown-ups' hands *inside* the boy's stomach, he kept quiet.

A faint tremor in the ground that might have been booted footsteps pulled Dunkirk out of his effort to remember what had happened.

His heart pounded in his chest. He whipped around, tangled in the undergrowth, looking desperately for any sign of movement in the fog-sodden trees. His hands were shaking.

I've never fought alone, he realized in a panic.

The glittering blue horn of his helmet caught in the low branches above him. It twisted around his face, blinding him. He wrestled it off and set his back to the trunk of a tree, trying to slow his breathing.

The boy on the table's breathing steadied, and Bowen let out a breath he hadn't known he was holding. Goodie Hazel wiped the sweat from her brow with the back of her arm. Her hands were red to the wrist.

"Think I might be sick," Oscar muttered.

"Don' you dare," ordered his brother. But both kept looking anywhere but at the wound where Goodie Hazel diligently worked.

Bowen didn't feel sick at all. He was captivated.

The forest was silent again. Dunkirk closed his eyes, leaning his head back against the trunk of the tree behind him.

Why can't I remember?

They'd been standing on the hill and then... and then...

They'd been standing on the hill and then the horns blew.

The enemy started marching.

They waited, watching rank upon rank of gray armored warriors advancing. Ten times their number.

And then she was there: the Blue Wizard's daughter. Walking among them. She spoke to them, whispered encouragements.

She put her hand to his cheek.

And then she was gone, and the Blue Legion answered the enemy's horns with the tolling of their great silver bells and began their charge.

He and the other trilsk quickly checked the straps of their armor and took up their spears. Some carried true spears to fight off enemy skirmishers. Some carried the curse staves, disguised to look like spears, to hide them from the enemy.

With a snap of their fingers and stomp of their feet, they burst forward on charms of wind and speed, rushing down the emerald hill towards trees at the edge of the battlefield, where they would disappear to set their staves. Long loping strides, quickened by the flitting of beetle's wings on their iridescent armor, carried them effortlessly down the hill and ahead of all the other companies of the Blue Legion. The thrill of the charge was all consuming.

It felt to Dunkirk like flying.

They'd nearly reached the trees and then... *This is when it happened,* Dunkirk remembered. *No, not again!*

A concussive blast of air knocked him to the ground and sent his companions tumbling in the dirt. Dunkirk's ears rang. He saw the front runners of the enemy's ranks collapse. *We've done it! Already? That can't be right.*

There were cries of alarm and confusion from both ends of the field.

Just as Dunkirk thought he might be able to pull himself to his feet, a shadow fell over the field, and with it an overwhelming pressure that crushed the air from his lungs and smothered all clattering of armor and cries of panicked soldiers in utter silence.

Gasping, Dunkirk rolled over, trying to see what was happening, trying to see why the sky had gone dark. He saw it then, cresting over the trees. A bank of fog that towered gray and angry into the sky.

The fog crashed into the emerald valley in a pitiless wave. Where it crashed upon the grassy shore, phantoms rose. Beasts of spine and tooth and horn, forming and reforming out of the mist, towering above the trees.

What kind of spell is this?!

Screams shattered the silence. Dunkirk scrambled to his feet and broke for the trees, the Legion in shambles around him. Great grasping arms—of and from the sea of fog like some deep ocean nightmare—plunged down the grassy bank, cutting them off from the forest. Shapes resolved in the mist. Phantom faces with horns and tusks and trunks and teeth—too many arms—too many eyes—all shifting and reforming all around them. His brothers tried to shout over the chittering chorus but the fog beasts echoed back, twisting their voices, mocking them.

Dunkirk saw the others disappear into the gray mist, the phantom beasts pouncing upon them in glee. He was surrounded in the eye of this terrible storm, a small clearing of green grass and blue sky. The phantom faces mocked and cajoled. His knees went weak.

Why don't they get it over with?

Something lunged out of the fog—not a beast! One of his brothers!

"Markus!" There was a crazed look in the young man's eyes. Clawed tendrils clutched his wrists and ankles, pulsing with a red mist and then dissolved as he stumbled into the clear, the flying charm of his winged armor stuttering.

There was a beat of silence as they stared at each other, breathing hard.

And then a greater phantom came, tall as a siege engine. It stretched four great arms, growling from a lion's head as other beastly faces burst from its neck like tumors. It lunged.

Dunkirk raised a fable hand to ward it off. He heard Eirik shout in panic as he ran.

But before those lunging jaws could snap, before the great claws could rend his limbs, this phantom too dissolved, leaving Dunkirk again in a fragile bubble of calm. He sank to his knees, breathing heavily.

A thin keening came from behind him. Slowly, he turned.

He could see a shadow in the fog. A smaller one. Human shaped.

"...Markus?"

The keening grew to a wail, a chorus of screams picked up and echoed by the fog.

Shaking and crying, Dunkirk ran.

～

The boy on the table whimpered while Goodie Hazel stitched. Even unconscious, the boy's hands clenched as he grasped at the pain in his belly.

Bowen imagined what it would be like to wield the needle himself—to be a healer. He still flinched every time the boy cried out, but Goodie Hazel was unflappable, almost serene. As she calmly and methodically closed up the wound, slowly the boy's struggling slowed, his chest rising and falling in ragged, gasping breaths.

～

Dunkirk sagged against the tree. *Then I was here*, he remembered. *Lost*.

Another tremor in the ground brought him back to himself. It was stronger this time, almost on the edge of hearing.

The low rumble grew louder and closer, and then Dunkirk realized it was not a sound made by boots on the ground. A great furrow in the earth was rumbling towards him, pushing aside root and tree. Dunkirk wiped cold sweat from his brow and braced himself, gripping his spear tightly in both hands.

A beast crested over a wave of earth, enormous.

Too many teeth. Too many eyes. Dunkirk could see the deadly spines on its back. He braced himself for its charge. And then it dived, burrowing deep into the earth, and disappeared.

Dunkirk stood his ground, choking back fear and frustration. He spun around, searching the ground everywhere and stabbing ineffectually at the dirt. But there was nothing, no sign of it, not even a tremor, until—

—until the ground exploded beneath him and the beast emerged, snorting clods of dirt from its gill-like nostrils, jaws snapping at his leg.

With a cry of pure terror, Dunkirk fell back, narrowly escaping the gnashing teeth.

He ran.

The beast stalked him under the earth. Dunkirk ran without pacing himself, without any effort to orient himself or keep track of where he was going. He simply knew he had to run, had to escape the great furrow in the earth, tearing up stone and sapling behind him. Every time he tripped over an unseen root or loose stone, another shout escaped his lips and hot tears of shame stung his eyes.

He was certain with each stumble that the great beast would erupt from the earth, and this time it would have him. The ground around him kept changing as banks of fog swirled. He found himself running through mud, then moss, then on parched earth, in open meadow, and then back in pine forest. And yet still he could feel the tremor in the ground beneath him.

The fog parted briefly, and through the gap, something caught Dunkirk's panicked eye. *Stone? A wall!* He wasn't sure but for a moment the stitch in his side seemed less, and he put on another burst of speed. The trees opened up and...

It was just here! I'm sure I saw it!

Dunkirk cried out in frustration and ran through the empty clearing.

It couldn't be that far. I'm sure it was just there. Maybe over that next rise.

He risked a glance over his shoulder. The furrow was falling behind, almost lost in the wisps of fog in his wake. He remembered himself. *I am trilsk. I'm a runner.* He was going to make it.

A root tangled his ankle and Dunkirk sprawled on his face in the mud. With a roar of triumph, the beast burst from beneath the earth and charged.

The boy convulsed on the table, wrenching upwards against the men who held him down and then collapsing again. Goodie Hazel stepped back, needle and thread still in hand. The wound was finally closed, but the boy was delirious, whispering and shuddering between fevered convulsions.

A gentle rain fell on Dunkirk's face as he lay beneath the carcass, slipping in and out of consciousness. He felt warm. *A rest. Just a rest and this stitch in my side will go away...*

∽

The boy shuddered as the old man mopped the fever from his brow. And then, mercifully, he slept.

Ogma half-woke to a confused jumble of children's voices and the sound of a fire crackling. She could barely open her eyes. She felt smothered, ice cold and burning hot at the same time. Her heart beat echoed in her chest, not pounding, not racing, but tolling... ever so slowly. *What if the bell stops?* she wondered. She felt a burning hand on her brow and succumbed to uneasy dreams.

Her sleep was fitful. She lost time between each heavy-lidded blink. Sometimes the room was darker, sometimes lighter, and the children's voices rose and fell from bright chatter to gentle murmurs.

Someone was humming a lullaby. A tune she remembered deep in her bones, whose words she couldn't remember. She opened her eyes. Daniel sat beside her, rocking gently in a chair, darning socks by the fire. The watch house was dark and quiet. After a moment he glanced up from his work and met her eyes.

"Hey, little grub." Setting aside the socks he got up from the chair and knelt at the head of her bed. "How are you feeling?"

"... 'm not a grub, *you*'re a grub," Ogma mumbled. He hadn't called her that in seasons. Daniel chuckled.

"Here, drink this." He held a warm mug to her lips. Ogma tried to lift her head, but everything felt too heavy. Daniel slipped his arm under her neck and lifted her up, murmuring,

"There you go, drink up now." The cider was sweet and warm, gliding down her throat and warming her from belly to toes. After finishing the mug she fell back against the pillow, lids heavy over her eyes.

Daniel sang softly as she slept.

Confused memories of the rescue—of blood and fog and glittering blue armor—faded from her dreams as Ogma woke again.

There was an unfamiliar bunk above her. Golden afternoon light was streaming through the shutters, filtered through drifting motes of dust, lit up like fireflies. Ogma propped herself up on her elbow, every muscle complaining. *I'm in Wheeler's bunk?* She sank back to the bed and remembered.

She remembered the boy in the strange iridescent armor. *I brought him in. Got back to the top of the wall.* She took a few more breaths and sat up slowly. She ached from head to toe. Wheeler and Brigid were standing by the fireplace talking quietly. Wheeler looked tired. *Well of course he's tired,* Ogma berated herself. *Someone's been sleeping in his bed.*

The blankets were stifling. She was about to push them back when she realized she wasn't wearing her nightgown. She blushed furiously. Peering over the side of the bunk she saw a neatly folded gown in Daniel's rocking chair. She grabbed it and pulled it on under the covers.

She swung her feet over the side and noted the absence of mud with some surprise. A quick check revealed that most of it had been washed off. The thought of someone washing her feet while she slept made her blush deeper. *What if it was Wheeler?*

She stood up and hobbled over to where he and Brigid were talking. Brigid was dressed in patrol leathers and holding a few of the vicious quills that had been scattered around the carcass of the beast.

"—the fog had already taken the clearing. I did find a few of these in the trees, though I'm surprised there was even this much left." Brigid stopped when she saw Ogma, and the normally grim girl smiled and surprised her with a hug. "You've been sleeping for days! It's good to see you on your feet."

"Days?!" That meant she'd slept through watch shifts, missed meals. She didn't have time for that now and pushed the thought aside. "How is he?"

Wheeler gave her a grin, the exhaustion retreating from around his eyes. "Up-and-at-em and no nonsense. That's the way, right, Ogma? Sleep well?"

She carefully ignored him, color rising back into her cheeks.

Brigid covered her mouth with one hand. "Oh dear, your hair—" she began.

"Well?!" Ogma cut in, blush deepening. She felt her hair, which was sticking out in strange ways, matted with now-dried mud. She tried to comb through the tangle with her fingers, but they stuck in the knots. She extracted them carefully.

"Is someone going to tell me—?" Her voice caught suddenly. "I mean, is he... did he—?"

"He's all right," Brigid said kindly. "At least for now. I checked in this morning after my patrol. Goodie Hazel managed to get the shaft out of his stomach and his fever broke."

Ogma grunted and turned to the embers in the fireplace.

"Goodie Hazel had him moved to the Old Man's cottage in case she needs room for new patients. Bowen's been visiting."

Wheeler patted her gently on the shoulder. "You did well. No one could have done better."

"Little grub! You're awake!" The young ones with Daniel giggled at the nickname as he shooed them inside and ran up to pull Ogma to his chest. He kissed the top of her head. A tension inside Ogma let go; her shoulders sank and tears flooded her vision.

"I was scared..." she whispered.

"I know, little grub. It's okay to be scared."

Ogma broke the embrace and turned back to Wheeler and Brigid. "I'd like to see him if that's all right."

He pursed his lips. "Goodie Hazel says we're supposed to let him rest. Actually, I was going to—" the rest of Wheeler's remark was cut off as he yawned enormously.

"Go to bed?" Brigid finished for him, a twinkle in her eye. She motioned to Ogma to grab his other arm and they marched him over to his bunk.

"Hrmph." Wheeler grunted and gestured imperiously at his mud-stained pillowcase. "Mutiny is what this is. Muddy, too. *Mud*tiny." He pitched onto the bed, grumbling incoherently, and was asleep almost instantly. Brigid dusted off her hands and gave Ogma a wink.

"That's one thing settled. Now then," the older girl turned and rummaged through a pile of satchels near the fireplace. "These are for Rora and Effie on the south wall." She handed Ogma two burlap bags filled with fruit pies wrapped in rice paper. They smelled heavenly. "They relieved Cole a few hours ago and they missed breakfast."

Ogma opened her mouth to protest. Brigid raised a finger to stop her.

"You can visit your rescue once you've dropped off the food. You weren't the only one who's had trouble with the fog. We had to step up the patrols. People are tired."

Ogma shut her mouth and took the bags. After a moment, she asked, "What happened?"

Brigid sighed and shook her head. "It... wasn't that bad. It was close, that's all." She paused. "The fog got through in a few places."

"Phantoms?" Ogma asked quietly.

"Big ones." Brigid managed a smile again. "No fear, right?" she quoted Wheeler. "Cole and the others told them off. No one was taken. At least it's finally clearing up."

"There's a fog break?" Ogma perked up.

Brigid smiled. "Why don't you go and see?"

Daniel put an arm around her shoulder. "Before you go... " He held up a comb.

Ogma rolled her eyes, "Okay, okay. I'm muddy, I get it." Then her smile softened. Restless as she was after days abed, she followed him back inside as he gently washed the mud from her hair with warm water. The feel of the comb on her scalp was deeply relaxing.

She gave him a hug and a small smile. "Thanks big grub."

Ogma emerged from the watch house door into the bright afternoon light. The sky was clear and the glare from the town's blue slate roofs was bright enough for Ogma to have to shield her eyes. The late afternoon sun was warm on her face. It had been dark and cold for so long that the feeling was almost unfamiliar.

She set an easy pace, enjoying the warmth as she walked through the cobbled terraces. From where the watch house stood by the northeast wall, she'd have to cross the entire village to reach Rora and Effie on the south span. She could have taken the rampart walk, but it was quicker to go straight through.

Her shoulders throbbed in a constant, dull ache, but gradually the warm sunlight worked its way into her stiffened muscles and the ache subsided.

The fields and gardens in the outer terraces were overgrown. With the fog as bad as it had been, most of the villagers had been unwilling to venture too close to the wall. From the look of it, the ermine moths had been at the crops as well. About half as long as Ogma's forearm, ermine moths were a common pest. Mice could be a problem in the granaries, but the big, fuzzy ermine moths would eat the grains right off the stalk. Sometimes they'd venture into eating other vegetables if an ambitious mood took them. They were nearly impossible to catch, but sometimes they'd get drunk off fermented grain piles and you could just pick them up off the ground. You couldn't eat them, but their wings made a decent leather. Ogma actually thought they were kind of cute with their fat, furry bodies and fuzzy antennae.

Among the crops, wildflowers that had been waiting for any hint of sunshine after the long rains had begun to open. A gentle breeze swept waves through the tall grain that lapped gently around a few old stone buildings standing empty on the edge of the village, only just outside the shadow of the wall. Ogma wasn't sure why they'd even been built; none of the adult villagers would risk living so close to the wall in case a fog phantom broke through. But under the clear blue sky and the warm breeze, they looked much more inviting, as if they were only waiting, not abandoned.

The next terrace was better cultivated, the houses occupied and carefully cared for. Even though it was still fairly close to the wall, there were many more houses here, some even newly built from stone and timbers scavenged from the abandoned buildings. As large as their village was, they still had to make careful use of the space. Mixed planting was the norm, with vegetables, grains, and climbing gardens filling in all the space that wasn't occupied by the houses or the cobbled paths. There were orchard trees of several kinds as well. The ones on Ogma's path had budded a few weeks ago and now hard green olives hung from their branches, not yet ripe.

Her step lightened by the sunshine and crisp air, Ogma

skipped up the steps to the third terrace. It was a higher climb than the rest, and more closely crowded, with some of the buildings reaching two stories. The few olive trees here were older and much taller. She set her bags down at the base of one of the trees that stood apart from the rest and started climbing. The very highest branches were just high enough for her to see over the edge of the wall.

The silvery bark of the olive tree was warm. The upper branches swayed gently, and the leaves whispered in the breeze. Ogma looked out over the wall and she felt something in her heart swell.

The fog really did *break! It's clear!*

Sometime in the early morning, the roiling, angry banks of fog that had besieged the town had rolled back, retreating over the landscape. Ogma could see for miles. The fog had changed the landscape as it retreated. The dead pine forest that she had caught glimpses of when the fog was thick was gone, and instead she could see bright, green grass. Wild meadows surrounded the village in gentle, rolling hills. Stands of proud, green trees swayed in the warm wind. And in the distance, Ogma could see the peaks of snow-capped mountains. The windmills on the wall were still.

She'd never seen the fog retreat so far. The only signs of it she could see were in patchy banks on the foothills of the mountains and drifting like low clouds in valley meadows.

Ogma stood on the gently swaying upper branch for some time, just drinking in the sight of it. She started scanning the horizon excitedly.

Maybe there's a town! We could trade—and that would mean a festival!

Try as she might, she couldn't pick out any man-made buildings in the distance. She hoped she might hear Enki and Enoch start tolling—that someone else might have spotted another village—but the great bells did not disturb the warm afternoon air.

In spite of this, Ogma felt a guilty sense of relief. Other towns meant festival and trade, but more often than not, it also meant the young men and women of each village meeting and *courting*... and, as often as not, leaving. And who knew if the two villages would ever find each other again.

So for all the color and noise and excitement of a fog break festival with another village, they were always sad.

Ogma shinned down the tree and shouldered her bag, reflecting on hazy memories of festival days from earlier seasons. *I guess it's not quite that bad. Sometimes we find the same villages again.* But there was no regular interval, and it was never certain. There was no way to predict when a given village might be brought close in the drifts. At least, not that anyone seemed to know.

She padded down the cobbled path towards the town square. Most of the buildings were two stories now, and some of those that lined the central square were even three. They were cleverly designed so that each building had an open balcony garden that overlooked the roof of the buildings below it. Even the path was divided to make room for a central planter. These were shared by the important craftsmen and village elders who lived in the center of the village, who didn't have enough open space for their own plots.

The village square was bustling. Hopeful villagers had assembled goods on carts and were gathered around the cistern wells, chattering about the possibility of a trade festival. Most of what they had for trade was food: fresh produce, preserves and pickles, and baked goods and pies. She also saw some homespun cloth made from plant fibers, and some pottery that the villagers made from the clay inside the walls. They looked up at the bell tower expectantly, but Enki and Enoch remained silent. No other village had been sighted.

A young woman that Ogma vaguely remembered as one of the older girls on the wall when Ogma had been very young saw her and waved. She bustled up as Ogma struggled to remember her name. She'd left the wall some five seasons ago.

"No village then, I guess?" the young woman said with a hopeful smile.

Ogma shook her head.

"Oh well..." She sighed, looking down at the folded linens she'd woven, ready for barter. "How's young Wheeler? Still doing his funny little shadow puppets?"

Ogma decided she didn't like the cheerful young woman.

"He's the oldest now, you know," Ogma said.

"Oh." The young woman's face fell. "Has it really been...? Is he coming off the wall soon, then?"

"I... don't know." Ogma worried her lip.

"Oh, that's all right... I'm sure he won't wait too long."

Ogma mumbled a goodbye and hurried on her way. Now that it was clear no other village had been sighted, she could hear the villagers beginning to argue the merits of going beyond the wall anyway to forage or hunt.

It'll come back, you know, Ogma thought. *It's still not safe.* Yet, if they caught something, perhaps they might have a feast. It seemed like the fog had been so close for so long that they deserved *some* kind of celebration. Ogma had only eaten meat once before, on a festival day several seasons ago when the villagers had killed a great antlered beast with three toes on each foot and bird-like talons. Goodie Hazel called it a hart. The juice had been sticky on her chin, but the saltiness of it was delicious. She was sick afterwards, but it was worth it.

Ogma's stomach rumbled.

She pulled herself out of her daydreaming and hurried on her way to the south wall. The north and south walls both had large gates so the stone steps to climb to the top were easy, if a bit steep. To get directly to the east or west spans, they had to either go around on top of the wall or climb a ladder onto the roof of a nearby building and take one of the connected rope bridges.

Rora and Effie were at the middle of the span over the gate when Ogma puffed up the steps to the top of the wall. Of an age with Ogma, they were cheerful mirrors to her own seriousness, and today they were smiling and enjoying the sunlight. Ogma chimed her chord and they turned. Effie's bell was clear and warm, and Rora's bright and pure.

"Hey! You're awake?" Effie waved.

"I'm here, aren't I?" Ogma replied, fishing in her bag for the pies. She tossed one to each of them.

Rora caught it easily. "Mmm... provisions!" She unwrapped the pie and took an eager bite. "Tanks," she said, crumbs tumbling from the corner of her mouth.

Ogma unwrapped one for herself and the three girls sat cross-legged on the wall, munching happily in the sunlight. They ate in silence for a while until Effie sat back with a sigh.

"Delicious. I think I'll have to be a baker when I leave the wall."

Rora snorted. "I bet. You don't know the first thing about cooking."

"I sure do."

"Yeah? What's that, then?"

"The first thing about cooking is that the cook eats first." Effie grinned and grabbed the burlap sack to root around for another pie. Ogma smiled and Rora laughed.

Brushing crumbs from her patrol leathers, Rora stood to glance over the wall. She shook her head in amazement.

"I've never seen it like this. It's so clear. And no fireflies, no other town, just *clear.*"

Ogma went to stand beside her, looking out over the hills. "It won't last."

"Oh, I know. Don't spoil it," Rora said with a sigh.

Effie popped up beside them, offering the half-eaten second pie first to Ogma, and then to Rora, who took it and finished it off absently.

"We should go out."

Rora shook her head firmly and Ogma spoke, "No."

Effie gave them a push. "Come *on*, you old grumps. You sound like the elders."

Rora stuck out her tongue at Effie. "We're on patrol."

Effie rolled her eyes. "*After* dummy. If it's even still clear by then." she sulked.

Rora hesitated. She was clearly tempted.

Ogma shook her head again. "Not unless we go in groups. And besides, if we go out, we should take the villagers and the carts. Bring back timbers and—"

"Ugh. *Yes, Wheeler.*" Effie threw up her hands, but she was smiling when she said it. "So we're going out then?"

Ogma blinked. "Wait. I didn't mean—"

Rora threw her a wink. "She got you there. Smarter than she looks, our Effie."

"Hey! Am not! Wait, I mean—"

Rora laughed and turned to knuckle Ogma on the shoulder. "Don't worry so much, Ogma. We're not going anywhere without talking to Wheeler."

Ogma relaxed a bit.

"It's just this sun—and the sky! It makes you giddy, y'know?"

"We've had some rough nights, that's all," Effie said more quietly. "A break is nice."

It took Ogma a moment to realize they weren't just talking about her rescue. "Brigid said you had trouble over here."

Effie nodded. "Same night as your rescue. We'd just got out here for our shift when we heard double-E start ringing the alarm." She jerked her hand at the bell tower standing above the blue slate roofs in the center of town. "And we missed Wheeler's shadow puppets *again,* by the way."

Rora picked up, "We knew *something* was happening on the north span from the alarm, but we stuck to our span. It was a good thing, too. It really started boiling then."

Effie nodded.

"We were sprinting up and down the wall clearing phantoms all over south and southwest."

"Phew—what a run. This is why we always win the Circle."

"Truth. Anyway," Rora continued, "Little Ambrose and Zachary were on southeast."

"We should have thought of it." Effie put in.

"They're still young. They didn't realize what was going on," Rora said. "They dashed right back off for the north wall when they heard the alarm. Left the whole span empty."

Ogma sucked in a breath, biting her lip.

"It's all right," Effie was anxious to clarify. "I mean—it worked out in the end."

Rora shook her head. "Only because they ran right into Cole coming the other way. He got them turned around real fast. But—"

"But some phantoms got over the wall," Ogma finished.

Rora nodded. "Three of them."

Ogma winced. "Brigid said they were big."

"Big ones are easy to spot though," Effie put in, waving it off. "But yeah—even the smallest one cleared the roofs by head and shoulders, easy."

Ogma didn't find that very reassuring. "What happened?"

Rora took a breath. "Well it turned out okay. Cole took the wall and Ambrose and Zach chased down the phantoms. Gave Old Keegan and Nan Aud a mighty scare, but they kept their heads. Left the house and ran further in."

"The old man was out there too. Not sure where he was going, but it's a good thing he wasn't home. I don't know why he lives so close to the wall." Effie shook her head.

"He was going to Goodie Hazel's, I think," Ogma put in. "He helps her with the medicine sometimes, and the boy we rescued was hurt."

"Ah. That makes sense, then. Ambrose said he was heading in that direction. He didn't even run from the phantoms." Rora sniffed.

"So you found a *boy*, then," Effie teased.

Rora rolled her eyes. "How is he?"

"I don't know. He looked pretty badly hurt." She described the spear wound and the carcass of the beast she'd found on top of him.

Effie whistled. "Gross! And not even a phantom, just some animal out in the fog?"

Ogma nodded.

Effie seemed almost wistful. "Wish I'd seen it."

Rora grinned and nudged Ogma with her elbow. "That's our Effie, more interested in strange beasts than strange boys."

"Don't you know it." Effie pulled Rora into her lap, "That's why I like *you*, eh?"

Ogma smiled. Watching the two of them together never failed to cheer her up.

"It was well done, Ogma," Rora said.

Effie nodded. "She always does well. That's our Ogma. Say —remember your first season? When that big phantom came right over the wall and made it all the way to the village square?"

"We were fetching supper for the watch," Rora remembered.

"And here it comes, all horns and arms and teeth, halfway as high as the bell tower."

"And Rora and I are just standing there, holding the soup—scared stiff. And what do you do?"

Ogma felt herself beginning to blush.

"You walk right up to the cursed thing and wag your finger at it!"

"It looked so ashamed before it faded! And you in your nightdress because you'd forgot your coat again."

"At least you're not doing that anymore," Rora chuckled.

Ogma's blush deepened.

"*No.*" Rora looked at Effie and they looked back at her in disbelief. "Is that why you caught cold?" Effie curled up laughing.

Rora tried to smother a laugh of her own. "We shouldn't. You were really sick." She snorted and fell over Effie, trying to hold back her giggles.

After a moment of heated embarrassment, Ogma started laughing too. It felt good to laugh. It replaced the pit in her stomach with a pleasant ache.

Rora and Effie's laughter subsided into chuckles and then yawns. Rora got up from Effie's lap and stretched.

Effie shook her head to clear it, short curls bouncing around her face. "Aren't we about done for our shift? Are you relieving us, Ogma?"

Ogma shook her head. "Sorry, no. But I think Brigid's sending someone soon."

"Where you off to, then? Back to bed?"

"No, I'm checking on the boy."

Effie started grinning again, but Rora elbowed her in the ribs and turned to Ogma.

"All right then. Hope you find him well. Thanks for the pie."

"Aye, thanks!" Effie waved and Ogma went on her way.

Ogma was a bit anxious about approaching the old man's stone cottage, which was almost in the shadow of the southeast wall. No one was quite sure why he'd decided to live there, but they let him be. He'd certainly never explained it—Ogma wasn't sure if he was actually mute or he just chose not to speak. The gardens and grain fields around his cottage were the best kept in the lower terrace, though, and while the other villagers had abandoned the rest during the weeks of heavy fog, he'd taken care of his crop.

The windows and front door were open and she could hear the quiet rustle and clatter of domestic sounds inside. She approached cautiously and paused a moment on the doorstep to calm her nerves. She'd asked Wheeler once what the man's name was. He'd shrugged and said he didn't seem to have one. When she said they had to call him *something*, Wheeler told her that Goodie Hazel had tried to give him one shortly after he came to the village, but he just shook his head. Apparently, he didn't seem to mind that they all called him "the old man."

He appeared on the threshold as if he'd heard her thoughts. He seemed entirely unsurprised to see her, just smiled placidly and gestured for her to come inside. The cottage had only a single room, but it was spacious. The old man went over to the sink and pumped water into a kettle while she looked around.

What a strange place. He had a bizarre collection of knick-knacks: old feathers, bits of rock with writing or pictures carved into them, and brightly-painted pottery animals, all cluttering the shelves and windowsills and hung from the walls.

He must have traded these from the Caravaners. I wonder if they do anything.

Movement in the corner of her eye caught Ogma's attention. The boy was lying under a threadbare quilt in the old man's bed. *He's awake.* His eyes were following her around the room. They looked at each other.

After an awkward pause, Ogma ventured an introduction. "What's your name?"

The boy's eyes widened and words began pouring out. Words that she couldn't understand.

"Du snakker! Så du kan snakke da. Selv om du gjør høres morsomt. Den gamle mannen har ikke sagt et ord!" He gesticulated in exasperation.

He doesn't even speak our language? Apart from Caravaners, there'd never been a wanderer or other village that spoke another tongue, though some spoke their familiar language rather strangely.

"Jeg trodde du ville alle være dum." He sank back on the bed. "Hvor er jeg? Hvordan kom jeg hit?" His voice was surprisingly soft and lyrical.

She'd thought he was a bit older than Wheeler, but now she thought he must be younger.

He sat up straighter, looking at her intently. "Er dette en beholdning av den Blå Legion?" His voice became more insistent. "Jeg advarer dere—jeg trilsk! Jeg trilsk." He was strangely proud, and defiant, when he repeated the last phrase.

Ogma was unsure what to say. "Trilsk? Is your name Trilsk?" She pointed at him.

He nodded vigorously and pointed at himself. "Trilsk." He pointed at her. "Er du en vasall av den Blå Legion?"

She looked at him in confusion. *There's something—I could almost understand that.*

"Den Blå Legion?" he repeated.

Ogma shook her head and pointed at herself. "Denbla lagoon? What does that mean? No denbla lagoon."

The boy seemed to be getting agitated. He sat up straighter. "Au!"

Well that's clear enough. "You should be lying down."

He clutched at his side and sank back onto the bed. The old man was watching silently, a mug of tea in each hand.

Ogma pointed to herself. "My name is Ogma. Ogma."

The boy pointed at her. "Ogma?"

"Yes, yes!" She nodded vigorously and pointed to herself again. "Ogma." She pointed to him again. "Trilsk?"

He began to nod, and then shook his head as if he realized some mistake. He pointed at himself. "Mitt navn er Dunkirk." He looked at her and nodded slightly, still pointing at himself. "Dunkirk."

Ogma pointed at him, "Dunkirk," and then at herself, "Ogma."

He pointed at her, "Ogma?" and then at himself, "Dunkirk." He watched her, and nodded when she did. He pointed at the old man and raised his eyebrows.

Well that's not going to help matters, she thought, *even we don't know his name.* She just shrugged and pointed at her mouth mutely.

The boy looked confused and frustrated, but then shrugged and began speaking again, as rapidly as the first time.

"Jeg må komme tilbake til den Blå Legion. Veiviseren datter. Hun er avhengig av oss. Vi må beseire fienden. Jeg må finne dem."

The words washed over her in an incomprehensible rush. He seemed to be asking for something. Pleading almost. *That last bit almost sounded like...* Ogma shook her head and waved away his words in frustration.

He kept talking at a desperate clip until at last the old man stepped in, murmuring soothing sounds until Dunkirk fell silent, and pressing a cup of tea into his hands. He turned and gave the other to Ogma, sitting her in a chair at his table. The last chair he took for himself. They sat in silence for a while, each sipping at their tea as the quiet drew on.

An approaching voice made them turn their heads in unison toward the door.

"—and then he started talking and talking, only I couldn't understand any of it, so I left right away to run and get you." Bowen's voice carried up the walkway to the house.

"Good of you to think of it, young Bowen," Goodie Hazel replied, and then she was in the doorway. She surveyed the room with an intimidating glare. Her gaze lingered first on Dunkirk, sitting up in bed, at which she clucked disapprovingly. She turned to Ogma next and smiled, but it was still intimidating.

"Come to check on him, have we? Of course you have." She bustled into the room and addressed herself to Dunkirk. "Awake then? Feeling better?"

Dunkirk said nothing this time. *Well... Goodie Hazel can do that to a person.* Ogma half-smiled to herself.

Bowen trailed in behind her and whispered conspiratorially while Goodie Hazel examined her patient. "There was a lot of blood." He chattered excitedly. "The spear was right there, right in his belly. They had to pull it out, but first they had to clean out all the splinters and stuff. Here, I've got a piece." He handed Ogma a glittering iridescent blue fragment. Ogma turned it over in her hands, studying it.

"It looks like—"

"—beetle shell! I know, right?" Bowen gestured in the direction of the boy admiringly. "I wonder where he got it?"

Still a stupid thing to use for armor, Ogma thought, and

went to hand the piece back to Bowen. Dunkirk squirmed as Goodie Hazel and the old man changed his bandages.

"Oh, you can have that one," Bowen said, pushing it back into her hand. "I've got *loads* more. Goodie Hazel let me keep 'em." Bowen was puffed up with self-satisfaction. Ogma pocketed the fragment, watching them unwind the bandage.

Bowen looked briefly disappointed with her lack of interest in the acquisition he clearly found rare and valuable. But then he shrugged and started narrating the proceedings, his observation of the surgery having made him a certain expert in his own mind.

"See—after they cleaned out the wound they just sewed him right up, just like Daniel mending shirts." He lectured with an air of clinical authority, as if it were something he'd seen a hundred times. "Only you have to sew the *insides* first, *then* the outsides so he doesn't keep bleeding inside and pop."

Ogma was rather sure it was more complicated than that.

"Au! Som gjør vondt. Når har du tenkt å la meg ut herfra? Jeg føler meg bra." Dunkirk seemed to be protesting the proceedings. He tried to get up from the bed, but Goodie Hazel pushed him firmly back down.

"None of that, now. Bed rest. *Bed. Rest.*" She spoke loudly and slowly.

It's not like he lost his hearing, Ogma thought. Dunkirk subsided sulkily back onto the bed.

Goodie Hazel turned to the room. "All right, then. On your way!" She shooed at Bowen and Ogma with her hands. "I'm sure you've got more important things to do. He needs his rest."

Bowen was already out the door. Ogma stood up quickly to follow.

"You'd best come by early," Goodie Hazel said as Ogma headed for the door.

"Sorry?"

"Your Wheeler says the boy's to move to the watch house tomorrow."

"Oh."

"I told him: I said he's plenty old enough to be off the wall—and for that matter Wheeler should be thinking about—oh well, anyway, he insisted."

She thinks Wheeler should be off the wall. Ogma pushed that thought away. She was impressed that Wheeler had managed to insist on anything with Goodie Hazel.

"But is he well enough?" Ogma asked, gesturing to the heavily bandaged Dunkirk.

"He will be. Those sutures came from Caravaner thread." Goodie Hazel sighed heavily. "Not much left, I'm afraid."

Ogma had a vague recollection that Old Keegan had once had a very serious accident, caught his arm in the windmill works or something, but after Goodie Hazel sewed him up, he was back at work in the village within a week.

"So you'll collect him early, then."

It didn't sound like a question to Ogma. She nodded and left. The boy's eyes followed her from the bed as she walked to the door, and the old man waved.

The golden glow of afternoon light was just fading to dusk as Ogma traced her steps back through the village. The villagers were lighting lanterns in their windows. Considering the late hour, there were more people in the streets than Ogma was expecting. Men and women were gathered in small groups just outside their doors talking in hushed tones.

"It's a whole *day* wasted, if you ask me," a man was complaining as Ogma passed by.

"Shh... I know," a young woman put a hand on his arm, nodding in Ogma's direction. "They're just being cautious."

"Hrm..." The man cleared his throat when he saw Ogma and lowered his voice. "It's just we could use the lumber. The roof's been sagging, Moll, and Kev's been hoarding all the timber we've got left."

"I know all that as well as you, Roose, you know I do." Moll replied, "and not enough leather for shoes either. But you heard what happened last night. They're tired." She gave Ogma another sympathetic glance.

Just at that moment, Enoch tolled: long–short, long–short. Roose and Moll disappeared inside their home, emerging a moment later with coats and bells. The village was gathering. Ogma heard the answering bells across the village, including the clear note of the watch bell. She added her own simple chime and hurried curiously to the square. There was already a fair crowd, and lanterns had been lit in the fading light.

The village elders were there: Old Keegan the weaver, the only man in the village with fully gray hair; Nan Aud the stone-mason, her hands as gnarled and bumpy as the cobblestone paths of the town; and Goodie Hazel, bustling into the square just a moment behind Ogma. Wheeler was there as well, for the watch. They stood on a small platform just below the bell tower as the stragglers filtered into the square.

Rora and Effie slipped in from the northern end of the square, Rora suppressing a yawn and Effie giving Ogma a smile and a wave across the crowd. They went to stand near the plat-form. Ogma was surprised to see them: she'd have expected them to go straight to bed after they were relieved on the wall. Wheeler usually took the meetings alone.

The sky faded to purple while Wheeler and the elders waited patiently for the last of the able-bodied villagers to arrive.

Nan Aud raised a bell in each hand, pealing first her own high chime, and then the powerful basso gong of the Elder's bell. She cleared her throat as the whispers in the square subsided.

"Welcome all!" The clarity and tenor of her voice belied her rough manner. "It has been twenty-four nights since our last meeting, forty days since the fog last broke, and almost four seasons since the fog last brought another town to us."

The villagers murmured their quiet hopes for the fog breaks to come more often.

"There is much news, but first, the reckoning of the stores." Nan Aud stepped back and Old Keegan stepped forward, ringing his three bells in their complicated discord.

Ogma had heard the village where he'd watched had been almost three times the size of their own, and so he was used to carrying more bells. He'd always kept his three even though no one else in the village carried more than two.

Ogma had once worked out how many villagers they'd have to have before they really needed three bells. With two bells from up to three octaves, and discords as well as true chords, and only some people's chords rung in unison, while others were rung broken... It had made her head spin, but the number was at least five hundred, she was pretty sure. The village needed maybe half that many at its current size.

Sums weren't Ogma's favorite thing, but she was fairly good at them. Still, thinking about that—or anything else—was more interesting than listening to the accounting of the stores.

Old Keegan's voice quavered, but he was still easily heard across the square.

"We have thirty tons of grain left in the stores, enough for half a season, and we should have our next harvest within ten days. We have twenty tons each of beans and squash, with more of that, too, to harvest soon. Other vegetables have been plentiful, with three full harvests this season, despite the rain. Our food stores are strong, and we have plenty to trade should a break bless us with another village."

The villagers murmured agreement, but some were shaking their heads impatiently. Rora was yawning again, which made Ogma yawn in turn. As important as the reckoning was, it was *boring*.

"We are low on tin ore and very low on iron. We must hope for trade or forage," Old Keegan continued, nodding toward Rowan and Isak, the village's smith and tinker, standing in the front row. "Down, cotton, and wool have all run low, and nights have been cold. We must hope for trade or forage. Leather stores are nearly empty. We should try to catch the ermine moths when we can."

Roose spoke up so the square could hear. "We should hunt, Keegan! We could use the hides."

There were murmurs of assent from the other villagers. Old Keegan raised his hands placatingly. "That is for young Wheeler to decide. He will speak soon."

"But—"

"He will speak soon," Keegan said firmly, and Roose quieted. "In the meantime, the stores are enough that perhaps we can leave some grain in the fields to ferment, to better catch the moths."

Nan Aud interjected with a gentle chime. "Food is not a thing to be wasted lightly."

Wheeler spoke up. "The youngest ones have been wearing through their shoes. Of all the stores, we have the most food. We always have."

Goodie Hazel agreed. "The watch must have their shoes." She looked to each of her fellow elders.

After a moment's consideration, they nodded, and together with Wheeler, rang their bells to affirm the decision.

"Good." Old Keegan continued, reciting the village's other precious stores.

Ogma's mind was wandering. She tilted her head back and watched the first stars come out. The ones directly overhead were still, though those on the horizon danced. The small disk of the moon's blue sister was high in the sky, though her larger sibling had yet to rise. She'd forgotten that the fog breaks stilled the stars. It was very peaceful.

Keegan had nearly finished. "Last, our timber stores are lowest of all. The reserve is nearly spent. We may have to salvage from the buildings closest to the wall." There were harsher murmurs at that. "We must hope for trade."

"Trade?" Roose called out again. "The other villages can no more afford to trade their timber than we!"

Other voices were rising in agreement.

Kev spoke up. "He's right, Keegan! We need to chop new timbers."

Old Keegan nodded grudgingly and stepped back, gesturing to Wheeler, who stepped forward.

He looked tired, and more than a little nervous. He stood as tall as most of the men in the square, a fact Ogma noted uneasily.

He cleared his throat. "I know the break has been tempting. I know you're eager to go out and gather." The villagers watched him grimly, nodding. "I'm sorry we haven't been able to send out parties yet."

A young woman's voice, Ogma couldn't tell who, spoke up. "These breaks hardly last more than a day most of the time. You know that. What if we've missed our chance?"

Worried calls of agreement rose up.

Wheeler raised his arms. "We've kept watch—there's still no fog within miles of the village."

"Then why haven't we gone out?" someone called.

"Please. The fog's been at the wall's edge for ten days, and even before that, the banks were thick and close. Every child's been on the wall. We're tired. I had to let them sleep."

The mutters quieted down again.

Nan Aud chimed her bell gently and stepped forward. "We know it's been hard. We thank you and the other children, Wheeler. We remember the wall."

The villagers called out their thanks, but many without feeling. Ogma could still hear them muttering about the wasted day. She could see Wheeler tensing on the platform.

Don't they remember? It's not that long since some of them were on the wall. Ogma felt anger unfolding in her chest. *We have to live it every day.*

Goodie Hazel's glare withered the unenthusiastic crowd. She drew herself up. "*Three* phantoms crossed the wall before the fog broke."

Faces in the crowd paled, and the muttering stopped.

Now you remember, Ogma thought with grim satisfaction. Goodie Hazel paused and let the words sink into the sheepish crowd.

"*And* a wanderer, lost in the fog, was rescued. I'm sure we're all *very* grateful."

Some surprised chatter broke out among the villagers who hadn't yet heard.

"Who'd we find? Someone from another village?" Moll called out.

"One of the badgerkin?"

"A Caravaner?"

Wheeler spoke up again. "A boy. About my age. He was badly hurt, though..." He looked to Goodie Hazel questioningly.

"He will make a full recovery," she replied. It had more the tone of a command than a statement of fact. "He's resting now."

"What's his name?"

Wheeler shook his head. "I don't know. I'm not sure he speaks our tongue."

The chatter rose in volume. Even the Caravaners only spoke in their own strange dialects amongst themselves. They at least *knew* the proper language.

Ogma, near the back, spoke up. "Dunkirk. His name is Dunkirk."

The villagers parted and turned, most noticing her for the first time. Ogma shuffled her feet, uncomfortable under their scrutiny.

"That's as far as we got."

Wheeler cleared his throat and the villagers turned their attention back to him. He continued, "He'll be joining the watch tomorrow. He's still of age to help."

Roose called up again, "That's all well and good, but what about this fog break?"

Kev added, "Aye. Are we going out, boy?"

Wheeler hesitated.

Rowan called out from the crowd. "It's up to you, boy. We'll abide." She'd been the oldest too, once. She knew the burden on him. Wheeler nodded and made up his mind.

"Yes, we'll go out tonight. But—" Excited voices cut him off. He raised his hands and shouted over them. "Please! But only a small party tonight. For lumber only."

"Bah," Roose sighed in frustration.

Wheeler's voice hardened. "It's dangerous enough in the woods at night. Harder to see the fog if it creeps up. If the break holds out, we'll send out more parties tomorrow."

Roose nodded grudgingly. "We'll abide."

"Rora and Effie will escort. No more than two carts and eight people." Wheeler finished firmly, "More tomorrow."

Goodie Hazel nodded her approval and stepped forward. "If the village business is done, then?"

Nan Aud and Old Keegan nodded and raised their bells.

"Then we are done. May the breaks be many, and the other towns near."

Nan Aud rang the elder's bell in benediction, and all the villagers rang their own bells in answer.

The villagers began to disperse. Ogma noted with a snort that for all the bluster in the crowd, Roose was having trouble finding volunteers to go out with the lumber party. Rowan and Isak had joined right away, and Kev was eager, but others were hard to come by. In the end, five men and three women stood by the carts, honing rarely-used axe and hatchet blades in the pools of yellow lantern light. Ogma sidled closer to the now empty stage where Rora and Effie were getting the party organized.

"One of us stays with each cart at all times." Rora gestured at herself and Effie. "We'll leave by the northern gate, and the carts must stay within bellshot of the wall *and each other*, got it?" She waited for each of the villagers to meet her gaze and nod.

Effie added, "We'll have an extra patrol at the north wall watching for fog. So if you hear the watch bell, or fog forbid Enki and Enoch, you drop what you're doing, grab the cart, and get back quick, right?"

The villagers all nodded.

"If you have to, you *will* leave the cart behind."

They nodded again.

"Right, let's go." The expedition trundled off, the hand-drawn carts rumbling over the cobblestones.

Ogma waited in the square, letting them get ahead. She'd have to walk the same direction to get back to the watch house, but she'd rather walk alone than with the adults.

Wheeler appeared at the edge of the lantern light. "Dunkirk, huh? What's he like?"

"He talks funny," she replied, considering the lilt of the boy's voice. "Almost like he's singing? Can't understand a word, though." She started walking the cobbled path to the watch house. Wheeler shortened his stride and walked beside her. The air was pleasantly cool, in contrast to the bitter cold of the previous night.

"It's almost worse during the breaks," Wheeler said distantly, then faded into a brooding silence.

After a moment, Ogma asked, "What's worse?"

"*This*," he said, gesturing vaguely at the village. "The fog. The watch." There was a bitterness in his voice she had never heard before. "It shouldn't *be* this way." He clenched his fists, nails digging into his palms. "All the grown-ups behind the walls while we train, while we patrol, while we skin our knees and break our bones, and fight the beasts outside, let alone the fog." Ogma had never seen him like this, never heard his voice quake with such anger.

She touched his shoulder gently "But it can hurt them. Kill them."

"I know! Of course, I do! I just..." He threw off her arm and sank down on his heels, arms wrapped around his knees. "Have you ever seen it? Seen what happens when the fog hurts someone?"

"I... we all know the stories—"

"—well I have! I've seen it." He rocked back and forth, his eyes somewhere far away. "It hurt her. It took her."

"...who?" Ogma asked gently.

"My—" He hunched his shoulders, started again."She always came to check on us at the wall when I was small. She played games with us. Sang to us." His voice was small. "She always had something special just for me."

He seemed to come back to himself, and stood.

"I'm sorry, Ogma. I shouldn't put this on you."

Wheeler's hands were shaking. It was the most frightening thing Ogma had ever seen. *What should I do? He's so afraid.*

"I try..." he whispered, tears streaking his cheeks.

Ogma hugged him fiercely, her own eyes stinging.

"You don't just t-try." She muffled her sob in his shirt. "You *do*. You're always there for us. You taught us everything—told us all the stories. Y-you're just getting older." She held him tighter. "We'll protect *you* now! All of us!"

Ogma felt the muscles in his chest tighten. After a moment, he put his arms around her. He was warm. He took a deep breath. She could feel his chest rise and fall against her cheek.

"Why don't you let someone else take over?" She asked quietly. She didn't want to ask. Didn't want him to leave.

"Who? Daniel? He's... he's too kind. Brigid's strong but she rubs people the wrong way. Rora maybe, but Effie brings out her worst. It would have to be... you."

Ogma broke the hug and stepped back, shifting nervously from foot to foot. She swallowed gruffly and rubbed the tears from her face, but couldn't meet his eyes.

"I-I..." She tried to steel herself, get the spike of fear under control.

"Not yet." Wheeler whispered. "A couple more seasons."

Ogma felt relief and guilt fill her all at once. She told herself she hadn't heard disappointment in his voice.

They stood quietly in the cobbled path for a while. After a moment, he relaxed slightly and exhaled.

"Why do we get *more* scared when we get older?" he asked quietly.

"We know better," Ogma said.

He smiled bitterly as she wiped her cheeks. They turned back on their way towards the watch house.

CHAPTER 3
STRANGE CUSTOMS

A soft tickling on her face woke Ogma the next morning. She opened her eyes. Feathery black antennae tickled searchingly over her nose. She and the ermine moth stared at each other for a moment.

"Well," Ogma started.

The unconcerned insect considered her in silence.

"I need to be going."

The critter fluttered its wings once, but did not take off.

"And if you don't want to be shoe leather, you should probably get moving too."

Ogma picked the moth up off her chest, sat up, and dropped the fuzzy thing back on her pillow. It fluttered its wings again but didn't fly away. It had a coat of white fuzz with black spots and was quite rotund. She wasn't entirely sure it could actually fly, though she supposed it must have to get up to her bunk.

"Ridiculous," she accused it.

It fluttered again.

"Suit yourself."

Ogma changed quietly and picked her way past the other

sleeping children. Effie and Rora were snoring in two bunks closest to the door. Wheeler's bunk was empty.

Brigid was tightening the laces on her patrol leathers. They were well worn and looked very warm. *They were Rowan's when she was on the wall,* Ogma remembered enviously. *They'll give me my own when I've stopped growing,* she consoled herself.

"We'll be rousing them in a bit." Brigid nodded to the sleeping children as Ogma approached. "Wheeler's organizing more gathering parties. It's still so clear out there. We'd better make the best of it."

Ogma nodded.

"You off to pick up the boy, then?"

"Dunkirk."

"So he does have a name. All right then, you hurry back. Maybe once he's settled in you can help us with one of these gathering parties."

"All right," Ogma replied, turning to head out.

"Ogma!" Brigid called after her.

Ogma made an about face just outside the door. "Wh—"

The coat Brigid flung hit her in the face.

"Mrmph—thanks," she said, pulling the coat off her head.

Ogma wrapped the coat tightly around her as she mounted the stairs to the wall. The air felt thin and still cold in the early morning light. She'd decided to take the rampart walk: it was longer, but it would give her the chance to study the strangely unchanging landscape outside the walls.

Free of fog, the landscape glittered with a pale frost. Ogma's breath hung in the air. The banks around the distant hills seemed to be thickening, but none were approaching the town as yet. She could faintly hear the foraging parties: gruff calls and the crashing of timber.

Back over the town, the dawn light was cold and pale as it

glinted on the blue slate roofs. Long shadows marched across the ground and the sun shifted on the horizon as the fickle landscape changed in the distance. It was disorienting, but she knew that in a few hours, once the sun was higher in the sky, it would chart a straighter course.

Ogma shivered and yawned. *Time to wake up.* She shook her head and set a quick pace along the rampart, rubbing her arms through her coat to keep warm.

She met Ambrose and Zachary on the northeast wall. *Wheeler's moved them closer to the watch house,* Ogma noted. They jangled bells at her and she chimed hers in return.

"Ogma! Did you hear? Did you hear?!" Ambrose was beaming from ear to ear. "I banished 'free phantoms!" He held up as many fingers. "I was just like you! I ran right up to them and—and—"

Zachary was looking sheepish. He was two seasons older than Ambrose, and it was clear he realized she'd have known better than to leave the span, like he and Ambrose had done that night.

"An' it had a 'fousand teef! And—and the other one had heads that kept arguing and biting each other."

"That sounds perfectly horrible," Ogma replied in an appropriately impressed tone.

"Yeah! It was terrible!" Ambrose responded enthusiastically.

"We'd better get back to patrol," Zachary said, coloring with embarrassment. He took the younger boy's arm and continued on their way.

Ogma walked on. The windmills were still. The wooden frames creaked as the cold and dew made them swell and settle. The canvas of the blades flapped gently in the breeze. She passed other children on patrol who rang their bells merrily as she approached. Each one gestured at the landscape beyond the wall in apparent disbelief. Ogma grinned back and kept on her way.

As Ogma reached the southeast span, she heard muffled shouts and the sound of a scuffle.

What's going on? Some animal from the outside?

A vision of the beast that had nearly killed Dunkirk loomed in her head. She broke into a jog along the top of the wall.

Cole was shouting down at someone at the inner gate.

"You can't go out without permission! You can't leave the walls!"

"Åpne de fordømte porten!" The boy—Dunkirk—was shouting back up at him. "Slipp meg ut! Jeg vil ikke være din fange!"

As Ogma ran up, Cole turned to her in consternation. "He won't listen! He's trying to leave!"

Ogma looked out over the edge of the wall. The old man was trying to hold Dunkirk back from the gate. Dunkirk was rattling the bar on the wicket, trying to shrug off the old man. He was barefoot and shirtless, bandages still wrapped around most of his midsection.

He's not even wearing his bells? She was flabbergasted. *Wait, did he even have any?* She combed her memory of the rescue: she remembered the spear, the armor, mud and quills, but no bells. The voice they'd heard—those cries in the fog.

We heard them for days. The same voice. Ogma couldn't believe it. *If he'd had a bell, we'd have known he was real! We would have gone out sooner!*

She was angry suddenly; it welled up inside and boiled over. She was angry at the foreigner's complete stupidity and ingratitude.

"Hey!" she bellowed down the face of the wall. *"You!* Dunkirk!" He looked up at her in surprise, one hand pulling at the bar on the wicket gate, the other frozen in the act of trying to throw off the old man.

She stormed down the stone steps, interposing herself between Dunkirk and the wall and jabbing him in the chest with a finger.

"What do you think you're *doing?*" Ogma asked. Despite his lack of understanding, her tone was perfectly clear. Dunkirk shrank back from her.

She jabbed him again. "I can't believe anyone could be so *stupid.*"

He withered under her glare, but then his expression hardened.

"Hva er galt med deg, dum jente? Kom deg ut av veien!" He shoved her aside and made for the gate again. The old man threw up his hands and looked skyward.

By the time Ogma picked herself up off the dirt, Dunkirk had the wicket gate open and had walked through. He was walking quickly but limping, favoring his injured side. Ogma ran in front of him and spread her arms wide.

"*No!*" she shouted firmly.

He took a threatening step forward.

"Jeg vil ikke være din fange. Jeg må finne den Blå Legion!"

"Blå, blah, blah. No. I know it looks clear, but the fog could come back any time. You can't just leave like this!"

He took another step forward.

"Look! Look. You don't even have a bell. You lost your bell!" Ogma pushed him in the chest where his bells should be hanging around his neck, and raised her own, ringing them under his nose. "You forgot your bell!"

Dunkirk made a wordless, angry noise and grabbed the bells out of her hand, yanking them to one side and hurling them away from him. Ogma was jerked off balance as the leather thong around her neck snapped. She fell to the ground and the bells clanked in the dirt.

She felt heat rising in her face and a red anger, hotter than any she'd felt before. Tears burned in the corners of her eyes. She blinked them away and stood up, running forward to cut the boy off again.

She stood facing him, chin thrust out defiantly, hands balled into fists at her sides.

"You're not going anywhere," she spat through gritted teeth. She wasn't as big as him. *But if I was strong enough to carry him out of the mud, I'm strong enough to knock him back down again.*

He gave her a contemptuous look and started to brush past her.

Her fist caught him square in the side, just above the unhealed wound. With a wheeze and a gasp of pain, he collapsed in the dirt.

"I *saved* you." Her voice was hard. "And like it or not, I'll save you again."

He wheezed in the dirt, face ashen, one hand to his bandages. She pushed aside a twinge of guilt. *Well I don't regret it.* She leaned down and helped him to his feet. Looping one arm around her shoulders, she led him back to the gate.

Cole's eyes were wide as they came back through. The old man noticed Dunkirk's labored breathing and clucked his tongue in consternation before stepping forward to help on Dunkirk's other side.

Ogma tossed her head to Cole. "Could you get my bells?"

Cole ran through the gate to retrieve the two bells from the dirt, whose melancholy minor chord sounded as battered as she felt. He tied the ends of the broken lace together and slipped it over her neck.

"Thanks."

He nodded and went to close and bar the wicket gate.

It was awkward for the old man and Ogma to try and support Dunkirk. The old man was so much taller than her that most of Dunkirk's weight fell on her shoulders. He turned them back towards his cottage.

"Wait - I'm supposed to take him to the watch house."

The old man glanced at her questioningly but took her lead. Dunkirk was still wincing with each step, but Ogma was still too angry with him to have much sympathy.

She changed course. The fastest way was straight through the village square, though it was also the most public.

"Hvor skal vi?"

"Hush. We're going to the watch house."

The village was bustling with all the craft and exchange of goods of any fair-weather day, plus clumps of excited bystanders waiting on the return of the foraging parties and their carts. Gossip and speculation were running thick and fast, especially given the fog's continued quiescence. A second full day of fog break was great luck, even if there was no other village close by this time.

Ogma saw Eve, a young woman who often made soup for the watch, chatting among a small crowd of people at the edge of the square. "I just keep hoping the fireflies will come. It'd be good to have a festival day."

"Aye, it feels like we should, with a break like this."

"Oh—!"

They noticed Ogma and the old man helping Dunkirk hobble into the square. They turned to watch in open curiosity, but made no move to speak or help.

When Dunkirk saw the villagers watching he shrugged off Ogma's and the old man's support to walk on his own. *Not hurt so bad after all, hm?* Dunkirk grinned smugly down at her, and then blanched as her elbow caught his ribs.

"Oops." Ogma smirked. "Come on—this way." She set a faster pace not waiting to see if he would limp after.

In the square itself, Roose was splitting lumber. He paused to stretch his back and wipe his brow.

"Good on you, girl! Getting him up on his feet already—ha! Why don't you help us with the lumber, boy? ."

"Hvem, jeg?" Dunkirk pointed at the cart and shook his head no." Roose laughed and they walked on.

As they reached the cobbled path that led to the northeast wall, they met a cart rumbling back into the village. Burly Rowan and Isak were hauling from the front while several others pushed from the back. Bowen was walking beside the cart. All were streaked with dirt and grime. The back of the cart was filled with dull gray and charcoal-colored lumps.

Bowen called out to Ogma. "It's ore! We've found iron and tin!" He waved something over his head. "And look at these!"

They looked like rusted iron bands to Ogma, but they were clearly man-made—something that had been lost in the fog who knows when. The metal was good salvage and the ore a rich find. Between that and the lumber, they'd be well equipped to trade the next time another village came near. She grunted an acknowledgement and waved at Bowen from under the weight of Dunkirk's arm.

"So that's him?" Rowan called out as the cart rumbled past. It was gone before Ogma could reply.

They walked the rest of the way in silence, pausing every now and again to catch their breath, and enjoy the light breeze.

The watch house was nearly empty. Most of the children were on patrol or assisting the foraging parties. No available hands could be wasted during a fog break. Of those who remained, most were the very youngest and those who had stayed to watch them, plus a few exhausted older children slumbering in their bunks.

A blanket fort was under construction in the corner. Young Emma seemed to be in charge, with predictable results: grandiose design but some difficulties in execution.

Daniel, yawning, watched them curiously and gave Ogma a wave.

Ogma and the old man sat Dunkirk down on a bunk near the fireplace, though Ogma made certain it wasn't Wheeler's this time.

Emma and the others had noticed them, but the sight of the strange boy and the old man kept them behind the safety of their blanket walls.

Ogma took a seat on a bunk across from Dunkirk. He avoided her gaze sullenly.

The old man watched them both for a moment, hovering by the fireplace. After a few minutes' silence, he came and put a hand on Dunkirk's shoulder.

"Safe," he said simply. They both looked up at him in shock. He smiled at them kindly, the corners of his eyes crinkling.

He was out the door and gone before they could reply.

"Safe?" Dunkirk repeated quietly. He said it strangely—more like 'saife'—but it seemed to Ogma that maybe he understood. He met her gaze, sullenness gone from his face, replaced by a simple, pleading query.

"Hvorfor?"

Ogma shook her head.

"Hvorfor?" he repeated, crestfallen.

Ogma didn't know how to explain the danger he only barely seemed to understand. She sighed, staring into the embers of the fire, watching the smoke curl up the chimney.

The glowing coals gave her an idea.

"Wait here," she told him. He looked on, puzzled, as she stood up. She ran over to the watch house windows, pulling them closed and shuttering them.

Still too bright, she thought. She cast around the room for a moment until her eyes settled on the blanket fort. Ogma presented herself to the cohort of youngsters.

"May I borrow your blankets?"

Emma drew herself up. "It's our *fort*. It keeps away the fog."

Ogma nodded with appropriate, solemn concern.

"Of course. Only I was hoping..." Ogma sighed in mock disappointment, watching curiosity war with possessiveness on the child's face. "I was hoping I could use them to cover the shutters... so I could make shadow puppets."

Emma looked at Ogma skeptically. "Are you any good?"

"Oh sure," Ogma lied brazenly. "Wheeler used to say I was his best assistant."

"Pff. *I'm* his best assistant," Emma said. "But I guess..."

"Thanks!" Ogma responded, gathering handfuls of blankets from the fort before the capricious child could change her mind. She returned to the shutters and covered them over as best she could. Some light was still leaking through, but the room was much dimmer.

"It'll have to do," Ogma said aloud, brushing off her hands. She jogged over to the fireplace and pulled the carven wooden screen across it, dimming the room still further.

She fumbled with the dark lantern for a moment, burning her finger with the taper before managing to get it lit. *What am I doing?* She sucked her burned finger. *I should have just waited for Wheeler. Too late now.*

Emma's cohort had wandered over with their pillows and they took up places around the bunk where Dunkirk sat. If anything, he looked even more confused. But he was watching.

Here goes...

She took the wooden silhouettes and arranged them in front of the lantern: the shadow of walls and windmills was projected on the wall behind her.

"This is why we watch the fog," she started. It was the only proper way to begin. "The village." She pointed to the silhouette and then gestured around the room. "The village."

Dunkirk nodded, relief passing over his face as he understood her purpose.

"Byen." He mimicked her gestures. "Landsbyen." He screwed up his face, trying to pronounce it as she had. "Vil-laj." It sounded thick and heavy on his tongue.

"Village," Ogma repeated.

"Vilaj," he said hesitantly.

Close enough. Ogma turned back to the shadow puppets. She picked up the metal basin and reached behind the fireplace screen for a coal. After several failed attempts, she managed to grab hold of one long enough to drop it in the basin.

"This is *boring,*" Emma complained. Ogma ignored her.

She hunted about a moment for a mug and scooped up some of the wash water. She poured it slowly into the basin and set it in front of the lantern and silhouettes, as Wheeler had done. The steam curled up and the shadow of the fog's gripping tendrils curled around the silhouetted ramparts.

"The fog. Fog."

Dunkirk looked confused for a moment. "Brann? Royk?"

Ogma grabbed several tree puppets and some mountains and shuffled them into and out of the steam. The shadows on the wall shifted and twisted.

Dunkirk understood. His expression tightened.

"Tåken," he said firmly. And then more hesitantly, "Fogg?"

"Yes, taken! The fog takes people." Ogma dropped the landscape silhouettes with a clatter and picked up doll figures. They made children-sized shapes at the top of the wall. She took one a bit bigger than the rest and made it walk awkwardly through the gate.

This is you, you stubborn clod.

She blew at the bowl of steam and the shadow fog billowed and twisted. The figure in her hand disappeared in the shifting shadows and she dropped it to the floor out of sight. She blew more gently, clearing away a patch of the shadow fog and the figure was gone. She pushed the wall silhouette away and picked up the trees and mountains again. She made them dance in the fog, and then picked up the small figure. She showed it drifting through the fog, wandering first one way, then another: popping up between the trees, and then atop the mountain.

"Fog. Tåken," Dunkirk said again, expression grim.

"Lost," she said firmly, shaking the small figure in her hand.

"Lost. Tåken."

Ogma hesitated for a moment. She wasn't quite sure how to do this next one. It was complicated. She shifted the wall and windmill silhouette to the middle of her scene. On one side she placed the outline of a cottage. She moved the bowl to the other side so that the fog billowed up against the wall.

She rearranged her figures. One child-sized silhouette stood in the house and an adult-sized shadow puppet stood on the wall.

She picked up the basin of fog and brought it level with the top of the wall shadow. With her other hand she picked up a grotesque, ill-proportioned shape. Wheeler only used it in his scariest stories. She blew into the basin again until the fog boiled over the rampart, surrounding the adult-sized figure on the wall. She brought up her other hand and the snarling, twisted shape coalesced from the fog.

Emma's group shrieked with fear and excitement.

Ogma made the horrific shape attack the adult figure savagely. The adult puppet did not disappear like the child had but was pulled to pieces instead.

Emma's cohort booed the beast's triumph. Dunkirk's hands were clenched on the blankets.

Ogma poured the phantom over the lip of the wall and into the village. She picked up one of the child-sized figures and marched it straight for the beast.

"Yeah! You get him!" Emma interjected. "That's me!"

Dunkirk looked on warily as Ogma marched the little girl purposefully towards the beast. When the two shapes touched, instead of attacking the child figure, Ogma dropped the monstrous silhouette and the phantom shadow instantly disappeared.

Ogma lifted the child figure to the wall and made it patrol. She picked up an adult-sized figure and put it firmly inside the walls.

She turned back to Dunkirk.

"Safe," she said grimly.

He met her eyes, and then looked away. "Saife."

CHAPTER 4
THE FESTIVAL

Ogma was wracking her brain, trying to figure out some way to explain the bells, when Mae and Maya burst through the front door.

"Caravaners!"

Two lumps in the upper bunks rolled over.

"Mmm... how long have we been out?" Rora asked groggily, looking around the darkened room in surprise.

Effie, the lighter sleeper, called down to Ogma. "I like what you've done with the place."

"I thought you were with the lumber crew?" Ogma asked.

"We were! That was *ages* ago. Wheeler has someone else out with the crews now."

"What's this about Caravaners?" Rora put in.

Mae and Maya continued chattering.

"We saw them from the west wall."

"They were out in the hills."

"They're definitely coming this way!"

Ogma was elated. "Real Caravaners? They're actually here?"

"Come see!" The twin girls turned and ran back out of the

watch house. Emma's cohort scrambled up, chattering excitedly. Dunkirk was looking panicked again.

"It's all right. It's Caravaners. It's trade." Ogma tried to make her voice soothing. She didn't want Dunkirk to mistake their excitement for danger. "Come on. Let's go see."

She gave him a hand up and went to find a coat that would fit him. Daniel was organizing the younger children.

"Everyone have your bells and coats? Let me hear 'em." There was a chorus of chimes. "All right, off we go." Daniel led the younger group out and up to the wall.

Ogma returned with an old ermine moth fur coat. It was about Wheeler's size, but he preferred his brown leather patrol jacket. This coat was white with black spots, and very dusty. After Dunkirk shrugged into it, Ogma suppressed a giggle.

"I think it suits him," Effie said with a grin.

Rora's eyes twinkled. "Aye."

Dunkirk eyed them warily.

Ogma's brow furrowed. "He doesn't have a bell."

"What? He lost it out in the fog, then?"

"I don't think he ever had one."

"Psh!" Rora shook her head in disbelief.

"Well... it *is* a fog break. And we'll be staying on the wall," Effie reasoned. "Come on. We can find Rowan later and ask about a bell." She snapped her fingers and grinned. "Or maybe the Caravaners will have one we can trade for."

Ogma hoped they'd have stranger things then bells.

They pulled Dunkirk along and followed Daniel's crowd out and onto the wall. As they walked along the rampart, they could see more of the foraging parties returning. The villagers were panting and grunting as they heaved the fully laden carts back through the north gate. They looked tired but satisfied. Every cart was full, either with timber, ore, or bundles of strange herbs and wildflowers that would be used to diversify the gardens.

The sun was high and still, and the sky was clear and blue. Even the cobblestones were warm. Ogma looked out over the fields and forests that the fog had left them with. She could see a few of the other carts, still out foraging among the meadows. Snow-capped mountains in the distance stood majestic against the sky.

But it looked to Ogma like the distant mountains had moved. *And I don't think that's the same valley that was there this morning...* Looking past the carts trundling through the meadows, she could see that distant banks of fog were cresting the hills. *It's getting closer.*

Dunkirk was studying the landscape as well. Looking from mountains to valley. He didn't seem to like what he was seeing. "Det er ikke riktig. Jeg kjenner ikke igjen noe av det," he said quietly. He looked to Ogma and sighed and turned away again.

Rora and Effie were watching them curiously.

"Come *on*. We'll be the last to get there at this rate," Effie said. She linked arms with a bewildered Dunkirk and pulled him faster along the wall.

Rora chuckled and did the same with Ogma, stepping up her pace as well. She nodded at Dunkirk's back. "He really didn't have a bell?"

"I don't think he knows what they're for. He acts like..." Ogma paused.

"Like what?"

"He acts like he's never seen the fog."

Rora was silent. They jogged along the top of the wall together, Ogma still watching the distant foothills as they began to shift in the fog. Green hills on the horizon were slowly replaced with stony, weather-beaten mounds overgrown with heather.

Effie was jogging along beside Dunkirk, carrying on a mostly one-sided conversation, and laughing at his bewildered replies.

"What could she be laughing about? She can't understand a word he says."

"That's probably what she's laughing at." Rora smiled.

They arrived on the west span to see a small crowd already gathered. Many of the children of the watch were on patrol, but enough of those who were not and those who had returned with the foraging parties were gathered there, talking excitedly and looking out over the rampart's edge. Many of the adults had crowded around as well, the more timid remaining inside the wall and those emboldened by the extended fog break standing atop the wall with the children. Effie and Dunkirk had paused under the windmill where the northwest span met the west. Rora and Ogma joined them.

"Look, just out there! Coming over the hill." Effie pointed straight out over the span.

"I don't see..." Rora shielded her eyes with one hand.

"There, by that old oak."

Ogma peered into the distance, trying to trace a line from Effie's outstretched finger to the horizon.

"Oh and there's a second cart!" Rora exclaimed.

"Hva er vi leter etter? Er vi under angrep?" Dunkirk said in confusion.

Ogma saw it. She wondered how she could have missed it before. The brightly-painted covered wagon was just trundling over the ridge in the dappled light under an old oak tree. It was drawn by two tall antlered shapes.

"Are those harts?" Rora asked.

"Vent, er at all? Det er bare en vogn."

As the first wagon crested the ridge and continued down the other side, another trundled over the ridge behind it. It was as brightly painted as the first and was being drawn by another strange shape.

"Pfsh—what's that?" Effie leaned out over the rail.

"I think that's a donkey."

"Are donkeys that big?"

"Ooh, wait a minute. Is that a horse?"

Ogma hadn't seen a horse before, but she'd been told stories. One of Wheeler's silhouettes was horse-shaped. *Is that how they're supposed to look?* Something about it wasn't right, but she couldn't tell from this distance.

Excited cries from the other watchers along the wall went up as they caught sight of the caravan as well. The watchers began ringing their bells, a simple cadence: *Hello! Welcome!*

Ogma strained to see any reaction from the caravan, but they were still quite far away. She thought she saw some activity at the front of the wagons, but she wasn't sure.

A moment later, Enki and Enoch boomed behind them, amplifying the message, pealing over the roofs, atop the wall, and over the open plain. It looked to Ogma like the clear pealing of the bells was carried on waves across the tall grass.

The Caravaners clearly heard them. Small figures unfolded themselves from the wagons to walk in the grass beside them. One figure stood in the foot box and waved while another drove. They were still too far to see properly, but even from this distance, she could see many-colored cloaks made of patchwork cloth and feathers—just as she'd imagined.

She turned to Dunkirk. "Caravaners!" The booming of the bells drowned out his reply. Ogma, beaming, turned back to watch the wagons.

As the caravan grew closer, the ramparts became more crowded, with children of the watch and adults all straining to see the visitors. Ogma hopped onto the rail for a better look and leaned out, steadying herself with one hand.

The first wagon was painted in pale purple and fuchsia. It almost hurt to look at, the colors were so bright. The roof was made of sod and overgrown with long grasses and mushrooms. Lanterns were hanging from the eaves at each of the four corners.

"Fireflies," Ogma breathed.

The second wagon was painted in a bright forest green with blue trim. It was the larger of the two, with lanterns on the eaves as well, and broad, shuttered windows. The roof was wood shingled, with gutter rails that seemed to lead to wooden barrels strapped to the back.

Those must be rain barrels.

Then Ogma realized, *Those are harts!*

A pair of them, both antlered, were drawing the first cart. They had gray coats with white-patterned underfur. Their chicken-footed gait was strange, but they seemed to pull the wagons smoothly. The driver was cowled and hooded, and there was something strange about his hands on the reins.

A woman walked beside the cart wrapped in a purple and yellow patchwork sari. Her skin was an earthy red-brown color. Her fingers were long, almost twig-like. Branches sprouted from her shoulders and hair. She was beautiful.

Ogma finally tore her eyes away to look at the second cart again.

Is that what a horse should look like?

It moved like an animal should move, trotting and snorting and tossing its mane. *But—it's made of wood. Wickerwork or something.* It was more like the skeleton of a horse, or a basket woven into the shape of a horse.

But it's breathing. How can it be breathing?

It couldn't be a living thing, but it acted alive. And it seemed to have no trouble at all pulling the larger of the two carts.

A small figure rode on the back of the not-quite-a-horse. It was dressed in breastplate and shield of the same wickerwork material. It wore a helm and had a wooden sword in one hand. It was small, probably no taller than Ogma, but there was something noble in its bearing. She couldn't make out the rider's features, though, as they were hidden in an inky black shadow beneath the helmet.

The villagers were cheering and ringing their bells in a hearty welcome. Despite the breadth of the rampart, the press of people was getting dangerous.

Ogma leaned back from the rail and pulled Dunkirk by the arm. "Come on! They'll have to come in by the gate."

They jogged back along the wall towards the gate in the north span. Ogma kept most of her attention on the carts below.

The shutters on the green cart swung open. At first Ogma thought someone was heaving moldy vegetables over the sill until she saw the eyes. It was a person, but barely. They were covered with lichen and fungus in mottled, unhealthy shades of brown and gray. Their eyes stared mournfully over the wagon windowsill.

Ogma thought she saw another shape moving in the shadows of the wagon, but someone jostled her elbow and she stumbled. The villagers, realizing as she did that the visitors would have to come through the main gate, had begun jogging along the wall top as well, shouting for the caravan below to follow them.

"This way." Ogma shouldered her way into the crowd, tugging on Dunkirk's shirt. Resigned to his confusion, Dunkirk followed. Some of the villagers were looking at him with almost as much interest as the caravan. Ogma had to push her way down the stairs as most of the villagers were still making their way up. Once they reached ground level, the path to the north gate was largely clear.

"Come on. If we get there early, we'll be closer when they

come through the gate." Ogma jogged along the cobbles, trying to slow her pace to keep from losing Dunkirk, but barely able to keep herself from breaking into an eager run. The Caravaners had always been her favorite part of Wheeler's stories.

They reached the gate. To their right, the watch house loomed over the overgrown fields against the northeast span. Ogma picked a spot a fair distance from the doors, but right beside the cobbled path, so the wagons would have to roll right past on their way to the village square.

Gradually, some of the other villagers also decided the ramparts had lost their appeal as a vantage point and came down to crowd around the gates. Ogma noted with a smile that Daniel had somehow managed to carve out pride of place in the center of the span for the youngest children of the wall. Emma's entourage chattered loudly over the general commotion. The clangor of bells rose to a greater height still, and then there was a clear, purposeful knocking on the gate. The crowd all turned to hush each other in a cacophony of harsh whispers and then gradually fell silent. Ogma heard a soft, accented voice calling clearly.

"My name is Nod, of the Caravan. I come with my companions and our humble wagons. May we have your trade, and your company, on this day between the fog?"

Before anyone else could say a word, Emma's voice piped up. "This is Emma of the watch and yes, you may!"

Ogma thought she heard Daniel laughing as the villagers on the ramparts cheered. The wooden gate swung open beneath its carven stone lintel, and the caravan clattered through.

The harts were taller than Ogma expected, striding through the gates with antlers almost brushing the top post. They had hare lips and short gray beards, and trotted forward on their strange chicken feet. Their eyes were wild as they shied away from the excited villagers coming down the steps. Ogma made sure not to stand directly in their way.

Nod's presence was hypnotizing, as he stood in the foot box of the first wagon. In sharp contrast to the brightly-colored painted wagons, he was dressed entirely in black, cowled and hooded. His face was largely in shadow, except for his enormous golden eyes that stared unblinking. The liquid pools seemed to be staring right at her, and Ogma had to look away.

The tree woman walked beside the cart. She was even more beautiful than she had seemed from afar. Her red-brown skin was smooth, but curled up at the edges like birch bark. She held her arms raised at her sides, her long twig-like fingers splayed in a way that would have seemed uncomfortable if it didn't look so natural on her.

Charms and ornaments were hung in the branches sprouting from her head and shoulders.

She smiled at Ogma as the wagon trundled by, leaves rustling gently.

The next wagon was stranger and more wondrous than the first, and Ogma finally got to see the wooden horse up close.

It was huge, bigger still than even the harts had been. But it was definitely made, not alive. She could see the broad wicker bands that formed its skeleton. The almost-horse tossed its head and snorted, chest rising as it danced to the side and pawed the ground.

Perhaps something can be made and *alive?*

"Wait, there are people in it! Look, look!" She pointed under the horse's belly.

Two shadowy black figures stood between its fore and hind legs, each operating a strange set of levers.

"It's a puppet!"

Dunkirk looked on in wonder as well. "Det er en hest marionett? Det er rart."

It looks so alive. It's breathing.

"Men de er bare leker!" Dunkirk was gesturing at the rider.

The noble figure was utterly silent, almost lifeless compared to the mount she rode. It carried a sword and shield, both made of the same wickerwork as the puppet horse.

"It's just a costume?" Ogma wondered, uncertainly. And yet there was something dangerous about the way the wicker knight carried herself.

The rider's features were still obscured beneath her costume. Something about the deep shadow beneath her helmet was unsettling.

The horse clopped past on the tail of the first wagon.

A doll-like figure walked behind the second carriage. She was perfectly, pristinely beautiful, but she moved very strangely, with a stutter-stop motion that looked awkward, almost painful. It was as if she were strung to a puppet cross and being played across the ground.

There's something about her eyes, too, Ogma thought, studying the woman's face. They had no depth, as if they had been painted on.

She almost didn't realize the woman was looking back at her. Suddenly graceful, the doll-like shape danced elegantly over to her and Dunkirk, and then the grace disappeared again as she turned a dramatic but jerky bow.

"Hello there, townie. Aren't you the serious thing?" The woman's lips didn't move when she spoke. "My name is Semane."

"O-Ogma," she replied.

"Pleased to meet ya. I see our puppeteers have caught your eye." She gestured to the knight. "She cuts a fine figure doesn't she? And the boys are stronger than they look—carrying her and pulling the cart and all." It was true, now that they were closer Ogma realized that neither the rider nor the two puppeteers in the horse were any taller than her. Semane winked one painted eye and she danced away.

Ogma looked at the second cart. A muddy swamp-water gaze glared out at her before the shutters banged shut. As the cart went by, Ogma noticed two short, wooly animals tied by leads to the back of the wagon.

One of the creatures looked at her with unsettling, square-pupiled eyes and *baaaed* balefully. Their limbs were chicken-footed, too, like the harts, both front and back. As they went by, one of them lunged into the tall grasses beside the path, straining at the end of its tether. There was a rustling and snapping noise and the goat returned, prancing and self-satisfied. There was an ermine moth firmly between its jaws. The other goat greedily chomped at one wing, and they squabbled until they'd pulled the moth clean in half.

Ogma took an immediate dislike to the creatures.

The caravan trundled to a halt in the open space, just before the steps of the outermost terrace.

Old Keegan, Nan Aud, and Goodie Hazel stood on the steps. They rang the elder's bell as the villagers gathered around the wagons.

"Welcome travelers!" Nan Aud spoke out in a clear voice.

Nod—the tall one, hooded in black—raised his hand and nodded.

"We are blessed to find you on this day of broken fog," Nan Aud continued. "We would trade with you and hear the stories of your travels."

"And we have goods to trade and stories to tell," Nod intoned ritually.

"Then let today be a festival! We have been many days in fog, but we find ourselves rich and in the company of friends. We shall celebrate a new season!"

The chatter soon became cheers and ringing of bells as the

villagers celebrated. It had been a hard season. The villagers were drunk on sunshine and broken fog and scattered to prepare the village square for the festival.

Rora had clambered partway up the steps to the rampart walk. "All right then! If it's a festival we want—I suppose we'll be running the Circle first?" she said it nonchalantly but grinned broadly. The Circle was her favorite festival activity and in recent seasons, she had always won. There were ragged cheers from the children of the watch.

"If we're to have a festival then we might as well have the games," Goodie Hazel grumbled, though she was secretly fond of the races. "But it'll be fair. Send out to the watch house for anyone who wants to join—"

"Beg pardon, Goodie Hazel," Effie put in, "but everyone's already here."

The stern elder gave her a brief glare and then gathered herself up. "Right then. A race it is to be. The full circuit of the walls. And *I'll* be the judge."

The villagers cheered.

"Now then—contestants to the wall! Anyone who's fit may join."

"Might we watch?" a solemn voice intoned. Nod had dismounted from the wagon and his golden eyes looked to Goodie Hazel.

"'Course you may," Goodie Hazel replied. "Our honored guests may watch right from the finish."

"How do you run the race? Just one lap?" the tree woman queried, leaves rustling.

Effie called down. "Naw, just the lap's too simple. That's just endurance. We do things a bit differently."

Goodie Hazel glared again. "Aye. That is to say, there are stages." She collected herself and then explained. "We have eight windmills on our walls, as you can see. Each windmill is a stage. We place a token at each—a scarf, a flag, something of that sort—and the winner is the one who finishes with the most tokens. Any who have the remaining tokens shall win as well."

Effie piped up, "And what is it we'll be winnin' this fine new season, eh?"

"All the winners shall eat first at the feast, and none will help with washing." Some muffled cheers went up, but most grumbled. After all, Goodie Hazel was really saying that most of them would be washing dishes.

"And the overall winner will have no patrols until the fog break ends," Wheeler called out.

The cheers were more substantial this time.

Watch children, and a few of the younger adults who weren't too fond of washing dishes, assembled atop the wall. Dunkirk was still looking around in some confusion, but he seemed distracted enough studying the strange Caravaners.

"Jeg burde be dem om nyheter om krigene..." Dunkirk muttered to himself, gesturing in Nod's direction.

"What was that?" Ogma asked.

Dunkirk pointed at the rider. *No, at her sword, I think.*

"Krigene... Krigene!" At her blank look he threw up his hands in frustration.

Nod walked around the wagons and rapped on the shutters, whispering in a tongue neither Ogma nor Dunkirk—given his puzzled frown—could understand.

Semane and the tree woman seemed eager to follow him to the top of the wall. A grumpy mutter was all Ogma heard from the second cart.

Nod hesitated, whispering something to the rider on the puppet horse. She shook her head, but hopped down and took off her helm. Ogma gasped. The rider's face was blank—a featureless expanse of inky black. Beneath the knight's costume, her whole body was the same: vaguely human, but softly rounded and shadow-dark.

The puppeteers in the horse emerged as well, and the horse became lifeless, suddenly nothing more than a well-crafted wickerwork costume.

Ogma studied the two of them. Each wore a belt and shoes, but nothing else. Each was an inky blob in human outline. They were impossible to tell apart. Their faces had no features that Ogma could see, nor any other difference to distinguish them from each other.

As she watched, one of them took a large iron ring from its belt. At first, she thought it must be a key ring, because of the many shapes hanging from it. But then it began flipping up individual keys, flashing each one to the other puppeteers, like semaphore. The other responded in kind, using a key ring of its own.

The small colored flags flashed by in a blur—too quickly for Ogma to make any guess as to what each meant.

The third puppeteer, the rider, still stood before Nod. He spoke softly and she responded in pantomime. In the end, she simply shook her head, pointed to her companions, and then back at the wagon.

"Talking with flags—funny little creatures, aren't they?" Semane said brightly to Ogma.

Ogma looked the doll-like figure up and down and raised an eyebrow?

Semane laughed. "I know, I know. I'm one to talk, right?"

"What are their names?"

"Well they don't use spoken names, but they let us give them some. That's Regal." Semane pointed at the rider. "And we call the boys Mane and Rump—but which is which..?" Semane shrugged and grinned, skipping away. Ogma wasn't sure she could tell *any* of the three apart.

The three inky puppeteers walked to the first wagon and went inside.

Ogma dragged her eyes away and found herself meeting the swamp-water gaze from before, staring out at her again. She quickly broke eye contact. *Whoever that is, he can stay inside.*

Nod was standing in the doorway of the wagon and shaking his head. He seemed to be arguing with someone. Ogma could just make out the low murmur of Nod's voice, but she couldn't hear any reply. He finally shrugged and bowed his head. An instant later, the wagon door swung wide and a shape emerged stranger still than any of the Caravaners she had seen yet.

It cast a stark shadow on the wagon steps—just the silhouette of something—but then—*No! It is the shadow!* The black, translucent shape unfolded itself from the wagon door and grew thin and tall until it towered to nearly half the height of the wall. To Ogma, it looked like a shadow cast at sunset or a dark shape caught in the corner of your eye.

There were gasps and fearful mutters from the assembled villagers. Something about it made Ogma's eyes cross when she looked at it. She could see through, to the wagon, but at the same time, when she tried to focus on it directly, it hurt her eyes.

Dunkirk muttered something under his breath. The villagers' gasps subsided to an uneasy tension as the shape turned its featureless face to look over the crowd.

It strode to the wall, placidly unaware of the panic it was causing as villagers dived out of its way. *I don't think it'd hurt you,* Ogma thought. *It's just a shadow.* The shadow took its place near the starting line of the race. The assembled children looked at it in fascination, but not fear, and soon turned back to their places. They'd fully expected the Caravaners to be strange.

"Come on, then." Ogma gestured to Dunkirk as Nod and his entourage mounted the broad steps after the shadow. "We can get a better view." She fell into step just behind the Caravaners, feeling rather brave and nonchalant.

The tree woman looked back over shoulder and smiled at them. "Will you be racing then?"

Ogma shook her head.

"Why not?"

"I don't want to be tired when I'm washing dishes," Ogma replied matter-of-factly.

The charms in the tree woman's branches tinkled. "My name is Melial."

"Ogma. This is Dunkirk," she said, gesturing at the boy, who was dividing his wary attention between the Caravaners and the crowd.

Melial waved, branches rustling. Dunkirk looked nonplussed. "Is he... quite all right?"

"Yes—er, no. He doesn't speak our language. We found him in the fog just before the break."

"Ah... I see." Melial studied the boy more closely. "You know, we may have something for that."

"For what?"

"For his *tongue*."

Ogma froze, watching Melial's back warily, and then shaking herself and continuing up the stairs.

At the top of the wall, Goodie Hazel was rallying help to set up the race. "Now then, we'll need a volunteer to place the favors."

"I'll do it, Goodie Hazel," Wheeler responded.

There were relieved faces around the circle. No one wanted to tire themselves out just by placing the markers. Wheeler was just about to jog down the span when Melial spoke up.

"Just a moment, please."

Wheeler hesitated.

"As we are your guests, might we provide the favors?"

Wheeler looked uncertain and turned to Goodie Hazel.

"Of course! Our guests may provide the favors if they wish."

Melial smiled. "All right then, hmm..." She studied the charms hanging from her branches. "How about these?" She counted out eight into Wheeler's hand. "And whoever takes them may keep them."

Ogma suddenly regretted her decision not to race. She'd always wanted something from the Caravaners.

Wheeler started an easy pace around the wall to set one token at each windmill.

Dunkirk was looking at the assembled crowd, and the children lined up on the wall. "Hva er det som foregår her?"

Ogma just shrugged.

"Er det et løp?"

Ogma could only shake her head again.

Fifteen minutes later, Wheeler puffed back to the assembled participants from the other side of the span. He wheezed a bit as he came up on the line.

"Gettin' out of shape there, big man?" Effie teased.

Wheeler held up a hand and caught his breath. He gestured at Effie, waving her closer. She stepped out of line to stand nearer and raised an eyebrow. He waved again. She leaned in and turned one ear toward him.

"GO!" he shouted.

The race began.

Effie fell over backwards and, when she took off running, she was several steps behind the pack thanks to Wheeler's trick. He grinned and waved.

Rora set up an easy loping stride in the center of the pack, as most of the younger children sprinted in an all-out dash for the first marker. Most of the older settled in for the long haul.

Cole claimed the first token. Ogma could hear his triumphant shout even from the starting line. But as she watched the group turn on to the second span, he fell behind. She'd have called that foolish, burning up his strength in the first eighth, but then again, he'd secured one of Melial's charms.

Rora started to pick up her pace on the second span, moving up through the crowd. She had a long, easy stride and looked entirely comfortable. Effie was a few paces behind, her form a bit more ragged, and chatting away at the other racers despite the pace.

One of the villagers, a young man recently off the wall called Eric, took the second token. The runners were then mostly out of sight in the distance.

"The tall girl has moved to the front," Nod's quiet voice intoned. His liquid golden eyes pierced the distance. He named the current standings of the runners.

"Det er et race!" Dunkirk said, finally realizing what was happening, and brightening up considerably. He shaded his eyes and looked out across the village in the general direction of the runners. Cracking his knuckles, he stretched his back in an unconcerned, casual way.

A moment later, he snapped the fingers of his right hand and beat two quick beats with his left foot.

There was a sudden *whoosh* of air and he burst forward on a gust of wind. He leapt from foot to foot, eating up twenty feet in a single bound, passing the first windmill almost before Ogma had realized what had happened.

Melial and Nod's eyes snapped to his back, and they watched him intently.

Goodie Hazel frowned.

"What was that?" a villager wondered aloud.

"Never seen anything like it. Some kind of charm?"

"Do you think he'll catch 'em?"

Ogma wondered. He was moving incredibly quickly, already out of sight beyond the second span. She watched Nod's face. He glanced into the distance in one place, and then some distance behind it. He repeated this several times, each time glancing closer and closer, until his eyes converged on a single point.

"He's caught the pack," he said simply. "The tall girl has a good lead, though. And the other."

Ogma wasn't sure whether she wanted to root for him to win, after catching up such an incredible handicap, or whether she wanted Rora to put him in his place.

The next few minutes were an intense waiting game. Ogma kept looking to Nod, but his features were inscrutable and he didn't volunteer the standings again.

"There they are!" someone called out.

Ogma looked. She could just see Rora rounding the sixth span. *She'll have the charm then. How many is that? Has she won?* Ogma was just guessing, but if she'd only taken the lead by the fourth or fifth span, she might only have two or three. If the sixth was her third, she'd probably win it, but if not...

Effie came into view, puffing along some distance behind. She was clearly lagging.

Next was... *Dunkirk.*

Unbelievably, he had nearly caught up with Effie. His long, gliding steps ate up the distance. The wind of his passing ruffled Effie's clothes and blew her hair around her face. She staggered to a halt for a moment in shock.

Rora still had a solid lead coming into the final span. She rounded the corner at the seventh windmill and grabbed the charm. Her pace slowed just a bit; she clearly anticipated an easy jog to the finish.

"No! Keep running! Behind you!" Ogma found herself shouting. She could see Effie shouting a warning as well.

Suddenly all the villagers were shouting: some for Rora and some for Dunkirk.

Rora glanced over her shoulder and nearly stumbled as she saw Dunkirk gaining rapidly. She put on a burst of speed, and suddenly it was an all-out sprint across the last span. Dunkirk was still gaining, and gaining easily, but they were running out of race.

In the last ten yards, Dunkirk burst past Rora in a single bound, sliding past on a gust of air that whipped round the assembled crowd. The dust made Ogma's eyes water.

Rora grunted and threw herself to the finish, reaching for the token.

She had it. Dunkirk had blown right past.

The villagers stared open-mouthed, not quite sure what had happened.

Dunkirk was wheezing, but had a cocky grin plastered across his face.

Rora was bent over double, dry heaving, but Ogma counted five charms clutched in her hands. Even without the one that Dunkirk had simply ignored, she would have won, easily.

Semane patted Dunkirk on the back. "Congratulations! You are the fastest loser I have ever seen!"

Dunkirk grinned widely.

Effie barked a laugh at that as she panted her way to the finish, and the rest of the pack followed soon behind.

The last of the racers—mostly the younger, and Cole with a stitch in his side from his initial sprint—finally trickled in.

Those who'd managed a token raised them triumphantly and rang their bells.

Cole had one, Eric had one, Effie had one, and Rora had five.

Dunkirk had none.

Goodie Hazel raised herself up, still eyeing Dunkirk. "We

have our winners! Cole, Eric, and Effie, with one token each."
She gestured to the three of them who, still panting somewhat,
raised their tokens and grinned. "And Rora, the overall winner
with five tokens!"

A cheer went up from the crowd.

Dunkirk's smile took on a puzzled aspect. He turned to
Ogma as the crowd jostled around them.

"Vant jeg ikke?"

"No," Ogma said simply, shaking her head.

Rora and Effie trotted up to them, Effie laughing between
wheezes.

"This one's yours by right," Rora said to Dunkirk. "You did
beat me on the last span." Dunkirk was still looking puzzled, so
she pressed the charm into his hand.

He held it up and watched it glitter in the sun. Ogma looked
at it longingly.

"Vil du dette?" he said, holding it out to her. "Vil du
dette?"

Ogma nodded. Dunkirk took the charm and threaded the
chain over her head and around her neck. Effie sniggered
behind her hand, and Ogma haughtily ignored her.

The sun suddenly dimmed, and Ogma realized that the
shadow was looming over them, casting the rampart in shade. It
flickered happily above Dunkirk.

Nod walked up, with Melial behind him. "Dunkirk, is it?"

He turned and nodded his head.

Nod gestured at himself and Melial. "Nod. Melial."

Dunkirk repeated them, nodding again.

Melial turned back to Ogma. "I think we *do* have something
for him. Find us in the market."

The villagers were still crowded around the parked carts as the race ended. The little puppeteers peeked out from the open shutters as the runners descended the wall.

Harts are nervous beasts, Ogma thought, watching the two animals standing in almost rigid attention and eyeing the crowds warily.

Then again, we might eat them for all they know.

In contrast, the two chicken-footed goats were entirely unconcerned. Ogma saw a scrap of apron hanging from the corner of one of the creatures' mouths and noticed that people were giving them a wide berth as they walked by. The other one was sleeping.

It's standing on one leg. The creature had pulled its other three chicken-footed limbs up against its wooly body and was snoring gently: a cotton ball on a single, spindly pedestal.

I wonder what would happen if I tipped it over.

As Nod and the other Caravaners returned to the wagons, the goat that was still awake chomped at Melial's ankle. Melial walked on as if she hadn't noticed, and the goat bleated a complaint.

Looks like it broke a tooth, Ogma thought, looking at the creature's dismayed expression.

The two shorter puppeteers emerged from the other wagon. *I wonder if one of them always does the front and the other the back, or if they switch off?* The inky shapes clambered into the horse puppet frame, and then the wicker horse tossed its head and shied away from the crowd, instantly transformed from lifeless shell to living, breathing animal as the puppeteers took up their work.

They began to strain forward, setting the cart moving. They were certainly strong. The wicker horse had no trouble pulling the substantial wagon to a rolling start. The harts seemed to have more trouble than they did.

Nod took up the reins of the first wagon and urged the harts to get moving again. They tossed their heads and stepped sideways in their harnesses, clunking antlers together.

"Bah." Nod clucked, and fought with the reins, trying to coax the creatures to move. Ogma couldn't help but stare; Nod's hands holding the reins weren't hands at all: they were talons, sharp and black, like crow's feet.

"He's not very good at that, is he?" Ogma asked Melial as he struggled with the harts.

Melial chuckled and leaned in conspiratorially. She smelled like woodsmoke and fallen leaves. "No, he usually leads them on foot."

"Does that work any better?" Ogma asked skeptically.

Melial laughed aloud. "No, not really. But once they get moving, it's all right." She gave Ogma an appraising look. "Would you like to ride?"

Ogma tried to sound nonchalant, though the offer had her heart racing with excitement. "I suppose it would save me the walk..."

Melial's eyes sparkled. "I suppose it would. Come on then."

She led Ogma over to the wagon and motioned for her to climb up next to Nod, who was still struggling. The step was taller than it looked, and higher off the ground than she expected. It felt like trying to take three stairs at once up the wall. She was just pulling herself up when the cart lurched forward.

Ogma lost her balance and fell, stomach dropping as she began to go over backward.

A black, taloned hand grabbed her by the coat and hauled her up into the seat.

Nod glanced at her with an inscrutable golden-eyed stare and turned back to the harts. Melial had walked up beside them and was now guiding them forward by the bridle. She sang softly to them and they quieted.

Ogma was too exhilarated to be concerned by her near accident. *I'm riding in a caravan!*

She was grinning foolishly, she knew, but she didn't care. The seat was padded and more comfortable than it looked. The roof of the wagon overhung the foot box—a sufficient, if drafty, cover from the weather. The old wood was smooth, paint bright but worn.

The harts didn't smell quite as pretty as they looked, though.

They trundled along the cobblestone road towards the town square, the caravan having become a parade as the villagers followed. Those who hadn't gone to the walls had gathered goods for trade and were bustling to the square.

Enki tolled brightly, calling everyone to the festival. Ogma rolled her eyes. *As if everyone isn't already here.*

Brightly-colored linen cloth, homespun quilts, and woven carpets decorated the square. They were arranged artfully, competing with each other for the eyes of the caravan traders.

Other villagers had set out stalls. There were fresh vegetables from their gardens, bread and baked goods, and tools and other handicrafts. People were bright and cheerful in the sunlight.

The caravan trundled to a halt just beneath the bell tower, and Ogma hopped down from her perch. Nod and the others dismounted and began opening shutters and unfolding the sides of the wagon cleverly, into a counter and awning. They began laying out goods of their own.

Some were as simple and normal as finely crafted pots and pans and cooking utensils. Some were of finer make—glass and porcelain. *What use is a cup that breaks if you drop it?* Some of them were beautiful though.

They also had reams of fabric and fine leather, stockings and shoes, gloves and coats, spices and dried herbs. They even staked out the two loathsome goats for sale, though Ogma didn't think they'd have much luck.

But what Ogma was most excited about were not the trade goods from the caravan's travels in other towns—no. What held her attention and wouldn't let go were the Caravaner-made goods: firefly lanterns, small folding tools, metal charms with strange symbols on them, colorful powders and potions, masks and old bones, bits of string, and—

Books! There was a small case with six or seven volumes bound in leather.

There was too much to take in all at once. She fingered the charm around her neck while she studied it all, wondering which treasures she would cherish the most, which would make the other children the most jealous, and then realizing, crushingly, that she didn't have much of anything to trade.

Ogma worried her lip as this disappointment dawned on her. *It's all right,* she consoled herself, *you just wanted to see them, right?* The thought rang hollow in the presence of these mysterious and beautiful things. *At least you have this charm.*

She picked up a translucent red stone and turned it in her hands. It looked like frozen tree sap.

"Amber," Semane said. The dancing girl smiled at Ogma. It was stiff and stilted like all her movements, but Ogma was beginning to like her.

"Look. Hold it up to the sun."

Ogma turned and did so. At first, the corona of the sun around the stone was too bright and dazzled her eyes, but her vision adjusted and she looked into the amber glow.

"There's something in there!"

Semane had a pleasant, tinkling laugh, like the sound of a babbling brook. "Yup, can you tell what it is?"

Ogma looked closer. "Some kind of bug."

Semane giggled, surprisingly girlish this time. "A blue beetle."

"How can you tell?" Ogma asked.

"See its horn?" Semane turned the amber in Ogma's hand, guiding her eye to it. "Only the blue beetles had those horns."

"Had?"

"They're all gone now. They died out a long time ago."

That's sad, Ogma thought. Dunkirk's bright blue armor came to mind and a strange melancholy came over her. She put down the amber.

"They're very beautiful," she said, gesturing at the collected treasures.

"Thank you. I collected most of these. If you'd like me to hold something for you..."

"N-no. No, thank you," Ogma replied, trying to disguise the longing in her voice. Some of the villagers were hovering nearby, their own precious goods in hand, clearly eager to browse the Caravaners' wares.

Ogma wandered away, promising herself she'd at least come back to look again.

Nod and Melial were walking the villagers' stalls while Semane managed their own. Nod handled the goods he was presented with carefully, turning them over, checking for imperfections, muttering mysteriously. Ogma thought she saw him *lick* a clay pot. The villagers were boldly hawking their wares, but those unblinking golden eyes made them nervous.

Melial on the other hand seemed almost too casual. She chatted gaily with the villagers, praising their wares, asking how they were made—from time to time mentioning something they had brought that she thought might be a fair trade.

They're very clever, Ogma thought. Just before she settled one of her casual deals, Melial always glanced at Nod. After a few stalls, Ogma had them figured out. Nod would pick up one item while Melial casually picked out the one they really wanted. Nod would study his item intently while the villagers tried to bargain with him, and Melial would negotiate for hers with apparent disinterest, as if the item were just a bauble that caught her eye.

If he thought the price was fair, he would simply meet Melial's glance, while still seeming to be deeply absorbed in the object he held.

If he thought it wasn't worth buying, he'd put the one he'd chosen back down early in the examination and they'd move on.

Very clever.

"Ugh, can you believe that—doll woman?" Effie announced loudly and leaned on Ogma's shoulder. Rora was with her, shaking her head.

"All we asked her is if these charms"—she dangled the token she'd won in the race from her fingers—"*do* anything."

Ogma tried not to smirk.

"You know what she said?"

"What did she say?" Ogma asked innocently.

"She asked me what I would trade to know!" Effie shook her head in disgust.

Semane's pretty clever too, Ogma thought.

"Why don't you ask Melial?" Ogma suggested. "She gave them to you after all."

"Who, the tree?"

Ogma winced, wondering if Melial had heard her. *How could she not? You can practically hear Effie on the south wall from inside the watch house.*

"Hmm..." Rora responded skeptically. "I figured they were just trinkets. This was Effie's idea."

118

Effie looked affronted.

"Do you think they really do something?" Rora asked Ogma.

Ogma shrugged. "I don't know." What she didn't say was, *I hope so.*

"Hmm..." Rora said again.

Effie grabbed her by the hand and dragged her towards Nod and Melial, who were apparently negotiating with Roose about how much leather his share of the ore was worth. Melial had a glint in her eye. Apparently, she could tell Roose was desperate.

Ogma shook her head.

"Shouldn't have let on, should he?" Nan Aud had walked up quietly and was watching the negotiations too. "Ah, there's Eve coming up. At least she has some sense." Nan turned and looked kindly at Ogma. "Enjoying the festival?"

"...Yes," Ogma said hesitantly, thinking longingly of the fantastic trinkets in the Caravaners' stalls.

Nan raised an eyebrow.

"No, I really am."

"I noticed you didn't run the Circle."

"I never win," Ogma responded.

"Does that bother you?"

Ogma considered it. "No. No one runs the tethers as well as me."

Nan Aud nodded firmly. "And that's the truth, as I hear it."

"Only—" Ogma started.

"Only there's no prizes for running the tether," Aud finished.

Ogma nodded lamely. "Except for the occasional stupid boy in the woods."

Aud smiled kindly.

"Can't trade him, though," Ogma said straight-faced.

The village elder laughed. "True enough! Though it seems he gave you that at least," she said, pointing to the necklace

Ogma wore. "Mayhaps it'll work out. Speaking of... where's he got to?"

"Um..." Ogma suddenly realized she hadn't seen Dunkirk since clambering aboard the wagon.

"Lost him, have you? Found him in all that fog, but can't keep track inside the village, eh?" She chuckled and patted Ogma on the shoulder. Her grip was rock steady. "There's more important things than trinkets, girl." She said it warmly, but firmly.

Ogma nodded. "I know." She meant it.

"Still, I remember a girl who was afraid the Caravaners would never come back to her town. Maybe you'll see what this is worth."

Nan Aud dropped a small, smooth object into Ogma's palm, and walked away before Ogma could say anything.

It was a small glass firefly, almost like the ones used in the shadow puppet props, only much more finely wrought. It was almost perfect in every detail, as if it could take off at any moment. Ogma's heart swelled. *Maybe I can trade it!*

"Thank you!" she called to Nan Aud's retreating back. Aud smiled and waved over one shoulder, disappearing into the crowd.

Ogma held the precious object tightly in her hand and looked again at the Caravaner's stall. She resisted running over and trading it for the first thing that caught her eye. She pocketed it for now and went to browse the stalls.

Nod was selling the virtues of the chicken-footed goats to Old Keegan and Goodie Hazel.

"They're quiet and companionable creatures. Almost pets," he said.

In the background, one of the goats head-butted the other and they tussled in the dirt, *baaing* loudly.

"Their fur can be combed for soft wool."

Travel dust and brambles had turned their coats an unpleasant mottled brown.

"There are no other creatures as adept at catching ermine moths."

One of the goats toppled over the other and they collapsed in an untidy heap, chicken feet cycling in the air as they *baaed* stupidly.

Nod kept his expression perfectly, inhumanly straight. His hand still stretched out as if presenting a glittering prize.

"They are carnivorous, but would never attack a human."

One of the goats snapped at his outstretched hand.

"All in all, a bargain at half the price," he finished.

"Don't you mean 'a bargain at twice the price'?" Goodie Hazel snapped sharply.

"Don't I?" Nod replied, not missing a beat.

Ogma tried not to laugh. Partway through the negotiations, Goodie Hazel threw up her hands and walked away in disgust. Old Keegan seemed to have made up his mind though, and he and Nod continued haggling. Eventually, they settled on a portion of grain and the goats were traded over.

One promptly tried to eat Old Keegan's shoelaces.

He and Nod both wore expressions like they'd been robbed by the end, but Ogma thought there was relief on Nod's inscrutable face as well.

Ogma found Melial hiding a smile behind her hand. "Why didn't *you* negotiate the goats?"

"Wouldn't be fair, taking what *I* could get for 'em." Melial winked.

"Will they really eat the ermine moths?"

"Oh that they will, including the wings if you're not careful, though they don't like them as much. You'd better gather them quick if you're planning to use the leather."

Ogma would relay that to Keegan later. It brought to mind

the white, spotted moth that had woken her up this morning. The fuzzy thing wasn't *that* bad. It certainly didn't deserve to be *eaten*. For that matter, she wasn't at all sure she wanted to see it harvested for shoe leather either.

Panicked shouts from the center of the square suddenly wrested Ogma's attention. They were coming from the bell tower.

"He can't do that! He'll break his neck!"

"Someone stop the foreign fool!"

Ogma trotted over to the scene of the disturbance. A small crowd of adults was gathered, and Roose was on his back in the dirt.

"What's happening?"

Moll and Isak turned to her. "Ah. Ogma, isn't it? Shouldn't someone be minding him?"

"It's that boy you rescued. He's climbing the bell tower!"

"He's doing *what*? Why?"

Roose picked himself up. "Search me. He was babbling in that foreign tongue of his. Wanted inside and wouldn't take 'no' for an answer." He rubbed his jaw. "Stronger than he looks." Roose seemed impressed.

"And he's in there now?"

Kev looked back from the tower door. "Yup. Made it up the stairs we had left. 'Course most of them are gone. We pulled down those timbers seasons ago during the storms. Needed 'em for firewood or we would 'ave all freezed to death, wouldn' we 'ave?"

Ogma wondered privately what they'd been planning to do if the bell-pull snapped.

"Anyway, he's climbin' the wall now. Don't make no sense, but he's going to break his neck, that's for sure."

Ogma ducked inside the tower.

It was by far the tallest structure in the village, though it wasn't the oldest. It was easy to tell because the stones were cut differently from the ones that were used to build the rest of the village.

The two thick ropes that were Enki and Enoch's bell pulls hung down from the top of the tower. A rickety wooden platform ran around the inside wall, but about halfway up, just as she had been warned, the timbers had all been removed.

In the dim light of the tower, it took a moment for Ogma's eyes to adjust. Once they finally did, she saw Dunkirk. He was almost three quarters of the way up, dangling from the anchor point where a wooden beam for the steps used to be.

He'd clearly been climbing from one to the other around the interior of the tower. They were easier handholds, but it was a much longer climb.

"Hey! What are you doing? Get down here!" Ogma's shout echoed up the tower. Dunkirk paused a moment in his climb, looking down over one shoulder.

"Jeg må se bjellene!"

He's not very good at this. She climbed the wooden platform, taking the creaking wooden stairs as high as she could. Once the stairs ran out, she grabbed one of the bell pulls and strung it through her belt and then clambered over to the wall.

The weight of the rope was uncomfortable, pulling her back towards the middle of the room. *Probably not the best idea I've ever had, but I'll just take my time and make sure my handholds are good.*

She felt out her first holds and began to climb. Instead of following the path of the old beam anchors, she went straight up the wall, finding plenty of hand and foot holds in between the rough cut stones. Dunkirk had a good lead, but he was a slow climber, and she began to catch up.

She was concentrating on making up the height, so she lost track of which side of the tower's interior Dunkirk was on.

Grunting with effort, she slid her hand into a crack in the wall and made a fist so that she could lean back and catch her breath.

A panicked yell made her heart skip a beat. She craned her neck, expecting to see Dunkirk plummeting to the stones below. He was dangling by one arm, only fifteen feet below the beam that held the bells. The old timber he hung from was rotten and had cracked.

Ogma cursed under her breath. He was on the opposite side of the tower and she wasn't sure how long he could hold on. It would take too much time to climb around the inside.

She decided to take a risk. She planted herself firmly with both feet and one hand, and pulled the end of the rope from her belt. She let most of the length dangle back to the tower floor and got a firm grip on the upper section. She took a deep breath, and then another, and pushed off from the wall.

She swung out into open space. A familiar fear thrilled through her as her feet and hands left contact with the solid surface, but her grip on the rope was good. The sensation of swinging out into the open air, even at that height, was as exhilarating as it was terrifying.

Ogma reached out for the far wall with one hand.

There was a deafening boom as the bellpull did its work.

Startled, Ogma scrabbled for purchase with her hand on the opposite wall, but too quickly she swung back out into space.

She could feel the noise from the bell vibrating in her teeth. In the enclosed space, it overwhelmed all feeling. Ogma's ears were still ringing as the bell boomed out again. Ogma grunted and locked the rope between her feet. She rocked back, trying to regain lost momentum, and swung forward again.

This time she went for the wall with both hands, rope still

firmly locked between her ankles. It wouldn't be pleasant if she slipped, but she probably wouldn't fall.

She caught the edge of the rough stones and was able to cling to the wall. Ogma could feel the mortar and grit in her fingernails.

"Ah—ya!" Another panicked cry from Dunkirk. He was hanging from three fingers and slipping. He looked around frantically and caught sight of Ogma below him. "Hjelp! Dritt—hjelp!

Ogma looped the rope across her body and began climbing again, as quickly as she dared. She was just about level with Dunkirk's knees when he jumped for the rope. Without warning, his weight jerked the rope back into the center of the tower and pulled her from the wall.

Ogma's hands wheeled desperately, reaching out for anything to hold onto. Enki boomed out again. She could feel herself falling, the rope slithering past her. She closed her arms quickly, hugging the rope tightly to her body. The friction rubbed her forearms raw, but she managed to halt her fall.

She looked up at Dunkirk. *You stupid wretch. You nearly killed me.* He was looking down at her with horror frozen on his face. It faded to relief.

"Er du godt?" He was clinging to the rope clumsily with both hands—awkwardly spinning as he craned his neck to keep her in sight. "Jeg er sa lei meg."

She motioned for him to climb down. He hesitated and then shook his head.

"What are you even doing?" Ogma yelled up at him.

He gestured upwards, at the bells.

"Disse klokkene! Jeg tror jeg kjenner dem." He turned and started clumsily climbing the rope.

"You're not even climbing the rope right! Lock your leg! Your leg—! Argh." Ogma broke off with a frustrated grunt and began pulling herself up the rope. She moved much faster than he did, but she'd lost ground in the fall.

Dunkirk made it to the support beam and pulled himself up. Ogma followed.

They straddled the beam, panting. Dunkirk glanced back down the tower and visibly paled.

"Jeg trodde ikke det var så høy." He whistled and dropped one hand.

"Yeah. It's a long drop." Ogma glared as she caught her breath.

Dunkirk leaned out to look at the bells. His eyes widened in disbelief. "Det kan ikke være. Jeg tror ikke på det."

Ogma had never seen Enki and Enoch up close. As it turned out, they weren't really a pair. More of a mismatched set. Enoch was the larger of the two bells, but more crudely fashioned. It was a dull bronze.

It's engraved, Ogma realized, leaning closer. There was a scene etched into the metal. Small figures stood on a stone rampart, erecting some tall shape. *The bell tower?* Ogma wondered. *No! They're building the windmills.*

She leaned out on the beam. It was a history of the town. There were more scenes engraved all the way around the bell. An early scene showed them carting stones to build the walls.

Huh—they built the bell tower before the walls, and before that... One scene showed a lone wagon wandering in the fog. Antlered figures dug up something from a mound in the other and put it in their wagon. They came upon a small gathering of humans inside a wooden pallisade. *A bell! They're giving them a bell. That must be Enki, the old one*, Ogma figured, *and then they made Enoch.*

She was so fascinated she hadn't noticed Dunkirk fall silent. He had no interest in Enoch; it was Enki that held his attention.

There was a frightening stillness in Dunkirk as he looked at the bell. His shoulders sagged and he began to shake.

Is he crying? Ogma looked at him in shock. She didn't know what he'd climbed the tower for, but this wasn't what she expected. Ogma scooted over on the beam to sit next to him. He sniffed, and wiped his nose with one arm, not meeting her gaze.

"Jeg kjenner denne bjella." He pointed to the bell and pressed a hand to his chest.

She looked at Enki. It was much more finely wrought than Enoch, that she could tell. Even though the metal was dark and patinated, it had a silver hue. And it was scarred—a jagged groove cut into one edge. *Even that crack looks old.*

As her eyes adjusted to the dusky shadows in the tower Ogma began to pick out details. The bell was engraved with a field of stars, and the moon and her sister—

—*is falling*, Ogma realized. *The blue sister is falling.* And the stars engraved beside it were marching below the horizon and onto the earth. That couldn't be. They had no stories of the moon falling. No stories of the stars marching on the earth. *It must mean something else.*

There was strange writing or perhaps decoration around the top of the bell, and more around the rim. Whatever it was, she couldn't read it.

Dunkirk tugged on her sleeve and pointed. There was another scene on the bell. He stood, balancing on the beam and hopping to one on the other side. He turned and held a hand out to her.

She took it cautiously and took an awkward half-step, half-jump across the gap. He steadied her and they sat down again.

"Ser du det?"

Ogma looked. The blue moon was just above the earth. A small group of figures stood around it, with human bodies and beetles' heads. *Or beetle's armor,* she thought, glancing at

Dunkirk. The figures raised their arms in supplication, or maybe worship. Silhouetted by the blue moon was a gowned figure.

"Jassike." Dunkirk turned to her, eyes red-rimmed, defeated. "Dette er datterens bjella."

Ogma ran her fingers gently down the engraving. "You know who this is?" She pointed at the gowned figure.

"Jassike." He nodded sadly, and then pointed at one of the beetle figures and then himself.

"Wait—you were *there?!*"

Dunkirk put his head in his hands. "Død. Omkom. De er alle døde."

Ogma's mind reeled. Enki was hundreds of seasons old, maybe thousands. If he'd been there before it was made... everyone he knew, anyone he loved...

She took his hand and squeezed. "I'm sorry."

"Oi! You lot ever coming down?" Rora's voice echoed from the base of the bell tower.

Effie's voice followed. "Not coming down until she's done with 'im, I bet."

There was a muffled *'oof'* from below—courtesy of Rora's elbow.

"We'd better go down now," Ogma said quietly, pointing to the floor below. They'd been up there for some time, Ogma letting him gather himself in supportive silence.

Dunkirk grunted and nodded vaguely. He laid one hand gingerly against Enki's surface, as if afraid—or hoping—that it would disappear. Like a fog phantom or a dream.

Dunkirk moved as if to grab the rope.

"Woah there. You just hold on a minute." Ogma pulled him back and held her hands up in his face in a 'stop' gesture.

"Before we do this, you're going to learn how to hold a

rope." Ogma caught the rope with her toe and pulled it up to them, pulling up some slack so she had something to work with. She demonstrated wrapping the rope around her feet and locking it with her ankles.

"See?" She pointed. "*That* is how you climb a rope."

Dunkirk looked unfocused, so she repeated the motion. He shook himself and then pointed at the rope and nodded.

Ogma passed the rope to him and made him practice several times until he got it right. She took the rope back, locked her ankles around it, and slipped off the beam. She swung in a gentle, controlled arc, the bell clapping only lightly—a warm hum hanging in the air.

She demonstrated how to move up and down the rope, adjusting her hold with her hands, and moving her foot lock up and down the length. Dunkirk studied her carefully.

"Okay, you ready?" Ogma asked. She gestured with one hand. He nodded.

Dunkirk gingerly lowered himself from the beam and eyed the bellpull skeptically.

"You're going to have to grab it sometime," Ogma said flatly. "Just reach. It's right there."

Dunkirk glanced down and gulped. Gritting his teeth, he managed to wrest one hand from his secure hold on the beam and grab at the rope. As he let go, the rope swayed awkwardly and the bell clapper clattered against the side.

Ogma watched critically. "All right, now just hook your leg around and—no, you've got it backwards again. Backwards!" While Dunkirk couldn't understand her words, her tone was clear. On the second try, he got it right, and they started making their way back down to the ground floor.

Ogma made it down first. She opted to skip the platform to nowhere and just took the rope straight to the floor. Dunkirk moved more slowly.

Rora and Effie were there to greet her as she dusted off her hands and shook the cobwebs out of her hair.

"So what was that about then?" Rora asked.

Effie started to grin, but she eyed Rora's elbow and kept her lips shut.

Ogma shook her head. "I—I don't think I can say."

Effie broke in. "So what? He just felt like climbing the belfry?"

"He—um—he knows the bells," Ogma said carefully. "Enki anyway."

"Huh," Effie replied, unsure what to make of that.

Rora only grunted.

A clomp of boots on the platform above them let them know Dunkirk had opted to get off the rope early. He practically flew down the steps. He shied back from the three girls and their critical eyebrows. His eyes were still red-rimmed.

Effie took pity first. "Cheer up, eh? You've given everyone something to talk about at least." She linked arms with the sheepish Dunkirk and pulled him back out to the square. Rora and Ogma followed.

The small crowd had grown a bit. Nan Aud had been holding them back from the tower, but they were clearly standing around expecting an accident. Ogma thought they looked almost disappointed when both she and Dunkirk walked out unharmed. But maybe she was just tired.

A small crowd of children, those who didn't have duty on the wall, had gathered as well.

"What d'you think you're staring at?" Effie teased. Ogma admired her unabashed charisma. "It's a festival day, isn't it? We have games to play!"

That broke the awkward silence. The crowd of adults turned back to their business in the square—setting up decorations, preparing for the feast, and carrying wares to trade with the caravan—as the children clamored for their favorite games to play.

"Stick ball!"

"Potatoes-in-the-cellar!"

"Fade the phantom!"

In this last game, one child was designated the phantom and stood in one corner of the square, while the other children split up into the two adjacent corners. The phantom's job was to run to the other corner before being tagged by any of the other children. It was a fun game, but it just didn't seem right with the sun shining overhead.

"No fog games!" Ogma called out.

Wheeler's voice rang out from the back. "Potatoes-in-the-cellar, for sure! *That's* my game." With Wheeler's endorsement, the rest of the children quickly relented.

"Who's It?"

Just about every hand was raised.

"What's 'tatoes-in-the-cellar?" a small voice asked. It was one of Emma's cohort. *Billie?* Ogma went up on her toes, trying to see through the crowd of kids. Billie was a small blonde child with big blue eyes. She and Clara, a girl about the same age but with brown hair and brown eyes, stuck to each other like glue.

"Don't you 'member that?" Emma said scornfully. "We played it last time."

"Nuh-uh!" Billie stamped her foot.

"Yeah we did, Billie, I 'member." Clara said. Billie was tearing up with all the contrary attention "Oh, don't cry. Actually, I don't 'member either."

"First, the rules!" Wheeler bellowed over their heads, as if he hadn't heard any of it, neatly circumventing the brewing spat. "Before I pick who's It, who can tell me the rules?"

Several of the older children started talking all at once—but not unexpectedly, Cole was the loudest.

"That's easy! Whoever's It has to go find a place to hide, while the rest of us close our eyes and count to one hundred. Then we all go looking for them. If you find them, you have to hide there too!"

"And...?" Wheeler prompted his self-styled lieutenant.

"And... the last person to find the others loses—and they're It the next time," Cole finished.

Wheeler eyed him up and down with an exaggerated air. "Correct. And for that, you're It! One! Two! Three!" Wheeler put one arm over his eyes, and the others scrambled to cover theirs when they realized the game was on.

"Hey—no fair!" Cole protested.

"Five! Six! Seven—!"

"All right, I'm going! I'm going!" Cole dashed for the edge of the square.

"And stay on the first terrace!" Wheeler yelled after him. "Back to the wall is cheating! Eight! Nine!"

Dunkirk was looking puzzled.

"Come on! Cover your eyes!" Effie picked up his hands and put them over his face.

"Bah! Dette er et spill for barn!" Dunkirk protested.

"I'll sit on you if you don't!" she threatened.

Dunkirk relented.

Ogma covered her own eyes and tried to listen for Cole's footsteps between the count. With all the adults in the square it was hopeless. "Twenty-seven! Twenty-eight! Twenty-nine! Come on, you guys, help me count!"

"Thirty!"

"Thr—Thirty-one!" The small children were just a beat behind; they were still learning their numbers.

"Thirty-two!"

"—two!"

"Thirty-three!"

"—free!"

Ogma felt her pulse quicken as the count approached one hundred. She already knew the first places she was going to look. *But I can't go there right away—have to make sure I'm not followed.* The chant hit a crescendo as they reached the end.

"Ninety-nine! One hundred!"

"Go!" Wheeler's voice boomed out from across the cobbles.

"You cheat!" Once the rest of them had picked up the count, he'd snuck his way to the edge of the square. The children laughed and protested as they realized what he'd done.

"Nothing against it in the rules!" He grinned at them as he disappeared down the alley. "My eyes were closed!"

Ogma laughed so hard she had to sit down. The other children scattered, some peeking in the bell tower to see if Cole had gone with the easy fake out, while others immediately sprinted for the alley after Wheeler. Dunkirk was looking puzzled again. *He does that a lot, doesn't he? I guess when you can't speak the language...* Effie ran off across the square.

"Come on! We have to find Cole!"

"Merkelig jente..." Dunkirk turned to Ogma. "Hva gjør vi?"

"Oh, come *on.*" Ogma took his hand and dragged him to the edge of the square. Emma, Mae and Maya, and Billie and Clara trotted after them. *You're supposed to look on your own, you know.* Not that she could say anything with Dunkirk in tow.

"Let's check in here!" The bakery looked deserted, but the smell of yeast and crusty bread hung in air that was still warm from the ovens.

"Is it *allowed?*" Billie and Clara stood on the threshold, peering inside the dim room.

"Sure it is!" Emma said confidently. "Now where's Cole hiding? Do you see him?"

A door in the back wall led into the attached granary, but it was dark and empty.

"Maybe he's in here!" The little girls started looking behind the boxes and sacks.

Ogma held a finger to her lips and backed slowly out of the bakery. Dunkirk, resigned to confusion, followed.

"That should keep them busy—come on!" They trotted back through the square. The crowd of children had really dispersed now. She saw small groups sneaking from alley to alley, but it seemed clear that some portion of the children had already found Cole.

One cobbled avenue looked even less trafficked than the others. *I thought so.* She looked behind them to make sure no one else could see them and darted down the alley. She sidled casually to the wells above the cistern that gathered rain from all the roofs in the square.

Kneeling down, she lifted the trapdoor set into the cobbles. Ogma guessed it was made to let them clean out the cistern if something fell into the wells. She peered into the shadows. As her eyes adjusted, she could see blue light lapping at the stones. One of the shadows moved.

"Quick—come on!" Ogma clambered down the ladder and Dunkirk followed.

Cole was there, as were Effie, Rora, and a number of the others. Ogma hunkered down next to them. The advantage of this hiding place was that there was plenty of space for the children to pack into. Dunkirk studied the ceiling, peering up the shafts of the wells, and then down into the dark vaulted chambers.

"Hvor langt går dette?" he pointed into the dark.

"Shh!"

"Greit! Jeg skal være stille!" He buttoned his lips with one hand and sat down next to Ogma, still muttering. "Hvor lenge blir vi her nede?"

Rora put a hand to her lips and pointed at the ceiling. A voice echoed down.

"Hm! I wonder where they went?" It was Wheeler talking in an exaggerated voice that let them know he was trying to throw off one of the other children nearby. He rang his bell, the tenor chime filling the cistern below. He snapped his fingers. "Maybe he's at Goodie Hazel's house!"

They heard footsteps pounding.

Ogma laced her fingers under her head and watched the strange blue light of the reflected water dance on the stones. One after the other, the children tried the cistern door and filtered inside. Even Emma, Mae, and Maya found it.

"Haha. We saw you, Bowen," Emma giggled. The boy blushed.

"Shh!" The girls settled down, but couldn't help whispering to each other.

"Ugh—where *are they?*" It was Billie's voice.

"I don't see *anyone.*" That was Clara. Her voice got louder as she peered over the edge of the well. "Cole must be good at hiding—oh!"

Two sets of footsteps ran to the trapdoor, and they heard it rattle as the girls tried to lift it.

"Me first, me first! I found it!" That was Billie.

"Nuh-uh! I did!" There was more rattling at the door until finally it opened and the two girls clambered down the ladder. Clara came down first, with Billie just behind her. Both little girls immediately sat down with Emma and the others.

Emma spoke up first. "Billie! You're the last one! That means you're It!"

"Nuh-uh! Clara was last!"

"Nuh-*uh.* She came down before you!"

Clara tried to mollify them both. "We came down together. Maybe we can both be It?"

"I don' w-wanna be It!" Billie was on the verge of tears.

Cole spoke up. "It's only fair, Billie, those are the rules."

"Oh shut up, Cole—she doesn't want to do it."

Dunkirk covered his ears as the argument echoed through the cistern. "Hva er barn krangler om?" Just as Billie looked ready to wail, a voice boomed out from the well above.

"What's this I hear?" It was Wheeler. *He must have heard the argument a mile away.* "Oh no! Why is the cistern door open?" He rang his bell. "I hope no one hid down there." He gave a stage gasp. "What if the *monster* gets them?"

There were shrieks and giggles as the smaller children rushed for the ladder, argument forgotten.

"No one *said* there was a *monster!*"

"Eek! Help! Let me out!"

"Wheeler! Help!"

The oldest children grinned at each other as the youngest scrambled up. Wheeler's face appeared in the hatch. "Quick! I've got you." He grabbed the young ones by one arm and pulled them up bodily. "It hasn't seen your face, has it?"

His voice was so mock-serious that Ogma couldn't help but giggle. Cole was looking half-concerned himself. He tried to hide it, but he kept glancing over his shoulder into the dark. Ogma giggled harder.

"Quick, you guys!" Billie called down. "The monster will *get* you!"

The older children tried to control their laughter as they clambered up the ladder after the little ones. Wheeler was hunkered down on his heels with a ring of young children around him.

"What is it, Wheeler?"

"Yeah! What's down there?"

"Does it have sharp teef?"

"Oh yes—very sharp teeth. And *huge* eyes—the better to see you in the dark." The children shivered. "And if it sees your face, you're *doomed!* Then it can follow you anywhere, even if you get out of the cistern. It didn't see any of you, did it?"

Wheeler looked at each of the terrified faces.

"No way. Not me!"

"N-not me either!"

The children all shook their heads vigorously. Wheeler sat back on his heels and sighed with relief.

"Whew. That's good. Because if it ever does find you—there's only one way to escape."

The children waited with bated breath for the secret knowledge that could save them from the cistern monster.

"Wait, do you hear that?" Wheeler held up one finger and the children fell silent. *Dun, dun, clap. Dun, dun, clap.* A rhythmic stamping and clapping echoed down the cobbles. Wheeler jumped to his feet and started jogging for the square. He waved them after him. "Come on! It's starting!"

"But *Wheeler!*" The children whined in chorus. "How do we 'scape?"

Wheeler paused and looked back over his shoulder. "That's easy! Just ring your bells!" He chimed his own tenor bell and turned back to the square. The children all rang their cheery chords and ran after him.

A number of the men of the village stood in a ring on wooden boards in the center of the square. The women stood in a circle inside, facing them. The men were stamping their feet and clapping their hands in rhythm. The women stood perfectly still.

Ogma and the crowd of children gathered in the square to watch. Even Dunkirk seemed transfixed as the rhythm grew louder and more complex. The women in the center circle slowly gathered themselves up on their toes, raising their bells above their heads. The stamping and clapping wove together in rhythmic crescendo—

Boom. Enki tolled once, the sound filling the square. The women brought their bells down, in alternating pairs, ringing chords in a lilting melody. The men began to stomp and clap again, shuffling around the outside circle as they kept rhythm for the women's bells.

The children clapped and cheered as the dance began in earnest. The two circles of dancers wove in and out of each other. Sometimes the women took their turn keeping rhythm while the men rang their bells, and sometimes there seemed no pattern to it—just the joy of the beat as they clapped and rang their bells together.

The children formed their own circle, Ogma with them, joining the dance with their cheerful chords. They danced breathlessly, forgetting the fog and fear for a little while. Wheeler linked arms with Ogma and they spun in a short circle, her melancholy chord a counterpoint to his clear tenor bell. They broke away and she linked arms with Bowen next, stamping their feet as he rang his bell in rhythm. Rora and Effie spotted Dunkirk tapping his foot on the sidelines and pulled him in to dance.

The sun was setting, the shadows of the buildings in the square dancing with them as the sun shifted on the horizon.

Boom. Enoch tolled. The circling dancers stopped and cheered, all bells ringing in a joyous clangor. Wheeler had Billie up on his shoulders and little Clara in his arms, laughing and cheering with the rest of them. *That's the Wheeler I know.* As the cacophony of joyful noise diminished, the villagers dispersed, gathering at the stalls to look at the wares on display and bustling off to long wooden tables to finish preparing the evening's feast.

Ogma was just wondering where she might find a place to curl up with a mug of cider and rest her aching limbs when she saw the old man rushing across the square. He was carrying an old chest with him. From the way he was puffing, he must have carried it all the way from his cottage.

After scanning the crowd, he walked over to Ogma. He set the chest down and sat on top of it, mopping his brow. He smiled placidly at her and they sat in silence for a moment. Dunkirk emerged from the crowd of children, grinning and breathless from the dance. The old man jumped to his feet. He ran over to the boy and took him by the arm, pulling him insistently over to where Ogma was sitting.

"Hva er det nå, gammel mann? Uuff."

Dunkirk grunted as the old man picked up the chest and tossed it to him. Smiling broadly, he gestured for both of them to follow. For once, Ogma's expression was as puzzled as Dunkirk's. She shrugged and followed Dunkirk after the old man.

Ogma realized that they were headed for the Caravaners' wagons. She began to get excited. *What could he want from them?*

The old man ambled across the square with his typical, eager gait, but his demeanor changed as they approached the caravan wagons. He seemed to stand a little taller and his hands were steadier.

He stopped just outside the area where the Caravaners had set up their stalls. A number of the villagers were still trading: those who'd been busy with work to prepare the festival, or who had come by earlier and were hoping the Caravaners would be more flexible on price at the end of the day.

Goodie Hazel was haggling over a variety of potions and

powders, though Ogma caught her glancing enviously now and again at a collection of fine, almost daintily wrought knives—surgeon's tools.

Brigid was there as well, dressed in her patrol leathers. She was talking quietly with Semane about a selection of bells. She picked them up in pairs and rang them together.

That one's Ambrose, Ogma recognized instantly. Brigid shook her head and swapped them, ringing the new pair. This one Ogma didn't recognize. *She's trying to find chords we aren't using yet.* Brigid picked up a new pair and rang them again. Ogma cocked her head. *That would work.* Brigid nodded and set the pair aside.

Nod came out of the back of a wagon, bolts of fine fabric in both arms. Ulfred the baker was there with his brother. He set down two barrels of the special ale he made whenever a surplus of grain stores allowed. Nod handed the fabric off to Oscar who was mournfully watching the barrels disappear into the wagons.

Oscar wasn't good for much, but he was a decent tailor when he wasn't drinking, so all in all Ogma thought it was a good trade.

Nod stepped back out of the caravan, caught sight of the old man standing there, and stopped in his tracks. They both stood perfectly still, watching each other across the stones. Nod moved first. He extended his arms broadly, and then—to Ogma's astonishment—bowed low to the ground.

The old man looked almost bashful. But not surprised. He quickly walked over to Nod and pulled him up by both arms.

They embraced warmly, and Nod began speaking in a language Ogma had never heard.

The old man responded in kind.

Ogma nearly had to pick her jaw off the floor. After his terse words back in the cabin, she hadn't expected to hear him speak again, let alone in Caravaner tongue.

Melial and Semane watched the exchange with great interest as well. Ogma started to think that the stories that the other children told about him might not be as far-fetched as she had thought.

The old man fell silent again, turning and gesturing at Ogma and Dunkirk. He grunted, bringing a hand to his throat.

Nod replied, "Yes, we thought so. We have a few things that might work." He held up one hand for them to wait and hurried back to the wagon. Dunkirk and Ogma looked at each other as sounds of papers shuffling and drawers slamming came from within the wagon.

Nod peeked his head out and waved his hands.

It took Ogma a second to realize he was motioning them to come inside.

I don't believe it. She'd always imagined what it would be like to travel with a caravan. She'd thought riding on the wagon this morning would be the closest she'd ever come, but this? She leapt up eagerly, barely able to resist trying to beat the old man inside. Dunkirk hefted the old man's chest and followed.

The interior of the wagon was surprisingly roomy. The walls were lined with a multitude of clever cabinets and storage nooks, which kept the center open. Nod had hastily cleared off a small table in the back of the wagon. Ogma saw stacks of books and bottles, and strange sheafs of paper, any one of which she would have given almost anything to have—just to remember them by.

"You remember Son." Nod gestured to the shadow already sitting at the table. Ogma hadn't noticed the shape at first. She wondered uneasily what would have happened if she'd accidentally sat on him.

But he must have been twenty feet tall outside. How does he fit? She tried to look at the place where the shade's head should be and her eyes crossed again.

Enthusiasm slightly dampened, Ogma slid onto the bench across from Son. His silhouetted shape flickered pleasantly. *How does something flicker pleasantly?* Ogma asked herself. But he did.

The old man gestured for Dunkirk to sit next to her. He sat down next to Son. *Is there really enough room on the bench for both of them?* She was reassured to see that while the old man took the seat without hesitation, he still looked askance at his bench partner. *So it's not just me.*

The old man took the chest that Dunkirk had set down and laid one arm protectively over it.

Nod pointed to Dunkirk, declining to speak, perhaps in deference to the old man's choice to remain mute. The old man nodded. Nod bowed again, and pulled down his cowl, turning to search among the cabinets and curiosities in the many hidden cubbies of the wagon.

Ogma was fascinated. This was her first opportunity to get a good look at Nod without his hood obscuring his features. His eyes were every bit as golden and owlish as they had seemed. His skin was dark, and apart from the eyes, his face was largely human. But at the hairline, behind the ears, and at the throat, she could see that he was Caravaner. Stubbly, almost scaly shoots seemed to grow from the edges of his face, spreading into dark, blue-back feathers across the back of his head and down his collar. His taloned hands were dexterous and even delicate, hovering over a series of drawers.

He seemed to find the drawer he was looking for, then pulled it out of the cabinet.

Ogma stood half out of her seat, trying to see what was inside, but rather than bring it over to the table, Nod discarded it on top of a pile of dusty old parchment.

He looked at them, golden eyes inscrutable, and then reached his hand into the cubby hole where the drawer had been. He reached his arm well past his elbow and fished around for a moment.

When he pulled it back out, Ogma thought at first that he must have made a mistake. It looked like he was holding a string of particularly nasty, shriveled garlic cloves or old onions. Then she realized what they were.

Seven tiny heads, shrunken, with leathery faces and wisps of hair tied up with beads, were strung together on a leather thong like a daisy chain. Several were the heads of small animals: rodents or weasels, perhaps. One was just a skull grinning a feline smile. Another looked like the head of an ermine moth with long feathery antennae. The last, apart from its diminutive size, looked human.

Ogma jumped back in her seat. *They're moving!* The leathery brown things were spinning gently on the end of the thong, but she was certain that one had opened its mouth. *They're... yawning?* Ogma shuddered.

Dunkirk had noticed too; she heard him suck in a breath and his hand clenched on the tabletop.

Then Nod did one of the most disgusting things Ogma had ever seen. He picked up the other end of the leather cord and tied the chain of heads around his neck.

The seven heads woke up. They started chittering to each other, snapping and arguing in small heated whispers. They shot wary glances around the room. The chipmunk head eyed Ogma mistrustfully and began whispering to one of its compatriots.

Nod whispered in the Caravaner tongue to the feline skull at the end of the chain. The whisper was passed down the line until it reached the shriveled almost-human face.

"With this voice, you could speak," the head intoned in a dusty croak.

At the same moment, the head next to it echoed, "Med denne stemmen, kunne du snakker."

With some shock, Ogma realized it was speaking in Dunkirk's tongue. She watched to see what Dunkirk thought of the offer, but Dunkirk shook his head vigorously, looking a little sick.

Nod looked disappointed. He raised an eyebrow and looked at the old man. The old man shook his head as well.

Nod shrugged, blinking owlishly, and untied the string of heads from around his neck. As soon as the knot was undone, the heads began yawning again and he gently tucked them away and replaced the drawer.

Ogma was vaguely disappointed. It had been quite horrible, and yet...

Nod rubbed his taloned hands together and frowned for a moment, casting about the room.

He picked his way through the cluttered wagon to a different cabinet, digging about inside. Ogma saw the glittering of silver and glass, and something seemed to glow. Eventually, he came out with a few objects in hand, which he brought over to the table.

Dunkirk shied away a bit as Nod approached, squeezing Ogma uncomfortably into the corner. Once she saw what Nod laid out on the table, she understood why.

Nod carefully laid down several objects rolled in bands of cloth. Unwrapping the first, he laid out a large curved needle and several pieces of what looked like jewelry. They were large-gauge shapes, carved from stone or ivory—Ogma wasn't quite sure which.

The next cloth roll was laid out to reveal a kit that was similar, but not precisely the same. There was another needle in this one, but this time straight, and set into a delicate wooden handle. Beside the needle sat a jar of ink, and beside that...

Is that a tongue?

Dunkirk recoiled in disgust. The leathery shape was black and cracked and dry.

"Ah. I'll be needing..." Nod said and got up again. He rummaged about in another cabinet. He returned a moment later with a mortar and pestle in hand.

Dubious was too mild a word for Dunkirk's expression. He was eyeing the implements with near horror. Nod spoke, and, once again, Ogma heard Dunkirk's language.

"Med denne stemmen, kunne du snakker." Nod patted the table next to the implements as he said it. He was speaking in his own voice this time. There was no visible implement translating for him as there had been with the heads.

It's like an echo. Underneath his voice, she could hear him saying the words in a different tongue, probably his own.

Dunkirk still looked skeptical. He gripped the edge of the table and looked down at the implements. Ogma could see him weighing it over in his mind.

"Jeg vil være i stand til å snakke? Jeg vil være i stand til å forstå?" Dunkirk asked.

Nod looked back at him with his unblinking golden eyes. With one taloned hand, he pulled down the front of his collar. A circular disk of ivory or bone was set into his throat. He gave Dunkirk enough time to look at the piercing to see that it had healed. Then he opened his mouth and stuck out his tongue.

His tongue was tattooed. Designs in black ink were crowded so tightly that his tongue itself looked black. Each design looked like a different word and, in some cases, written in a different alphabet.

Can he speak all those? Ogma marveled.

Dunkirk hadn't relaxed his grip on the table, but he wasn't shaking his head either.

"Hva må jeg gjøre?" he asked Nod.

Nod turned to the old man. "First we will need to settle our bargain. We can only trade a greater charm for its like."

"Why?" Ogma interjected. "If the charms can help people."

"It's our law." Nod spoke firmly.

The old man looked back at Dunkirk and held his gaze for a moment, then nodded. With a small sigh, he took a key from around his neck. The old chest unlocked with a well-oiled click, and he pulled the lid open.

Ogma craned her neck to peer inside.

"Hei, vent litt! Det er min!"

An iridescent blue reflected on the faces assembled around the table. On top of the collection of objects, half covered by a silk cloth, was the backplate of Dunkirk's armor.

The old man ignored Dunkirk's outburst and lifted the plate out of the chest. While the front plate had a jagged hole punched through it, the backplate was entirely intact. It wasn't just the color of a beetle's shell, it *was* a beetle's shell. Despite Dunkirk's muttered protestations, the old man laid the plate down on the table.

He ran his fingers over the surface, and with a small grunt, worked his fingernails into a crack running straight down the middle of the plate. He carefully levered the two halves of the backplate aside. Gossamer, iridescent wings unfolded from the armor.

If Nod was impressed, he didn't show it. But the reflection of the blue beetle shell glittered in his golden eyes. Casually, he leaned over the table, inspecting the beetle shell carefully, as if looking for imperfections.

What does he think he's looking for? I bet not even the Caravaners have anything like it.

Nod reached for the armor plate, but paused, looking to the old man. The old man nodded and waved his hand.

"Det er min!" Dunkirk repeated. He snatched it up and held it to his chest.

Nod raised an eyebrow. "Have you anything else to trade? Har du noe annet å bytte?" *That echo again.*

Dunkirk's scowl faded. "Nei... nei jeg har ikke noe annet." He bit his lip, still hugging the armor to his chest, and then sighed and held it out to Nod.

Nod's eyes glittered. He lifted the armor and spread the blue outer shell further. The gossamer wings unfolded, and then fluttered with a gust of wind that tugged at Ogma's clothing and scattered old papers and scraps of cloth all over the wagon.

As everyone looked at the armor in wonder, something else caught Ogma's attention. The gust of wind had blown loose some of the silk cloth that hid the rest of the contents of the old man's treasure chest.

Inside, partly covered by black rags, was a beaked bird's skull, big enough to be worn as a mask. The old man saw that she had noticed. He calmly replaced the silk cloth and closed the chest. He and Ogma traded a look.

Nod was still absorbed in tinkering with the beetle shelled armor plate. The wings fluttered again. He nodded. Son flickered merrily. Nod turned to Dunkirk and the old man.

"This will be fine. Too much in fact. Dette blir bra. For mye faktisk," he repeated for Dunkirk " He held up one hand and untied a beaded bracelet from his wrist.

He then counted out three beads onto the table. The old man looked up at him. Nod counted out a fourth bead and then the old man nodded, gesturing to Dunkirk to take the beads.

Dunkirk was still muttering as Nod closed the deal, folding up the beetle wing armor and tucking it away in one of the many cubby holes in the wagon.

Nod reached for one of the glittering implements, and then

snatched his hand away at a knock on the door. He turned to look at it, blinked, and the knock came again.

"Sorry. Is Ogma here?" It was Wheeler's muffled voice.

"Yeah! I'm here," Ogma called out. She gave Dunkirk a push so that he would let her off the bench and ran over to the door.

"What is it?"

"Sorry, Ogma. I promised that you'd take the feast shift on the west wall."

"Oh." Ogma's face fell a bit. She looked back inside the wagon, trying to commit every detail to memory.

"You've been off patrol for a few days, and with Rora, Effie, and Cole all off for the night..." Wheeler was kind but firm.

"Sure. Of course." She turned back to the others inside the wagon. "Sorry. I have to go." She waved to Dunkirk and the old man and bowed to the Caravaners. Son flickered and Nod inclined his head. She hopped down from the wagon step.

Wheeler was already jogging away towards the watch house, likely to gather up more children to patrol the walls. His promise that the Circle winners wouldn't have to patrol meant that finding children who hadn't already been on double shifts would be difficult.

He'll probably take a shift himself. I bet he hasn't slept. Ogma sighed and resigned herself to a long night.

The light was fading. Tables had been brought out and set in rows in the square. She could smell the feast being prepared, the savory smell of vegetable stew, and a spicy mulled cider. There were other spices in the air that Ogma had never tasted before, newly traded from the caravan. Ogma's mouth watered and her breath misted in the air.

At least I've got my coat this time. Ogma pulled it tightly around her as the stars began to dance in the deepening blue sky.

CHAPTER 5

BLANK FACES

It was Daniel's watch on the north wall. He looked back over the village. The festival had gone on long into the night, but now, well past midnight, most were sleeping. Only the most committed revelers were still gathered around the fires, laughing and carousing. Outside the walls, fireflies winked green and yellow in the meadows.

The fog was coming back. It wasn't yet thick and close, but it rolled across the landscape in great banks, and the valleys and meadows that had almost become familiar were giving way to a patchwork of forest thickets and bare earth.

A small yawn and the pattering of feet made him turn.

"I brought you dinner!" It was little Emma, barefoot but bundled tightly in a coat a few sizes too large for her.

"Oh did you now? And who sent you—is that the stew from the feast?" Daniel swept the bowl up and slurped it down greedily. The warmth spread through him.

"*I* sent me. It was my idea."

"Well, you're a wonder then." He savored the delicious broth. "And why are you awake, little one?"

"I'm here t—to patrol!" She yawned.

"How about this? How about we patrol together?"

She frowned and considered this.

"You can tell me how the festival was."

"Oh yeah! It's the best ever. I won the Circle!" she lied outrageously.

"Oh you did, did you? The whole thing?"

"Well, I won *three* stages. I mean *two*." She generously revised her claim to a level she thought he might believe.

He smiled and let her chatter on, interrupting now and again to ask her questions about the wall patrol.

"All right, so we're coming up on the northwest windmill. And what do you do when you reach each windmill?"

Emma looked at him like he was stupid. "Ring my bell."

"...and?" he prompted.

"And..." she continued her bluster, but faltered.

"And you wait until you hear the other patrol ring theirs."

"Well yeah! That's *obvious*." Emma rolled her eyes at him. Daniel shook his head as she picked up her irrepressible chatter.

"*Anyway*," she continued, "after I won the Circle race..."

Daniel chuckled to himself.

A muffled, metallic rattling noise suddenly distracted his attention. "Huh. Wh—what's that?"

Daniel stepped to the edge of the wall and leaned over. The newly fog-sculpted landscape had no landmarks, so it took a moment to get his bearings. And then he saw movement: huddled shapes at the edge of a stand of trees. He saw the flutter of a cloak and the edge of what might have been a cart.

"Daniel, what is—"

There was a rush of air as something flew past Daniel's face.

With a dull metallic thunk and a muffled cry the little girl collapsed to the flagstones.

"Emma!" Daniel's heart leapt into his throat and he fell to his knees next to the little girl.

A heavy iron hook on the end of a rope had struck her in the temple. She'd fallen in a jumble of limbs. Her hair was matted with blood.

"No—no, no, no..." Daniel cradled her slight frame to him. Her head lolled unnaturally, but he thought he felt her heart flutter against his chest. His eyes burned with furious tears.

The rope pulled taut and the iron hook skipped along the stones. Daniel rolled out of the way, Emma still held to his chest. The hook clipped him on the leg, jerking him towards the wall's edge and tearing a burning gash on his calf before he pulled free.

"Shh, shh. Emma?" Daniel wiped the blood from the girl's temple with his hand and gently tapped her cheek. "Can you hear me? Emma?"

His heart was pounding so hard he didn't hear the metallic clatter as several other hooks were thrown over the wall.

Emma's eyelids fluttered, but didn't open.

Daniel put his ear to her chest. Her breathing was coming in short, quick flutters. He took a deep, shuddering breath. "Okay, okay. We need help."

He lifted his bell and started ringing out the alarm.

What was that? Ogma tore her eyes away from the landscape beyond the western span and listened. She strained to be as quiet as possible until the rush of blood in her ears sounded like a river, but whatever she had heard had been carried away on the wind.

I thought I heard a bell. Ogma worried her lip, but if there were an alarm, the larger bell at the watch house should be relaying it out so all could hear.

It couldn't have been Mae or Maya. The two little girls were patrolling the northwest span tonight, but they had two bells each, and they were high-pitched, merry chords.

The bell I heard was deeper.

Ogma peered into the dark towards the north wall. The fields were black pools in the night. The few stone buildings she could see in town were dark and empty. Hollow, black windows against black stone.

In the far distance, near the northeast span, she could see the faint outline of the watch house against the sky.

The shutters are closed. She could probably have seen the firelight through the cracks in the shutters if she were closer, but in the hazy, frosty air, she couldn't make out a glimmer.

Ogma tensed and waited.

Come on, you two, she silently urged the twin girls, *give me something.*

Daniel was still ringing his bell wildly, cradling young Emma in one arm. A grunt and the sound of booted footsteps on the wall made him tear his eyes away from the injured little girl.

A broad figure stood on the edge of the rampart in a patchy, many-colored cloak. Two more pulled themselves up from the other ropes.

Daniel's vision went red.

"You did this!" Daniel shouted.

The central figure stepped back a pace, and the shadowy cowl turned towards the fallen girl. The figure hesitated.

Daniel threw himself at the shapes, beating with his bare hands and tearing with his fingernails, his breath coming in ragged gasps. He fought with no technique, no purpose. The three figures were caught off guard.

"How *could* you?"

The hood of the cloak fell away and Daniel faltered,

surprised. Inky black hands closed around his arms like iron bands as the two cloaked companions took hold of them. Daniel struggled, kicking, twisting, and pulling against them.

Two pairs of bells chimed a panicked query from the western side of the wall.

"Mae! Maya! Run!" Daniel shouted himself hoarse and struggled harder.

The thing that Daniel had been fighting drew its cloak back about its face and advanced on the twin girls.

Daniel tore free and launched himself at its back.

"Run! *Please!*" Daniel called out desperately. "Just run!"

Mae and Maya were staring in shock. He hit the thing in the fluttering cloak at an awkward angle. It was like running into a stone wall. The hulk swatted him away like a fly. Daniel stumbled sideways and tripped.

He felt a lurch of vertigo as he fell backwards over the edge of the wall. He heard Mae, or maybe Maya, screaming.

As the wind of his fall rushed through his ears, his last thought was of cold, hollow eyes in a blank face.

Ogma had jogged to the windmill on the corner between the west and northwest spans. It was the closest she could get without leaving her post.

The creaking of the windmill frame and the flapping of the canvas blades made it harder still to hear what was going on. Ogma pulled the main lever of the mill with a grunt of effort. With a solid mechanical *clunk*, the mill locked in place.

She heard Mae and Maya's bells chime a query. There were muffled shouts coming from the north. Ogma's heart pounded.

Calm down, Ogma scolded herself and drew a slow breath. *It could be anything. I have to hold my post.*

Ogma glanced behind her. The fog was still drifting in

menacing banks, but it hadn't gotten closer to the wall yet—at least not where she was.

Come on. Where are your bells?

She raised her own bells and chimed her minor chord loudly: *I'm here. All's well. And you? And you?*

There was no response.

Maya was shocked into action first. She watched in horror as Daniel stumbled over the edge of the wall and fell. Mae was screaming. Emma was lying in a broken heap at the edge of the wall. And three shapes in brightly-colored cloaks were turning on them.

Maya grabbed Mae's hand and turned to run.

She made it about two steps and then Mae's hand slipped from hers with a sudden jerk. Maya didn't stop running. Hot tears burned on her face and she sobbed in ragged gasps as she ran. She glanced over her shoulder.

The cloaked shape had Mae.

Maya sobbed and ran on.

There! Ogma strained. *Those were bells, weren't they? One of the twins. Why'd she stop?*

Ogma opened the storage door on the mill and pulled out a tether and harness, strapping herself into it, and looping the tether around one arm.

Just in case. She glanced nervously behind her at the lonely western span she was supposed to be guarding.

Who's on the north? Where are Mae and Maya?

Ogma's palms twitched. She was desperate to do something, but she didn't know what was wrong—or if anything *had* gone wrong.

I don't think this is a phantom. An unpleasant prickling ran up her arms. Ogma moved from foot to foot anxiously and began pacing in a quick, short circuit on the rampart. She glanced outward again, compulsively, to make sure the fog hadn't stolen up. It was still distant, and still divided into several banks rather than one great rolling wave, but it seemed to sense something as well. It roiled and bubbled, gathering like a storm. She could sense a gleeful malice.

Too fast. Ogma shook her head. *It's moving too fast.*

She wanted to shout with frustration. Then the distant cries grew louder, and now Ogma could hear it clearly: bells ringing in frantic alarm.

Maya was running so fast that she missed the top of the stairs in her haste. She had to double back and clattered down them as fast as she dared. She fell on the second landing, scraping her knees. She looked at Daniel lying at the edge of the cobblestone road. He wasn't moving.

Maya shook the tears from her eyes and ran on and on. She took up her bells and rang out the alarm cadence frantically, as loudly as she could.

Attack! Alarm! Attack!

She heard the gates opening behind her; the sound of wagon wheels on cobblestone.

A shadow in a many-colored cloak pointed her out to its companions and they charged towards her.

Ogma heard the bells. *Maya's bells. She's here! Why is she off the wall? Where's Mae?* The bells came from inside the village, below the wall, to Ogma's right. She turned and peered through the dark, trying to place the sound.

Suddenly the watch bell began ringing—the large bell booming clearly through the night air. The cadence was strange. Ogma almost couldn't place it for a moment.

Alarm! North wall! The bells rang out clearly, and then... *Caravan! Alarm!*

Ogma had no time for her shock to sink in. She saw someone moving in the dark. Only it wasn't Maya. It was a tall figure in a brightly-colored cloak, stalking through the buildings.

Bile rose in the back of Ogma's throat. She lifted her bells and rang out her chord. *I'm here! Ogma. I'm here!* She kept ringing it, hoping it would distract the figure. Hoping Maya would be able to find her in the dark. She heard a cry and then saw the little girl sprinting from the buildings through the field towards her.

The cloaked figure saw her too. With an inhuman growl it leapt after her.

He's going to catch her!

There was no time. Ogma snapped the tether catch onto the railing and jumped from the wall.

She paid out the line too quickly and jumped too far. With a hard grunt, she jerked at the end of the tether, breath knocked out of her body.

"Here—" Ogma broke off in a fit of coughing. She cleared her throat. "Maya, *here!*"

The girl saw her. She altered course, sprinting for Ogma as quickly as she could.

The cloaked figure changed course as well.

Ogma scrabbled in the dirt for something, anything.

Her hand closed around a loose stone. She hefted it and took aim, waiting for the figure to get closer.

She threw, whipping the stone forward from above her shoulder. It struck home with a crack and the cloaked figure tumbled to the earth.

Maya was choking and gasping, trying to catch her breath. Her face was red and tearstained.

"Shh, shh—hold on," Ogma said. She turned and hoisted Maya onto her back. The girl was still small, but Ogma wasn't that much bigger herself. "Hold tight, okay?"

Not waiting for an answer, Ogma began pulling them both back up the wall. It was a slow, tough climb. Ogma's limbs were burning when they reached the top.

She set Maya down and took her by the shoulders.

"Are you okay?" Ogma asked.

Maya shook her head no.

"What happened?" Ogma glanced down the wall, trying to keep her voice calm. The brightly-colored heap was picking itself up from the weeds.

The girl sniffed and the words tumbled out all at once.

"They hurt little Emma, and—and they pushed Daniel off the wall."

"They did wh—"

"They have Mae!" the girl wailed.

Ogma's stomach dropped. *They're taking the children. They're after us. The caravan is taking us!*

"Shh... hush now." Ogma tried to calm the girl down. "This is very important, are you listening to me?"

The girl hesitated, but nodded.

"Okay—here's what you need to do." Ogma thought fast. "I need you to go to the village and tell them we need help. If they heard the alarm, the adults will be staying away from the walls and we *need* them, right?"

Maya looked like she was going to cry again, but she blinked back the tears and nodded.

"Good girl," Ogma said. "You're strong, you're brave. You can do this. Don't worry, I bet Mae's giving them a good kicking, huh?"

Maya choked out a desperate laugh. "Yeah."

"All right, you have to get moving. Stay on the wall until you get to the southwest, then make a break for the square, okay?"

"O—okay."

"No bells until you get there, all right? And tell them to send someone here to the west wall, too."

Maya nodded. She looked at Ogma pleadingly.

"I'm going after Mae," Ogma said, hoping she sounded more reassuring than she felt.

Maya nodded in relief and turned to run.

Ogma turned to jog north, glancing down. The cloaked figure in the field was gone. She froze, scanning the shadows for the tatterdemalion invader.

The watch bell rang out—*Alarm! Help!*—and then went silent.

No, no, no! Ogma sprinted north.

Rora set down a mug of cider, and cocked an ear. "Hey Ef, do you hear that?"

"Hear what?" Effie queried over a mounded plate of potatoes and berries and onions. The villagers who were still awake were laughing and swapping tired old stories from previous fog breaks, previous harvests. Some were telling tales of the villages they'd left when their time on the wall was done.

Old Keegan had his flutes and was piping a merry rhythm while a small group of the more adventuresome young adults still danced.

"There it is again!" Effie said, cocking her head to the side.

"What are you talking about?" Then Rora heard it too, and her face went ashen. "The watch bell."

"Alarm. And something else!" Effie scrambled to her feet, overturning Rora's plate as she clambered on top of the table.

"Alarm! Alarm from the wall!" Effie shouted. "Everyone quiet!"

The merry celebration suddenly died into a tense silence. The watch house bell echoed, distant but clear.

Alarm! North wall! Caravan! Alarm!

And then then just as suddenly the night was quiet. Shocked faces stared at each other over the cooking fires.

"What does that mean?" Rowan asked.

"Is it a phantom?"

"What's going on?"

"Everyone quiet!" Wheeler shouted over the noise. The villagers fell silent. Wheeler cocked his head, listening for the bells to start again. They did not.

"Is something the matter?" Melial's voice called out across the square. Her shadow seemed to sway in the wind just outside the darkened caravans.

"You tell us!" Oscar was deep, deep into his cups and showed no sign of slowing down. He sloshed to his feet, cup still in hand. "Th' alarm said caravan! Foes!"

The gathered crowd began to mutter.

Wheeler ran up to Rora and Effie, his voice frighteningly level. "I don't like the look of this. We don't know what's going on. Might be just one of the little ones decided to ring the bell, who knows." From the grim set of his jaw, Effie and Rora could tell he didn't believe that. "I'm going to check on it."

"We'll come with you," Rora piped up at once.

Wheeler shook his head. "Not just yet. We don't know where the danger is. They could have relayed the alarm from the south wall for all we know. Stay here and I'll go and ring the alarm again if we need you. I'll tell you where to go."

Wheeler gave Rora a hard look.

Rora nodded.

Wheeler turned to the other girl. "Effie—help them sound Enki and Enoch. Just an answering bell to let them know we've heard, and then keep everyone quiet so you can hear me."

Effie nodded and turned towards the nearby tower.

"Wait—once it's sounded, find Goodie Hazel as soon as you can." He eyed the drunken man who was muttering to the other villagers. "We may need her to keep them from doing something stupid."

Effie nodded and jogged away.

"It'll be all right," Wheeler assured Rora. He turned and started to run for the watch house.

"No it won't," Rora whispered, dread heavy in her chest. It was a fog break, a *festival*. There shouldn't *be* any alarm.

Enki and Enoch boomed out a moment later, pealing clearly into the night. *Alarm! We hear! Alarm! Need help? Alarm! Need help?* And then went silent.

"Wh—what is happening?" A soft voice spoke tentatively at Rora's elbow. Something about it buzzed strangely in her ear, as if another voice was whispering just out of hearing, exactly in time with the words.

"Dunkirk!" She turned to the boy in surprise. "You can talk?"

"Yes—I could talk before?" His voice buzzed again and he rubbed his throat.

"But I mean, I can understand you."

"The Caravaners gave me this." He tilted his head back and Rora could see a small disc on his throat.

"Yugh! Is that a piercing?" She reached out one hand.

"Ah—still sore! Why did the bells ring?" Dunkirk gestured at the tower.

"We're not sure. We heard an alarm from the watch, but they're quiet now, it could just be..."

"It's them! Thieves and witches all of 'em. They done something." Oscar raised his voice, and this time other villagers stood up too.

Melial had not left the shadows. Her silhouette swayed like a willow in the wind, and her charms tinkled faintly. "Whatever is happening, we've had nothing to do with it."

Oscar sneered. "So an alarm on a clear night is jus' coincidence, is it?"

"Perhaps we can help."

"Help?" He scoffed.

"Oscar!" Goodie Hazel's voice rang across the courtyard, and even though it wasn't directed at her, Rora felt rooted to the spot. "Leave these people alone."

"Y've no right to tell me what to do—" Oscar began.

Effie jogged up to Rora. "Oof. This won't be pretty.."

Melial and Nod stood in the shadow of the wagons, the villagers facing off against them. The puppet-horse shied and stamped the ground.

"You're a drunk and a lout! Where's your brother? At least that one has some sense. He's probably asleep, I'd guess, like you should be. Sit. Down."

Oscar drew himself up, chest inflated with alcohol fumes, and unleashed a string of profanity about Goodie Hazel's meddling that made Rora gasp. She held her breath, waiting for the explosion from Goodie Hazel that she was sure would send Oscar rocking on his feet.

And then a chord chimed on the western edge of the square. It was Maya. The villagers turned in surprise. The little girl burst into the square, panting, and tried to catch her breath.

Rora and Effie sprinted over.

"Rora! Rora! The Caravaners! They hurt Emma. They pushed Daniel off the wall!" The girl was crying piteously. "Th-they have Mae!"

161

Rora stared in shock and then quickly hugged Maya to her.

Goodie Hazel rocked back on her heels. For the first time in Rora's memory it looked like she didn't know what to say.

The villagers turned back to eye the darkened wagons.

Oscar grew bolder. He pulled a burning brand from the bonfire and pointed it at the wagons. "Knew it. I've always said that's what they do—stealin' kids."

Effie cursed loudly and creatively, ignoring a disapproving glare from Goodie Hazel. "Look, would they still be here if they were stealing children?"

"She's right." Semane kicked open the wagon door and strode into the square, hands on hips. "If someone's taking your children, we can help. Let us help!"

Rora held Maya to her chest, smoothing back her hair. "We'll get them back. Just hold on." She looked up at Effie and Dunkirk. "We don't have time for this."

"I say we hold these 'uns til their friends give our children back." Oscar slurred. Several of the other villagers muttered agreement.

"You'll do no such thing." Goodie Hazel had recovered and had stepped between the mob and the caravan, a steely glint in her eye.

Rora turned to Dunkirk and Effie. "We've got to get to the watch house. If they're taking the others—"

"What are we waiting for then?" Effie said. "Come on! Let's go!"

Rora made to stand, but Maya clutched her tight. "W-wait. Ogma says someone needs to go to the west wall. She's going after Mae."

"You saw Ogma?"

Maya nodded. Rora wasn't sure whether she was more relieved that Ogma was on her way to help, or worried that Ogma would get taken too.

"That's good," she told Maya. "That's real good." She called out to Effie, who was already ten paces up the path. "Sorry, Ef, we need someone on west."

Effie came back shaking her head. "Eric just went to take some soup to Jory on the south. I'll go there first, have Eric take the west, and then I'm coming after you."

"Right." Rora gave her a peck on the cheek and jogged to the edge of the square, peering into the night.

While the belligerent knot of villagers was arguing with Goodie Hazel and threatening the wagons, another group was picking up broomsticks, ladles, knives, cookware—whatever came to hand—and went to join Rora at the northern edge of the square.

"What're you doing?" Rora asked Roose, who seemed to be leading the group.

"We're coming with you."

Rora shook her head. "The fog break's just about over. It'll be right back at the walls by now." Some of the villagers paled.

"We're coming with you," Roose said firmly.

Rora nodded and sprinted ahead. Dunkirk jogged up beside her and she gave him a grateful smile.

They turned the corner at the edge of the square onto the main cobbled path. A hooded figure in a particolored cloak peered out from behind a building a hundred yards ahead. Seeing the angry pack of watch children and villagers advancing, the figure turned and ran back towards the wall.

Rora turned to Dunkirk. "Get 'em."

Dunkirk nodded, grinning broadly. He took a deep breath and held his right arm parallel to the ground. In one smooth motion, he snapped his fingers and beat his left foot on the cobblestones—two quick beats. He burst forward on a gust of wind, each leap eating up the distance.

Rora settled into her long, steady lope, pacing herself for the wall. In five impossible strides, Dunkirk caught the fleeing foe. The patchwork cloak fluttered in the air as Dunkirk hit it in the back. They both went down in a pile.

Ogma careened past the second windmill and on to the north span. She stumbled, almost becoming tangled in the tightly braided tether she still carried, but managed to recover and keep running.

The span over the north gate was empty. The moon was setting, but the long shadows it cast seemed only to deepen the gloom, giving the angular surface of the stone wall an unearthly silhouette.

Ogma sprinted on toward the watch house where it lay below the inner edge of the northeast span. Red firelight glowed around the edges of tightly sealed shutters. Shouts and the sound of splintering wood urged Ogma to greater speed despite the burning stitch in her side.

Come on, come on! She rounded the windmill at the span's corner. *They're inside!*

There were two wagons below the watch house—large and open-topped—much more like the wagons the villagers used to haul timber than the brightly-painted carriages of the caravan. They were being guarded by three immensely tall and rail thin figures in patchwork cloaks.

A shout of defiance echoed from the watch house.

She looked across the gap in time to see one of the brightly-cloaked figures crash backwards over the verandah railing. Its cloak snapped and fluttered in the wind as it fell, silent until it landed with a heavy thud on the cobblestones.

Serves you right. Ogma moved quietly, trying not to draw their attention as she crept across the span. A female voice shouted and grunted with effort. There was a smack of wood on flesh.

Brigid. She finally reached the center, just across from the watch house roof. Her view was obstructed, but she could still hear the muffled thuds and angry cries from inside. With a clatter, the rear watch house shutters opened.

Zachary, Trot, and Billie appeared at the window. The young ones were struggling to get the end of a long ladder over the sill. Ogma saw immediately what they were trying to do.

Smart, Brigid, Ogma thought. *Just hold them off a little longer.*

They were the youngest children in the house, faces frightened but determined as they struggled to tip the ladder over the edge.

They're not strong enough, Ogma realized. "Psst. Here! Zach! Trot!" Ogma called out in a harsh whisper.

Zach and Trot looked up.

"Ogma! Ogma! They've come to kidnap us! Brigid says we have to get out da window!"

"I know, I know! Here, tie this to the end of the ladder!" Ogma threw the end of the tether to the children. They fumbled the catch and Ogma reeled it in to throw again.

This time they caught it.

Ogma gritted her teeth, willing the children to move faster as they clumsily tried to tie a knot.

"Zach, remember? The tether knot." Tying knots was one of the skills they learned from an early age, but Ogma knew they were struggling with it.

Zach nodded and changed his tactics, reciting a rhyme to himself.

"Right over left, left over right..."

Come on... come on...

There was a *shing* of metal on metal from inside the watch house, and then someone screamed.

"...makes a knot both tidy and tight," Zachary finished.

Ogma heaved on the tether. It held. She pulled the ladder fully across the gap from the window to the wall and steadied the makeshift ramp. The incline was about forty-five degrees with nothing but open air between the children and the ground, but it would have to do.

"Come on, then! Come on!" Ogma whispered as loudly as she dared. The children started moving out onto the ladder. Ogma tried not to think about one of those small bodies falling to the ground below. "That's right, hands on the outside edge. Just slide 'em up as you go. You never have to let go."

Zachary and Trot went first, and Ogma could see a queue of frightened faces behind them. They moved resolutely from rung to rung and were soon safely across. Ogma gave Zachary and Trot instructions to lead the others south along the wall and then make for the village square.

Enki and Enoch boomed out into the night again.

Alarm! We hear! Alarm! We hear!

Little Carson, a quiet member of Emma's cohort, was halfway across the ladder when the bells rang out. He froze, two more children behind him on the ladder and more still waiting in the watch house.

"Come on, Carson, keep going" Ogma urged him on.

"I *can't*," Carson cried. "I'm g-gonna *fall*."

"No, you won't, sweetheart, it's okay."

Damn it, Carson, move! A cry of pain echoed out the watch house window, and the sound of fighting lulled. *Brigid!*

"Hurry *quick*," Ogma said. She clambered out onto the ladder and tried to help Carson along.

"Come on, now, I've got you, just start moving your hands and—"

"No! I'm gonna *fall.*" Carson had his eyes screwed shut and was gripping the ladder tightly.

Ogma took a deep breath and patted the frightened boy on the back.

"No you won't. Now listen. What would Wheeler want you to do?"

Carson kept his eyes screwed shut.

"He'd want you to lead the others out and take care of them, right?"

Carson started to shake his head again, and then hesitated. He gulped and scooted his hands forward, making his way across the ladder by feel, eyes still screwed shut.

Good enough. She led him back up the ladder and to the wall.

"Ogma, *help!* They're here!"

With a curse, Ogma turned back to the ladder. The children were being pulled away from the windows in a flurry of many-colored cloaks.

Ogma scrambled back onto the rungs just as Billie, who'd been waiting for Carson to finish, was snatched off the windowsill. She was halfway across when a cowled figure filled the window. Ogma growled a wordless challenge and surged to her feet, running from rung to rung.

The figure calmly raised a boot and kicked the end of the ladder, shoving it out into space.

With a cry of dismay, Ogma fell.

She woke a moment later in a bare patch of dirt, dizzy and nauseous. Her right arm throbbed painfully beneath her. She shook her head, trying to clear her vision.

That was a mistake.

If the ground had been cobbled rather than dirt, she might

not have woken up. Blurry shapes swam in her eyesight and the stars danced above her even more than usual. She could hear muffled shouts ahead of her.

The wagons, Ogma thought groggily. She stumbled to her feet, trying to get her bearings. Through the wooden pilings that held up the watch house, she saw a still figure in the dirt. A vicious quill protruded from a patchwork cloak.

Brigid got one of them, at least. Ogma shook her head again, more gently this time, and though her stomach roiled, her vision began to clear. She started jogging for the north gate. After ten paces, she was jerked to a halt by the broken ladder, which was still tied to the end of her tether. With a curse, she pulled it to her and undid the knot with clumsy fingers.

Looping the tether loosely around her arm, Ogma ran for the gate. Her elbow was throbbing and the stitch in her side came back instantly. In the middle of the cobblestones, there was another still shape.

Daniel. Ogma realized in shock. *Oh no... he's not moving.* Ogma felt angry in a way she'd never felt before. It was like a fire roaring in her chest and flickering behind her eyes.

She tore her eyes away from Daniel's still form.

The wagons had already passed through, and they were nearly fifty yards past the gate. They'd trundled to a stop—there was some kind of struggle going on. A tall young man from the village was wrestling with one of the figures.

Wait! That's Wheeler!

The older boy was shouting and pushing back at the cloaked figures who'd surrounded him. He had a long wooden plank in one hand that he was swinging wildly. The cloaked shapes stood in a ring around him, trying to close.

They're not guarding the other wagon! The cloaked shapes were so busy trying to subdue Wheeler that their second wagon stood alone. Ogma looked desperately from Wheeler to the huddled children in the wagon. A bank of fog was boiling and rolling around the edge of the wall from the west. The combatants hadn't yet noticed.

Ogma made up her mind. She snapped the end of her tether to a hinge on the gate and sprinted for the unattended wagon.

Wheeler had knocked two of the cloaked figures to the ground when another jumped on his back. He cried out and fell, the plank falling from his grip. He hit the ground struggling as the other figures piled onto him.

At about thirty yards out, Ogma hit the end of her tether. She shrugged out of her harness and sprinted the remaining distance.

She spared a glance for Wheeler. He looked dazed, shaking his head from side to side, his hair matted to his forehead. His eyes found Ogma's between the limbs of his assailants and widened in unlooked-for hope. He hesitated for just a moment, and then started kicking and shouting again, trying to hold his attackers' attention. Blows rained down on him.

Ogma winced and turned away. Frightened faces stared out at her from the back of the wagon. The children were bound and gagged. Emma was sitting in the middle of the row, supported by two of the others. Her eyes were unfocused and it seemed like she was having trouble supporting her head.

Damn them!

The children's feet weren't bound, but they couldn't clamber over the wagon's sides with their arms behind their backs.

Ogma climbed into the wagon to muffled cries of relief.

She started helping the children over the wagon edge. It was awkward and more than one wound up sprawled in the dirt with a scraped knee.

"Quick!" Ogma instructed, a wary eye on the wall of boiling fog that was drifting closer. "That way! I've left a tether on the ground. Run for the village, and if the fog comes in before you get there, just grab it and hold on tight."

The children nodded fearfully and ran.

Ogma went to Emma. "Can you walk, little one?"

Come on, you little brat, she thought, with tears burning in her eyes, *please don't do this.*

Emma's eyes were still unfocused, her chin on her chest. "Ogma?"

Eyes still burning, Ogma lifted the girl in her arms and struggled out of the wagon. She glanced at the fog.

It's too close, she realized, heart sinking. The gray wall was towering, boiling into wicked, massive shapes with horns and teeth and claws.

It was already closing on the north gate. It would cut them off.

Ogma stumbled to her knees at the end of the tether and strapped little Emma into the harness.

"Sh... sh... just hold on. Can you walk that way? Follow the tether. Can you do that?"

Emma stood there, blinking dumbly and then sat down hard on the ground.

Hot tears ran down Ogma's cheeks. Two of the children further down the tether glanced back and saw Emma. They ran back to help the little girl.

Ogma looked past them.

A figure burst from the gate at a run, and then stumbled to a stop as it tried to make sense of the chaos.

"Rora!" Ogma could just see the older girl's face turn towards her before the fog boiled between them. The end of the tether seemed to be stretching away into nothingness: an endless gray bank.

Ogma's heart leapt into her throat. Trot and Carson held

tight to the tether, steadying Emma on her feet, and they disappeared into a pocket in the fog.

Please, let it hold. Don't take the walls away. Not yet.

The gray bank boiled closer and closer to where Ogma stood. Horned, grinning faces cackled, throwing phantom cries and melting away. Great amorphous beasts coalesced out of the fog, tore furrows in the earth, and charged the crowd of many-colored cloaks.

Wheeler!

Ogma turned to run for him, knowing she wouldn't make it. The fog boiled past her and around her and the whole world went white.

CHAPTER 6

LOST

Ogma trembled as the gray-white emptiness swarmed and swirled around her. She had a bubble of about six feet in every direction that the fog couldn't touch, but beyond that, it made an impenetrable wall. She could still hear terrified voices crying out in fear and panic, answered only by chittering cackles and roars.

"Wheeler!" she shouted. *Come on, where are you?* Ogma ran, stumbling over grassy fields, then tangled tree roots, then scrambling up a scree slope.

"Wheeler!" she yelled again.

"Is someone there?"

"Yes! It's me! It's Ogma!" She ran in the direction of his voice, heedless of everything around her, not realizing that the panicked cries and the shouting and the screams had disappeared, not noticing the silence and what it meant.

"Please. Where are you?" Wheeler's voice came again.

"Here! I'm here!" She ran on.

"Please! I'm—I'm afraid..." His voice broke and he seemed to be drifting farther away.

Ogma sprinted forward. She could see a silhouette in the

fog. "I'm here!" she shouted desperately.

The shadowy silhouette turned towards her. A cackling laugh erupted from the fog, and the shape swirled into nothing.

Ogma's heart was pounding. In shock, she turned in a slow circle, straining to see anything in the fog. There was nothing but gray emptiness.

My bells, Ogma realized, crestfallen. *I forgot to ring my bells. That was a phantom's voice.*

With a sick feeling in her stomach, Ogma hoisted her bells in hand. Her mournful minor chord rang out thinly in the close air. There was no response. No other bells.

Why are we more scared when we get older? Wheeler's moment of fear echoed in her memory.

She noticed the quiet then. The perfect stillness around her. No sign of the wagons, or the other children, or even the hateful brightly-cloaked figures.

How could they do this? Ogma still burned with anger.

The fog continued to drift around her small, untouchable pocket of air, circling like a predator. She sat on the stony ground and hung her head.

What am I going to do? I'll never get back.

"No," she said aloud. "I will make it back. I will."

She thought of the other children who'd still been in the wagons when the fog came. She wondered if Emma and the others on the tether managed to reel themselves back to the town.

"I'll find them," Ogma whispered.

The fog whispered back with sibilant, taunting nonsense. Ogma glared and put her chin in her hands to think. The ground was cold, hard, and uneven. She pulled an offending rock out from beneath her and tried lying on her back.

It was worse, but it distracted her from her throbbing elbow. In the first panic of the fog, she'd nearly forgotten her fall. It'd been a bad one. *I'm lucky it's not broken.* As it was, the slightest bump was sending pins and needles shivering through her fingertips.

I've had better days.

She closed her eyes and rested for a while, not quite sleeping, but firmly denying the fog any satisfaction of her fear.

When she opened her eyes, the fog had thinned somewhat. Through the wispy tendrils, the moon's blue sister winked down from a sky of dancing stars. Ogma propped herself up on her good elbow. She could see shapes drifting by as the landscape shifted. Mostly trees, but some of the shadows might have been moving on their own.

No more faces or phantoms. Good, it's calming down.

She could hear the sway and rustle of leaves. There was a snap and then the sound of some small, startled creature sprinting through the underbrush. Strange, almost-human cries sounded mournfully.

Owls? Or it could just be the fog again.

Still, Ogma waited, hoping the fog would clear further, and hoping more deeply still that when it did, she might see windmills in the distance.

"Don't hold your breath," she berated herself.

Gradually, stiffness from sitting on the stony ground sunk into her bones and amplified the aches and pains in her joints. She tried to think of something to distract herself, but her thoughts kept returning to the frightened faces in the back of the wagons, the dazed look in Emma's eyes, and the abject fear on Wheeler's face as the fog rolled over him.

Ogma shook her head. *Not now, come on. No time for that.*

Ogma felt the hair on her neck prickle. There was a new kind of stillness in the fog. The feeling was hard to place, but something about it was almost a relief, as if the fog were no longer quite so empty.

There's something out there!

Ogma bit her lip, wondering whether to sound her bells. *If someone else is lost...* Ogma thought. *But if it's not a person...*

Another crunch and rustle of undergrowth echoed indistinctly in the fog. It was accompanied this time by a snuffling snort, and the sound of something pawing at the ground.

Maybe it's a hart? Visions of the beast that had nearly killed Dunkirk were running unbidden through her head: rows of eyes and teeth.

So just keep quiet then, Ogma scolded herself. *It'll probably pass right by.*

The pawing and snuffling sounds were getting closer. Ogma could see the fog swirling as some large shape displaced it. A shadow loomed against the gray.

Slowly, Ogma got to her feet, sidling away from the dark shape. She tried to watch where she stepped to avoid any twigs or loose stones, but her eyes were riveted to the menacing form.

A thundering feline *yowl* from deep within the fog toppled Ogma to the ground. The ill-formed shadow bolted into Ogma's personal clearing. It was some relative of the harts, a hoofed deer that leapt clear over Ogma's head, eyes rolling in terror, fleeing something else.

Before Ogma could think to run, an even larger shape burst from the fog in hot pursuit. The cat rippled with muscle, easily as tall at the shoulder as Ogma. It stopped its chase short when it saw her lying on the ground directly in its path.

The great cat brindled, tilting its head and eyeing Ogma warily. Despite its size, it was difficult to see against the fog, even from this close. Gray and black patches on its fur drifted and rolled across its chest, camouflaging it against the swirling mist. As Ogma watched, the creature tilted its head even further until it was completely upside down, mouth above eyes, tongue lolling from a wide crescent of teeth.

Ogma scrambled up and ran, the vision of those disembodied teeth against the fog burning in her mind. A mewling growl and the scrabbling of claws against dirt and stone followed her.

Ogma turned sharply, deliberately running through a thicker drift of fog. She felt the wind of the cat's passing as its pounce carried it through the spot where she'd been standing.

Her pounding heart made it hard to hear where it landed behind her, or even to hear herself think.

I don't think it saw me before it broke into the clearing. It might look like the fog, but it can't see through it any better than I can.

Unfortunately, her very presence was enough to push the fog away. Her age saved her from the fog's touch, but it also meant she carried a clearing with her. She had to get far enough away that the grinning cat couldn't find her again.

Ogma dived to one side at random. She heard another frustrated yowl as the creature hurtled past her yet again.

Too close.

Ogma put on speed, stumbling over mossy stones and moldering leaves. The fog seemed to be thinning.

Of course it starts to clear now, Ogma groaned. She found herself willing the wisps of fog in front of her to slip behind, to cover her trail. Tendrils began to curl towards her.

The sound of those scrabbling claws was still close behind when Ogma found herself at the edge of the bank, a forested glade before her. A round weather-beaten boulder, covered in a spongy moss, stood half-buried in the loam.

Now what do I do? It was too exposed.

Ogma turned and ran parallel to the edge of the glade, dodging trees and trying to crash through the bushes as quietly as she could, and then dived back into the fog.

She was gasping for air but tried to calm her breathing. Her heart was pounding so hard she was sure it could be heard for a mile.

The beast crashed and crackled through the brush, spitting and yowling. Ogma waited, straining to hear which way it moved. Over the rush of blood in her ears, she could just hear the creature padding in a circle on the edge of the fog bank, sniffing at the ground.

I'll just stay right here. I'm in no hurry.

The scrabbling sound faded to nothing, and still Ogma waited.

Is it gone?

She sucked in a breath as the beast passed close enough that she could see its mottled flank through the fog, and then it melted away.

Ogma stayed where she was, just to be sure the hungry creature wasn't circling around again. She was cold, and bone tired, and her arm was still aching from her fall, but she kept still.

After the better part of an hour, when all around her seemed quiet again, she got up the nerve to push out of the fog bank.

To her surprise, she emerged again in the forested glade, or at least, one that looked the same. It was hard to tell with only the pale glow of the moon and her blue sister to light the clearing.

It is the same though. I remember that old stone. The half dome of rock dressed in its shaggy moss stood just at the edge of the glade.

Deep shadows were painted under the trees. Ogma peered into them uneasily, wondering whether anything was staring back at her.

Better than back in that fog. Ogma steeled herself and walked into the woods.

The trees were old, haggard-looking things. Curtains of

moss hung from them like beards and shaggy clothes. Rotting fruit and old nuts mixed with moldering leaves on the forest floor. The smell was musty and the air close, but it was an earthy odor, not too unpleasant.

I hope Emma's all right. She remembered the dazed look in the little girl's eyes and felt tears coming again. *No. Rora and Effie found them. I'm sure they did.* Trying to burn away the tears with anger, she thought again of the cloaked figure speared by the quill under the watch house.

I wish Brigid had killed more of them. I hope she's okay.

Ogma sniffed, thinking about the soft beds in the watchtower, and warm cider, and shadow puppets in front of the fire...

I'm never going to get back.

The tears came then, running down her face, warm against the pinched cold in her cheeks. She wandered through the woods, not really caring where she was going, just putting one foot in front of the other, letting the tears fall freely.

Darkness deepened, and Ogma curled up on a bed of moss and cried herself to sleep.

Before long she woke, damp and shivering in the cold. She'd been dreaming—bad dreams—and it was some small mercy that she couldn't remember them. Ogma rubbed her arms with both hands, breathing on them and sticking them in her pockets.

There was an unfamiliar shape in her right pocket and she pulled it out. It was the glass firefly that Nan Aud had given her.

She couldn't go on, so she leaned against the bole of a tree and sobbed quietly.

A light in the corner of her eye made her blink and look up. She saw nothing but the shadows between the trees at first, but then a greenish-yellow light winked to life.

Firefly, Ogma thought, sniffling. She wiped her nose on her sleeve and turned to watch it. Another came out, and then another.

Beautiful, Ogma thought, sniffling again. She glanced down, melancholy, and noticed a glimmer between her fingers. She opened her hand. The glass firefly was glowing with a faint green and yellow light.

The true fireflies winked out and then came closer. Before long, a small swarm had filled the forested glade with a soft, gently shifting glow.

They're dancing. Like the stars. She found herself wondering if that's all the stars were, just fireflies, far and high in the night sky.

The fireflies danced and swirled around the clearing. After a few moments, the light in Ogma's hand faded, and the small swarm of fireflies started to drift away.

"Wait!" Ogma called out. "Don't go."

Don't leave me alone again.

She ran after them, following the little lights as they winked in and out, each time a little further away.

"Please wait!" She called after them.

She followed as quickly as she could, climbing over fallen trees and clambering over old stone piles covered in vines. She was halfway up one such pile before she realized it was made up of blocks, hewn by human hands from pale white stone. The fireflies were retreating through a gap in a wall so old that the moss had covered it in green, the white stone only visible as a scar where it had recently crumbled.

Into the ruin she went, after the fireflies, picking her way carefully over the wall. Weeds and moss sprung up between the cobbles of the courtyard. Great trees grew here, lonely giants filtering the moon into a soft green light, their gnarled roots overturning wide pavers and raising ridges in the cobbled ground like ripples on a pool.

Oh no... where have they gone? Small green and yellow lights winked faintly here and there, but the great cloud of fireflies had dispersed.

Ogma jumped. A woman stood in a corner of the courtyard, dressed in rags of green slime and clinging vines, like some ghost story from the bottom of a well.

It's just a fountain, Ogma scolded herself.

As she stepped closer, the statue became less frightening. Beneath the algae and the pond scum was a young woman, very beautiful, and not wearing very much.

She looks cold, Ogma thought, eyeing the scanty costume critically. Ogma pulled her coat more tightly around her. The woman was holding a silver basin, but where once she might have poured water, she now poured out a vine with small white flowers.

Pretty.

Ogma realized then how thirsty she was, but as she leaned over the lip of the fountain, the cloying scent of water lilies almost overwhelmed her, and she saw a stagnant pool choked with algae.

Trying to ignore her parched throat, she walked on through the courtyard. From the pattern of stones, she realized that there must have been other fountains and maybe gardens once. There were paths laid in concentric rings, all leading to one place.

Ogma found herself clambering over broken flagstones and picking her way through low branches of old, bearded trees. Parting the curtain of a willow, Ogma found the center of the courtyard where a ruined tower stood.

Well, used to stand. Must have been tall. She tried to guess how tall from the piles of ruined stone heaped around what remained. *Could have fit the whole of Enki and Enoch's tower, for sure. Maybe twice over.*

The great piles of stones were covered with climbing vines,

blooming with more of the delicate, star-shaped white flowers, incredibly fragrant in the night air. The forest ruled here.

The base of the tower still stood, more or less. There was still a ring of stone anyway, though it had an uneven crown. The highest parts of what remained might have come about halfway up the windmill walls, though the lowest portions had crumbled nearly to the ground.

Better be careful. Those stones will probably come right down on my head.

She chose one of the smaller piles and clambered over the dusty blocks, curious to see what, if anything, remained of the interior. At the top of the heap, she paused to clap the chalky white dust from her hands and clothes.

Wait—what is that?

A single tree grew in the center of the ruined tower. It was a small, gnarled thing, hardly even worth climbing. *Looks like a plum tree.* Certainly it was a fruit tree of some sort; Ogma could see the plump fruit hanging from its boughs. But hanging was clearly the wrong word. It looked like the swollen fruits were pulling the boughs *up*, as if they were going to float away into the sky.

In fact, as Ogma looked on in astonishment, one of the plums burst free and lifted off into the air. It rose a few feet from its branch, and then began to gently circle the tree, floating well above the ground. Another, and then another pulled themselves off their branches and joined the strange orbit.

Ogma was still staring, flabbergasted and rather delighted, when suddenly one of the orbiting fruits wobbled in the air, and began to glow. Before Ogma could guess what was happening, the overripe plum erupted in flame and crashed to the ground, where its wet wreckage smoldered in the leaves.

What in the fog's name just happened?

And then she heard the voices.

"Hup! There's another one!" a tiny voice cried.

"Another crop lost!" called out another.

"Ach. Wretched," called out a third, and notably grumpier, voice.

At first Ogma couldn't tell where the voices were coming from, and then she noticed movement around the roots of the tree.

She slid down the side of the pile of crumbling stones to get a better look.

"Yipes—lookout! Here she comes!"

"There she goes!"

"Here we go again," finished the grumpy voice.

A small trail of leaves beneath the plum rustled and danced.

Are they invisible?

Ogma walked cautiously closer to the tree. "Hello?"

"Yes!"

"No!"

"Goodbye!" The three voices cried in unison.

There was a rustling in the leaves and three small shapes disappeared around the trunk of the tree. Ogma caught a brief glimpse of a tiny pair of booted feet sticking out from between the tree roots before they disappeared.

She crept closer. It was hard to make out anything at first, but it was getting easier by the second. Ogma glanced up. The sky was lightening; it was finally dawn.

"I won't hurt you," Ogma said lamely, unsure how to reassure them.

"See! I told you."

"Lies!"

"I should hope not!" squeaked the last indignant voice.

A tiny wrinkled face, about the size and shape of a walnut, peeked up from among the roots, and then promptly disappeared.

"We won't hurt you neither," a little voice spoke.

"Yes we will!" said the grumpier voice.

"Oh *mercy,* shut up, you two," said the third.

Ogma picked her way carefully through the leaves to the trunk of the strange tree. The wreckage of a burning plum still smoldered. She had to duck out of the path of another strangely orbiting fruit that wobbled dangerously as it passed. She peered cautiously around the trunk, but whatever had been peeking out had hid itself elsewhere.

"Is this your tree?" she asked politely.

"Oh most certainly."

"Absolutely not."

"It's *complicated!*" the three voices chorused.

"Um..." As Ogma glanced about in confusion, another small, wrinkled face caught her eye. It seemed to be peering up at her from the gnarled tangles of the plum's roots. Ogma tried not to look directly at it.

"Well, she don't look like much." The voice was surprisingly gruff for such a small sound.

"She's *bootiful,*" intoned another voice somewhere in the branches above her. Ogma glanced up casually and saw a frumpy, rumpled hat sticking out from the fork of two gnarled old branches, and a pair of moony eyes looking back at her.

"Still too tall," said the third voice with a sigh. There was a dramatic rustling of leaves, and at last, one of the creatures burrowed its way up and stepped into view.

He could barely climb out of a boot if you dropped him in. And he was certainly a 'he' if the beard was any indication. His skin was a deep, ruddy purple—almost brown in fact. His only clothes were a pair of overalls and an elaborate, if *tiny,* tool belt.

The diminutive creature studied her up and down, and then smiled broadly. Its whole face crinkled up, but there was an undeniable warmth in its wizened eyes.

"You'll do, though." The gnarled little creature beamed up at her.

"She's *perfect*," said the moony-eyed one still sitting up in the branches.

"Well, if it's the best ye've got," said the third voice amid the roots.

The one in the tree scrambled out from behind the upper branches and began to climb down. This one appeared to be wearing a blue nightgown to go with his nightcap, and was carrying...

Ogma peered closer.

...a very tiny stuffed bear?

To Ogma's surprise, the little gowned figure leapt from the bole of the tree, landing spryly on one of the orbiting fruits.

His weight bore the plum down to earth, and he tumbled to the ground as it crashed into a cobblestone and burst into flame.

Ogma began to giggle, and then clapped one hand over her mouth. *I shouldn't offend them.* She tried to stop herself laughing but even covering her mouth, she only managed a stifled choke.

The kindly one with the tool belt looked up at her in obvious concern.

"Are you all right, dear? Ooh. I think she might be sick."

"Diseased, I've no doubt. And horribly contagious, I'm sure." The last of the absurd creatures clambered over the roots he'd been hiding in and toddled towards her.

Oh no, what is he wearing?

If anything, he was even shorter and rounder than the other two. He wore neat trousers and a jacket with tails, and had a jeweler's glass in one eye, which magnified it hideously as he glared up at Ogma.

Ogma collapsed. She couldn't help it. She was laughing so hard she could hardly breathe.

The one in the nightgown with the moony eyes stared at her in some surprise, and then ambled over to pat her knee in a reassuring way. This only caused Ogma to laugh harder. She could barely resist picking the tiny creature up and tickling it under the chin.

The other two crept closer, expressions more perplexed than anything else.

"You've broken her," the one in the tool belt said critically.

"No! She's just very happy to see us!" replied the one in the nightgown, who redoubled his efforts to pat her knee comfortingly. It tickled awfully.

"Broken before she got here, if you ask me."

It was probably ten minutes before Ogma finally exhausted her laughter. As her giggling subsided, tears dried on her face and she lay back in the leaves watching the plums orbit the strange tree.

A cautious moment later, after waiting to make sure she was truly finished with her fit, something tickled her side and a small figure climbed onto her stomach. A concerned face in a night cap peered over her chin.

Ogma stifled a resurgent giggle and looked back at the creature.

"Who *are* you?" she asked, sitting up on her elbows.

"*Us?* Oh mirthful one?" asked the one in the gown.

"Oh here he goes," said the grumpy one.

"Oh hush," said the third.

"Well, who else would I be talking to?" Ogma went on, bemused.

"Who *else? Who else?*"

"Oh now you've done it."

"*Anyone else,* I should think."

"Never mind," Ogma said hurriedly. The wrinkled creature

on her stomach was still gasping in philosophical distress at the depth of her question. "Just tell me who you are."

"Ah..." The poor creature's mask of distress dissolved, and it bowed deeply. "We are *plummers*."

He held his bow, clearly waiting for some reaction from Ogma that was not forthcoming. He tilted his head back and waggled his eyebrows at her significantly.

"Oh."

"*Gnomes*, more generally," added the kindly one.

"Never mind who we are, we should be asking the same of you." The preposterous gnome with the jeweler's glass stomped his foot.

"My name is Ogma."

"*Ogma*," said the silly gnome in reverent tones.

"What's an Ogma s'posed to be?" the grumpy one asked. The kindly one only smiled.

"I'm a person," she said.

"Oh *you're* a person, eh?" The grumpy one cut in. "What are we, I suppose? Rubbish and refuse?"

"Er, no—that's not what I meant." Ogma stumbled over the words. "I'm lost."

"Alas! A lost child." The gnome in the nightgown began to sob. "Alone in these dreadful woods! Helpless! Timid! Afraid! Fearful that rescue shall never come!"

"I am *not* helpless," Ogma replied sternly, her blood suddenly up. "Or timid, or afraid... and if it comes down to it, I'll be rescuing *myself*."

The flighty gnome was lost in its sobbing, but the kindly gnome nodded and smiled.

"Oh *sure*. All well and good, rescuing yourself. If you're not eaten of course. And so long as the fog don't put a cliff one step in front of you. And if you don't wake one of the Sleeping Ones.

And so long as the Olden Times stay where they belong. And if the plums don't start another forest fire—"

The dour creature looked as if he would continue indefinitely.

"Oh hush. I'm sure she'll be fine." The kindly one patted Ogma on the knee. "Won't you, my dear?"

Ogma nodded diffidently. "Y-yes."

"Besides, you'll be staying with us awhile," he continued. Ogma hesitated.

"Oh don't ye fret. We have food aplenty, and plenty of warm leaves to sleep in, so long as you're 'ware the plums."

"I..." Ogma considered. *It's not as though I have somewhere else to go.* "Yes. Thank you. Erm—do you have anything to eat?"

The gnomes, or plummers, were gracious hosts in their own way. They brought Ogma nuts and fruit that they had foraged from the forest, and small thimbles full of a cordial that had a fizzy, fiery flavor to it.

"This is delicious."

"Brew it m'self." The grumpy one blushed, shuffling his feet.

Ogma whiled away the morning with the wrinkly gnome folk, feeling much better to have someone to talk to after her hours spent wandering alone. Gradually, the warm light and the soft whisper of the trees made her eyelids heavy. The small creatures piled up a bed of warm leaves around her, and she slept.

"Quick! Awake, awake!" an anxious voice wrested Ogma from a pleasant dream.

"Hmung? How long have I been asleep?" Ogma muttered, opening her eyes to pale late afternoon light. There was a rustling noise, and the leaves that covered Ogma's head were brushed away.

An anxious face peered into Ogma's eyes. "Awake, awake!"

"What is it?" Ogma sat up. The leaves they had carefully piled, that had seemed so comfortable before, now seemed a meager protection against the coming night. The gnome in the nightdress was biting his fingernails nervously. The surly gnome was warily studying the edges of the ruined tower.

"What—" Ogma repeated.

"Shh..." The kindly one's voice spoke softly from behind her elbow. "It's the *king*."

What's a king, that they are so afraid?

There was a gravity in how the kindly old gnome spoke. Something much more serious than their playful and ridiculous banter that morning, and an undertone of fear.

Ogma fell silent, trying to keep perfectly still. *If it's just another gnome, it can't be that impressive.* Her bravado felt hollow. The ruined courtyard was frozen, expectant. Ogma felt like a deer startled in the thicket, every fiber ready to run.

She studied the trees at the edge of the tower intently. Drifts of fog had crept up, the mist padding softly around the edges while Ogma slept. There was a rustle of bushes somewhere in the undergrowth, the sound of a branch bending and whipping back into place.

"There he is," the grizzled gnome hissed, dropping his eyes to the ground in a fearful bow.

A king's a person, then. Still, she couldn't see him. Her eyes flitted from budding leaves to hoary lichen, peering through the twisted branches trying to find—

There! I'm sure I saw something. If that's another gnome, then I'm a pickled onion.

Ogma caught glimpses of the figure through whorls of fog. Twigs snapped. With a creak and groan even the gnarled trees were bending. The king, whoever he was, wasn't pushing through the undergrowth, nor was he picking his way carefully around it. The trees and branches were moving on their own.

They're bowing, Ogma realized with a shiver.

His clothes hung with shaggy curls like birch. His skin was the mottled color of moss and lichen. He was tall. Taller than any person Ogma knew in her village, but not quite *too* tall. Moss grew in a beard that hung from chin to belt.

"Mmm? What have we here?" The shaggy green man picked his way through a gap in the stone wall and loomed over Ogma and the genuflecting gnomes.

"A visitor, your majesty."

"A trespasser, more like. But she knows 'er cordials," the grumpy one admitted reluctantly.

The gnome in the night cap simply cowered.

"A trespasser, is it?" The old man's voice was deep and grave. He blinked, ripples in amber pools, as he considered Ogma. "How very serious."

He stared at Ogma for an uncomfortably long moment. *I don't think he talks to anyone very often.*

Ogma drew a breath. "Thank you for the shelter." She thought it best to start things off politely. "This is your, er— tower?" She gestured lamely to the ruins.

"My tower?" he rumbled, looking around in some surprise. "Is it mine?" Deep lines creased around his features like the bark around knotted wood. He stared in apparent bewilderment for so long Ogma was worried he'd forgotten she was there. "I remember it being rather taller."

Ogma startled. There was a twinkle in the shaggy man's amber eyes. She relaxed a little. *Maybe he's not that... mad.*

The old king casually plucked an orbiting fruit from the air, biting into it with evident pleasure. The pit of the plum glowed like a coal. "How have my subjects been treating you?"

"Your subjects?"

He gestured toward the plummers with his half-eaten fruit. The kindly and grumpy gnomes were standing in solemn attention, watching the conversation intently. The sillier gnome had prostrated himself on the cobbles and stayed there.

"They're very kind."

There was a tiny snort from the grumpy gnome.

"What does it mean that you're their king? You don't much *look* like a gnome," Ogma said, frankly.

The shaggy man chuckled. "Hmm... no, I don't suppose I do." His expression hardened. "But I am a king. A king *rules*."

I don't like the sound of that.

"Bring food and cordial." He said it kindly, but with a certain imperiousness. The little gnomes bowed hastily, trembling. They disappeared into the roots of the tree.

The old man sighed, leaning heavily on his staff.

"I suppose a fire's in order," he said significantly.

Ogma raised a skeptical eyebrow. The old man glanced at a pile of leaves under the wall and then back to Ogma.

Ogma sighed. "Could I help?"

The man brightened. "Ah, what a kind young child you are. There's some lumber just over there."

Beneath the leaf mold, Ogma found dried boughs, sheafs of bark, and fallen logs that had been stacked rather neatly under the wall. None of it was hewn, though; it all appeared to be deadfall.

She carried a bundle into the center of the courtyard and started clearing a space in the leaves.

"Ah." He cleared his throat. "Just here."

A circular fire pit had been made with the fallen rubble. Ogma started building the fire, hoping the old man at least had a flint.

"So is this what it means to be a king? Other people make your fires?"

"Just give it here, then," he said, pointing at the tinder bundle Ogma had made. She handed it over to him. She didn't see him strike the spark, but a moment later, he was blowing gently into the bundle and it burst into a merry flame. He added it to the fuel wood, and soon the fire pit was burning brightly.

The gnomes—or *plummers*—returned. Each had rigged up a sort of stretcher that they dragged behind them, with bundles of small pastries, berries, and more of the delicious cordial.

"We'll be... back soon... with the rest," the kindly one puffed. The others only wheezed and turned back for the gnarled tree.

The gnome king was staring into the fire, the carefully prepared food forgotten beside him. He looked very old as he brooded. The deep lines in his face looked much less like the gnarled wood of an old oak, and much more human. *He really is, isn't he? Or he was, anyway... and whatever else he is now, he's certainly half mad.*

Ogma warily walked closer and sat down beside him.

"Hm?" As if he hadn't drifted off for even a second, the old man scooped up the small pile of food and gobbled it down. Then he paused, remembering his manners perhaps, and offered some of the food to Ogma.

"No, thank you," she said.

He shrugged and munched away at the rest. Silence fell again, though Ogma was getting used to the old man's strange lapses. Even when he seemed present, he held his gaze uncomfortably long. *Not staring, really. Watching. He just watches things.* He watched the orbiting plums, or the wind stirring the fallen leaves, or a bird come to perch on the stone wall. He watched her the same way, like she was just another bird perched on the rubble.

The gnomes emerged again with more food, which he ate, and this time Ogma had some as well. They behaved with a stiff and careful reverence around their unlikely king, but the kindly one patted Ogma gently on the knee before they retreated once more to the roots of their tree.

The afternoon passed quietly, Ogma and the shaggy old man saying little. Ogma tried to maintain idle conversation, if only to keep the old man from brooding.

There was something about his eyes when he fell to brooding for too long. The whole courtyard seemed darker, like a shadow passing over the sun, a shadow of something hard and proud behind those amber eyes. It made Ogma shiver.

"Wait! I've just remembered—"

"Hm?"

"It—there was an old story—shouldn't you have a crown?"

"What?" The old man stirred but didn't turn to look at her. The shadow in his eyes flickered.

"I mean... if you're a king. Shouldn't you have a crown?"

The old man turned and stared at her. *Has he forgotten that I'm here?* There was something utterly uncomprehending in his gaze. And then all at once, his face relaxed into pleasant wrinkles and the warm glow in his eyes returned. "Of course I have a crown."

Ogma looked at his shaggy curls and raised an eyebrow.

"Er—don't I?" The old man patted his head with one hand. When it was apparent he wore nothing at all on his head, he jumped up. "I—I must have dropped it!" He started shuffling the leaves about with the end of his staff.

His antics brought a bemused smile to Ogma's face, and then her expression froze and it felt like the ground was falling away beneath her.

The staff, Ogma realized, suddenly remembering which of Wheeler's stories had featured the kings-before-the-fog. There'd been another prop in that story besides the crown.

"The staff—you're a wizard!" She clapped a hand over her

mouth, not meaning to say it out loud. *Idiot, of course he's a wizard—and a mad one at that. But how could he be? They all died before the fog.*

The old wizard in the shaggy, mossy robes crouched at the edge of the broken courtyard, his back still to Ogma. She watched him warily.

He must have heard me. I'm sure he heard me...

The old man's shoulders fell. He leaned heavily on his staff.

"You remind me so much of her..." he whispered.

"Who do I remind you of?" She asked softly.

As if he hadn't heard, he raised his voice. "We fought over the bones of giants."

A wind picked up, and the trees in the courtyard sighed.

"We raised things from the deep places." With a sputter, water trickled from the silver basin of the fountain into the stagnant pool. The wizard in his shaggy robes glanced at the statue of the young woman. His bark-like color gave way to careworn lines, and his eyes that had been amber pools were blue and cold. "We squabbled in the dirt, thinking ourselves mighty."

The shadow over the courtyard deepened.

It wasn't my imagination. Ogma looked for the sun between the falling leaves. It still shone: there were no clouds, no reason for the shadow, but even as she watched, it seemed smaller and colder. It was dimming.

The old man stood taller and straighter. His voice had changed. It was stronger and crueler. "But we *were* mighty. We divided the world." He tilted his head back to stare at the sun. "The stars were mine..."

He raised one hand and slowly closed his fist. A wave of nausea crashed over Ogma and she fell to her knees. It was as if the air itself was crushing her. Her fingers went numb and began stinging with cold. Her breath frosted in the air.

What has he done? She looked up.

The sun had disappeared and the stars stood clear and bright and utterly unmoving. Tears of pain and fear froze on her eyelashes.

A small hand was tugging at her leggings urgently.

"He's remembered! He's remembered!" The silly gnome in the cap wailed and cowered, shivering violently.

"That's it for us, then. I knew it'd come some day." The grumpy one stamped and puffed.

The kindly gnome clambered to her shoulder and whispered in her ear. "Quickly then, you must distract him."

"W-W-What do I do?" Ogma's teeth chattered, her breath a glittering cloud.

"Call to him! You must call to him."

"What d-do I s-say?"

The small gnome creature worried its lip. "Call him 'Father!'"

"What? W-Why?"

"Come on, girl!"

Ogma staggered to her feet and shouted into the cold. "Father!"

The proud figure of the wizard started and turned. His hand relaxed and then a warm wind filled the courtyard. The sun was shining again. He blinked at her, a wrinkle of confusion on his proud brow.

"My daughter—is that you?"

"Y-yes, Father, I'm here," Ogma stammered. She whispered to the gnome out of the corner of her mouth. "What do I do now?"

"It's done now, my dear." The kindly gnome patted her on the cheek and scampered down her back to the ground. "So sorry."

"At least she came here on her own," the grumpy one said diffidently. "The last one took ages. That were a *cold* time."

The silly gnome in the nightdress was sniffling and boohoo-ing, but even he had turned away.

A chill that had nothing to do with the cold crawled down Ogma's spine. *They were expecting this to happen. They wanted this.*

"Come to me, my daughter." The proud voice spoke sternly.

"Just—just a minute, Father."

Those ice-blue eyes hardened. The fire died to embers.

"What have you done with your hair?"

"M-my hair?"

"I made it spun gold, my daughter. Yet it's dun and dull when I look at you."

Ogma backed up slowly, wondering if she could make a run for the trees. Something caught her eye.

"What are you wearing? Where is your gown? I stole the twilight for it." Suspicion crowded the old wizard's features. He glared down at Ogma coldly.

Ogma bit her lip and said nothing. The shadows were gathering again in the clearing. The ruined tower and the courtyard looked vague and unreal in the frozen gloom.

Wait! What's that? There was a glimmer of yellow-green light deep in the fog.

"Tell me your name, my daughter."

"My name?" Ogma's heart pounded.

"Have you grown stupid, daughter? What is your name? Remind me of it! I've... forgotten."

Ogma's cheeks burned; she was shivering with fear and anger both. The light in the distance twinkled and then went out.

He's going to kill me.

CHAPTER 7

THE SHEPHERDS

"Hail! Father of stars!" The voice came from behind her, thin and muffled by the cold, but familiar. Even before the taloned hand went protectively around her shoulders, Ogma knew it was Nod. Ogma could see a glimmer of confusion in the old man's eyes. He tilted his head as if struggling to remember something.

Nod bowed deeply. Somehow he pulled Ogma into the folds of his robes and she found herself standing behind him, shielded from the wizard's view. If he noticed her absence, he gave no sign of it.

"Psst!" Semane was standing behind a gap in the ruined curtain wall of the tower across the open yard. She gestured at Ogma to wait and looked back to the wizard.

"What do the Twisted Ones want of me?" The proud voice intoned.

"We Shepherds know your greatness, Old Father." Behind the ruined curtain wall, Semane made a face. "We come to pay homage to your working in the stars." Nod gestured up at the sky. The old man turned and looked up as well. Ogma took her

chance and ran across the open courtyard to the wall where
Semane was waiting.

"Hush now," the dancer doll whispered. "We'll have him
quieted down in no time, don't you worry. Nod's just keeping
him busy. Look there." Semane nodded towards the trees.

At first Ogma couldn't see anything, but then she caught the
glimmer of a silver charm in the shadows. Melial was stealing up
behind the wizard. Nod continued his performance, but his
tone of voice changed suddenly.

"Where is your crown, Old One?"

"My what?"

The old man turned, confusion on his face. He leaned a bit
more heavily against his staff.

"Have you lost it, majesty?"

"Have I lost..." he trailed off, puzzled. The mossy green hue
of his skin seemed to return. And then a hard glint suddenly
took hold in his eyes, and the cold snap deepened.

"My daughter! Where have you taken her?" He stood proud
again and raised his staff, eyes flashing.

Ogma flinched back, stories of the wizard's curses wheeling
through her mind.

Before he could bring the staff to bear, Melial stepped out of
the shadows and dropped a crown woven of white branches on
his head. The old man staggered, as if an enormous weight was
crashing down on top of him. White flowers blossomed on the
crown, and green roots grew into his tangled hair. All at once,
his clothes looked shaggy and ragged again, his beard mossy.

The sun again returned. Ogma nearly fainted in relief.

Melial caught the old wizard's elbow. His face was bark-like
and careworn again.

"There now, Old One, why don't you sit down?"

"Hm—what? Oh yes." The man was again bent over with

age, leaning heavily on his wooden stick. His eyes were deep pools of amber. They looked kind, if bewildered.

After a moment's rustling in the leaves, he looked up again. "You've come to visit me." He smiled.

"Indeed we have."

"We've brought you presents."

"Oh!" The shaggy old man's voice brightened.

Nod and Melial each pulled a few small things from their clothes: a few loaves of bread, some trinkets, nothing that looked valuable.

"And one for your subjects."

"Phah, oh *them*," the shaggy old man dismissed them with a wave of his hand. "What is it? What if I like it better?"

"Never you mind!" Melial laughed.

Ogma held her breath and waited for him to explode, but he just smiled placidly and started picking through his own gifts. Melial smiled over her shoulder and went to lay a small box at the base of the tree.

"We must be going, Old One," Nod said carefully.

"It's been wonderful to spend so much time with you—the whole day!" Melial lied easily. "But we must be on our way."

"But there was..." The old man's face fell. He muttered to himself in confusion. "Someone I wanted you to meet."

Nod gave Melial a significant look.

"Another time then. Farewell, Old Father."

"Farewell, young Nod."

Semane tugged at Ogma's elbow. "Time to go."

They slipped off into the trees.

Ogma heard the old man just once more before they were out of earshot of the clearing. He sounded unsure of himself, and almost plaintive. "I—I thought I had a visitor."

Nod and Melial soon appeared at Ogma's elbow as Semane hustled her quickly through the trees. The fog mewled and chortled around them. A strange draft blew in from in front of them, a salty taste in the air. Ogma was certain the fog was about to cut them off from the wagons.

"No. Not this time." Melial's typically serene voice was breathless. She raised one of the charms on her branches, a plain pebble with a hole bored through the center. She muttered to herself as the fog thickened.

"Come on... come on..." Semane was watching Melial.

Ogma suddenly felt the world stretch. She felt like she had back on the wall when it seemed like her tether was stretching for miles. Whatever Melial was trying wasn't working. She felt Melial and Semane pulling away from her, even though they were standing right next to her. She closed her eyes and concentrated on the landscape she had just seen, willing it to stay present.

"*No!*" Vertigo made Ogma stumble as the wooded ground snapped back into place. She recovered and they burst through the trees into a clearing. The caravan wagons were there, on the side of a small, mossy track through the woods.

Ogma staggered thankfully into the pool of firefly light from the lanterns at the fore of each wagon and sat herself down on a half-buried boulder.

"What just happened?" She panted.

Melial let out a deep breath. "A charm. Do you see this stone?" She dropped it in Ogma's hand. The pebble was smooth and cool. Ogma held it up to one eye and looked at Melial through the hole in the center. "You need two like this. The same kind of stone, found in the same riverbed. The fog tends to keep twinned charms together while we sail the fog."

"Though they don't usually work so well," Semane added, giving Ogma an odd look.

"There are charms to keep people together in the fog?" Something ached in Ogma's chest. *If we'd known about those...*

Ogma thought of what might have happened if every child on the wall had one of these charms. *I might've been able to go home!* She looked at Melial accusingly, tears in her eyes again.

Melial read Ogma's face and shook her head sharply. She bent to take Ogma's hands in her own. "No. No, dear, I'm sorry. We couldn't have." Her hands felt like birch bark. Charms tinkled softly in her branches as she looked into Ogma's upturned face. "They're very rare. You see the hole? You can't carve them that way—it has to be done by the river. Do you know how rare it is for that to happen to two stones together?"

Ogma nodded mutely. She didn't really know, but she'd never seen a stone like that before.

"Even if you do have a pair, they don't always work. We've lost some of our own who wandered too far from their wagons, thinking the charms will bring them back."

"Not many of us are lucky enough to find them," Semane continued. "Melial has our only pair."

Ogma looked at Melial searchingly, but she saw compassion, not deceit, in those sap-green eyes. Ogma sniffed and wiped her cheeks.

Semane patted her kindly on the shoulder. "We wouldn't keep it from you. We trade the children the best we can."

"Wait, the others—!" Visions of many-colored cloaks, and Emma's head lolling to the side, blazed through Ogma's brain. She jumped to her feet and backed to the very edge of the lantern light.

"What did you do to them? Where are they?"

"Sweetie, we didn't hurt—"

"Don't call me that! I'm not your *sweetie*, or your *dear*, or your—your anything!" The tears were back and they burned hot on her face.

"Y—you hurt Daniel. You pushed him off the wall."

"We did *no such thing*." Melial's eyes blazed. "We haven't hurt anyone."

"Or taken anyone. Ogma, you have to believe us, we don't do that. Those are just stories."

"*Why* are there stories then? I saw you! I saw the wagons and the cloaks—"

"You saw what?" Melial and Semane shared a look.

"Swee—Ogma, what did they look like?"

Ogma described the motley patchwork and the two open wagons. She didn't want to tell them. She wanted to run away—run into the fog—away from these people who betrayed her. *But they saved me too. And if I left.... I don't want to be alone again.*

"They didn't take me. I just—when the fog came—I was too far from the wall."

Melial's expression was cold and she was looking at Semane. "We tried to warn them."

Semane fumed. "We offered them help. We could have done something!"

"Stop talking like I'm not here!" Ogma sobbed. "*What happened?* Who were they?"

Melial sighed. "Anyone can wear a cloak or ride in a wagon. Sometimes..." she hesitated, but met Ogma's eyes and continued. "Sometimes accidents happen. Children wander too far from their walls on forage—or they just all grow up—or the villagers find they can't have children anymore, or the ones they do have need constant care."

"What does that have to do with *us*?"

Melial pursed her lips. "Well... whatever the cause, if a settlement loses its children, how will they defend themselves? How can they keep the fog away?"

"So they take *us*? They kidnap children? How can they do that?"

Semane touched her on the shoulder. "They're desperate.

They're afraid. Some people—good people—are so afraid of the fog they'd do anything." The memory of the fear on Wheeler's face as the fog closed over him came unbidden. Ogma shook her head.

"But no—why would they dress like you?"

"Well... people are afraid of us already, aren't they? There are enough stories told about us—and if they succeed and save their own towns, they'll want to be able to trade."

"But.. But—maybe that happens. But that wasn't it this time. I don't think these were... they were like you."

Semane sighed, "Well, maybe they were like us. I doubt it, but maybe. But they weren't *us*. You believe that, right?"

Ogma looked at them, anxiety tight in her chest. Finally she nodded. Melial looked to Nod. He was scanning the tree line behind them, his owl-like face turning rather farther on his neck than Ogma thought it should.

"We'd best be moving." He blinked and stared into the trees. "He may still try to follow."

He's talking about the wizard. A thrill of fear ran through her, but also pity. She remembered the bewildered expression on the shaggy man's face once Melial had put the crown on his head and he'd forgotten who he was. She remembered how lonely his last words had sounded. *Of course he deserves it, the way he treats the plum folk.* She shook her head and put those feelings away.

"Who was he?" Ogma asked. Nod's eyes were inscrutable pools as Semane looked from him to Melial.

"Surely you'll tell her!" Semane said.

"No time. We've stayed too long already," Melial said before turning back to Ogma. "We can talk as we ride. But look here—" Melial put an arm around her shoulder. "You see that stone you were sitting on?"

"Yes?" Ogma replied.

"Do you really see it?"

Ogma looked again. It was a large boulder, weather-beaten and sunk well into the ground. Though as she studied it, she realized that it was a remarkably smooth shape: a nearly perfect half dome, in fact.

"Wait! I've seen this before! When I was lost. I was running from this *cat* and—and I found this just before—"

"—just before you found the tower," Semane finished.

Ogma nodded. Something on the stone caught her eye, and she scraped away the moss with one hand. A many-pointed star was carved into one side.

"What does it mean?"

"The stones are markers. We use them as guideposts and warnings—of anything or anyone we must be careful of. If you find another one—"

"But it's so old!" Ogma interrupted. "That one must have been there a hundred seasons!"

"Many hundreds."

But that means the old wizard... Could anyone be hundreds of seasons old? Or more?

"—just stay away," Semane finished. "If you find a marker, whichever side the picture is on, go the *other* way."

Ogma nodded. She filed that away with the rules she'd learned when she'd first begun to patrol the wall. "But wait, why wouldn't the fog just take the stones away? Put them in the wrong places?"

Nod clucked his tongue and waved for them to get moving.

Melial nodded wearily and climbed into the wagon foot box with Semane close behind. Ogma clambered onto the coach seat after her. Nod climbed up beside her to take the reins. The harts snorted and the caravan creaked forward.

"Some places..." Semane seemed like she was struggling to find the words. "Some places are whole. They're singular. Even though they might take up a lot of ground, they're only one place."

"So the fog can't move them?"

Semane shook her head. "No... it can. But it has to move the whole place together. Like your village."

"But we keep the fog out of our village," Ogma protested. "That's *why* we watch the walls."

"You watch the fog to keep it away from the adults—to keep them safe. Even if the fog rolled in, it could only move the village as a whole. It couldn't take just one house or just one part of the wall."

Ogma thought about this in silence for a moment. "But—if *you* made the markers..."

Melial nodded, urging Ogma on.

"If you made the markers as a warning, then they weren't a part of those places. So did you *make* them part of those places, somehow?"

"Ooh! You're a *smart* one. It was seasons before I asked that question." Semane smiled at her.

"We did make them." Nod spoke from where he'd sat silently driving the harts. "At least, our stories say we did. But all the stones we know of were made a long, long time ago. We've forgotten how."

Ogma propped her elbow on the side of the wagon and watched the trees pass by, turning the strange revelations over in her mind. That the Caravaners had some secret knowledge of the fog was no surprise. She'd always imagined they must know secrets that let them travel the fog. She hadn't imagined there were things that even they didn't understand.

The wagon rocked back and forth as it rolled along the uneven ground. Something always seemed to be creaking or settling and the lanterns swung gently with the rhythm of the wagon's sway, casting languid pools of light. The harts pulled them on, silent and uncomplaining except for an occasional *whuffle* or a twitched tail to dislodge a fly.

Ogma's eyelids drooped. She barely felt it when Nod put his cloak around her shoulders.

A vision of the proud old man squeezing the sun in his fist as the clearing dimmed consumed her dream. She felt cold again. The chill was creeping into her bones. Ogma's eyes shot open, her heart pounding. The cloak had slipped from her shoulders.

No—it's dark again!

She turned and looked behind them, scanning the trees for that mossy beard or that haughty face.

"Is he—? Did he—?" she whispered.

"Hush... no." Nod's voice was steady and soothing. "Night has fallen. That's all."

"Night?" She shook the dream from her. "Right. The sun was setting." Ogma took a deep breath and let it out slowly. Then another.

When did I get so scared? Ogma scolded herself.

The fear wasn't new, but it had never stopped her from being the first to run to the wall at the sound of bells. It had never stopped her from facing down a fog phantom. She took a deep breath again, watching the blue disc of the moon's sister between the trees.

I'm brave. No fear. Just like Wheeler always says.

Her eyes stung a little.

"You snore, you know," Nod commented mildly.

"What?"

"You snore. In your sleep. Quite loudly."

"I *do not!*" Ogma felt her cheeks flush. *Someone would have told me.* Nod was inscrutable as ever as he looked at her. "*I'm* going inside." She huffed and opened the hatch behind the coach seat to let herself into the wagon.

The small door opened to a cozy interior. This was the same wagon Ogma had been inside at the festival, though it took her a moment to recognize it. It had the same honeycomb of nesting boxes and shelves along one wall, but the table where they had sat was folded away, along with the benches. There was a wood burning stove in one corner, crackling merrily.

Semane lay on a bed of cushions where a panel had been slid away in the floor, reading a book. Melial stood by one of the shuttered windows, rinsing dishes in a small sink that also seemed to fold out from the side of the wagon.

There's a lot more space in here than shows from the outside. Ogma wondered if that was due to more Caravaner charms. Could they charm the inside of a place to be bigger than the outside? She shook her head. *It was just made by someone clever.* Melial looked up from her dishes and smiled as Ogma stepped inside.

"Tea?"

"Yes, please."

She pulled open a cabinet set up along the ceiling and pulled out a bright copper tea kettle. She filled it at the tap.

"Where does the water come from?"

"The roof of the wagon has rain catchers," Semane replied, nose still in her book. "And we fill them from streams or cisterns every chance we get."

More cleverness.

The kettle was full, and Melial turned to put it on the stove. It was built up vertically, with a main firebox for fuelwood at the bottom, and then two sets of oven shelves.

"Couldn't you pipe the water past the stove to make it hot?" Ogma asked.

Melial turned to stare at her and Semane looked up from her book in surprise. Ogma could just feel the heat in her face again when Semane started laughing. Melial looked chagrined and impressed.

"We probably could," she admitted.

Semane wiped her eyes from laughing. "Oh me... can you imagine when we tell Nocker?" Seeing Ogma's confusion, she explained, "He builds the wagons for our caravans. He'll be so angry he didn't come up with it himself. He's so proud of his wagons."

Melial was sizing Ogma up. "I think we should keep her."

Ogma's heart skipped a beat before she saw the twinkle in Melial's eye. Then it was her turn to be chagrined, and Semane broke up laughing again. Semane had a surprisingly throaty laugh for her dainty, doll-like form.

Ogma basked in the warmth and the company of the wagon while they waited for the kettle to sing. She wanted to let that warmth stretch out as long as she could because she was dreading asking what she had to next. Melial seemed to realize something was troubling her, but she waited for Ogma to speak.

At last the kettle began to whistle and she poured each of them a steaming cup. Ogma accepted hers gratefully and wrapped her hands around it, pulling in the warmth. Looking at her feet, she finally asked.

"Can you... can you take me home?" She kept looking firmly at the floor, afraid to see pity in their eyes.

The answer took too long in coming—and that was answer enough. Ogma's shoulders shook and warm droplets spattered the floor.

"It's not that we don't want to," Melial said softly.

"We will if we can, Ogma. We will try," Semane cut in.

"It's just that your village—it's harder to find than many. The fog doesn't break as often, and you drift more than the other towns."

"Something to do with the windmills, we think. It could be many seasons before we find it again." Semane said.

Ogma sniffled, still looking firmly at the floor, trying to keep her bangs between them and her tearstained face. *But the windmills keep us safe. How could they make it harder for me to get home?* Ogma wiped her face with her sleeve and took a sip of the tea. She managed to look at them again. Thankfully, there wasn't too much pity in their faces. She took a deep breath and changed the subject. "The old man in the fog. He's a wizard, isn't he?"

The two Caravaners looked at each other significantly. Melial started. "We're not supposed to—"

"Oh fog take 'supposed to.' The poor child will be with us long enough, we should just tell her what we know. That's little enough anyway." Still, Semane hesitated.

"He's one of the old ones, isn't he?" Ogma asked. "The ones the stories are about."

"He is," Nod stated flatly.

Ogma hadn't heard him come in—hadn't realized that the wagon had stopped.

"But—I thought the fog destroyed them."

Nod blinked slowly. "We know that when the fog came, the wizard's war was nearly done."

Semane closed her book. "There were only three left alive then. That's what we think, anyway. If any of the others were still alive, they'd had their powers stolen by the three."

"In any case," Nod continued, "by the time the fog came, the land was already scarred, already broken. She-who-was-third-to-last had lost the sun to the Blue Wizard, and he and the Forgotten were turning on each other."

"The Forgotten?"

"He and the Blue were allies once—for however long it took

to crush the others. His name was destroyed. He cannot be remembered."

"So say our histories, anyway," Melial cautioned. "It was a long time ago."

"But the wizard in the tower—you saw! He tried to take the sun." Ogma shivered.

"Yes, we saw," said Semane. "That means he is the Blue." She said it almost with satisfaction.

"You were right," Nod admitted.

"But how do you *know* him?" Ogma replied. They were talking over her head and in riddles. "You called him Old Father! You put that crown on his head and made him forget! How did you know to do that?"

The wagon fell silent for a moment. Semane was glaring at Nod, so Ogma turned to face him full on.

"It's against our laws to say."

"Iona's sake! What could it hurt?" Semane objected.

"Hush," Melial scolded.

Nod cleared his throat. "Melial, will you drive the wagons?"

"I surely will. Get some sleep."

Nod pulled aside one of the wooden panels in the floor and lay down in one of the cushioned compartments. Melial leaned over and whispered to Ogma as she made her way to the front. "Why don't you come sit with me?"

Ogma followed Melial back out to the driver's box. That sat in silence on the bench for a while, watching the landscape drift by in the fog. *What did Melial call it? Oh yes—sailing.* It was a strange word.

"What are the other towns like?"

"Hm? Oh, they're alike enough. Sometimes the walls are made of stone, sometimes brick, sometimes wood—"

"Are we the only one with windmills?"

"The only one I know of. Most have nothing but their patrols. One or two try to keep the fog away in other ways."

"Like with firefly lanterns?" Ogma gestured to the lanterns at the corner of the wagon.

Melial nodded. "A few. They can be hard to care for though."

"What are the other children like?"

Melial smiled. "What are children anywhere like? Fearless, rambunctious... and much too curious for their own good." Ogma blushed at Melial's gentle teasing. "They're also responsible and fair and kind. It's a hard life. You do well to take care of each other. It seems like everywhere we go, the children want a keepsake from the wagons. Sometimes they'll try to trade their shoes, or food, or small things they made." Melial fished a small, crude carving out of her pocket.

"Is that supposed to be a rabbit?" Ogma eyed it critically.

"It's a bit hard to tell, isn't it? Well, she was young." She pocketed the small carving again. "And every once in a while, some little one is just so sure they have nothing worth trading so they... *borrow* one. They never think to just ask." Ogma was aghast, but Melial laughed. "They don't know what the charms *do,* of course, but something catches their eye or they just *have* to have something to remember us by."

"But aren't some of the charms dangerous? Someone could get hurt."

Melial's eyes twinkled. "I just make sure to put out the ones I want them to take, and keep the others locked up safe."

"You put ones out to get stolen on purpose? What do they do?"

"Most of them are simple enough things. Charms against fever or infection. Do you remember the ones we used for the race in your village?"

Ogma nodded.

"Some of those will keep a person warm. Others will keep your feet from aching."

Ogma's hand went to the charm around her neck that Dunkirk had given to her. *Is that why my feet feel better?* She thought about the handful that Rora had won. *I'm sure she gave them away.* Rora was like that.

Melial sobered a bit. "We didn't used to just put them out like that. It was Semane's idea after someone took something truly dangerous." Her expression darkened. "Actually, it happened in your village, about ten seasons ago now. That was the last time we found it."

Ogma straightened in surprise. "Someone from *my* village took something? Who was it?"

"A little boy, I think. We never found them."

Ogma searched her memory, but she couldn't think of anyone in the watch house who had anything that might be a dangerous Caravaner artifact. With all of them living together so closely, it was hard to keep secrets. *Of course, ten seasons ago... whoever it was would probably be off the wall by now. Wheeler or Daniel are the only boys even old enough.* Ogma felt a pang in her chest. *Daniel...*

She remembered the soft lullaby he'd hummed by her bedside. She hoped—she hoped he wasn't— *please be okay, Big Grub.*

Ogma shook her head.

She looked up at Melial. "What did the boy take?"

"I'm not sure I should say." Melial looked uncertain, but she soon relented and leaned in, lowering her voice to a whisper.

"Do you know how it was that the wizards conquered?"

Ogma had heard stories, but she doubted any of them were true. She shook her head.

"They took the names of things. *True names.* They took the

idea of a thing and made it so only they could use it. They wrote them down and made special charms—phylacteries."

Ogma's eyes widened. "What do they look like?"

"Oh, they're small things. Just a little glass phial with a scrap of paper inside."

Ogma frowned. "So you had one of those phyl-act-er-ies." The word tripped up Ogma's tongue. "And someone stole it. Someone from *my village*. What were you going to do with it?"

"The same thing we do with every other dangerous thing we find that we don't know how to destroy. Bury it. Bury it deep."

"What did it do?"

Melial sighed. "We don't know. We can't read them."

"How did someone manage to take it from you?"

"It never should have happened. We didn't even know that it *had* happened until we were miles away."

"Why do you think it was one of the boys?"

"I just remember one little boy, he must have been maybe six seasons? I went round to shutter the wagon and there he took off like a rabbit. I'd thought he was just peeking through the window. I didn't realize he'd already been inside. We kept them —" Melial paused and shook her head. "We kept it in what we *thought* was a very safe place. Hidden. We didn't even think to check there until we were long gone."

She said we kept 'them'. They had more than one of the phylact-thingies. Ogma kept that to herself. She didn't want Melial to realize she'd let slip another Caravaner secret..

"Wait. These phials could control anything?"

She thought of the forgetful, shaggy old man in his ruined tower that they called Old Father. She remembered how he'd seemed to clench the very sun in his grip; how he'd made it disappear from the sky.

"That means *he* has one. The Blue Wizard! He has the sun!"

Melial nodded shortly, her lips tight. "Yes, he must. Although, we didn't know that until we found you there. He'd never woken that far, not since I've been old enough to shepherd."

Her bark-like brows knit in consternation.

"We're not sure where he's keeping it. He's been searched before."

"I might have an idea," Ogma murmured, thinking of the plummers. She explained how the little gnomes secreted things away in the roots of the tree.

"Hmm... if so, we'll need to send someone for it. It's too dangerous to leave with him, even if he's forgotten again." At Ogma's look of horror, Melial hastened to add, "Don't worry. We won't go back ourselves. That would be more dangerous still. Something about you makes him remember. We won't take you back."

Ogma sighed with relief.

"The next time we find another caravan, Nod and I will put out the word. Hopefully the next Shepherds to find him will make it safe."

Ogma's mind was racing with speculation about the wizards, wondering what other phials they might have used to fight their wars. *Is there a phial for the fog somewhere?* Most of the stories said the fog was what ended the wizard's war, though, not that one of them controlled.

The moon rose as the wagons trundled through the dark. After some time, Melial reined up.

"We're stopping?"

"I don't know about you, but I'm getting hungry."

Ogma's stomach rumbled and Melial laughed.

She opened the door. Nod was awake and he and Semane were gathering supplies.

Semane smiled at Ogma as she came inside and gave Nod a

significant look. He blinked owlishly. The look became more of a glare. Finally, Semane sighed and spoke. "Nod has decided to tell you more about us. Haven't you, Nod?"

Nod hesitated, and then said, "How much do you know, Ogma?"

"About Caravaners, you mean?" Ogma wasn't sure what he was getting at. "We have lots of stories."

"Do you know what we call ourselves?"

Ogma hesitated. "Melial called herself a Shepherd?"

Nod raised an eyebrow at Melial, who pretended not to notice.

"Shepherds of what?" Ogma asked.

"Shepherds of the beasts of the fog, of things that claim the woods and mountains as their own, of older things that sleep... and must be kept sleeping."

"And of things that have forgotten themselves," Melial added.

Like the wizard.

"How do you shepherd them? Why? I don't understand."

"It's not easy to explain."

"Nor quick." Semane snorted.

"Come help set up camp. Then I will tell you the story." Nod opened one of the main doors on the side of the wagon and stepped outside. The inky, blobby figures that wore the horse puppet had already unloaded their costume. They were setting up a small camp of their own near the second wagon. Something about them made Ogma uneasy. She wondered what they ate. Or if they ate at all. The windows of the wagon were not shuttered and swamp-green eyes were watching her. The shadows flickered behind them.

Nod was picking up deadfall with his taloned fingers and bringing it back to camp. Ogma went to gather some of her own, making sure not to stray too far from the light of the firefly lanterns. She found several smooth, round stones as well, and brought them back to make a ring around the fire pit they dug out in the dirt.

As she was laying out the stones, she noticed a thin, wavering shape: a shadow cast on the air.

"Oh! Your name is Son, right?" He was much smaller than at the festival.

He flickered and again she could sense a friendly candor in him—though *how* that came across she was still unsure.

Melial stepped down from the wagon carrying a tripod that would let them hang a cauldron over the fire. Semane carried a basket of chopped vegetables.

"Better get that fire lit."

"Do you have a flint?"

"Right pocket."

Ogma reached into Semane's apron pocket and retrieved the flint and steel. It took two strikes to light the tinder and soon she was nursing the bundle into flame.

They set up the cauldron and set the vegetables to stew. The puppeteers came over to join the bigger circle. Ogma had trouble telling which was which, but Regal was a bit taller than the other two. *Still can't tell Mane and Rump apart.*

The three of them bowed to her, holding happy-face masks in front of the featureless expanses that were their heads. She nodded back, some half-formed idea itching in the back of her mind.

Once everyone was settled comfortably around the fire, Nod cleared his throat and began to tell his story. "Now then... this is why we watch the fog."

Ogma startled. She knew those words. That was how all their stories started on the wall, but she hadn't expected the Caravaners to say them, too.

215

"Just you wait a minute, Nod!" a voice growled from behind them.

"Here we go..." Semane whispered. "That's Tramet."

These were the swamp-green eyes that had watched Ogma from inside the wagon. Tramet stepped into the firelight. He looked strange: like an old man who had fallen asleep in the leaf mold for seasons upon seasons. Mushrooms and lichen covered him all over. His skin seemed to be made of shelf fungus and chaga. His nose and ears were too large for his face, and his back was bent with age. Smaller fungi in his dank hair were sporing in clouds of white dander.

"You know fair well that the histories are forbidden from the *townies*." He spat the word.

Semane piped up angrily. "And why should that be? Maybe if they knew more about us, they wouldn't be making up *nonsense* about us stealing children. Maybe half of them would stop trying to run us out of town every time we come to trade!"

"It's the *law!*" sputtered Tramet, shaking his finger at Semane. "We're all very sorry for the little girl, I'm sure, but we should be dropping her off at the first town we see, not telling her our secrets."

"My name is Ogma."

"Eh, what's that?"

"I said my name is Ogma." She kept her voice level. "Not 'little girl.'"

"Phah." He threw up his hands. "On your heads be it. I'll suffer no exile for you." He stormed off in a cloud of spores and slammed the wagon door. Son flickered with agitation. The party around the fire fell silent.

One of the puppeteers pulled a mask from its pouch and capered around the fire. It was an old man's face in a horrible grimace. He pantomimed shaking his finger and storming away in disgust. The other blobby puppeteers fell over themselves, spinning the rattles that they used to laugh.

Ogma giggled and Semane started laughing as well.

"Well that's that, then," Melial said with a smile. "Go on, Nod."

Nod, silent throughout the preceding argument, turned his liquid eyes on each of them until they got their laughter under control, and then began again.

"This is why we watch the fog. We are Shepherds. It is given to us to watch."

"Before the fog, when the wizard's war had just begun, there were those who would not fight in the wizards' armies. Peace-loving people who fled their conquered homes to hide in stony valleys, eking their living out of war-torn fields so ravaged that they were abandoned by the victors who claimed them. They were the first of us."

~

Iona paused at the top of the stony ridge. Her back ached with the weight of her pack. Everything she had left she carried with her. She wiped the sweat from her brow and the soot left a smudgy black smear on her hand.

A column of smoke rose behind them: a scar on the sunrise. Being the first to crest the ridge, Iona took the time to catch her breath and watch the weary black dots on the valley floor below. Each of the other refugees wore a heavy pack, their clothes soot-stained and torn. She took a quick headcount.

"We all here?" Cob puffed to the top of the ridge and glanced behind him as Iona counted.

She nodded shortly. Not everyone had made it out of the wooden palisade that had sheltered them in the forest, but all who she'd counted leaving the gate were still here on the trail. No survivors had fallen behind.

Cob offered her a canteen of water. She took it gratefully, but only let herself swallow a mouthful. They'd had no time to fill up on water before they fled their homes. Her canteen was dry and she wasn't ready to halt the line and take stock just yet.

Cob started off down the other side. Iona stayed at the top to help the refugees, young and old, scrabble over the stony ridge. Soon, Moug arrived: a bear of a man, half again as wide at the shoulder as any other man in the party, and half again as tall. Nevertheless, his hand shook as Iona took his arm and he wouldn't meet her gaze.

She watched his back as he went down the other side of the hill, his shoulders rounded, eyes never lifting from his feet. He was a broken man. Iona sighed and shook her head. She couldn't blame him. They were fleeing again; another home had burned. Not one of them knew where they were going. She had expected some of them to argue, as they had argued before when they found the old orchard in the woods and built their palisade.

But this time was different. There were no arguments about which way would best hide them from the marauding armies. No debate about which lands were blighted by curse. There was nowhere left. And so they walked because they weren't yet ready to die.

Someone patted Iona on the arm, breaking her morbid train of thought. It was Old Ilka, who, despite her small frame and frail appearance, wore a pack as heavy as any of them, and she was not the last straggler in the line. She gave Iona's arm an encouraging squeeze, her grip not yet weakened by age.

"We'll carry on. We've rebuilt before."

"So they can just burn it all to the ground again?" Iona's eyes blazed, and the old woman's face fell. "I'm sorry, Ilka. I'm just tired of running from them. I don't think they even knew we were there. They just set the whole forest to burning."

Ilka shook her head and sighed. "They'll tire of war. You'll see."

"Well, I'm tired of running," Iona said firmly. She shooed Ilka down the hill. "Go on. We've a long day yet."

Iona helped the last of the stragglers over the ridge, and then plodded along at the rear of the line, trying to encourage those in the back to pick up their pace a little. They were strung out enough as it was, and she didn't want anyone to lose sight of the person in front of them. After all, they weren't following any roads. The roads were never safe.

It was hard to fault the ones who had fallen behind. They were hollow-eyed, wracked with coughing fits and spitting up black phlegm or nursing burns. She did what she could, lightening the load of their packs into her own.

"Wagons," she muttered to herself. "We need wagons."

She tried to lighten their burdens with idle conversation. Not that there was much to talk about. The landscape held nothing but barren scrubland and stony hills as far as she could see. As the sun climbed, it grew hot, sticking Iona's shirt to her back. The sweat ran down their faces, washing the stinging black soot into their eyes.

Iona kept as careful a watch as she could, pausing at the top of each ridge to make sure they weren't followed, and to look for any signs of other threats that might find them. The armies that ravaged their homes had treated with dark things, enslaving demons and lesser gods to fight for them. All too often they broke free, roaming the wild places and taking their vengeance on anyone unfortunate enough to cross their paths.

∾

"What are gods?" Ogma asked, interrupting Nod's story. "Wheeler used to tell us stories of the monsters the wizards had made. He said some of them still lived out in the fog. But he never talked about gods before."

Nod inclined his head pensively.

Melial spoke up. "It's an old word. In Iona's day, before the fog, gods and demons were everywhere. The wizards used them to destroy each other."

"But what *are* they?"

Nod spoke. "Gods are... very old. Older than the bones of the earth. Older than mountains."

"I've never heard of two the same. There are gods of anger, or peace, of quiet places—or of a single tree," Melial added.

"Not that we've seen many," Semane interrupted. "Or maybe any. We call the bad ones demons, and the good ones"— Semane made it clear she was skeptical that there was such a thing—"those we call gods. The thing about gods and demons is they all call *themselves* gods."

"If they can speak at all. Either way, it's best to keep them sleeping."

Semane nodded, allowing the point.

"So they're just monsters then?" Ogma said.

"No—not that. All gods have two things in common: they're all dangerous and—"

"They can all be appeased," Nod finished. "May I continue?"

Ogma nodded.

The land itself was as dangerous as anything that roamed it. Cob did his best to route them around the worst of it, but even in these forbidding, infertile hills, they still found themselves forced to pick their way through battlefields, wondering with every step whether some malicious spell carelessly left behind would blind them or wither their bones or worse.

They passed through the splintered wreck of a village. There was nothing left but rubble. Matchstick beams stuck up out of cracked earth. The ruined wood was petrified, though the war had only started two winters before. They circumvented the well. Of the whole village, only the ground around the well was clear. They knew better than to try to drink from it.

As the rest of the line went around, Iona crept closer to the well to peer in. Thick, ropy cobwebs with strands as big as her wrist filled the well from top to bottom. It sent a chill down her spine. She backed away carefully and piled several stones on top of each other just at the edge of the cleared area. With the point of her knife, she carved a crude spiderweb facing the well. She bowed and whispered a respectful entreaty that whatever displaced demon lay inside it would leave them be.

They found no water that day.

As they set up camp for the night, they said quiet prayers to small gods remembered from their villages. Village gods were humble, and they gave humble offerings: small stacks of stones, or bundles of faded flowers plucked from the stony ground. Food and drink were common offerings, but they had so little Iona forbade it.

The next day's journey was wearier, though the ground was flat. It was hot again and the air was choked with dust. Even redoubtable Old Ilka bent under the weight of the sun as they trudged through the scrubland.

When they paused to adjust the packs on their shoulders, one of the wounded men at the back of the line wheezed, "How much... further...?"

"Not far," Iona replied, trying to put some genuine feeling behind an encouraging smile.

He smiled weakly, too tired even to disbelieve her, and they staggered on. Iona knew they wouldn't get much further without water.

"Today. We'll find it today," she whispered to herself.

At midday, one of the refugees screamed. It was a parched croak, a tearing cry that made Iona's throat ache in sympathy. Sluggishly, she tore her eyes away from the heat mirage on the horizon to look back over the line.

A shadow passed over the sun—an instant of shade and relief from the glare—and then was gone.

One of the refugees was pointing at the sky. Iona's tongue stuck to the roof of her mouth. A headache throbbed behind her temples.

"What is it?" It came out more croak than question.

The shadow flickered over the sun again. Dust rose in a cloud. The refugees panicked. Parched cries carried thinly over the stony plain as the line broke and scattered.

Iona watched the burdened figures scrambling through the dust, running in all directions. Some stayed in their line, too weary to care what troubled the others. Iona's head was fogged with fever and pounding headache.

A shadow passed over the sun again. Finally, she looked up.

Its wingspan was nearly a quarter of a mile wide from tip to tip, so large that in Iona's heat-stricken state, she found it hard to judge how close it was. It was silhouetted against the sun, and the shadow on the ground spread like a stain. Fear for the others won through Iona's heatstroke.

"Run! Please, run!"

Some of the soot-stained faces looked to her and tried to pick up their pace, but not all. The heat and the thirst were too much.

The great shape crashed to the dirt, raising a cloud of dust that stung Iona's eyes. The god—or demon—had a desert serpent's body with the diamond pattern that warned of venom. She couldn't see its head among the knots of coils, each three times a person's height. Its thrashing shook the ground, and it dropped iridescent feathers longer than she was tall.

Iona scanned the horizon, desperate to find someplace that they could shelter from the serpent. Mirage pools reflected ruined cities and cool oases, which Iona ignored despite her fever. A scar in the parched earth caught her eye.

"Come on! Follow me!"

She ran on trembling legs, hoping the crack was more than it looked. It was. It was a narrow canyon, maybe the bed of an old river, long dried up. She stood at the canyon's mouth and helped the other refugees inside.

"Damn you, Moug! You can run faster than that! Rogan! Get a move on! Yulia! Help Aphis, you know his knee is bad. Come on!"

One by one, or supporting each other by the arms, the panicked refugees found her and squeezed into the crack in the earth and disappeared into the cool shadows.

"Cob, where are you?"

Ilka hadn't made it, nor several of the others who'd been nursing injuries. The great feathered serpent was slithering closer on its coils. Iona's eyes were too dry for tears as she turned away.

"Now just you wait a minute, Iona!" Ilka emerged from a cloud of choking dust. She was dragging Cob by his arms. "Well are you just going to stand there? Help an old woman."

Iona wrapped Cob's arm around her shoulder and helped Ilka pull him into the canyon. He was unconscious.

"What happened? Was he crushed?"

"Just the heat, I think. He collapsed right in front of me."

The rest of the refugees had disappeared into the gloom of the canyon. It went much deeper than Iona had thought, with only a glimmer of sunlight filtering down across the striated stone walls.

Suddenly the walls shook and even that glimmer was cut out. Diamondback scales roofed the cavern.

"We should move."

Ilka nodded. With one arm, they supported Cob's limp form and with the other they trailed their fingertips along the walls, stumbling through the dark.

As her eyes adjusted, Iona realized there a a faint glimmer of light. Some phosphorescent spores were glowing. There were voices ahead, distorted by the twisted stone walls into ghostly wails and moans.

She reached the first of the survivors then. The most infirm were crouched in a huddle, hugging their knees to themselves.

"Is there a way out?"

The soot-stained faces looked at her blankly.

"The canyon, does it go anywhere?"

"They're tired, dear." Ilka sighed. "For that matter, I am too. They're just going where you tell them."

Iona nodded and they limped on with Cob still slumped between them. He was muttering feverishly, his skin still hot to the touch despite the cooler canyon shade.

The distorted voices resolved themselves into an argument.

"We can't go on like this. We need water."

"It's right there, maybe if we—"

"If we what? With that... demon waiting for us?"

The knot of desperate faces noticed Iona in the phosphorescent gloom.

"Iona! You've got to do something."

"You promised us water! What'll we do now?"

Iona faltered. Her heart was weary and her headache pounded.

"That's enough!" Ilka stared them down. "It wasn't one of

you who saved this many from the village. It wasn't one of you who found our home in the forest. And it wasn't one of you who stayed to help the children and wounded out of the smoke when the armies burned it." Ilka withered them with scorn. "It wasn't one of you who saved us. That was Iona alone."

Even Moug, twice the size of any of them, looked broken and defeated. He turned his tearstained face to Iona. "Please... my mother's dying."

Iona sighed. "If I had any water to give..."

"No—you don't understand. There's water here! Can't you hear it?" Now that he said it, she could hear it: a trickling of water.

"Well, where is it? Where's it coming from?"

Moug and the others looked stricken. "I'll show you. You'd better leave Cob here."

Iona was perplexed, but she didn't argue. Gently, she set Cob down.

"Will you stay with him?"

"Of course." Old Ilka sat beside him. "Go on and find this water they're fussing themselves about."

Moug motioned Iona to follow him deeper into the tunnel. After a few bends, the phosphorescent light began to fade and the canyon opened up to daylight again. Moug put a finger to his lips, peeked his head around the corner, and then pulled it back again and sank heavily to the floor.

Iona tilted her head in query.

Moug only shook his head.

Gingerly, Iona peered around the bend of the canyon wall to see what had so frightened Moug. After the gloom, the light of day made her squint. She blinked away the spots that swam in her vision.

"But—it's beautiful." The canyon opened into a perfectly protected bowl, carpeted with soft grass. Statues of white marble striated with gold gathered around a central fountain, where pure water trickled into a pool. One statue of a young woman carried a basket of bread and fruit. Another led a marble stag on a golden cord. Dozens filled the courtyard.

Iona's heart nearly stopped when she finally lifted her eyes and saw the face of the feathered serpent staring down. She realized that she'd gone several steps into the soft grass, the diminutive statue of a young rabbit just beside her right foot. Heart pounding, she scrambled back around the canyon bend.

The vision of enormous eyes, liquid green, transfixed her. Moug met her gaze, the fear she felt reflected in his eyes.

"I have to think."

Iona stayed apart from the others and ordered each of them to stay away from the mouth of the canyon and the god's statue garden that waited there. She sat beside Cob's fevered body, alone with her thoughts until night fell.

When moonlight glimmered at the mouth of the canyon, she stood and walked into the garden.

Nod leaned back from the fire and fell silent for a moment.

"So the... god... was there? It was guarding the spring?"

Melial answered, "It's more that it *was* the spring. With many gods, they're tied very deeply to a place."

"Or they're just greedy," Semane muttered.

"What happened then?" Ogma looked to Nod expectantly, the flames reflected in his golden eyes. Minutes passed.

"Um... Nod?"

"We don't know what she thought of. What private hope told her she could do what she was about to do."

Ogma waited.

"She bargained with the god."

～

When dawn came, and Iona had not returned, Old Ilka went to Moug, who was waiting patiently beside the canyon's mouth. "We have to follow her."

"We can't. You don't know what's there. She'll come back."

"She's not coming, Moug."

"She will. My mother's sick. She'll come."

Old Ilka sighed. "Well I'm going. I'll not stay here and die afraid."

Worry creased Moug's brow as the old woman picked her way past him and turned the bend. After a moment, he followed.

In the garden, the great serpent was still. It had turned to stone: white marble, streaked with gold. And a new statue stood at the lip of the pool. It was Iona.

～

"No! But after all that—" Ogma's eyes burned with frustration and sorrow. "Why couldn't she—?"

Melial spoke quietly, "Some of us call the serpent the Gift-Giver. But there's always a price to be paid."

"But why would it turn itself to stone?"

Melial sighed. "We don't really know. We think it was tired, or afraid—"

"—or angry." Semane muttered darkly.

"Afraid of what?"

"The war. So many of the gods were being twisted. So many bound. So many demons put in collars and chains. The world was getting smaller. Carved into kingdoms. Perhaps the Gift-Giver was afraid of who would come for its gifts next. Perhaps it wanted a gift for itself: to sleep. To be made safe."

"—only it couldn't pay the gift-price for itself." Semane glowered.

"But—"

"I haven't finished yet," Nod said quietly. "Would you like to hear the rest?"

Ogma hugged her knees to her chest and stared into the fire. "Yes, please."

~

When Ilka and Moug had dried their tears, they went back for the others. Reticent at first, fearful of the holy ground, they did not want to leave the canyon mouth. But soon the sound of water was too much to bear, and they came forward.

Ilka was first to taste the water. She made the others wait in case it turned her to stone as well.

"It's clean. The water's good. It's safe!" Her joy and relief echoed through the canyon. After a moment's hesitation, others rushed to the edge of the water to drink and fill their canteens. They brought the water back to those too afraid to approach its shore.

Moug carried his mother—and then Cob—to the water's edge. Bathing their brows, he cooled their fevers, and ladled water to their lips until they woke.

Cob shook himself and plunged his hand into the water. He cupped and brought it to his face, drinking down the cold, sweet water.

Those with injuries and those wracked by heaving coughs that brought up black phlegm and blood—they too drank, and, in drinking, were healed.

For three days, the refugees rested. Neither the serpent nor Iona woke. They cooked the food they had brought with them, cleaned their clothes, and gradually hope returned to their faces and laughter to their lips.

The children who they'd saved, few and precious, played in the garden among the statues, dressing them in flowers. Ilka, Cob, and Moug sat in the grass and watched.

"We're safe here now. This can be home for a while," Cob said quietly.

"We'll need food before long. And there's not much to forage in the scrublands," Ilka noted practically.

"What of Iona?" Moug asked, tears standing in his eyes as he watched the children play.

"I don't know." Cob shook his head.

Children's cries stole their attention.

"Hey! You moved her!"

"I did not! You did!"

"Nuh-uh!"

"Hey! What's all this?" Cob strode to where the two children argued next to Iona's statue. One was holding a daisy chain accusingly.

"She moved her! She was holding my daisies and now she's dropped them!"

"I did not! She moved on her *own!*"

Cob froze. Now that he looked, it did seem as though Iona's pose had changed. Where both hands had been held palm outwards, one now fell beside her hip.

"Ilka! Moug! Come look!" Cob gestured them over excitedly. "She's moved!"

There an uproar among the refugees, and arguments broke out about whether the statue had moved at all, or if they were misremembering. So many had been suffering from fever that no one felt sure of how she was standing before, except the children.

Finally, Cob waved them all to silence. He picked a blossom

from the grass and laid it in Iona's other palm.

"If you're there, show us."

All that day and late into the evening they watched the statue, waiting to see if Iona would move. But she did not. Finally, the weary refugees fell asleep.

"Wake up! Wake up! She's moved again!" The children shook Cob awake and ran from person to person until the whole camp was roused.

Rubbing the sleep from his eyes, Cob stumbled to the edge of the pool. Iona stood there still, white marble skin unchanged. But she had moved. Her hands held the blossom to her nose, and she smiled. They spent that day in celebration, though they had come to the last of their food.

That night, Iona spoke to Cob as he slept. And in the morning, he gave her instructions to the others.

"We will watch the Children. We will shepherd dead gods to their rest. We will find the old, the forgotten, the broken. We will make offerings and sing songs. We will respect all, but worship none. We shall put the dangerous to sleep. What cannot be made safe we will bury.

We will be Shepherds."

Nod fell silent. The vision of the story that he had told slowly faded, as Ogma stared into the dancing flames of the campfire. She wanted to jump to her feet, full to bursting with even more questions.

"But how did you change? How did you become like this?" she asked, and then fell quiet, realizing her question must be deeply rude.

"Iona's bargain was the beginning," Melial said gently. "She was the first of us. She gave instructions and the others followed."

Semane shook her head. "We don't really know that she said anything."

"Nevertheless, that is how the story is told," Nod continued. "After Iona was changed, she sent the others out into the world. They foraged for food and built new homes to protect their children. But the first Shepherds never stayed in one place."

Semane spoke next. "You have to understand. Food was scarce. All the world was still being torn apart by the wizards' war. They did their best just to survive, and to aid any others they found who had not aligned themselves with one army or the other."

"Our bodies didn't change all at once," Melial added. "A shepherd would try to till a battle-torn field and get snared in a half-buried curse. Or they would make other bargains with the wakened things that roamed the land."

"We sought them out. And one by one, every Shepherd changed." Semane shook her head. "But even to us, this is just a story. Some of us tell other stories."

Ogma was silent for a moment, staring into the embers. *I bet that's the right story though. It feels true.* Still, she asked aloud, "What do the other stories say?"

"Depends who's telling," Semane replied. "Some say it was the fog that changed us. That one of the wizards made it as a weapon against their enemies. Most adults it would simply kill, but we weren't part of any of the armies, so when it broke free, it simply changed us."

Ogma looked at Nod again. "But you tell this story. Why?"

Nod smiled. "I like this one best."

"Oh phah." Semane threw a bread roll at Nod and started ladling out bowls of stew.

231

"This one has something of all the stories," Melial said, accepting a bowl. Ogma's mouth watered as she waited for hers, and she ate eagerly, sopping up the gravy with the rolls that Semane provided.

"But in all these stories, you were people," Ogma said around a mouthful of food.

"We still are, dear," Semane said wryly. "Just not... *human* people."

"We're born this way now," Melial continued. "Every generation since the beginning."

"And you never look the same?"

"No two alike is what they say. Though that's not quite true either, is it Melial?"

Melial nodded, swallowing her mouthful. "There are resemblances sometimes. There are some of us who are like the trees. Or the birds." She gestured to Nod. "But the shapes don't run in families."

"Children are hard for us," Nod said quietly. "Some of us... can't."

"But we call *you* the Children," Semane perked up. "Not just you young ones. All you townies behind the walls. You're still the Children to some of us. Those of us who follow her story, at any rate. If Iona's story is true, you're all descended from the children the first Shepherds protected behind their walls."

Ogma leaned over to Semane and hugged her fiercely. They ate in companionable silence. The fog drifted around them through the trees. Ogma was startled to realize she'd hardly noticed it. It was quiet. It paid little attention to the Caravaners, even with her among them. She yawned mightily and her eyelids drooped. She felt Semane's porcelain arms surround her and lift her up.

CHAPTER 8

FACELESS

The sea of fog was calm the day after Nod told his story. Ogma sat beside him again as he drove the wagon and bit her nails. It was a newly acquired nervous habit, which she found quite annoying. The panic that had threatened to overwhelm her before the caravan found her was gone, but every time the wagon creaked to a stop, she couldn't shake a creeping dread.

Pools of green and yellow light rocked back and forth as the lanterns swayed with the movement of the wagon. The firefly lights burned off the fog in front of them, but outside their reach, it was a wall of gray.

It's quieter out here. It's not... talking or watching me. Ogma had always felt the fog as a *thing*—a malevolent presence focused on her or the town—but here she felt nothing. The fog drifted around and over them. It passed them over like a predator already sated. She'd never felt the fog seem so... disinterested. Still, every once in a while, she felt the gaze of phantom eyes, and then the fog would lick its chops and move on. She made a face at it every time she felt the eyes on her.

She distracted herself by trying to pry information out of

Nod. He didn't seem to mind her company or her questions, though sometimes Ogma felt like she was talking to herself.

"Where are we going?" she asked him. "Won't the fog just take us anywhere?"

Nod flicked the reins. "Perhaps."

She was about to prod him further when Nod reined in the harts. She heard the second wagon rumble to a stop behind them. Nod rang the bell he kept in the coachman's box and the carriage behind rang theirs in turn. The wagon bells were unpleasant, clangorous things, better suited for livestock than people. She knew they had better ones. She'd watched them sell them to the children of the watch, but they never seemed to carry any on their persons.

If it were me, I'd carry them. Then again, they stay in eyesight all the time except when they're on the move.

Nod seemed to guess what she was thinking.

"The fog rarely mimics our voices. Some of our kind carry the bells as you do, but with Melial's charm—ah, there we go." Without explanation, Nod started up the wagon again, clanging the wagon bell and hearing the one behind. Ogma was baffled by the apparently unnecessary stop. Several more times that day, Nod stopped the wagon. Other times, he chose to turn off the track they followed. Once, Nod stopped and turned both the wagons around completely.

We go in circles more often than not as far as I can tell. But she kept it to herself.

Melial often preferred to walk next to the wagon. The harts moved slowly enough over the uneven and ever-shifting ground that she had no trouble keeping up. She never made a sound among the trees, though she was careful to keep within reach of the lantern light.

Ogma liked to watch her, especially when Nod was not responding to her queries. The dappled shadows made her blend in so well she almost disappeared, but the silver chains of the charms she hung in her branches glinted in the firefly light.

Melial would occasionally appear at the edge of the foot box and whisper to Nod, who would make a slight change of course. One of these times, Nod stopped the wagons and they had a whispered argument. The fog had brought them to an open meadow, and Nod was making for a track in the distance. Melial shook her head. She sorted through the charms hanging from her branches until she found one. She took it, tapped it to her forehead and then let it drop. Instead of falling, it swung out into the air tugging gently in the direction of the bank of fog to their right.

Wordlessly, Nod turned them in that direction.

They all have charms, Ogma realized, *not just Melial. The others are just more sneaky about it.* Nod kept his hidden in the voluminous folds of his robe until he needed them. Semane kept hers tucked into her apron. *Tramet probably has some too, though I bet he'd never share them*, Ogma groused. Peering back over her shoulder, she caught the hoary old Shepherd watching her from inside the wagon. She waved impishly and he *harrumphed* and closed the shutters.

Ogma wasn't quite sure what all the charms were for.

Many seemed to be simple enough things to help with household chores. There were lanyards that Nod tied over the drawers in the wagon, which seemed to help keep their contents from tumbling about and the latches from coming undone.

Semane had a simple charm that shed water from their clothes, which she used after Ogma helped her with the washing, or when it had been raining heavily and whoever was driving the cart—usually Nod—finally came inside to rest.

Most of the charms, Ogma was nearly certain, were for navigation—to keep the caravan as a whole from getting lost. *Not like we're actually getting anywhere though.* Despite the

Caravaners' frequent consultation of these precious charms, the fog brought them nowhere. *I still can't see how they know where we're going.*

It didn't seem like they were sure either.

Nod and Melial continued their whispered arguments, and even Nod was getting irritable. She could see no rhyme or reason behind the decisions they came to. Sometimes they would try to dodge the banks of fog, trying to stay in whatever grassy plain or hidden valley the fog had brought them to. Other times, Nod chased the fog deliberately, and they passed from canyon to mountaintop to pine forest a dozen times in one day.

Caravaners are just strange, Ogma decided. *Well, yes, of course they are,* she thought peevishly, *just not the way I expected.* She'd always thought they'd be strange: exotic and exciting, or even alien and frightening. And yes, they *looked* strange, and they knew secret, ancient things, and they spoke in a strange accent, and at night they often played strange instruments, and they traveled with featureless inky blob folk who made puppet costumes come alive, but what was truly strange was how human they were. How much they were a family, no matter how different they looked.

They could be solemn and distant at times, Nod especially, but there was warmth and genuine affection for each other.

"Ach, phthooh!" Tramet spat as the wagons circled up, while Nod and Melial argued the way to go once again. "It's this child making the fog restless. We'd be on our way by now if not for her."

All warmth and affection, he is. Just to spite him, Ogma stalked over to the wagon he lived in while he was busy arguing with Nod and Melial. *If he wants to avoid me,* he *can stand out in the rain awhile.*

The wickerwork horse whinnied and whuffled when she approached. "How do you do that?" she asked them, not

236

expecting an answer from the mute puppeteers inside. Outside of their puppet, Mane and Rump were quite friendly and helpful around the fire, but inside the puppet...

The horse puppet snorted and stomped its foot and flicked its tail. Even the eyes, just holes in the wickerwork frame, seemed to watch her.

It really does breathe. The chest was rising and falling and she could feel warm breath on her face. The horse puppet turned to her, nose to nose, and whuffled over her face, mussing her bangs.

"Ow! Don't bite my hair!" She glared at the unruly creature.

A horrible grinding rattle startled her. She turned. Regal, wickerwork helm under her arm, was spinning her laughter rattle.

"Hmph!" Ogma turned up her nose and stalked over to the wagon. She'd opened the door and climbed inside before she'd really thought about what she was doing. *Don't know why she's laughing at me. It's her stupid horse misbehaving.* She stopped just inside the threshold atop the wagon steps. *This is Tramet's place.* Ogma bit her lip.

It was dim inside the wagon. The windows were shuttered. Ogma could see nothing but dark shapes at first as her eyes adjusted. It smelled musty and earthy, but in a surprisingly pleasant way, like soft ground after a cool rain.

As the room came into focus, Ogma noticed a soft glow emanating from the corners of the wagon.

It's covered in mushrooms! Dozens of different varieties grew in small, sculptured gardens. Some of them were phosphorescent, filling the wagon with a soft blue light.

And look at all this stuff! Crates of trade goods, piles of furs and leather—all sorts of things—stacked from floor to ceiling at the back. She saw finely worked tin pots, jewelry, wooden dolls.

Those are from my village. She remembered seeing Eve bring them to the festival to trade.

One side of the wagon had a long wooden bench with clay vessels, mortar and pestle, and dried herbs hung from the rafters. It reminded Ogma of Goodie Hazel's house back in the village. On the other side was another workbench, with wood-working planes, small saws, and other more delicate tools. There was a silver bell on the bench. Ogma went over and picked it up.

It was beautiful. The handle was still raw wood, unstained, but it had been carved with delicate motifs of flowers. The bell itself was being engraved as well. Delicate designs and geometric patterns covered roughly half its surface.

A shadow detached itself from one corner of the wagon. Ogma jumped.

"Oh it's you!"

The shadowy silhouette flickered and nodded.

"I forgot you were here. I'm sorry."

The shadow flickered cheerfully and came to stand behind her.

"This is beautiful," she said, gesturing to the bell. "Did you make it?"

Son flickered sorrowfully.

"Oh, you can't speak, can you?" Ogma flushed. "I'm sorry."

The shade raised the silhouette of an arm towards Ogma. It passed right through, though it left a companionable warmth behind.

He can't touch anything either. She bit her lip and tried to think of something to say.

"Wait. Did *Tramet* make all these?" She gestured broadly to the workbenches and the exotic miniature gardens.

Son flickered in the affirmative.

"Oh." Ogma wasn't sure what to think about that. She looked at the bell again, turning it over in her hands.

"Do you know where the clapper is?" she asked. She wanted to hear the bell ring.

Son flickered for a moment, considering.

He stepped forward, standing *in* the workbench, and drew himself up. He stretched into the rafters. He pointed at a rack in the shadows.

Ogma peered up and could just see other unfinished bells hanging above. Silver clappers, like teardrops, hung next to them. Ogma clambered up onto the workbench.

She was just reaching to take down one of the clappers when the door slammed open.

"Ey! What're you doing up there! Come down!" Tramet stalked into the room, swampy eyes blazing, mushrooms across his face and shoulders bursting into spore.

"Uh—uhm, I'm sorry," Ogma stammered, clambering hastily down from the workbench.

"What are you doing with that?" he said, snatching the bell out of her hands. "It ain't even been charmed yet! Ye can't go touching it with bare hands. It'll tarnish!"

He picked up a cloth and began buffing the bell furiously.

"I was only holding the handle," Ogma objected, her face hot. "I just wanted to hear it sound."

"Well it's not yours to sound!" Tramet growled.

Son flickered unhappily.

"And don't *you* start scolding *me!*" Tramet said, waving his hand through the unhappy shadow.

Son retreated into the dark.

"Have you had your fun, girl?" Tramet spat. "Come to laugh at old Tramet and his silly mushrooms?" He glared at her.

Ogma clenched her hands into fists at her sides. "They're very beautiful," she said coldly and stalked outside, slamming the wagon door behind her.

She ran past Melial and Nod, who were still arguing, and

straight into the other wagon. Semane was inside, reading another of her books.

"What happened?"

Ogma stomped across the boards, hot tears on her face, and slid open the floor panel that hid her bed cushions. She curled up inside and slid the panel closed, trying to disappear in the small, dark space.

There was a gentle knock on the wood above her—a muffled voice came through.

"Ogma, what happened?"

"I don't want to talk about it!" Ogma shouted, burying her face in the pillows.

"Ooh. It was Tramet, wasn't it?" Semane bristled. "When I get my hands on him..."

"No!" Ogma shouted. She hiccuped. "It was-wasn't him. It was my fault." She burrowed deeper into the cushions. Semane was quiet for a moment. Then she slid open the floor panel, just a crack.

"Well at least keep this open a bit. You'll get too hot in there," she said quietly.

Ogma said nothing. *I want to go home.*

She woke sometime later, feeling better.

You haven't had a tantrum like that in seasons, she scolded herself. *What would Wheeler think?* Wheeler would have tried to comfort her, she knew. It would have been Brigid who scolded her and told her to act her age. *As she should.* And Rora and Effie would have teased her for it, but gently, to cheer her up. And Daniel would have brought her tea.

Ogma's heart ached as she remembered Daniel combing out the tangles from her hair. She felt something welling up inside her.

I'm going to find those who did this, she told herself, anger burning in her heart. *I'll find them and then... and then...*

She didn't know what she would do after that.

The wagon swayed and rocked beneath her. *At least we're moving again.* Ogma sighed and pulled open the floor panel.

Semane looked up from her book, and Melial came over with a cup of tea. Ogma averted her gaze. They said nothing, for which she was grateful.

The wagon door opened. Nod was walking beside the caravan as they trundled along. She could see the fog billowing in clouds at the edge of the lantern light.

"Awake?" He cocked his head quizzically and blinked at her.

Ogma nodded.

"Walk with me?"

Ogma furrowed her brow, but nodded again.

"When she's finished her tea," Melial said firmly.

Nod bowed and closed the door.

Ogma sat and drank her tea in awkward silence.

Finally, Semane said, "Some folk are just hard to live with."

Ogma nodded miserably.

"They're not bad folk, they're just not good at people, 's all. Here—" Semane rummaged in the pantry and brought a small pitcher to Ogma. "While you're out there, you can feed the fireflies."

"Milk and honey?" Ogma asked, remembering her favorite story.

"Now how'd you know that? Oh of course, he lives there now."

"Who lives there? You mean the old man? You know him, don't you? Nod *bowed* to him."

"Not my story to tell, and I bet you know as much as I do, besides. Go on. The flies need feeding."

Ogma took the pitcher, grateful for something to do. *I'll ask Nod about him sometime,* she promised herself as she opened the wagon door. The wagons were moving slowly, but watching the ground drift past the wagon steps still gave Ogma vertigo. She stood on the last step, trying to figure out how to dismount, before she finally decided just to jump.

She landed awkwardly, bobbling the small tin pitcher in her hands. In the time it took to catch her balance, the wagon rolled on, so she had to skip to catch up with the front again.

Nod was on foot, leading the harts by their bridles. They were uneasy with the fog so thick. It blanketed everything around them so that Ogma could hardly see what the landscape looked like. Trees and boulders seemed to loom out of the banks and then disappear.

"Semane said I should feed the fireflies," Ogma explained as she came up beside Nod.

As she reached the front of the wagon, the fog billowed away from her. Nod pointed at the fog bank retreating in front of them. "Oh? You do a better job than they do."

She thought he was smiling as he said it, though on Nod's face it was hard to tell.

"Though Semane's right, we should give them their supper. Just pour a little bit in each lantern."

Ogma made her way to the lanterns on all four corners of the wagon. It took her a moment to figure out how to put the milk and honey mixture in without letting all the fireflies out. They buzzed softly, climbing around the inside of the lantern. Now that she could study them, she noticed that each lantern had a small collection of twigs and ferns—almost a miniature forest in each one. They looked like the gardens that Tramet built.

After some difficulty, she found that one of the panels on the top of the lanterns opened to reveal a fine mesh that she could pour through. She poured a generous helping into each of the lanterns on her wagon, and then made her way to the one that followed.

With the fog as thick as it was, the other wagon followed close. The wickerwork horse was a frightening shape in the mist, and Regal looked stern and proud in full knight's costume. But as she walked back between the wagons, the fog retreated from her and the shapes softened. The wicker horse whuffled and nudged her shoulder as she passed. Regal nodded.

Ogma filled the other lanterns, watching the shutters nervously, hoping that Tramet wouldn't choose now of all times to open them. He didn't.

She trotted back up to the first wagon when she was finished and knocked on the door. Melial opened it with an amused expression. "We don't usually knock."

Ogma puffed. "I'd rather not try to climb back on till we stop." She handed the pitcher up to Melial and jogged up to Nod. The fog was getting worse. *It would have been lapping right over the walls at home. I can't believe they just walk out in this.*

Even in the light of the fireflies, Nod's back almost seemed to disappear as he led the harts carefully forward. Ogma came up beside him and the fog retreated. He patted her on the shoulder gratefully and picked up the pace now that they could see a bit further in front of them.

I'm good for something, at least, even to a Caravaner, she thought as they trudged along. *And the ground is softer than the wall.* She had never gotten used to how the stonework of the wall always made her feet ache.

The next day, the landscape was strange: red earth and scrubland. Sheer walls appeared beside them, and then they'd find themselves climbing down into narrow canyons and out the other side.

In one such canyon, the walls rose steeply on both sides. The fog retreated behind them even as the walls closed in. Ogma studied the striated rock as they trundled forward.

Abruptly, Nod stopped. It was a dead end. He sighed heavily. "We'll have to go back."

"But it's too narrow to turn around..."

Nod sighed again and took the harts by the bridle. "Tell the other wagon?"

Ogma nodded. She trotted back, her shoulders barely brushing past the wagon on one side and the canyon on the other. The shutters opened as she passed. Ogma ducked, narrowly avoiding being hit in the head.

"Why the stop?" Melial asked, leaning out the window. She pulled back when she saw how close the wall had come.

"Dead end. And it's too narrow to turn around."

Melial shook her head. "We'd better get out and help. The harts don't like to go backwards."

She and Semane disembarked to help Nod with the animals. Ogma trotted back to Son and Tramet's wagon. Regal had already guessed the difficulty. The horse puppet stomped and snorted and slowly began to push the cart backwards.

It was slow going. It would have been impossible if the wagon hitches weren't built so the carts could be backed up. They wrestled with the harts and stony ground for almost an hour before the canyon opened enough to turn the wagons again. Another hour later, there was still no sign of the entrance.

"How can that be?" Ogma asked Semane. "We'd only just got into the canyon." She knew the answer before Semane said it. "The fog, I know, I know. Why are you always traveling in it?" Ogma asked with exasperation. "Why don't you build towns of your own?"

Sure, the fog wouldn't attack them directly the way it attacked other adult humans, but it still made a nuisance of itself. She'd almost prefer that it send a phantom after them rather than wander in the endlessly shifting landscape.

Semane hesitated before replying. "We could build homes, I suppose. We could build towns and wall everything out, like the Children" She tilted her head to one side. "But we're Shepherds. There are things to be done out in the fog. Things that need to be made safe."

"And there's trade to be done," Melial added. "Yes, the fog sometimes brings the towns together, but many of the villages are like yours—drifting for seasons at a time."

"We do need the trade," Ogma admitted.

"Besides. These are our homes." Semane patted the side of the wagon fondly.

Several hours later, the canyon walls finally fell away and they found themselves in open fog again. Ogma was weary from walking beside the wagons. She clambered into the coachman's foot box and dozed off.

An abrupt halt jerked her awake.

Nod had stopped them again. The fog before them had gathered into an enormous bank. *It's more like a thundercloud.* Ogma had never seen it like this, but Nod seemed perfectly calm. The bank split, revealing a new landscape behind it. It took Ogma a moment to understand what she was seeing.

Though it was daytime on this side of the fog, on the other, perfectly still stars stood in a sky with no moon. Glittering black sand seemed to reflect the starlight above, and dunes and stony crags stretched for miles in the distance.

"Wait. Can it do that? I've never seen the fog go to a different time of day before."

Nod didn't answer—he stood perfectly still and waited.

"Are we going there?"

Still Nod didn't move.

They waited for almost half an hour, until at last the fog rolled closed again, and seemed to dissipate, leaving them in the scrub pine that they'd been traveling in. Finally Nod spoke. "Always let the desert pass you by."

Ogma wrote the warning in her memory.

The harts snorted and pawed the ground. Ogma jumped down to help Nod coax them forward. She murmured to them softly, "Come on then, time to go." She stroked the doe's neck. The harts had a coarse outer coat over soft inner fur. They had a musky scent, but Ogma was used to it now. In fact, she had come to like it. It made them seem that much more real out in the fog where things changed so rapidly. The doe nuzzled her forehead and began to strain forward, the one on Nod's side following suit.

"They like you better than me," Nod bemoaned. He sounded so glum that Ogma had to suppress a laugh. He sighed and strode forward.

Ogma whispered to the harts, "You could be a little nicer. He does feed you, after all."

The doe nearest her snorted and shook herself.

With a creak, the door behind the foot box opened. Melial emerged with an anxious look on her face, scanning the pine scrub on either side of their path. A moment later, she noticed Ogma, and her face smoothed to a pleasant smile.

She's worried. I wish they wouldn't hide things from me.

"We're lost, aren't we?" Ogma asked. "I mean, more so than usual for the fog."

"You *are* a bright one. Yes, we are."

"Is it because I'm here?"

Melial shook her head firmly. "No."

"But Tramet keeps saying—"

"Tramet is just a grumpy old man," Melial interjected. "You're too young for the fog to be interfering on your account."

Ogma wasn't sure about this.

"It happens sometimes. The fog is fickle. Sometimes it's months before our caravans can get back on track."

"Months?" Ogma repeated, her heart sinking.

"It's not easy, sailing the fog, but some good may come of it. Sometimes we find new paths or settlements."

Ogma nodded and resigned herself to a long journey. There were distractions enough to keep her occupied.

That night, as she was helping Melial set up the tripod over the fire at camp, she noticed one of Melial's charms softly glowing.

"Does that mean something?"

"Hmm...?" Melial pulled the charm from her branches. "Cheshires!"

Semane dropped the kettle she was carrying and grabbed Ogma by the elbow. The others scrambled to stamp out the cook fire and carry things inside.

"What's a cheshire?" Ogma asked as Semane hustled her into the wagon and shuttered the windows.

"Remember the cat that chased you? How its coat blended into the fog?"

Ogma nodded.

"One of those."

"Oh." Ogma swallowed, remembering the big gray cat whose mottled fur shifted and rolled to blend with the fog.

"They usually hunt in packs. We'll wait it out inside the wagon and they'll move on."

"But what about the harts?" There was no way the big animals could shelter inside the wagons.

"Nod and Melial will do what they can to run 'em off. Do you know how they hunt?"

Ogma could guess.

"A lone cheshire, like the one you saw, will keep silent and sneak up on its prey in a fog drift. But when there's a pack..."

Several yowls and hisses sounded in the fog outside. Semane looked grim.

"A pack will try to confuse their prey. One or two will sneak away and make a bunch of noise in one direction while others circle around the sides. They try to frighten their prey into running into their ambush."

"But if the harts don't run? I mean—they can't, they're hitched to the wagons. Will they leave them alone?"

Semane shook her head grimly. "Not if they're hungry. If the prey doesn't take the bait, they'll come in from all sides and try to drag one of them away. They can be in and gone before you turn around. They're clever enough to chew through the hitching cord."

"But won't Nod and Melial need help?"

Semane shook her head. "Not from you. Small as you are, the cheshires would go for you for sure. The fireflies will give them some warning before the beasts can pounce."

The pools of firefly light barely reached a few paces in front of the harts with the fog as thick as it was now.

"I'm better than fireflies," Ogma said firmly, making for the door at the front of the wagon. She burst through to hear a howl and a cry of pain. A cheshire had Nod by the leg, while another spat and hissed. Nod's talons had elongated and were covered in dark blood.

Melial arrived at his side, tearing a charm from her branches and holding it before her. An enormous flash of light exploded outwards, leaving Ogma blind. She heard injured yowls and the scrabbling of claws. Blinking rapidly, Ogma tried to clear the purple spots that swam in her vision.

Nod was free and Melial was helping him to his feet.

Ogma realized the danger immediately: the fog was drifting close to the hart's unprotected flank. She jumped down from the wagon and stumbled forward. The mist rolled back to reveal four more of the fog-brindled animals, muscles rippling as they prepared to pounce on the hart's unguarded side. Seeing the powerful cats, the harts reared and stamped at the ground.

The cheshires hesitated, confused that their cover had just drifted away. They looked at Ogma and began to growl. *Now I've done it.* Ogma slowly backed away towards the wagon. She heard more yowls behind her, and the shadows danced as another bright flash went off. Melial was busy, and that probably meant that Nod was too.

The largest of the cheshires had old scars in fur that otherwise rippled in brindled gray and black. It grinned at her, mouth widening impossibly to show row upon row of teeth.

Ogma shrank back, the beating of her heart in her ears growing so loud it seemed to echo through the clearing—no, it *was* echoing.

Before Ogma could turn to look, the great cat pounced. In slow motion, the widening mouth filled her vision—

—and then a lance speared the beast through the side. It tumbled from the air, sprawling in a heap of limbs and fur, and then went still. Ogma wiped the cat's spittle from her face, still rooted to the spot.

Thundering past on the wickerwork horse went Regal in full knight-puppeteer regalia. The horse reared in a tight circle, kicking and biting as Mane and Rump fought like a living thing. Regal sat her mount easily. She slashed at another cheshire with her wooden sword, the lance abandoned in the first. Despite its blunted edge, the sword left deadly slashes in the beast's side.

The cheshires scattered, screaming and yowling into the fog. The warhorse stamped and pawed the ground as the knight puppeteer sheathed her prop sword.

Melial came around the side of the harts, supporting Nod on one shoulder while the frightened animals shivered and snorted. She saw the carcass of the cheshire transfixed by the puppeteer's lance. Its fur still shifted color.

"Thank you," she said wearily.

The charm that had started glowing at the cheshires' approach faded to dull silver. Ogma turned back to the wagon. Semane was standing in the foot box, clutching a kitchen knife. She looked ready to use it.

"No more?"

Ogma shook her head. Semane grinned. She pointed with her knife at the dead cheshire. "I like your way better than hiding in the wagons."

"Yes, thank you, Ogma," Nod said weakly. "It would have been me or one of the harts, I think."

"I didn't do much—" Ogma started.

The puppeteer knight shook her head and gestured to the fog.

"It's true. They couldn't have charged in blind," Semane explained. The knight saluted Ogma and trotted back to the rear wagon.

She thought about this, as they calmed the harts. *I did help. And next time, I'll do better.*

Once the harts had stopped shivering and rolling their eyes in fear, the caravan got underway again. Melial sang to the harts softly as they rode and gradually they forgot the big cats and settled into their plodding but steady pace.

For two days, Melial and Nod took shifts driving the wagon. When Ogma wasn't helping lead the harts, she borrowed one of Semane's books or helped with the chores.

Son had taken to joining them at every evening meal.

Though he couldn't eat anything himself, he sat next to Ogma and flickered happily.

"The stars are beautiful tonight." Ogma lifted her chin to a cloud-free sky. She tilted her head back and watched the stars dance above the trees.

Son drew himself up to look—and stretched, and stretched, and stretched until his wavering shadow towered over the branches. Ogma giggled.

Nod beamed at her.

"Oh come *down* from there!" Tramet snapped.

Son shrank below the tree level to look down at them, flickering uncertainly.

"You don't need to impress a *little thief.*"

Son shrank unhappily.

"We'll be dropping her off at the first town we get to, mark my words, so don't get too attached!"

Son flickered miserably, smaller now than even his usual size, and drifted back to the other wagon.

The puppeteers put on their frowning masks and glared at Tramet before stalking off.

"Can't an old soul eat his soup in peace?" he lamented to unsympathetic ears and began slurping noisily.

Ogma was furious. *That bully! It's bad enough picking on me, but Son can't even fight back. I'm gonna—*

Semane stood up suddenly. "Ogma, will you help me with the dishes please?"

Ogma, distracted by indignation, didn't answer at first.

"Er—" She glanced over.

The dancer doll was winking broadly.

"Okay." Ogma stood, glaring scorn at Tramet's back as she and Semane retreated into the wagon. As anger faded, homesickness took its place. "Do you like being a Shepherd?"

Semane was filling a bucket at the tap. "Sailing the fog all the time you mean?" She turned the tap off. "Sure, we like it well enough. We find hidden places, secrets... things that must be made safe. It's important work."

She peered out between the shutters. "Even with the company we keep."

"But do *you* like it?" Ogma repeated.

Semane turned and gave her a smile. "I used to. Oh, I still do, I suppose. But it's the towns I love the most. All the bright fabrics, strange food, and funny accents. And no two towns the same, just like us. And the festivals! Games and music and *dancing*. I love to dance."

Semane paused her usual herky-jerky movements and set the bucket aside. Then she spun, her dancing lithe and graceful. She turned a complex step, and a pirouette, and Ogma laughed with delight.

Semane smiled as she twirled to a stop and sighed as her hands moved into stutter-stop motion again as she stooped to pick up the bucket and set it by the windowsill.

"Do you like bein' a townie?" Semane asked.

"I—of course I do." *Don't I?*

Semane chuckled. "Said with confidence."

Ogma blushed. "I mean. I hadn't *thought* about it much. It's just who I am. Who I was anyway." She thought for a moment. "I guess... when I was little..."

"Yes?"

"We used to pretend to be Caravaners. To go out on an adventures in the fog. To find charms and turn into—er.."

"Strange shapes like us?" Semane arched a brow, but she said it kindly. She went to one knee and patted Ogma's arm. "Think of it this way. What if you hadn't been attacked? Hadn't been lost, all on your own? What if you'd just come with us? Wouldn't that have been your adventure?"

The thought took Ogma off guard. She considered for a

moment. "I-I guess so. Especially if I could go home at the end. I *do* miss them. Even the grown-ups."

Semane smiled and stood again. "You're usually so happy to see us. Even the grown-ups. She twinkled. But the expression on her porcelain face fell as she leaned back, resting her palms on the countertop behind her. "Except... three of the towns drove us off this season."

"They turned you away? But you bring seeds and animals and trade goods! All the towns hope for trade."

Semane shook her head. "Some of the towns are just like that. They're suspicious. Insular. We try to leave something outside the walls and usually they'll take it, but they never let us in."

"But this was different? Had they been attacked? Like... like we were?"

Semane nodded. "Two of the towns were regulars on our trade routes. As easy to find in the fog as your windmill town is hard. They were afraid. Called us *child stealers.*" She spat the words with disgust. "We have enough trouble without these *blighted* raiders stealing children in our name!"

Ogma shrank in on herself, remembering particolored cloaks and frightened faces.

Semane threw her hands up and stalked over to the window. "Phah! There he is!"

She grabbed the bucket and pitched its contents over the windowsill with a splash. There was an indignant shout and a puff of spores. Ogma could hear the laughter rattles of the puppeteers. Semane stuck her head out. "Whoops! I guess I didn't see you there. How *inconsiderate!*" She slammed the shutters closed and turned back to Ogma with a sour triumph on her face. "That was supposed to cheer you up."

Ogma smiled wanly.

The wagon door opened and Melial and Nod entered.

Melial started to scold, "I know he deserved it, but he'll be a terror for a *week* after that, Semane—what's wrong?"

"Oh, it's nothing." Semane wiped her painted eyes with the corner of her apron. Her tears were porcelain blue. "It just makes me so angry."

Nod looked puzzled.

"We were talking about the... raiders," Ogma said quietly.

Melial sighed. "We should warn the others."

"The other Shepherds?" Ogma asked.

"Them *and* any other towns we find. Maybe if we warn them of the impostors first, they won't end up trying to ban our kind entirely."

Nod spoke quietly. "Nothing we can do tonight. We should rest."

They were a sober crowd as they finished the cleaning, and then slid open their cushioned cubbies in the floor for the night.

How many other towns have lost their children?

Ogma woke the next morning with the warm glow of a pleasant dream fading. She opened her eyes. *That's not right.*

The crude pictogram that little Ambrose had drawn above her bunk was missing. The wooden boards were blank. The wagon hit a bump in the road and Ogma nearly knocked her head on the ceiling.

Oh... Ogma sighed, remembering where she was.

Rubbing the sleep from her eyes, she opened the panel of her cubby. *No one here? But we're on the road.* If Nod wasn't here, he was probably driving, and it was usually Melial that helped to navigate.

So where's Semane? Maybe she needed something from the other wagon. The thought of Semane facing down Tramet made her grin. She went to the door at the front of the wagon to see how they were getting on.

Nod was on the seat as she expected, and there was Melial leading the harts. But Semane was on the road as well, dancing down the path in front of them. She spied Ogma mid turn, and waved, grinning from ear to ear.

"You're awake! Good news!" The exuberant doll danced and twirled back to the foot box of the wagon. She clambered up breathlessly next to Ogma. "We're not lost!"

Ogma must have looked dumbfounded because Semane laughed and hugged her. "Did you hear me, sleepyhead? Melial's found a marker. We're on the way again!"

Ogma looked up at Nod, not sure what to believe.

"You remember the warning stone outside the Old Father's ruins?" Semane asked. "This is another one. A *very* old one."

"Isn't that... dangerous? Aren't the markers warnings to stay away?"

Nod inclined his head. "They can be. But most of the dangers they mark are sleeping—or long gone. We call these older markers sleeping stones. We can often use one to find another."

"Couldn't we have done that with the Old Father?" Ogma asked.

Nod shook his head, but this time it was Melial that spoke. "We tried. But the wizard's marker was made many seasons after the fog came, that makes it fickle. This one's much older. Should be more reliable."

"Like your twinning charm?" Ogma asked.

"Exactly."

The ubiquitous pines had finally turned to something else. The trees were bigger here, *much* bigger, and broad-leaved. The canopy was dense; only a gentle green glow filtered down. The ground was covered in a soft, springy moss. The air was warm and close. It felt like hallowed ground. It made Ogma want to speak in whispers.

Nod set a faster pace and the harts seemed to like the springy ground. Melial jogged beside them through the trees. Ogma bounced along in the coach box excitedly. They were finally getting somewhere.

It was late afternoon when something caught Ogma's eye. It was old and worn—barely recognizable as a deliberate shape. *Is that it? It looks man-made,* she thought. It was another half dome of stone, or had been once, worn and covered in moss.

She pointed it out to Nod. "Look! Is that the next one?"

Nod urged the harts in that direction. When he reached the marker, he reined in and the wagons creaked to a halt. He frowned.

"What's the matter?" Ogma asked.

Nod whistled low in the dark and clambered off the wagon.

"What's wrong?" A soft voice rustled from the branches. Melial's sap-green eyes emerged between twigs and bark, where she'd been running beside them. Nod gestured to the moss-covered broken shape mostly buried in the earth.

"We've just passed the stone again."

"Again?" Ogma interrupted. "What do you mean again?"

Melial studied the stone, a concerned look on her face. She turned back to Nod. "Do you think it's awake?"

"It may be."

Ogma realized with dread that the seasoned Shepherds had both started whispering.

Melial explained in a hushed tone, "Shepherds have passed this way for seasons out of memory. The sleeping stones are *essential* to our navigation. They're the oldest of our markers." She looked to Nod, as if for permission to tell her something.

He inclined his head.

"*Every* time anyone has passed *this* stone, at least in recent memory, it's been quiet. Safe."

Then why are we whispering? Ogma wondered silently. "But how could we have passed it twice?"

"It's hard to say. But if whatever slept here has woken up, it may be pulling us to it."

"What for?" Ogma asked.

"It depends who—or what—it is," Nod said quietly. He knelt in the earth and began scraping away the moss that covered the stone. Time and weather had worn away the stone considerably. Most of the carving was worn smooth. "Ah, there it is."

Melial swayed above, leaves rustling, as she leaned in to study the carvings. Her green eyes widened. "I don't know it," she whispered.

Nod turned to Ogma. "Stay there."

"But—"

"Stay in the wagon." His voice was firm. "Please."

Ogma relented, sitting back on the wagon seat. Regal was leading the second wagon forward. There was just enough space on the path for both wagons to fit side by side. The knight puppeteer nodded to Ogma and cocked her head.

Ogma shrugged and pointed to Nod and Melial, who'd stepped someway off the track and were having an apparently heated discussion.

"Why've we stopped?" Semane popped out of the wagon and joined Ogma on the coachman's seat.

"We've passed the same marker stone again. Nod and Melial are trying to figure out what to do."

"Well what's all the fuss about?" Semane hopped off the wagon and went to examine the marker stone. She stood quickly and gestured for Ogma to stay where she was. She joined the others.

Well great! I'll just stay here then. Ogma fumed quietly. She kicked her feet on the footboard of the wagon. The puppet horse stamped and whinnied.

Tramet had clambered out of his wagon and was stalking over to the rest of the Caravaners. Ogma stuck her tongue out at his back. It made her feel a little better. After a moment, even Son emerged from the other wagon and made his way to the small crowd around the stone. The horse nickered and tossed its head.

What are they so afraid of? Ogma slid off her perch on the footman's seat, hopping to the ground.

Just as she landed, a tremor went through the earth like a ripple in a pool. Ogma froze.

Something burst from the undergrowth with a raucous *caw*, flapping into the trees. The hairs on the back of her neck prickled. She peered into the gloom beside the track. The shadows seemed to darken and lengthen.

Hurrying her steps, Ogma jogged over to the gathered Shepherds and squeezed between them. She felt safer with them standing around her. Then she knelt in the dirt to look at the stone.

"You should have stayed on the cart," Semane whispered, eyes scanning the treeline with concern.

The marker showed a squat, round figure, but it was too vague to show much detail about the god's form. Ogma could see that one arm hung low, well below the level of its feet. The other seemed shorter, though still low enough to drag on the ground. Where the head should be, there was only a blank expanse.

Someone tried to scratch it out, Ogma realized with a creeping dread. *Someone scratched out the nothing where its head should be.* A clawed hand descended on her shoulder and she jumped. Nod frowned and hid his talons back under his cloak.

"Keep quiet," he whispered.

"Back in the cart, dear."

Ogma was too spooked to be annoyed with the diminutive.

Melial crept into the tree line in perfect silence. She never stepped on a single twig; the only sound she made was the rustling of her own branches and the faint tinkling of the charms she carried with her.

Ogma climbed back onto the cart, with a bit of a boost from Nod. She was embarrassed that he'd made her jump. She knew his hands were a sore spot for him. She even liked them. *He just startled me.* She didn't want him to think she was scared of him.

"It's awake, isn't it?" she asked. "What *is* it?"

Nod hesitated.

Ogma crossed her arms. "I'd be safer if I knew."

Nod was silent for a long moment, owlish golden eyes looking at hers.

She met them stoically.

He relented. "I don't know. There is one old myth: Faceless..." Nod stepped away, sentence unfinished.

He and Melial went back to their whispered conference with the others. Semane detached herself from the group and came to sit next to Ogma. She wrapped an arm around her shoulders. "Don't fret. Old gods are drowsy creatures. One lullaby and they go back to sleep for a hundred seasons."

Ogma wasn't reassured. The conference of the other Caravaners had drifted closer. "—won't take one of us!" Melial was saying.

"*If* the words are true..." Tramet nodded in Ogma's direction, and the others glanced at her.

"What does that mean, *if* the words are true?" she called out loudly. They quieted and turned to her.

"This is caravan business, young Ogma," Tramet grumbled.

"Only it sounds like it's not. *What* won't take one of you?" Ogma replied pointedly.

Melial spoke up. "This one's been asleep a very long time, dear one. We don't know how to quiet it."

Tramet rasped in a hoarse whisper, "The words say—"

Semane cut him off. "Oh hex your words! For one as old as this, they're not worth spit. It may not be the right myth."

Tramet's muddy green eyes were fixed unblinking on Ogma. She cuddled back into Semane's protective embrace.

"Whatever the words say, we'll have to speak to it. We're not giving it"—Melial glanced at Ogma—"anything."

"Agreed," Nod said, firmly. "We go and treat with it. Ogma and the puppeteers stay with the wagons."

Ogma was too shaken to argue.

Semane gave her shoulder a squeeze. "Don't you worry, we'll be back before you know it."

The Shepherds trekked off into the woods in single file. Even Son flickered after them.

Someone tugged at her clothes. It was Regal. The friendly puppeteer had pulled some folding chairs out between the wagons and started a fire. Ogma clambered down and accepted a chair gratefully.

"At least we'll wait in comfort?" They sat in silence for a moment. "It's like they still don't trust me. As if I won't be stuck in this stupid caravan for the rest of my life."

Regal listened politely.

"I wish they'd tell me what they were trying to do. I could help. Or maybe I should just... leave. The first town we find, I could—bah." Ogma gave up and settled in to sulk.

Mane and Rump ambled over, chatting away with their key ring semaphore. Every once in a while, one of them spun their winding rattles—laughing.

Regal moved about the fire, setting up the iron tripod from

which the kettle or cooking stove could be hung. Ogma studied Mane and Rump's chatter. She thought she recognized some patterns of the brightly-colored semaphore, but they spoke to each other much too fast for her to learn. They could understand her speech well enough, it seemed, but they only had the flags to speak to each other. From time to time, they'd take a mask from the pouches on their belts and raise it to their faces, usually to emphasize some emotion, Ogma thought, but often they reserved the masks and props for interacting with outsiders.

Not being able to understand their jokes, or the rattling laughter, made her worry they were laughing at *her*.

Regal mostly didn't talk to Mane or Rump. From time to time, she would throw up some signs of her own, but generally she left them to their conversation.

Ogma wished she could understand them.

An hour went by with no sign of the Caravaners returning. And then another. *What do I do if they don't come back?*

The fog kept its distance. There were wisps here and there, but the landscape didn't change. The stillness was disquieting.

A crash shook the forest.

Something was moving through the underbrush, moving too fast for Ogma to react. The treetops beyond the wagons swayed, though the air was still. With a great *whump,* one of the wagons shook. Hitched to the other wagon, the harts shied nervously. Ogma froze. *What was that? Where are they?*

Mane and Rump carefully stood up, pocketing their semaphore rings.

A loud snuffling came from behind the wagon and it was buffeted again. Visions of the beast she had found beyond the village walls, the one that had almost killed Dunkirk, ran through Ogma's head.

Something was scrabbling searchingly around the edge of the wagon. Long, ragged nails gouged furrows in the wooden trim. The hand was enormous, covered in coarse, dark fur except for the palm, which was black and leathery.

The snorting, snuffling sound came again and the hand turned suddenly, palm outward. Ogma realized with horror that there were two slit-like nostrils in its palm. It swung back and forth around the edge of their wagon, sniffing at their camp.

Ogma stood as still and quiet as she could. *What good's that going to do? I can't hide my scent.* But still she didn't move.

The bulk of the thing was still behind Tramet's wagon. It grunted and the wagon's lanterns rattled as it strained to reach its arm further into the camp. At the second wagon the harts strained against their harness, whickering as their eyes rolled back in panic. The arm turned towards the sound, snaking towards them and snorting through its palm.

How can its arm be so long? It's bigger around than I am.

Ragged claws on the ends of its fingers just brushed the nearer hart's flank. The air of its breath stirring its fur. The hart reared, clawed toes pawing the air as it tried to pull away. It leapt against its mate, trying to clamber over the harness to the other side, at risk of tangling in the harness. The ragged hand huffed and turned away.

It wants something else. Ogma realized with creeping dread.

The arm rooted through the camp, triple-joined. It snuffled right into the fire, scattering embers like so many dry leaves, apparently unhurt. Mane and Rump tripped over each other as they scrambled out of the way.

One of their laughter rattles clattered.

The arm swung suddenly towards them, nostrils flaring. The fingers grasped in their direction as it inhaled. Mane and

Rump clung to each other. Regal flashed her semaphore, signaling for them to keep still.

The arm snuffled at them again, fingers clenching and reaching in their direction.

As Ogma looked on in horror, it found them, grasping blindly at the ground at their feet, and then clasping their pudgy, inky limbs. It walked its fingers over their bodies as if searching for something. When it reached one of their heads, the hand snorted and whuffled excitedly and the fingers darted around the smooth featureless face.

What it found there made it furious.

Wood splintered as it struck the wagon angrily, and threw the hapless puppeteer aside. The enormous hand scrabbled across the ground to the other. It snuffled furiously, fingers almost completely enveloping the puppeteer's head.

They have no faces. It wants their faces.

Another frustrated *bang* behind the wagon splintered wood and made the harts jump in their harness. The creature's fist was starting to close around the puppeteer's head.

"No!" Ogma stumbled forward.

The arm released Mane (or Rump) and swung suddenly around to face her. Ogma stumbled back, scrabbling through the still-warm ashes of the fire.

It picked along the ground, walking on the tips of its fingers like a spider, snorting and sniffing closer and closer as Ogma tried to crawl away. She watched the embers flare orange-hot as it tried to suck in her scent above the ashes. It reached for her, the many-jointed arm stretching to its limit.

For a moment, Ogma thought it couldn't reach her, and then the long-nailed fingers closed around her ankle and dragged her forward through the dirt and ash.

Ogma kicked out with her other leg and tried to dig her hands into the spongy moss. The fingers tried to adjust their grip and Ogma pulled free. She scrambled just out of its reach, her back to the second wagon as the arm strained, fingers grasping and tearing furrows in the dirt.

Frustrated, the arm retreated, craning back to the first wagon where it gripped the wooden beams firmly. A second hand, just as hairy and leathery, but squat and muscular, took hold of the eaves. The wagon shook violently, rocking on its wheels. It threw the wagon over. The violence of the splintering wood mixed with a discordant clangor that filled the clearing as the wheels snapped and the beautifully painted caravan crashed into the dirt. *Tramet's bells. His beautiful bells.*

The harts bolted. With breathy screams they strained against the harness and set off at a gallop. Nod's wagon careened into the trees as they broke through the brush and dragged it deeper into the forest.

Ogma held her breath as the thing stepped over the wreckage.

It was squat and broad. Its legs were short, and it stood on the knuckles of its feet. Its left arm brushed the ground, thick and solid as a tree trunk. Its right was impossibly long, with too many elbows, and corded with muscle. The beast had pulled it back now and was holding it folded and bent above its shoulders with the open palm facing forward.

Where its head should be. Ogma's hackles rose. *It has no head.*

Instead, shoulder met shoulder in corded muscle. The nostrils in its palm flared and snorted and the arm snaked out again. The beast lumbered forward blindly behind it. It stumbled, getting tangled in the spokes of a splintered wheel.

Ogma dodged to one side as the beast smashed its way free, trying not to breathe too loudly.

Before she could decide whether to hide under the other

wagon or make a break for the woods, the arm snaked around her.

Ogma froze.

The creature gathered itself behind its snorting arm, rising to its full height and towering over Ogma. The hand snuffled closer and closer to her face.

She had nowhere to run, so she closed her eyes. She could feel the fingers gently brush over her features, almost caressing. The nostrils snorted wetly against her cheek. She braced herself, waiting for the fist to close—wondering if her head would pop like a grape or be spit out like the pit of an olive.

She was suddenly yanked backwards. She opened her eyes to see Regal standing in her place, wearing the coat and hat that Ogma had, as always, left forgotten somewhere in camp. The puppeteer raised a grinning wooden mask to her face.

The arm pulled back in confusion, and then drifted closer, snorting and snuffling again. Ogma could feel the breath of it tugging at her clothes as it inhaled, but the scent on her coat held its attention. It poked and prodded at Regal, almost knocking the slight puppeteer to the ground.

It knows something's different, but it can't see.

Eventually the hand worked its way back up to the mask Regal held over her featureless face. It ran its fingers over the carven features hesitantly.

Ogma held her breath.

It made up its mind. The clawed fingers closed around the edges of the mask, nails digging into smooth, inky skin. The slight form fell to the ground as the mask was ripped away. Ogma crawled to Regal's side, where she was huddled in a ball of pain. She winced in sympathy at the gouges around the edges of Regal's gentle, bulbous face.

A low, gravelly noise filled the ruined camp. Ogma could feel it buzzing in the ground. It grew louder and louder. It was coming from the beast. Ogma looked over her shoulder at the misshapen giant cradling the mask in its arms, stroking the edges of it protectively.

It's purring, Ogma realized with horror.

Ogma tried to pull Regal's huddled form out of the camp. She panted, dragging the limp puppeteer over mossy stones and knobby tree roots.

We have to get out of here before that thing—

Something bumped against her shoulder with a nickering sound. Mane and Rump had unhitched the horse puppet from the wagon and put it on. The horse nosed Ogma's shoulder, hollow eyes pleading. It whinnied and shied away, trotting to the edge of the trees. It kneeled.

Ogma picked up Regal's slight form and carried her the few feet to the horse. Regal weakly grasped the pommel while Ogma pushed from below. She pulled herself up behind—and she had barely got her seat before Mane and Rump broke into a trot into the woods.

She risked a glance back at the thing. Still crooning, it folded its twisted arm back over its shoulders. It held the mask where its head should be. The creature turned its new face to look at her. The wooden mask grinned.

Ogma dug her heels into the sides of the wickerwork warhorse and they took off at a gallop. She could only stare at the thing. It turned its new face to follow them as they left the clearing. The wooden grin widened and it gave chase. It lumbered, three-limbed with a rolling gait, easily dodging the second wagon and the trees at the edge of the camp.

The chest of the horse heaved under them as they leapt over fallen trees and splashed through glassy pools. Ogma scanned the undergrowth desperately, looking for some shelter, some place to hide. *Even the fog. Anywhere but here!* There was nothing.

From the crashing and lumbering thuds behind them, Ogma knew the thing was still on their tail. Glancing over her shoulder, she caught glimpses of the wooden mask, grinning hideously.

A flash of color in the undergrowth rushed past them.

"Wait!" Ogma shouted. "Wait—turn around!" She kicked her heels in the puppet's sides. "That way! Back that way."

The horse puppet reared and thundered in the direction she was pointing.

Where was it... I'm sure I saw—Ogma nearly cried. It was just a tree, but its smooth red bark looked so much like Melial. Ogma bit her lip in fear and frustration.

A gentle chiming jerked her chin up. Green eyes winked from the shadows at the edge of the glade.

"Quick!" Ogma bounced her heels against the wickerwork sides, urging the puppet horse to speed again. Melial swayed, arms cleverly pointed back over her head, pointing out a path between the trees.

Ogma burst past her, not wanting to draw the thing's attention to her. She looked over her shoulder. The beast lumbered past Melial's hiding place without slowing.

Swamp-water eyes saw them next.

"Go on, girl. Run!" Tramet waved them on, throwing a small leather pouch up to Ogma. She nearly fumbled it as they galloped on. Knuckling on three limbs, and crashing through the brush, the thing began to fall behind. Semane and Nod stood in the next clearing, waiting in the open. They pulled up.

"Quickly now," Nod said. "You'll have to circle back."

Semane spoke up. "This whole place belongs to it. It keeps the fog out at the edges. You'll have to find the path."

Ogma wrung her hands. "It smashed Tramet's wagon. And the harts bolted."

Nod's expression fell.

"No matter, now," Semane went on. "You've got to go. Circle back. We'll distract it. Make for the fog at the end of the path."

Mane and Rump turned beneath her and began to trot through the clearing. The lumbering gallop was getting closer.

"How will I find you again?" Ogma shouted back. A crash shook the clearing before Semane could answer. The war horse bolted.

The last thing Ogma saw as her view of the clearing disappeared was Son, stepping out of the shadows and unfolding until he brushed the tops of the trees.

They galloped on.

Regal seemed to be getting stronger. Her back straightened and she leaned low over the horse's head. She urged Mane and Rump to a burst of speed and then they were back at the camp. The one wagon was a shattered wreck, the other sitting forlornly on the loam.

Mane and Rump cleared the wreckage in a single leap and their hooves pounded down the path. Moss-covered trees whipped by in a blur.

There's the stone! Ogma marked it as they passed.

She could see a gray wall of fog in the distance.

What are we doing?

She braced herself and they plunged into the gray mist.

They rode in urgent silence, still moving as fast as they dared. The landscape shifted and melted beneath the horse puppet's hooves. One moment they were galloping over a stony plain, the next through brambled thicket, the next on a narrow track with a sheer drop on one side and a mountain face scraping painfully against Ogma's knee on the other. A great bank of fog poured over the edge.

"Wait! We'll fall!" Ogma waited for the ground to crumble

beneath them. Her stomach already seemed to be dropping away.

The mist rolled away again and they were thundering through a narrow canyon passage. Its mouth opened onto black dunes, cold stars standing like diamonds overhead.

"No! Regal, turn around!" Mane and Rump stumbled and Ogma was nearly thrown. Ogma could feel a sandy grit stinging against her face. "Go back!"

Regal realized the danger that Nod had warned against. She reined up hard and turned them, galloping back into the canyon, searching for the fog to take them out again. The horse puppet slid to a stop. Ahead of them was a blank canyon wall.

CHAPTER 9
THE THIRD-TO-LAST

Nod's warning echoed in Ogma's mind. *Always let the desert pass you by.* The warhorse stamped and snorted nervously. Regal shrugged and brought the horse's head around. She turned back in the saddle, looking at Ogma, as if asking what to do.

Ogma worried her lip. Suddenly she remembered the small leather pouch that Tramet had thrown to her. She opened it. A small stone with a hole through the center was strung on a leather cord. She almost laughed. *It's the twin to Melial's charm! The one that keeps the two wagons together.*

"Look!" She raised the charm excitedly. "If we can just get back to the fog, we're bound to find them. Let's just go on. We'll take the first bank of fog we see."

Regal nodded and they rode out onto the cold dunes. Black onyx sand glittered under a midnight sky. The desert was empty from horizon to horizon.

Ogma was freezing. It was bitterly cold and Regal was shivering in her arms. Ogma and Regal huddled together as the warhorse plodded on. She hoped the puppet was keeping Mane and Rump warm.

Strange formations broke through the dunes. They appeared first as gaps in the stars—malformed shadows clawing at the sky—but as they plodded on, the shapes got closer. The stone looked almost liquid, as if it had splashed up from the ground and frozen, running in rivulets between the dunes. They were pockmarked and scarred, some with deep shadows hinting at deeper caves.

Ogma's teeth were chattering. Her fingers ached and then burned. There was a constant wind that cut right through her and peppered her face with sharp grains of onyx sand.

"It's too cold!" she shouted to Regal over the wind. "We need shelter!"

Regal, shivering violently, pointed to the distant, stony shapes. Ogma nodded. *I'll take anything at this point.* She flexed her aching fingers and blew on them, trying to warm them up. She tried to remember the taste of warm cider and the feel of warming her hands on a fire.

It only made her feel colder.

The shape on the horizon was further away than it had seemed. It took the better part of an hour for them to finally reach it. It was another stone spar, jutting out of the earth at a strange angle. The horse's hooves clip-clopped as the black sand gave way to an island of stone.

Regal and Ogma dismounted and split up, circling the stony outcrop. Ogma rubbed her arms and peered into the shadows, but none were more than shallow facets in the rock face. *Come on. Just a small cave? Anything to get out of this wind.* She almost bumped into Regal coming the other way. The puppeteer was nearly invisible in the dark.

"Nothing?"

Regal shook her head.

Ogma's teeth chattered. "Well we c-can't go further tonight."

A snort and the sound of hoof pawing stone turned Ogma's head. Mane and Rump were pawing at a small divot in the stone face. As if liquid rock had flowed and crashed like a river and then frozen in place.. Ogma eyed the space skeptically. *Maybe it'll keep out the wind.* She ducked inside and pressed herself against the far wall to make room for the puppeteers. Regal followed and huddled against her. The cold, gritty wind still licked around the edges of their shallow shelter. The horse puppet knelt at the face of the stone depression, cutting the wind further.

Mane and Rump bowed out from beneath the wickerwork frame. Ogma was again struck by how the living, breathing horse became nothing more than a lifeless skeleton of woven cane. The two puppeteers hunched over wearily, and almost immediately began to shiver. Still, they stood apart from Ogma and Regal, huddling with each other at the edge of their shelter.

"Come on—d-don't be stupid. We need to s-stay warm."

One of them turned and flashed its key ring semaphore at Regal.

Fingers clumsy with cold, Regal replied.

Still Mane and Rump did not move.

Regal repeated her sign, angrily.

Mane and Rump hesitated and then shook their heads. They pointed at Ogma and Regal both and then crossed their arms over, swapping which hand was pointed at which.

Regal raised herself on one elbow and cocked her head at Ogma.

"What—?" Realization struck. *They don't want to touch her.* Ogma nodded and switched places, putting Regal against the wall and herself between Regal and the reticent puppeteers.

"Satisfied? C-come on, then."

For a moment it looked as though Mane and Rump would still protest, but then they relented and huddled close against

Ogma's side. With four bodies in the small space, it gradually got warmer, though never warm. Ogma closed her eyes and tried to sleep. *It'll be warmer when the sun rises.*

The stony ground was unforgiving beneath her back. Ogma fidgeted, trying not to disturb the others. She thought longingly of the feather cushions in the caravan sleeping cubbies. Mane and Rump nodded off first, and Regal's breathing eventually settled. Ogma sighed and blew out a breath between her teeth.

She tried gingerly to roll onto her side, but that left her arm trapped uncomfortably beneath her. *I swear, this ground isn't level.* Ever so slightly, the slope pitched towards the opening on her right, just steep enough to require a tension in her muscles to keep from rolling into Mane and Rump.

Ogma's only sign that she was dozing off at all was when she shivered herself awake.

The night went on.

Whenever she woke, Ogma looked out at the unsettlingly still stars, searching for any sign that the sky was lightening. *They* are *moving,* Ogma realized the third such time she woke. They weren't dancing the way she was used to, but they were slowly wheeling across the sky.

Regal curled up against her on one side with Mane—or was it Rump?—on the other, and at last Ogma felt warm.

It seemed only a moment later when a clattering on the stone woke her. Ogma's eyes shot open. The stars still slowly wheeled outside the mouth of their shallow cave.

Rump—she was pretty sure it was Rump—had rolled over in his sleep, and his semaphore flags rattled against the stone.

The three puppeteers all sat up at once, roused from their slumber.

Ogma yawned and blinked blearily. Sleep crusted her eyes. *That can't be right—I can't have been asleep for more than a few minutes.* Nevertheless, she felt almost rested.

Rump was pointing to the starry sky and flashing his semaphore at Mane in confusion. Mane shrugged. Ogma clambered over the frame of the horse puppet and stood up, stretching her back. It was dark but not as dark as it had been before. They stood in the shadow of the stone outcropping, and a pale, cold light shone against the black sand.

Moonlight. The wind had died as well. It was no longer cutting right through her clothes.

The sun should be up by now. Then Ogma remembered that it had been daylight when they'd galloped headlong into the desert... and night as soon as they entered. *How can that be?*

She thought of the old wizard clenching the sun in his fist and shivered.

Regal touched Ogma's elbow, holding out Ogma's coat. She'd worn it ever since she'd interposed herself between Ogma and the faceless thing.

"Are you sure?"

Regal nodded and Ogma shrugged into her coat gratefully. Mane and Rump joined them, looking around curiously. Mane pointed one arm in a broad arc—*I am beginning to tell them apart,* Ogma realized—and flashed his semaphore flags, cocking his head towards Regal.

Regal flashed her own semaphore back, and then tossed her head in Ogma's direction.

"Hey, wait a minute, don't put me in charge. I don't know where we are either."

They looked at her with their blank, featureless faces.

"Oh all right... let's see what we can see."

Ogma walked around the stone formation out of the moon's shadow. The moon hung full and pregnant on the horizon, larger than Ogma had ever seen. Its craters stood clearly on its surface, as alien as the desert on which she stood.

Beautiful.

A blue glimmer on the horizon showed that the moon's sister would soon follow.

Ogma looked up at the stone formation they had sheltered under and considered how easy it might be to climb. Like the other formations they had seen, this one was pitted and ragged. Spurs jutted off at strange angles, and it seemed to fold back in on itself.

Plenty of handholds. She craned her neck and looked up at the top of the spire. *Not much higher than the wall.* That settled it. Ogma peeled off her coat and bundled it onto a shelf of rock. Steeling herself, she clambered up to her first handhold.

The moonlight was bright enough to make it easy to find holds: brighter certainly than the last time she had made a climb like this. *When I rescued Dunkirk. I wish I had a tether this time.*

The black stone was sharp. She found a shelf in the rock where she could rest her legs and evaluated her cuts and scrapes. Her hands were raw and she'd skinned her knees, even through the thick canvas of her clothes.

She glanced over her shoulder. The blue sister was rising. The two moons were perfectly still on the horizon as they ascended, not moving as they usually did when distant fog changed the landscape.

The fog must be very far away.

Ogma watched the sister rise for a moment longer. The blue light over the black sand and the liquid stone spars was truly beautiful. Finally, she picked herself up off the shelf to resume her climb. A gust of wind tugged at her clothing. It was cold.

I better come down quick once I see something. She didn't fancy trying to climb back down with frozen fingers.

At last, she was at the top of the outcrop. There was no shelf here to sit on, but she had a fairly stable place to wedge her knees, and she wrapped her arms around the spire. The stone was cold against her cheek, but her arms needed the rest. She scanned the horizon in all directions. The black sand stretched endlessly.

It may be beautiful, Ogma thought, *but will I still think so when I'm trying to drink it?*

She shifted around the edge of the spire, looking for anything but sand and stone outcroppings. *Nothing. There's nothing out there.* Her throat felt parched. Suddenly she couldn't help but think of water. *Wait!*

"There," Ogma croaked. She cleared her throat and repeated, "There! Out there!" The puppeteers scrambled to the other side of the stone spire below her.

"Do you see it?" she called down.

Regal's semaphore flashed up at her.

I'll take that as a yes.

What at first Ogma had overlooked as merely a shadow on the horizon was actually something else. *It must be.* It was a great square of black against the starry sky: a mesa. *There might be water there.*

She started climbing down the craggy spire. It was tricky going. Her fingers were cold, and getting colder, which made her move from handhold to handhold faster than she should have. She nearly slipped twice, but managed to catch herself with nothing worse than a scrape on her forearm to show for it. When at last she was on the ground again, she sat down heavily in the black sand and leaned against the spire. Sweat from the exertion cooled like beads of ice on her skin.

"I just need to rest a moment." She closed her eyes and leaned back, licking her cracked lips. A small hand touched hers and she opened her eyes. Regal had a waterskin.

Ogma took it eagerly. From the weight, she judged it was about half full. With great effort, she restrained herself from gulping the whole thing down. She poured a small amount into the cap instead and drank that. It felt like her parched tongue absorbed the water before it ever hit her throat. She capped the skin and handed it back to Regal.

"We'd better save that."

Regal nodded and slung the skin over her shoulder.

Ogma looked up at the three puppeteers from her patch of sand. "I suppose we'd better get moving. Do you want to leave the horse? It must be tiring to carry so much weight."

Mane and Rump shook their heads firmly. Regal flashed semaphore at Ogma, making each sign slowly and deliberately. It reminded Ogma of how Goodie Hazel had spoken loudly and slowly at Dunkirk, as if that would somehow bridge the language gap.

"I'm sorry, I don't understand."

Regal pointed to Mane and Rump and pantomimed riding a horse. Then she flexed her bicep.

"Oh, I see. It makes them strong?"

The three puppeteers nodded hastily.

Of course it must. How else would they pull the wagon?

"So you could keep carrying us, even?" Ogma asked hopefully. Mane and Rump nodded. Ogma sighed with relief.

That seemed to be what she needed to finally clamber to her feet. Mane and Rump scampered around the base of the spire, and a moment later, the wickerwork horse trotted back to them and nosed at Ogma's shoulder.

Regal mounted up and helped pull Ogma up behind her. They could just make out the mesa on the horizon. It looked like a long way away.

They started off.

The pace seemed interminably slow, but Ogma knew that Mane and Rump were saving their energy. By the time the moon had reached its zenith, the wind had picked up again. Ogma draped her coat over herself and Regal, trying to shield them from the bitter cold. The gritty sand was getting every-where and Ogma's eyes stung.

After another hour or two, they were forced to take shelter under another one of the twisted spires. This time they fared better—there was a proper cave. They clambered inside and while it was still cold, they were completely out of the wind.

Regal offered the waterskin to Mane and Rump. They each took a single capful. She took none for herself, and Ogma asked for none either. They huddled together, and again they arranged themselves so that Mane and Rump weren't touching Regal.

"Why won't you touch her?" Ogma asked suddenly. She blushed, realizing how rude it was. "I—I just mean. When we're trying so hard to keep warm... is it a Shepherd thing? Because I've seen Nod and Melial touch before and—"

Regal's rattle laughed. Ogma's blush deepened.

Mane and Rump were looking from Regal's face to hers and back again. Regal took out her semaphore and flashed them slowly to Ogma, and then gave up and slumped in consterna-tion. She cocked her head to one side, leaning her cheek on her hand. Finally, she nodded once and stood up. Cupping both hands around the divots where her eyes should be, she stared at Ogma.

"I still don't get it."

Regal's shoulders slumped. She perked up and held her wrists to her temples, splaying out her fingers in all directions. Her pudgy fingers stretched and bent at the joints. Some kind of recognition tickled Ogma's brain, but she couldn't quite figure out Regal was pantomiming.

The puppeteer cupped her hands around her eyes again.

Ogma shook her head.

Finally, Regal dropped her hands and turned in pirouette.

"That's Semane!"

Regal cupped her hands around her eyes again.

"Nod!"

Then splayed her fingers above her head.

"Melial! Okay I get it!"

Regal nodded excitedly. Standing in one corner of the cave, she made the signs of each of the three Shepherds again, and then she moved to stand next to Mane and Rump. She pointed first to where she stood when making the signs, and then pointed to herself and the other puppeteers and shook her head firmly.

Ogma's brow furrowed. "You don't get along with them?"

Regal shook her head.

"You don't live with them?"

Regal shook her head again. "You don't... you have differ-ent... traditions?"

Regal paused at this. She nodded once, then shook her head again.

"You're different—well, of course you're different, Melial said no two Shepherds are the same, but—wait!"

Regal was nodding vigorously. Ogma looked from one inky black face to another.

"You're not Shepherds!" All three of them nodded this time. "But—" The squat, round shapes were definitely not human either. "What are you, then?"

At this, Mane and Rump took laughing and crying masks out of their pouches and capered.

"You're puppeteers? That's what Melial called you, but—wait, that's what your people are called? There are *more* of you?"

All three nodded vigorously again.

"...and you have different traditions than the Shepherds. Your women can't be touched?" This seemed foreign and unfair to Ogma, but Regal was shaking her head slowly. Hesitantly, almost sheepishly, she reached into her pouch, and placed something on her head.

It was a crown.

Ogma's jaw dropped. It was woven of cane, just like all their puppet costumes, but as with those, as soon as she put it on, she looked even more noble and aloof.

"You're a king! Er, I mean..." Ogma searched for the word from her old stories. "A queen!"

Mane and Rump were kneeling on the stone floor, heads bowed.

Ogma's mind reeled. "And that's why they're not supposed to touch you?"

Regal nodded, taking the crown from her head and putting it away.

"But then... why do you travel with the caravan?"

Regal deflated sadly.

"Were you lost?"

Regal shook her head.

Mane flashed his semaphore to Regal, too quickly for Ogma to follow. She flashed hers in return and then nodded.

Regal went to stand with Rump in the center of the cave. Mane stood deep in the gloom with his back to them. They stood for a moment, as if waiting for something.

It's a play.

Rump and Regal pulled grinning masks from their pouches. They capered in an exaggerated way, dancing happily around each other and twirling their laughter rattles. Each time they took the grinning masks from their faces and put them back, their mannerisms changed slightly.

They're playing different people. They look happy.

Rump continued to caper, changing his mask and pantomiming tasks of daily life: carpentry, fishing, washing clothes.

Regal took off the grinning mask one more time, and put on her crown, standing elegant and tall. Rump looked up from his work, and she extended a hand to him as if inviting him to dance. Rump eagerly rushed forward, and then stumbled over his feet in a pratfall. Regal simply started to dance without him. Rump changed his face, playing a new puppeteer again, and comically tried to rejoin her. Each time he would trip over some uneven patch of floor, or turn the wrong way, just as he would have caught hold of her and joined the dance.

Ogma had a fit of the giggles, which stopped abruptly when she glanced into the shadows.

Mane stood in the dark at the back of the cave, perfectly silent, facing the wall. He seemed stretched and thin, somehow taller than he usually was. Slowly, almost so slowly that it was hard to see, he turned in place. Ogma gasped. The mask he wore looked almost human, carved with a stylized beard and eyes crazed and cruel.

He crept up on the puppeteers as they capered, but they didn't see him. Rather than stepping forward into the starlight, he seemed to pull the shadows with him. He joined their dance. They capered and fell around him, just barely missing him as he stepped inexorably closer—a shadow they danced around but could not see.

He slipped behind Rump, mimicking his dance perfectly. He wove his arms beneath Rump's and leaned his face over Rump's shoulder. Rump's dance changed. He jerked, like a doll on strings. *He's taken control of him.* Ogma shuddered.

Mane shuffled Rump forward, his knees behind Rump's joints, his hands on Rump's wrists.

Regal's dance faltered. She watched Rump shake and jerk, straining against the shadow that held him. Regal turned her face to the mouth of the cave, only for a second, but when she looked back, she was crying; she'd changed her mask.

Rump reached out to her—almost in supplication. She stretched her hand back to his, and there was a moment of contact. And then Rump lunged as Mane thrust him forward to grab her. Regal fell back, ducking under the grasping arms, and ran from the cave.

Mane released Rump, their drama complete, and Regal came back into the cave, her masks and crown already put away. Ogma remembered to breathe.

"I'm sorry."

Regal shrugged sadly.

The mood was somber after that. With the wind howling at the mouth of the cave, they curled up and tried again to sleep.

Some hours later, a glimmer of blue light woke Ogma. The sister was setting on the horizon. The puppeteers were snoring softly, curled up together again in their pleasantly rounded normal shapes.

Groggy, Ogma picked herself up and stepped outside. With both moons set, the black dunes glittered coldly under the stars.

She scanned the horizon, trying to pick out the black patch against the sky that marked the mesa's location. It didn't look much closer. Ogma ducked back into the cave and gently shook the puppeteers awake.

"We should get moving."

Regal sat up. The puppeteer's inky hand went to her water-skin, and she looked at Ogma. Ogma licked her cracked lips.

"One cap each, I think," she croaked. They passed the waterskin around. It was an effort to cap it again, but little remained.

Regal and Ogma decided to walk beside Mane and Rump that night, at least at first. *Better we all get tired at the same pace. They're as thirsty as we are and working harder.*

The landscape was as beautiful, alien, and unchanging as it had been before. There was no sign of the fog. It seemed the expanse of glittering black sand blended seamlessly into the night sky—as if the stars were marching to earth.

As they walked on and on over the dunes, Ogma lost all sense of direction and time. Steps became stumbling, pace after pace. The tug of a small hand brought her back to herself.

Regal cocked her head quizzically.

Ogma looked behind her. Starlight illuminated their path: a single line of lonely footsteps that stretched forever to the horizon. About fifty paces back, Ogma's footprints had separated from the others.

"I must have been asleep on my feet." She shook her head and stumbled back over to where the wickerwork horse pawed the ground. She put her hand on the horse's neck so she wouldn't wander and again they set off.

The next time she woke to the tug of the smooth, inky hand, Ogma's world spun. Her stomach heaved, but was empty of anything to bring up. Glints of white light swam in her vision. It took her a long time—too long—to realize that she was on her back in the sand, staring at the stars, and not on her feet plodding through the dunes. The warhorse nosed her palm, while Regal shook her shoulder gently. Ogma pushed herself to one knee, sand cold between her fingers, and then staggered to her feet.

The puppeteer held out the waterskin to her.

Ogma stared at it blankly.

Regal poured a capful and held it to her lips. The moisture was enough to rouse her and she drank greedily. She managed to bring the dunes back into focus and took a step forward, groping blindly for the horse's neck. The horse didn't follow.

Ogma turned back.

The horse snorted and shook its mane.

Regal pointed to the saddle and cupped her hands for a boost.

"No. It's not fair."

The puppeteers didn't budge.

Ogma's temples throbbed, and she felt nauseous again. She relented and climbed onto the horse. Regal led them forward. The journey became a haze of fitful dreams: visions of fog phantoms stalking the black land in between brief bouts of wakefulness when Regal shook her and made her drink again.

She woke with a jolt when Mane and Rump stumbled, making the bells around her neck chime. The endless black plain and cold stars stretched before her. A black hole, carved into the sky itself, towered above them.

"The sun... he stole the sun..."

Regal shook her again and pointed. In that black void was a crack, even darker still.

Ogma fell from the saddle.

She dreamed of soldiers in slate-gray steel drowning in black sand as blue beetles flitted from helmet to helmet. She dreamed of Iona's pool, sinking into its cool depths, and drinking deep, clear water. She could hear it trickling down the canyon walls.

Ogma woke with a sudden and powerful need to go to the bathroom. She sat up awkwardly and blinked in confusion. The moon hung above her, and she could hear rushing water. She was lying on a bed of reeds, and to her right she could see the moonlight reflected in a stream that rushed quickly between the rocks and fell splashing into a shadow in the earth. All around her, walls of striated stone towered. There were no blue beetles, no soldiers in gray steel, and no hole in the sky where the sun should be.

It was the mesa on the horizon. We were close. They must have carried me.

Ogma stood and saw Mane, Rump, and Regal lounging

upstream by the water's edge. They jumped up upon seeing her. She held up one hand and motioned for them to wait. Her bladder couldn't. She minced her way hastily downstream, past the crevasse into which the water disappeared, and found relief behind a large boulder.

She emerged feeling much better and went to join the puppeteers. "You carried me."

They nodded.

Her eyes filled with tears. She couldn't believe she had any left. She knelt and hugged each one of them. They patted her on the back as she hugged them and held their smiling masks to their faces when she pulled away.

Ogma sat and watched the stream babble by, listening to the faint roar as it tumbled into the crevasse. She gathered her composure, realizing how lucky they had been that there'd been any water at all. The mesa might have been dry rock.

Of course, most of it seemed to be just that. She craned her neck to look at the striated stone walls in the moonlight. She was lucky that the puppeteers had managed to find this canyon. She hadn't seen any cracks in the mesa's forbidding face from the distant spire of rock when she'd first sighted it.

"How long was I asleep?"

Regal cocked her head and held up two fingers.

"Two days?"

Regal shrugged and pointed to the moon.

"Two moon rises, then."

The puppeteer nodded. She pantomimed filling the water-skin from the stream and giving it to Ogma.

"Thank you."

Ogma stood.

"Well, we may have water, but there's no food and I, for one—" Ogma suddenly remembered the charm, and patted her pockets frantically. At last she found it hanging under her shirt on its leather thong beside her bells. She sighed with relief.

"I, for one, want to find the caravan."

Regal nodded, while Mane and Rump tumbled to their feet.

"That's the way we came in?" Ogma asked, pointing downstream.

Regal nodded again.

"Then we go this way. Maybe it'll take us out of the desert." Ogma started walking upstream. Mane and Rump scrambled into the warhorse puppet, while Regal followed Ogma.

"Have you explored this way?" Ogma asked.

Regal hesitated, then shook her head.

The stream tumbled down a series of cataracts, curving through the narrow canyon. It was more difficult ground than the bank beside them had seemed at first, and Ogma found that her legs were weak. *How long have we been lost?* She was too tired to work it out.

Eventually, the hike burned the shakiness out of her muscles. They climbed over the tumbling rocks along the edge of the stream, stopping whenever they felt winded to drink, or simply rest. Ogma kept an eye to either side of the path for anything that looked edible, but there was nothing but grass and small woody shrubs.

The hair prickled on her neck, and Ogma looked up, scanning the craggy canyon walls around them.

It feels like someone's watching.

High above, there were deep shadows in the canyon walls. *Anything could hide in those caves.*

The feeling passed. Ogma shook herself and realized that Regal was looking at her, head cocked to the side in concern.

"It's nothing. Let's keep going."

As they hiked on, Ogma found herself jumping at shadows. In places, the stream widened into slower-moving pools.

It was quieter there, though sounds echoed strangely on the rock.

The moon passed out of sight over the roof of the canyon, and the blue sister emerged over the wall's edge. *The canyon walls don't look so high anymore. We must be getting closer to the top.* She yawned and wiped sweat from her brow. Regal tugged at her sleeve.

"Hm?" Ogma turned around.

Regal pointed to a shelf under the canyon wall beside them. The ground was silty. At some point, the stream must have been eating away at the stone before a rockfall changed its course. Regal laid her cheek against her hands like a pillow.

"Sure. Let's rest." *At least the ground is softer.*

Ogma nodded wearily to Regal and curled up under the ledge. There was enough room for the four of them to lie down, though Mane and Rump had to leave the wickerwork puppet outside. The silty ground was smooth and free of rocks.

I'll just close my eyes for a bit. I've been sleeping too long as it is. Her eyelids drooped. *We should keep... moving...*

She slept fitfully. She felt dark shapes looming in the shadows of the canyon walls, watching her. Voices whispered just out of earshot. A cool stillness lapped against her feet.

The stream is overflowing, Ogma realized with the unconcerned detachment of one who dreams.

She felt herself floating as the stream gently carried her away.

A voice—a woman's voice—whispered soothing sounds, but Ogma couldn't understand the words. The current caught her and she drifted faster. *This isn't right,* Ogma thought, almost stirring to wakefulness, but the voice whispered soothingly.

Hush child…

Ogma relaxed, letting the voice rock her gently in the cradle of the stream. Down she fell over the first cataract, the wind and the spray cool on her face. The stream caught her and she rushed on.

Ogma opened her eyes. The stars were a river above her, a mirror to the stream that carried her. *It's just the walls. It's just the canyon walls against the sky.* Over the second cataract she fell.

Silhouettes loomed over the river of stars. She knew them. They'd been watching her from the caves. The night was their time. They leaned out from their warrens, studying her with their glittering eyes, steepling their many fingered hands with delight.

She knew if she looked, she would see their reflections in the stream that carried her. She'd see the hands grasping for her. She'd—

Hush, child. Do not fear them. The voice was deep and old.

Ogma struggled in the water. *Let me go. I don't want to be here.*

The voice chuckled, a deep and terrible sound. They will not harm you. They are **mine**.

No! I don't want to!

Ogma tumbled from the third cataract. She felt her arms float into the air. She was falling. The crevasse at the base of the mountain loomed before her. The water rushed into it endlessly.

It's thirsty… so thirsty… I don't want to go!

The darkness swallowed her, and still she fell. The water roared and a silvery mist filled the chasm. *The fog!* Ogma reached for her bells in panic, but couldn't find them around her neck. *Where are they?*

The mist billowed and swirled as she fell. She saw a vision in the dark: Daniel falling. "Help me, little grub!" She reached out a hand for him. Tears welled up in her eyes, floating beside her cheeks as they fell with her.

The mist swallowed up the vision and left another in its place.

It was a grove; broad-leaved trees shaded a mossy forest floor. Brightly-painted splinters of wood littered the ground.

Faceless!

Someone fell into the clearing, scrabbling to get away from something just out of sight. It was a boy, holding a broken spear.

"Dunkirk!" Ogma shouted.

Suddenly Rora was there, pulling Dunkirk up by one shoulder. She was crying. They turned and ran.

A shadow fell over the splintered fragments. Ogma heard a snuffling, snorting sound as a huge arm, black and hairy and jointed in too many places, snaked across the ground. Broad shoulders covered in coarse dark fur followed.

Ogma's throat closed up. Her lip trembled.

It held something in its other hand. She watched as it swung its trophy into the air, holding it high so that it could see over the broken wagons. Black-nailed fingers were tangled in long hair.

No!

The thing paused, as if it heard her cry. Fingers twisted and the head slowly turned to face her. Ogma closed her eyes, not willing to see whose face the creature carried, whose head it was now using as its own.

Still she fell, the water tumbling beside her. As the spray fell, it changed, the droplets turning to glittering black sand.

Suddenly she felt it. She felt the weight of it dragging her down. The ground was rushing up to meet her. This was it. She was going to hit—

Her eyes snapped open.

~

Ogma was lying on the cool, silty sand by the bank of the stream. She was alone. She slid out from under the shelf in the canyon wall.

Starlight filled the canyon, reflecting off the smooth water of the stream. A whisper faded into the dark. Ogma followed the stream. She wasn't afraid, even with the dream fresh in her mind. There was something strange about that, but her thoughts were hazy.

I should be afraid.

She heard the whisper again.

"I'm coming!" she called absently. *Now where is the—?*

A staircase in the stone led up the wall to where the stream tumbled into the canyon from above.

Why didn't I see that before? Something pulled her on. She climbed. The stairs were so steep, they were more of a ladder in the stone. All she could see above her was the black line where the canyon wall ended, and an endless expanse of stars began. At last, she felt the top of the wall with her fingertip. With a sigh of satisfaction, she pulled herself up over the edge.

She stood on an endless plain. Stars spread above and below, twinkling against the blackness. Ogma felt the whispering again. She stepped forward, looking for the source.

"I'm here," she called, and then louder, "I've come!"

No NEED TO SHOUT, CHILD. It was a woman's voice, rich and deep. I CAN HEAR YOU.

"Where are you?" Ogma asked hesitantly. She scanned the top of the mesa in all directions, but she could see nothing but stars.

I AM HERE. The voice came from everywhere at once.

"Who are you?"

I AM NOT AS I WAS. The voice rumbled. I AM WITHOUT NAME, BUT I HAVE NUMBER.

"I don't understand."

IT IS NOT GIVEN TO YOU TO UNDERSTAND! The voice crushed Ogma with shame.

"I'm sorry!" Ogma fell to her knees, shaking her head to try to clear her mind. A ripple spread out on the field of stars.

Oh, it's a lake. It's just the reflection. The voice took no note of her discovery.

I WAS OF YOUR KIND ONCE, the voice sneered BUT **GREATER**!

Ogma started looking for the source of the voice again.

Now I AM... ELSE.

"Oh, I see."

YOU DO **NOT** SEE, IGNORANT CHILD. IT TOOK THE GREATEST TWO THAT WERE LEFT TO BRING ME LOW! IF THEY HAD NOT JOINED AGAINST ME— The ground shook as the voice growled.

Ogma shrank back. The shaking stopped.

MM... YOU ARE YOUNG, the voice purred. THEIR CRIME IS NOT YOURS. I CAN BE JUST. POOR CHILD... The voice was gentle. Ogma felt a warmth surround her. She started to relax—

"Why am I here?" Ogma wondered suddenly.

DO NOT TROUBLE YOURSELF, CHILD... the voice soothed, liquid soft.

"But how did I get here?" Ogma could feel panic rise in her chest. She couldn't remember. "I—was I lost?"

YES, CHILD, YOU WERE LOST, the voice purred. BUT NO MORE.

"I remember..." Ogma shook her head again. There were hazy visions in her mind. "There was a fog..."

The voice rumbled. MANY ARE LOST IN THE FOG OUTSIDE

MY REALM. FEW ARE SO FORTUNATE AS TO FIND THEIR WAY
TO ME.

Ogma nodded. "Yes... you found me." Something was
itching in her brain.

I WILL PROTECT YOU, CHILD, the voice whispered. JUST
SAY YOU WILL STAY WITH ME.

The cool night air buzzed with anticipation. Ogma felt
dizzy. The stars wheeled above and below.

Something's wrong. Where is Regal? And the others? Ogma's
hand went instinctively for the bells around her neck. She
grasped nothing.

"No..." Ogma said softly.

I COULD RAISE YOU UP, CHILD. The voice thundered in
her head.

Ogma covered her ears and fell to her knees in the pool.
Nothing she could do could drown out the sound.

"No! Please go away!"

The voice growled. I WOULD HOLD YOU. I WOULD KEEP
YOU. YOU WOULD BE SAFE!

"You're too loud!" Ogma shouted. "I don't want to stay
here."

The voice became smooth, cajoling. THERE ARE OTHERS
HERE, CHILD. YOU WOULD BE HAPPY.

Black silhouettes of child shapes blotted out the stars along
the horizon. Hollow laughter and sing-song voices echoed in her
ears. Ogma blinked and they were gone.

That was not the childhood she knew. She shook her head
from side to side. *"No!"*

MINE IS A GOOD HEAVEN! The voice shattered her mind
like glass.

She knew it spoke the truth. She could feel an overpowering
sense of peace weighing her down, pressing on her until she
could hardly breathe.

It would be yours if you were mine.

"*No. No!*" she shouted back. "I am my own!"

Suddenly Ogma saw it, the source of the voice: a shadow on the horizon, a black silhouette against the stars. Ogma took a step back.

What would you have instead? There are others who would take you if they could.

A vision appeared in the center of the lake. It was a town, though not her own, and it was burning. Giant, crooked machines stumbled and lurched beyond the walls like wooden towers on chicken feet. Platforms held catapults which threw clay pots over the walls into the town. Inky black figures clambered over the enormous, ungainly machines in fluttering brightly-colored cloaks.

"Puppeteers—no! They were—" Ogma thought back to the attackers who had stormed her village: how they never spoke, how they stretched tall and wrapped Wheeler in arms like bands of steel, how she could only see inky blackness beneath their hoods. *Did Regal know? Was it her people who took my friends?* More ripples spread in the starry pool as tears fell from Ogma's cheeks.

My children! the voice roared. They forget me. Someone else has made them bow, and now he makes them steal your kind. There was a dark satisfaction in its voice. He has my name—the one they took from me. He was as lost as you are. Out of time and out of place. But with my name in hand, the cursed fog brought him to my children. The voice cackled, madly. Now they find they are not so strong without my protection.

Ogma was barely listening, though the voice rang in her mind. She was watching the vision—watching the children on the walls flinging stones and arrows at the lumbering machines.

The older villagers fought desperately to control the flames, unable to aid the children on the walls.

A wickerwork bridge crashed down atop the rampart and inky black shapes dressed in bright Caravaner clothing poured out onto the wall. These puppeteers were bolder, their shapes twisted. They were tall, monstrously stretched, with limbs long and spindly, like spiders. Their disguises were perfunctory now. Whoever controlled them was bold or desperate. They looked so different from the small, gently rounded shapes of Regal, Mane, and Rump.

What happened to them? She watched as they snatched the children, binding them with ropes and sacks over their heads. Many of the children fought and were clubbed down. Ogma's blood ran hot with rage.

The vision pulled back. The fog was thinning where the desert met the hills.

Ogma's heart skipped a beat. *The way is open.*

Then she was rushing backward into the night, hills and trees blurring past until Ogma was flying over glittering black sand. She caught a glimpse of one of the strange desert spires with an eye like a needle, and then all at once she was back at the edge of the pool, facing the dark shadow.

The deep, female voice whispered hoarsely. Even now your fog has brought this to my northern border.

Ogma's head snapped up.

Even now, this is all that waits for you.

Ogma stepped back. The voice cajoled, quiet and syrupy sweet. I do not miss them, it whispered. Their servile whining bored me.

Ogma took another step.

You are a much better child, the voice purred. Yes, I can see that. You are strong.

"I won't stay with you."

Aʜ, ʙᴜᴛ ʏᴏᴜ ʜᴀᴠᴇ ᴄᴏᴍᴇ ᴛᴏ ᴍʏ ᴘʟᴀᴄᴇ, ᴄʜɪʟᴅ. Yᴏᴜ'ᴠᴇ ꜱʟᴇᴘᴛ ᴏɴ ᴍʏ ɢʀᴏᴜɴᴅ ᴀɴᴅ ᴅʀᴜɴᴋ ᴍʏ ᴡᴀᴛᴇʀ, the voice dripped. The shadow shape on the horizon grew larger—closer. I ᴀᴍ ᴏᴡᴇᴅ. There was a triumphant thunder in the voice. I ᴀᴍ ᴏᴡᴇᴅ. Yᴏᴜ ᴀʀᴇ ᴍʏ ᴄʜɪʟᴅ ɴᴏᴡ. I ᴡɪʟʟ ʜᴏʟᴅ ʏᴏᴜ. I ᴡɪʟʟ ᴋᴇᴇᴘ ʏᴏᴜ ꜱᴀꜰᴇ.

Ogma recoiled as the dark shape moved closer, blotting out more and more of the stars with each step.

"No! I'm sorry I took your water. Please let me go."

I ᴀᴍ ᴏᴡᴇᴅ, the voice insisted. Panic rose and Ogma's heart pounded in her ears. The black silhouettes of the child shapes were getting closer.

"I'll give you something else!" Ogma brought up her arms to ward off the angry shade.

Yᴏᴜ ʜᴀᴠᴇ ɴᴏᴛʜɪɴɢ ᴇʟꜱᴇ.

"Your name!" Ogma shouted. "The name that was stolen from you! I'll bring it to you."

The shade retreated, gathering itself into a dark cloud.

"Let me and anyone I call friend go, and I'll bring you your name."

The cloud considered. Ogma could feel her fate teetering on the edge of its capriciousness. *Come on, you greedy thing. You want your name more than me...*

Fɪɴᴇ.

Ogma shook her head. "No. Swear. Swear on your name."

The shadow swelled and a gale rose, whipping the pool to white caps. Ogma stood firm.

Dᴏɴᴇ. **I ꜱᴡᴇᴀʀ ɪᴛ!**

The voice thundered and Ogma leapt back in fright—and found nothing but open air beneath her.

She fell.

∼

Ogma woke on the silty shore of the stream, and almost banged her head on the ceiling of the stone shelf. Cold starlight filled the canyon with a soft, white glow. Her heart was pounding, and her hand went to her throat. Her two small bells tinkled in their familiar chime.

I'm really awake this time? Ogma didn't know if she'd ever feel sure of that again. She grabbed Regal by the shoulder and shook frantically.

"We have to go! We have to get out of here now!" The shadow grew closer and larger in her mind. "We shouldn't have come here. We have to run!"

Mane and Rump were waking groggily, but Regal was already on her feet.

"Quick! As fast as we can!" Ogma's voice broke with panic. Mane and Rump stumbled to their feet and flashed questioning signs at Regal. She cocked her head to Ogma.

"You don't understand! We have to go. Your mother is here!"

Regal dropped her semaphore in shock. Mane and Rump cowered, shivering. Ogma knelt in the sand and scooped up the semaphore, pressing it into Regal's hand.

"Please. We have to go."

Regal gathered herself and nodded. She put a hand on Mane and Rump's shoulders and nodded to the warhorse. The touch from their queen shook them out of their fear. They clambered into the wickerwork warhorse. Regal climbed into the saddle, Ogma quick to clamber up behind.

"Go! Go now!" Ogma kicked her heels against the puppet's sides.

The pale starlight was undisturbed; nothing moved in the canyon. Yet she could feel the shadow rising behind them. Mane and Rump must have felt it too—they burst into a gallop and plunged through the canyon.

Ogma didn't dare look back, didn't dare believe that the dark thing would hold to the deal she had made. Her heart was in her throat. *She'll catch us! She's going to catch us!*

She was terrified that Mane and Rump would break a leg; they were careening down the steep slope at breakneck speed. They scrambled over silt and loose stone and leapt down the sheer drops next to tumbling cataracts.

The ground rushed past in a blur. It felt like the canyon walls were narrowing, like black shadows were closing in to catch them. *Come on! Come on!* Ogma urged silently.

Mane and Rump splashed into the stream, galloping through the shallows, each stride sending the reflected starlight scattering. In the distance above, the river of stars poured out into an ocean.

Are we already out? The wind of their passing rushed in Ogma's ears and her hair flew in wild tendrils around her face. The rushing grew louder.

Wait. Ogma realized the danger as she felt the spray of water and saw the growing patch of darkness in front of them.

"Jump!" she shouted.

She felt her heart stop. Time seemed to slow. She could feel a shiver go through the wickerwork horse as Mane and Rump gathered themselves to jump.

They leapt. The chasm yawned below. Everything seemed to stretch as she watched the gaping shadow drift below them—

—and then they were on the other side and Ogma's heart started again. The puppet horse's hooves pounded hard-packed earth and then glittering black sand.

"North! Which way is north?" she gasped desperately. At home, north meant the direction of the wall with the main gate by the watch house. The fog shifted the landscape all the time, so there was no direction outside the walls. She had no idea what 'north' meant here.

The war horse reared and came back down, turning in a tight circle.

"Wait, that way!" Ogma pointed to a twisted stone outcropping against the stars. It had a hole through the center like a needle. She recognized it from when the vision on the mesa had rushed back over the desert.

She pointed and they charged at a full gallop.

The moon rose, enormous on the horizon, illuminating glittering black sand kicked up from the horse's hooves that stung Ogma's face. Dark stone spires drifted past them. With a direction to follow and Ogma's fear behind them, the warhorse flew across the dunes.

Ogma could only hope that Mane and Rump could keep up the pace. *If they go down, we're done for.* She didn't think she could survive another day in the desert.

She urged them on silently. She was afraid the fog would carry away the besieged town before they reached it. *If we can find the other puppeteers, maybe I'll find my friends.*

Ogma didn't know how many of her friends had been taken, and how many had made it back to the village before the fog came. She didn't know how she would face whatever force corrupted the puppeteers. And she didn't know how she would fulfill her bargain with the dark shape—but the seed of an idea was growing in her mind.

She was thrown out of her racing thoughts, and nearly out of her saddle as well. Mane and Rump had stumbled. There was a crunching sound that made Ogma wince.

Regal reined the horse in. Mane and Rump limped to a stop. Ogma and Regal dismounted on stony ground. *We're out of the dunes!* The change was probably what had caught Mane and Rump off guard and made them stumble.

The two puppeteers were quivering inside the horse

puppet. There was an oily sheen on their inky, featureless faces in the moonlight. The frame of their left foreleg had snapped.

Ogma groaned with despair. *We're* so *close!* She could see gentler silhouettes on the horizon. *Hills. Real earthen hills and trees too, I bet. The town can't be far—if the fog hasn't reached it yet.*

Regal pulled the wooden prop sword from her belt and snapped it over her knee.

"What are you doing?"

Regal pulled a length of twine from her belt and began winding it around the forelimb, making a crude splint. When she was done, Mane and Rump gingerly took a few steps forward. They limped slightly, but the splint held. They trotted in a short circle and the horse tossed its mane and snorted.

"Can we still ride?"

The horse nodded and stamped the ground with its good forefoot.

"Please try not to hurt yourself. If we have to stop—"

The horse snorted loudly and Regal shook her head.

"Okay." Ogma and Regal mounted up and they set off again. It was a slower pace, a sort of mincing trot that favored the foreleg, but it was still much faster than they could have walked.

Ogma glanced to her right and saw the sun just cresting the horizon. She sagged into the saddle in weary relief.

We're out of her desert. She can't catch us now.

The pink-golden light illuminated the hills in front of them as baked earth gave way to scrub grass.

Trees! However gnarled and bent the scraggly things were, Ogma's heart sang for joy. As they crested the hill, Ogma could already smell smoke. *The fog hasn't taken this place yet.* They paused, looking down on a patchwork landscape. There was a stark line where scrubland gave way to evergreen forest in the valley below. In the distance, a column of smoke was rising.

Ogma scanned the trees, looking for some sign of the wooden contraptions that had, according to the visions the god gave her, besieged the town. *Where are they?*

She could see smoke rising from the trees. *That'll be the town,* she thought grimly. Nearby trees bowed and bent at the edge of the valley, their thick trunks waving like grain in the terraced fields at home. Something very large was moving through them: the walking towers.

"There!" she said, pointing the way. "We have to follow them!"

Already tendrils of fog were drifting into the valley, threatening to cut them off. Ogma patted the horse puppet's neck. It whuffled and pawed the ground.

"I'm sorry, I know you're so tired. Just a little further. Can you take me there? We'll rest soon."

The puppet horse whinnied softly and trotted down the hill towards the woods.

Almost there. Now what will I do when we catch them?

CHAPTER 10

THE PUPPETEER

A sh, curling with red edges, drifted like snow on the wind. Mane and Rump picked up speed as they entered the shadow of the tree line. The acrid smoke of burning pine filled her nose and stung her eyes. She could hear a distant bell sounding the alarm for fire, and panicked voices shouting.

"We've got to find that town," Ogma whispered in the horse's ear, "but stay out of sight."

The puppet snorted and trotted into the woods, following the sound of the town bell. Each trunk was thicker around than the caravan wagons were long. *The trees are even bigger than I thought.* The great redwood boles stood even taller than the towers. Her only hope to track them if they'd already left the town would be by the wake of broken limbs they left in the trees. Ogma coughed and pulled up the front of her shirt to hold over her nose and mouth. The fire must have been burning a while: the air was stiflingly warm, and the cloud of ash thickened, dusting the warhorse, her hair, her eyelashes.

The valley, too, was larger than it looked from the hills. *How long does it take them to raid a town?* In the vision, the attack on the town had already been well underway. And the attack on her own village had happened so fast.

I hope the fog break holds.

Ogma peered into the dark between the trees for any drifts or tendrils that might carry them away. It seemed clear, but with ash swirling in the air and her eyes stinging, she couldn't be sure.

Regal's smooth, featureless hand tugged at Ogma's shirt. The puppeteer was pointing ahead of them. *There it is!* Patches of brown stone, smeared with ash, appeared through the gaps in the trees ahead. Regal looked back at Ogma and cocked her head.

"No, keep your distance. They might mistake you for raiders." Regal hung her head while Ogma dismounted. "I'm going to take a closer look."

Mane and Rump stamped nervously, and Ogma could feel Regal watching her.

"I'll be right back."

The knight puppeteer nodded, patting her wickerwork warhorse on the neck in a soothing way.

Ogma picked her way through the brush, wishing she had anything like Melial's grace. After snapping her fourth twig in as many steps, she gave up trying to be quiet and simply tried to stay out of sight. The flames no longer licked the sky, but she could hear the crackle and hiss of steam as the villagers dashed bucket after bucket from their cisterns over the smoldering buildings inside.

She pressed one hand against the stone wall. She couldn't tell if the warmth of it was from the fire or just her imagination.

A crash in the trees ahead stole her attention.

It must be one of those towers. When did they build those? The carts the kidnappers used at her village were perfectly ordinary, apart from the gaudy fabric that had thinly disguised them as caravan wagons.

What if this isn't them? Ogma tried to push the thought away. *It's got to be. I'm sure of it. I am.*

But she wasn't. If these weren't the ones who stole her friends, the ones responsible for Daniel's broken body on the cobblestones, the ones who beat Wheeler while she tried to rescue the others... if this were some new enemy—*then I'm just lost again.*

Ogma pictured herself wandering from town to town through the fog, never finding her friends or the new family she'd made among the caravans again.

No. Not this time.

Maybe twenty yards from where she'd left the puppeteers, the forest opened up. The undergrowth had been burned away, leaving drifts of ash and blackened stumps that glowed orange at the edges. Ogma peered around the skeletons of the trees and eyed the ramparts above.

No windmills, she noted first. *Or lanterns. It's taller though.* She had to crane her neck to scan the ramparts at the top of the wall. *No children on patrol either.*

The villagers inside still gave hoarse and weary shouts as they directed the bucket brigade. Columns of smoke still rose from inside the walls. *How* could *they? How could they start a fire?* She asked herself the question angrily, but she knew the answer: the blaze kept the adult villagers at bay while the puppeteers kidnapped the children.

Ogma tried not to think about what would happen when the fog came with no children to guard the walls.

Nothing I can do by myself. There's no time. I have to catch those towers. I have to.

She could hear the crash of timbers falling as the great towers pushed them over. They were moving fast—much faster than she'd thought such large structures could move. This village's children were already taken, and once the fog returned Ogma's chance would be gone. Ogma turned and sprinted back to the warhorse, scrambling over brush and slipping in warm piles of ash.

She clambered up behind Regal, kicking her heels. "Hurry!" Mane and Rump leapt into a trot, and they sped through the trees below the wall.

As they rounded the corner of the town, a wave of heat crashed over them. A section of the town wall had collapsed completely, spilling stone and smoldering timbers into the undergrowth that flared up again in the clear air. A furrow of splintered limbs and trampled brush where the great trees had been pushed over showed the way the trundling war machines had gone.

"There! There they are!" In the distance, two of the great, spindly machines had come to a halt. Fire from the raining ash had caught a patch of forest, and the path they'd carved through the ruined trees was blocked. The siege towers were being forced to carve a new path out of the valley.

"Look!" Wagons covered in tattered, faded fabric were following the machines. Ogma could just make out frightened faces, grubby with soot, in the back. The wreckage of trees was making the wagon travel nearly impossible. Inky black figures heaved at all four corners to force the wagons over the wreckage.

Whatever was pulling one of the wagons reared up as it heaved its burden over the shattered bole of a massive tree. The beast was huge and inky black, with a dozen pulsing limbs and three heads. One of the axles was clearly broken, but the thing dragged the wagon like a toy.

Ogma felt Regal take her by the hand and squeeze *hard* when she saw the puppeteers swarming over the wagons. They heaved at the corners, lifting stuck wheels off of broken ground, struggling to keep pace with the walking towers. Now that they were this close, she could see their twisted shapes more clearly. Where her friends were short, soft, and round, these looked wrong. They were stretched thin and hunched over, and something was wrong with their faces that she couldn't quite make out at this distance.

Regal nodded sadly. She hung her head and ran her fingers down her cheeks like tears. It nearly broke Ogma's heart.

"I'm sorry. I didn't mean to take you back. But they took my friends! I have to find them." She took a deep breath. "I need to see them again. I need to stop this. Whoever did this to your people—whoever's taking my friends—I'm going to stop them."

Regal studied her face for a moment, and then gestured helplessly at the towers and the swarming puppeteers. Her shoulders sagged.

Ogma put her hands on Regal's shoulders and turned to face her. Mane and Rump snorted angrily from the wicker horse and bumped her with one shoulder.

Ogma dropped her hands hastily. "Right. I'm sorry. Forgive me."

Regal waved them off and nodded to Ogma.

"I made a deal... with your mother."

At this, the noble puppeteer leapt back. One hand went for the wooden sword that was no longer there. Instead she grabbed a fearsome mask in a warrior's grimace and brought it to her face.

"Wait! Please—!"

The war horse reared with an anguished scream. She fell back and waited for its hooves to trample her.

Regal leapt forward, blocking the angry war horse with one harm. She took it by the bridle, gaze not leaving Ogma's face.

"Thank you." Ogma said from the ground. "Will you hear my plan?"

Regal considered her a moment, then took off the grimacing mask and nodded.

Ogma let out a breath. "Okay. I made a deal—but! I made her promise. If I bring her what she wants, she'll let me and anyone I call friend go. *Anyone*. She can't take you." She looked at Mane and Rump, and then gestured to the tortured puppeteers clambering over the towers. "Any of you."

The puppet horse stomped and snorted.

Ogma swallowed nervously, "That is... as long as you're still my friends." She had never felt so small.

Regal's posture softened. She crouched on her heels and put one hand to her heart, nodding. The lump in Ogma's throat grew. She raised one hand to her face and traced the tears down her cheek with her fingertips. "Thank you."

Mane and Rump nosed her hair and whuffled.

Still, Regal opened her hands in a questioning gesture.

"I made her swear on what I promised to bring her. On what's being used by someone in those towers used to control your friends." Ogma took a deep breath. "Her name."

Regal grew still and looked at Ogma gravely.

"And here's how we're going to get it."

Ogma explained her plan.

Slowly Regal's hand went to her belt, and she pulled out another mask... this one grinned a wicked grin.

Ogma grinned back and leapt to her feet. "We've got to follow them."

In the distance, the towers were on the move again.

Mane and Rump loyally, if wearily, waited for them to mount.

Ogma eyed the fallen timbers and shook her head. "This won't work. You'll break another ankle."

She led them into the trees beside the broken path and the puppeteers minced their way after her. It was dark, and the underbrush tangled beneath the canopy, but at least the ground itself was more or less flat. Ahead of them a drawn-out creak turned into a crash as one of the mighty trees fell.

"Maybe we can't see them from here, but we can surely hear them," Ogma muttered.

Once on level ground, Mane and Rump fared better. They kept to thickets and brambles to keep out of sight, the wickerwork shell impervious to the thorns. They circled wide of the wagons trailing behind, staying well out of sight and following by sound alone. This close to the siege engines, each crashing footstep shook needles from the trees. Dust devils swirled with twigs and ash that stung Ogma's eyes.

They shadowed the lumbering platforms through the valley. Ogma could still see no way to get closer without giving themselves away. Tendrils of fog had begun to creep up around them and the burning village disappeared behind them.

Maybe Regal could tie me up. Bring me in like one of the other prisoners. But what if they realize she's not one of them? Ogma wracked her brain for any other way onto the platform. And then she saw another tower in a clearing up ahead. They'd caught up with a third siege engine. This one had been waiting well away from the village.

Ogma stopped dead. This tower carried an enormous windmill on its back. Homesickness crashed over her in a wave. It was as big as the ones on the wall of her home village. Maybe bigger. She could see pulleys and tethers disappearing inside. She could only imagine the poor creatures who had to turn the mechanism.

It blew a huge column of air in front of the convoy, keeping the probing tendrils of fog from closing the path that the machines had taken.

As she surfaced from memories of home, she could almost hear the bells of her friends.

Wait a minute.

"Do you hear that?"

Regal cocked her head. It was hard to hear anything over the sound of the great machines crashing through the trees, but as the two other siege engines caught up, the great machine with the windmill lurched to a halt. The wagons with the children bundled in the back rolled to a stop in the clearing. Ogma strained to listen—she was sure she'd heard something.

Suddenly a much louder bell rang out with a crude and harsh clatter from the forward tower. In response, she could hear a cacophony of chimes drifting down from the others.

"Ambrose! That's Ambrose!" Ogma bounced on the balls of her feet. "They're here! They're here!"

Regal touched Ogma on the arm and held a finger to her lips.

Ogma tried to contain herself, but with her friends this close, a nervous energy buzzed inside her. *That means there are other children in the towers. So how will they bring the new prisoners inside?* Ogma studied them carefully and wondered whether she would be able to follow.

Frightened faces, grubby with ash, stood in a ragged line next to the wagons. Corrupted puppeteers walked up and down the line, some stalking on two feet, while others loped on four, jabbing and prodding the children into order. Some of the children were still in the back of the wagons, bound and hooded.

Those are the fighters, I'll bet. She cheered them on silently. *Good on you. I hope you saved some others before they took you.* Ogma remembered the way Brigid had fought when the puppeteers attacked their home. *Make it so they'll never forget.*

The many-limbed, tar-black beast that pulled the wagons was straining at its tethers and snapping at the half-circle of puppeteers that stood in a ring before it. It keened and wailed in strange echoes and discords. Ogma's hackles rose. She'd never heard a puppeteer make a sound. For some reason, the chorus of its voice was more disturbing than all the other corruptions she had seen of the puppeteer race.

Regal's grip on Ogma's shoulder tightened, and she turned her face away, running her fingers down one cheek.

A large hatch opened beneath the lowest platform of the last tower, and a wooden cage suspended on four hooks slowly descended to the ground. It was strangely constructed, and it took Ogma a moment to understand why.

The puppeteers pulled one of the hooded children from the wagon. The child was smaller than Ogma, but she kicked and threw her elbows against her captors. They dragged her to the back of the cage, which opened into a smaller cell.

One of them pulled off her hood and shut the cell door with a *thunk*. Her hair was matted and tangled and her eyes wild.

"You better let us go!" She kicked at the bars. "Augh! You'll be sorry!"

The ring of puppeteers that held back the ravening tar shape dispersed into two lines, flanking the distance from the wagon to the cage. A hunched and leering puppeteer collected the hoods from each child still held in the wagons—the fighters —so they could watch as the beast was untethered.

With a piercing howl in three discordant voices, the beast surged forward. It seemed for a moment that it might break free of the lines and turn on the row of children. It knocked one of the puppeteers to the ground, and two of the others jumped forward with spears in hand, jabbing at it as it snarled and tried to burst past them.

With a hiss and a final swipe at the spears, it turned towards the unguarded girl in the back of the cage. The beast poured itself inside: a roiling boil of fluid limbs.

Ogma could feel the impact as it slammed into the wooden bars that separated the inner cage from the outer. *If they were just feeding her to it, there wouldn't be a second cage.* The whole structure shivered as the beast slammed into it again. *I hope the bars are strong enough.* The girl was screaming, pressing herself against the back wall as the thing reached for her between the bars.

Ogma shook with anger and silently willed courage to the girl. *They're just trying to scare the others. It can't hurt you.* Ogma hoped that was true. The bars shook again and again as the beast slammed against them. The girl's friends were shouting at the puppeteers. She could hear the little ones crying.

"Let her go!

"Ollie!"

"Let her out of there!"

A pure, clear chord rang out over the frightened cries as one of the children rang her bell. In a wave, the others began ringing theirs. Even from above, in the towers, Ogma could hear the chimes of other bells ringing down. It brought tears to her eyes and it was all she could do not to ring her own.

The beast growled and snapped and gradually subsided in its cage.

Two of the twisted puppeteers slammed the outer cage door shut, locking the beast inside, while others unlatched the massive hooks from the cage and began attaching them to the corners of the first wagon. Ogma craned her neck to peer up at the hatch from which the cage had descended. *That must be how they load the wagons onboard.* Still more of the misshapen puppeteers began hooding the children and loading the ones that had been made to watch back into the wagons. The bells faltered as the children were bound again, but then one more chord beamed out like a smile, a bright chime that rang softly from the girl in the inner cage. Ogma cheered inside, and some of the children began to struggle again.

Good for you. Keep them busy. Ogma turned to Regal,

Mane, and Rump. "I don't think we're going to get a better chance. We'll just have to slip in during the confusion."

They nodded, and if they doubted her, they didn't show it. She was grateful for their grim determination.

"You'll need to tie me up. We don't have a sack, so you'll have to tie my coat around my face. Once we're inside, do you think you can blend in long enough to do your part?"

Regal hesitated, and then nodded shortly. Mane and Rump patted the horse puppet fondly, silently saying farewell. *The others aren't wearing costumes*. The corrupt puppeteers seemed not to carry the props of their people.

"I'm sorry." She hugged each of them and kissed them on the cheek. "Maybe you'll find it again."

They shrugged and shook their heads sadly. Wiping a tear from her eye, Ogma shrugged out of her coat and knelt on the pine needles, putting her hands behind her back.

She took a deep breath. "Okay, we'd better go."

Regal wrapped the coat loosely around her head, tying the sleeves together to hold it in place. Ogma felt goosebumps rise on her arms in the chill air, but with the coat wrapped around her face, her breath was hot and close. Her coat had too many layers of fabric for her to be able to see anything through the weave.

Mane unwound twine cord from the wickerwork structure of the puppet and Regal bound Ogma's hands. She did it gently but firmly. When she was done, she tucked the knot between Ogma's wrists. Ogma groped at it for a moment until she figured out that it was a simple slip knot.

Good, I can get out quickly if I need to.

She clambered awkwardly to her feet and felt Regal's hand on her elbow. Not for the first time, she wondered how she could so easily tell it was her. Another bulbous puppeteer hand took her other arm. *Rump, I think?* She mused on how she could possibly know, distracting herself from her quickened heartbeat.

What am I doing?

They nudged her gently and hurried her out of the treeline to the last wagon in the row. She could hear half-hearted kicks and nervous crying above the clatter of hooks being fixed to the forward wagon. She felt her shoulder bump into the wagon boards and Mane boosted her over the lip. She felt a chill arm against her side and the children shifted to make space for her. *At least with the hoods they won't realize I'm not from their village—at least not yet.*

She could hear the creak of rope and frightened gasps as the first wagon was winched into the air. She felt Regal and the others slip away. *I hope they make it.* The prisoners around her were quiet apart from the occasional shuffling of feet and anxious whispers quickly hushed by older children.

At last the puppeteers were ready for Ogma's wagon. They rolled it forward and she heard the clatter of the large hooks being attached to each corner. A ratcheting sound echoed from above as the wagon was winched into the air.

It swayed unsettlingly and she felt the warm touch of some-one's knee as the children huddled closer to the center.

After a climb that felt like forever, Ogma felt the wind die. *We're inside.*

The wagon swung to the side and they were lowered onto a platform. She felt hands—human hands—help her over the boards. She didn't dare move for fear of the opening they'd been loaded through, somewhere in the floor. The hand led her by the arm into something that felt like a smaller room. The others were led in behind her. She could hear footsteps retreating and the room fell into a hushed silence.

The sound of the winch began again. Ogma could hear a rattling and a growl rise somewhere below them. *They're winching up the cage.* At last, there was a hollow *thunk* and the winch fell silent. The beast's quiet keening was unutterably eerie in the dark.

"Well that's enough of this." Ogma pulled the cord of the slip knot tying her hands and untied the coat from her face. She blinked in the harsh brightness of lamplight. There were no puppeteers in sight, only the other children in their hoods.

Looks like a pantry. It was a small room, just off of the loading platform they'd been winched up to. Through the doorway, she could see the wagons side by side, and the top of the cage, which was level with the floor. A canvas covering had been pulled over it, and the beast inside was silent for now.

Ogma turned to the other children. "Let me get these off you." She started pulling the hoods from their faces and unbinding their arms.

"Are you all okay? Is anyone hurt?" The first boy Ogma untied had dark skin and a mop of curly hair, maybe a season older than she was. He looked at her with a blank expression.

"Well come on, then. Will you help me with the others or not?" The rebuke spurred him on, and he started unbinding the others. As the hoods came off one by one, the children clustered together. Ogma could feel them watching her.

"You're not from the village." The gangly boy she'd untied first spoke up. "Are you... with them?"

"Do I look like one of them?" Heat rose in her face. *I'm here to rescue you!* She bit her tongue.

After they were all free, Ogma picked her way carefully onto the lower platform, where the top of the cage filled the loading hatch. Apart from a cold draft from the floor, the tower platform was surprisingly warm. Another wooden door across the way looked like it led to a second pantry. A steep flight of wooden stairs led to another level.

Jointed wooden beams and ropes as thick as Ogma's waist

entered through the ceiling and disappeared through the walls and the floor. Strangely, it reminded her of the wicker-work mechanisms in the horse-puppet that Mane and Rump wore. *That must be how the towers walk.*

Ogma turned her attention back to the cage and chimed her bells softly—*I'm here, how can I help?* She heard a muffled chime from the bells of the girl in the cage below—just her simple name chime.

Our bell signs might be different. Ogma chimed her own name and knelt next to the cage. "Ollie? That's your name, right?"

A grubby face looked up at Ogma between the bars and nodded.

"I'm Ogma."

"I think it's sleeping." Ollie barely breathed the words.

"Okay. We need to get you out of there." Ogma studied the top of the cage. There was a hatch over the inner cage so that someone could be put in without opening the main door. *What a horrid way to punish someone.* The latch was a simple peg and mortise, but a box had been built up around it so that whoever was inside couldn't reach. Ogma knelt and opened it, stretching down to grasp Ollie's arm.

The girl's fingertips were icy. A draft billowed the canvas covering on the cage. *It's open to the air!* Through the wooden bars Ollie was standing on, Ogma could see the ground a good forty feet below. Ogma's vision swam and she nearly toppled headfirst into the cage. She tipped herself back and fell painfully on her tailbone instead, pulling Ollie most of the way up with her.

Ollie was trying to lever her legs up onto the floorboards when the door at the top of the stairs opened.

"Hey—! What are you doing? Get away from there!"

Ogma ignored the voice and continued to help Ollie to her feet.

The voice broke low. "You'll be punished if they see you."

Ogma turned to confront him. "*No one* is getting left in that cage."

She shooed Ollie towards the pantry, and then crossed her arms and studied the new boy critically. He was maybe a season older than she, and he needed new clothes; his sleeves and pant legs were too short and he was barefoot. He wore a ratty wool cap and had a bit of fuzz on his cheeks and upper lip. *He'd only have a few more seasons on the wall at home.*

He was staring down at her with a dumbfounded look on his face.

"Ogma?"

At that instant, the tower lurched into motion. The boy nearly fell off the stairs, but managed to catch himself on the top step. Gears clacked and ropes creaked and the whole platform swayed. Ogma fell backward onto the roof of the canvas-covered cage. The puppeteer beast inside raged, shivering the walls. Ogma rolled to the side, heart pounding. The echo of a sound rang in her mind.

Was that...?

She tried to clamber to her feet. The swaying motion of the tower's lurching steps was deeply uncomfortable. It felt as though at any moment it would tip over. She could hear the bells of the other children jangling together as they fell over themselves.

Ogma turned to look at the gangly older boy as he hopped down the stairs. He was surprisingly graceful on the swaying platform, running eagerly to her side.

"Ogma, is it really you?" His voice was bright, the dull resignation she'd heard before temporarily displaced.

It can't be. It's just a boy with the same bells.

"Don't you remember me? Y-you look exactly the same."

Ogma reached up and chimed her bells softly. "Ambrose?"

The boy reached inside his shirt and chimed the bright chord that Ogma remembered from the eager, chubby-faced boy out on his first patrols. "Ogma—it's me."

The children gathered around, steadying themselves against the empty wagons as the tower lurched and swayed, watching them warily.

Ogma studied the boy's face. His hair was too dark... and he was too lean and wiry... but there was a roundness in his cheeks that might fill out if he were better fed. And something about his eyes, so open and honest...

Ogma ran forward and threw her arms around him. "It *is* you! *Ambrose*—I never thought I'd see you again! Are any of the others here? I mean—I heard your bells from below—I was lost in the fog—but you're so *old!*"

Ambrose—this new, older Ambrose—laughed. "Slow down, will you?" His eyes were shining with tears, but he was smiling. There was fuzz on his cheeks. "*I'm* old? You mean you're young! It's been six—maybe eight!—seasons. You haven't changed a bit. How did you find us?"

"*Eight seasons!*" Ogma sat down on the floor heavily. "But we were only just attacked." Her mind raced, a wave of emotions welling up through her chest. Just seeing one of her friends again—*but it's been so long for him.*

She took a deep shuddering breath. "I've been lost. The fog took me."

Ambrose sat down beside her. "All these seasons, I just told myself to do what you would do. We tell stories about you! Especially to the little ones—try to teach them to be strong. I can't believe it. You're just the same."

Ogma's throat felt tight. She remembered the charcoal

drawing on the ceiling of the watch house above her bunk. Ambrose had practically been a toddler when he drew that.

"Was it a bird or a mule?" she asked suddenly.

Ambrose blinked at her. "What?"

"The drawing you made over my bunk."

Ambrose looked puzzled for a moment, and then the memory dawned behind his eyes. "I'd forgotten about that." He blew out his breath between his teeth and studied his hands. After a moment he chuckled to himself. "Y'know, it was supposed to be a goat."

"A goat?" Ogma raised an eyebrow skeptically.

Ambrose laughed. "Well I'd never seen a goat before. And I've *still* never seen a mule."

Ogma smiled. "Me neither."

They sat in silence for a moment.

"The others are here," Ambrose said quietly. "Some of them, anyway. Billie and Clara are in this spindler—" Seeing Ogma's confused expression, he blushed. "It's what the young ones called the towers and it stuck. Mae's in the second one. I don't see her much, but I can hear her bells."

Ogma remembered Mae and Maya patrolling the walls together; the girls had been so excited by it all. So... *Mae might be eight seasons older than her sister now.* Ogma shook the strange idea from her head.

"Cauly and young Isak are there too, I think. We don't see them much."

"Is that everyone they took?" Ogma asked. There had been others when the fog caught them out in the open, but Ogma wasn't sure who was taken, who made it back to the village, and who'd been lost as she was.

Ambrose looked grim. "Cole was here too—"

The door above the stairs rattled.

Ambrose looked up, panic in his face. "Oh no. I took too

long. I'm supposed to be telling the new ones how this works."
He leapt to his feet. "Look, Ogma, we'll talk again soon, just
don't—just don't do anything that might upset them."

The hatch opened and a taloned, inky black foot stepped
onto the first rung. Three of the twisted puppeteers Ogma had
seen with the wagons descended into the room. Up close, their
resemblance to Regal and the others was even stranger. She
could see how they might have been normal puppeteers once,
but their stretched frames looked corded and tense. Their verte-
brae stuck out like quills along their backs. Both feet and hands
ended in talons. The soft hollows of their eyes had sunk into
deep sockets. Where normal puppeteers had no mouths, they
had inky black gashes.

The newly captured children retreated to the pantry, the
smaller ones breaking into sobs. *It must seem just like a story to
them. Monsters come to gobble them up.* The children who had
been most tightly bound—the fighters—arrayed themselves
across the pantry door. Ogma stood up and tried to keep her feet
on the swaying platform.

Ambrose pattered over to the twisted puppeteers. He spoke
in soft, pleading tones. "I am not done with them yet." He kept
his voice low. "There are too many of them. It takes longer to
show them—"

One of the twisted shapes growled low in its throat.

Ambrose fell silent.

That's wrong—they shouldn't be able to make sounds.

The twisted puppeteers stalked into the room. One bent
low over the cage and prodded at the beast within. It whined
and rattled the bars. The puppeteer grinned a horrible, tar-drip-
ping grin. Another went to inspect the row of children standing
across the pantry door. It loomed over them, absently flexing its
talons. The last walked over to where Ogma stood alone,

cocking its head and peering into her eyes with its hollow sockets.

Ogma set her jaw and glared back, though its attention made her skin crawl.

Ambrose opened his mouth to speak, but his voice cracked. He cleared his throat and tried once more. "Welcome to the spindlers." It sounded like a speech he'd given before. "I know you're frightened, and afraid of being lost in the fog. But here you are safe." His voice cracked again. "This is your new home. You'll learn to turn the gears, to gather food, and how to fog watch from a moving tower. There are no adults here to protect. We care for each other."

He paused for a moment. The children had drawn together and were watching him. Some faces frightened and others defiant.

"These are the blots." He gestured at the twisted puppeteers. "They built the spindlers. They don't speak—" He looked sideways at one of the grinning shapes. "But they can get their point across. Do what they tell you and they'll feed you and keep you safe."

Ollie and some of the braver children were bristling.

He held up his hands and pleaded. "Make trouble and you'll be punished."

The twisted puppeteer—the *blot*—that stood by the cage rattled the bars again, and the thing inside surged upwards, growling in three voices. The platform shook and inky tendrils grasped through the bars.

The children eyed the cage warily, but some still had their jaws set. *Good for you.*

Ambrose continued his speech. "If the punishment doesn't teach you..." He let the words hang in the air for a moment, so they would really hear what came next. "They'll give you to the fog."

Where the threat of the monster hadn't done it, that worked. The last of the stubborn children subsided, faces haunted.

"Life on the spindlers doesn't have to be hard. There are many others here from villages just like yours. We will all be safe if we each do our part."

Ambrose met Ogma's eyes.

"This is why we watch the fog."

For the next two days, Ogma had no time to speak to Ambrose again. Despite his initial enthusiasm at their reunion, she could tell he was avoiding her. She saw him often enough, but he was always busy instructing the new children in their duties on the spindler. Every time she tried to catch him alone, he found another crisis to run off to.

Not that there weren't crises aplenty. After his initial speech, they'd all been led up into the main platforms. The tower was larger than Ogma realized. There were four levels at least, and it took nearly thirty children to keep it running smoothly. With all the children underfoot, it seemed hardly an hour went by without someone making one of the blots angry.

Ollie was put back in the cage again after one of the blots tried to separate her from a child no more than five seasons old. They put the child in with her. They weren't let out until someone else did something to upset the blots and went in instead.

Ogma tried to count the blots that guarded them, but it was like Mane and Rump all over again. She just couldn't tell them apart. She thought there were maybe twenty of them on this tower. They seemed to live on the highest platform, where the children weren't allowed to go.

Thinking of her puppeteer friends made Ogma anxious. She hadn't yet seen them since they'd left her by the wagon.

The new children, the ones from the village where Ogma had caught up with the spindlers, were split up and grouped with others who'd been here longer. Supposedly, it was so they could better learn the work that kept the towers running, but Ogma suspected that it was meant to keep them from banding together.

Ogma's first task was simple enough—doing dishes. She was put with a crew of five others, three of whom were the younger recent captures. Just old enough not to need supervision, but not yet strong enough for heavier labor. The other two had been on the spindler a while.

The eldest was a girl who clearly ruled the kitchen. Her forearms were wiry and strong, and she seemed to know without looking exactly where to reach for any given kitchen implement, and where to put it away.

Ogma's face was screwed up in concentration as she tried to clean a difficult bit on a large crockpot.

"Ach, use this y'stupid girl." The older girl was standing over her shoulder. She threw a scratchy bristle brush into the crockpot, splashing water down Ogma's front. "Can't ye even clean a pot?"

Ogma fumed but the older girl had already turned away. *Well maybe I would have if you'd given it to me sooner.*

The other veteran child, who had close cropped dark hair and a rosy complexion, met Ogma's eyes and shook her head. Ogma turned back to brushing furiously at the pot.

They were running low on water, and what they had was lukewarm at best. The oldest girl began muttering angrily to herself.

"These new ones just don't know how to do a thing properly." She tapped a foot, impatiently looking at the door, and then made up her mind. "I'm going to the winches t'see what's become of that stupid boy and our hot water. I'll be back *presently*." She glared at the new faces to make it clear that if they stopped scrubbing for even a minute, she would know.

They ducked their heads and kept working.

As soon as she was out the door, the rosy androgynous child came over to Ogma. "Sorry about that. Grace ain't as nice as her name. She's from Twigs. A lot of the ones from Twigs are like that." She spoke at a breakneck pace. "I'm Nute. You're from Windmill, right?"

It took Ogma a moment to realize that Nute was giving names to the villages. Her village had no name, but it made sense for these children from different places to call them something. Ogma opened her mouth to respond, but Nute chattered on.

"I'm from Muddle... well it's Mudhole really," Nute chuckled. "Not a very pretty name, but that's what we had. We made clay, we did." They nodded vigorously. "Traded with the caravans. Anyway, Clara said you were from Windmill like her and Billie. And Ambrose too, I guess."

Ogma straightened up. "You know Clara?"

"Course I do. Anyone who's been here that long... I'm not sure if Twigs or Windmill was the first, but they both sure been here a while. How'd you end up at Tallstone with these?"

They gestured to the other children who were still washing dishes. Ogma gathered that Tallstone was what they'd decided to call the most recent village.

"I—I was lost."

"In the fog?" Nute's eyes were wide, and the others were looking at her with something like awe.

A vengeful shadow appeared in the door.

"What is *this*?" It was Grace, glaring at them with her hands on her hips. She stalked over to Ogma, apparently ignoring Nute. "Why aren't you *scrubbing*?"

"I *am*." Ogma looked up from the crock where she was dutifully, if half-heartedly, scrubbing with the brush.

Grace rolled her eyes and gave an oath. "*Remember Cole.* Here, give that to me."

Ogma's blood ran cold.

Grace grabbed the pot out of Ogma's hands. "I won't have you in my kitchen no more. I'm sending you to the winch team. We need water and that stupid boy wouldn't listen to a word I say. Just started crying." She rolled her eyes and sighed heavily.

Can't imagine why. She didn't dare ask what the girl had meant by the oath. *What happened to Cole? Is that why Ambrose won't talk to me?*

"Do you remember where the winches are?"

Ogma nodded, mind racing. The big winches were on the second level above the cargo platform, along with the cistern barrels.

"Well, go on!" She shooed Ogma with her hands.

Ogma clambered to her feet and darted out the doorway before Grace could change her mind. *Anything's better than that.*

She was nearly bowled over by a skittering blot. This one had four limbs and seemed to prefer crawling along the ceiling.

Ogma shuddered, hoping again that Regal and the others were okay.

Working the winches proved to be more pleasant. As soon as Ogma came down the hatch, the team of children chimed their bells at her. She chimed hers in return.

"You're Ogma, right?"

She nodded.

"I'm Kit, and this is Connor." He pointed at the boy next to him. "We're from Lanterns. Tera over there's from City, and

323

Loll's from Stilts." Ogma tried to keep the names and villages straight. *So that's six villages? Seven? How many villages have they taken from?*

"I'm from Windmill."

They looked at her in some surprise.

Loll spoke up. "Didn't you come in with Tallstone?"

Ogma shuffled her feet uncomfortably, and Kit broke in again. "Well, never mind, Grace won't wait for us to chatter."

He waved over his shoulder and led Ogma down to the cargo level. The cage had been winched over to the side, and the central hatch was open to the air. The spindler had come to a stop, straddling a small river. Ogma crouched down to get a better angle through the hatch, but she couldn't see from here if the other spindlers were stopped as well.

Thin tendrils of fog curled around the stream, but either the presence of so many children, or the windmill on the back of the other spindler, kept it at bay.

"Pretty simple really." Kit slapped the side of a cistern barrel, which was suspended by a winch over the opening. "We winch it down, dip it in the stream, and pull it back up. Only reason it's taking so long is the stream's too shallow. I'm afraid if we winch it down too far, we'll break it on the rocks."

Ogma studied the stream below. Parts of it looked deep enough, but she could imagine that with the barrel spinning on the end of a rope, it'd be hard to aim. "Do you have a tether?"

Kit raised his eyebrows. "D'ya mean to go down with it? You won't be able to run, if that's what you're thinking."

Ogma shook her head.

His young voice was stern. "It's just the fog out there—or the desert."

Ogma looked at him sharply. "The desert?"

"Sure. Black sand, night sky. Spooky place. Likes to follow

us around a bit, seems like. We've never been in it though. The blots keep us well clear."

Ogma filed that away. "I won't try to run. If you've got a tether, I can go down and guide the barrel to a deeper spot."

Kit eyed her skeptically. "Well... tethers we've got. We mostly use 'em to gather food when the fog's too thick to let down the wagons, but it ought to work for this." He considered for a moment. "All right. We'll do it. I'll let the others know."

He disappeared upstairs to where the others waited next to the winch mechanism.

Ogma fished in her shirt and brought out the small leather bag with the twinned charm. Now that she was out in the fog again, maybe Melial could find her.

She worried her lip, the shape of an idea in her mind. *If the fireflies make paths through the fog, and twinned charms want to come together...*

Footfalls warned her that Kit was coming back down the stairs, so she tucked the pouch away. He tossed her a harness on a braided tether and a pair of heavy gloves.

The design was very similar to what she used at home. She stepped into it and snugged up the straps. She then paid the full length of line through her hands, looking for fraying, and inspected the knots.

Kit was watching her with growing respect. She gave the anchor knot one last jerk to confirm it was secure.

"Can you pull me back up?" she asked.

He shook his head. "No need. We can use these." He took the other end of the tether from her hands and started winding it through a smaller winch set in the floor. "Just need to thread the tether through here and I can crank you right back up."

Ogma studied the mechanism. It was unfamiliar, but it looked sturdy enough. "Okay. I'll go down first. Wait for me to call up before you send the barrel."

Ogma looked over the lip of the platform, peering at the ground below. A howl and a crash made Ogma jump, and she nearly tipped over the edge. Wheeling her arms, heart pounding in her chest, she tried to lean back. Kit grabbed her by the coat and pulled her in, eyes wide.

Ogma carefully took the tether from his hands and snapped it to the ring on her harness.

She took a deep breath. *Just like flying.*

She turned around, meeting Kit's still-wide eyes, and jumped off the platform, slowing her descent with the one gloved hand on the tether. From where she swung, she could see the other two towers ahead. The second tower was further upstream on the ridge of a small hill, and the windmill spindler was beyond that. It had turned back and was blowing air across them both.

The breeze was cold but refreshing after being closed inside the wooden tower. The small river ran down a stony rise where scrub pine grew in sparse patches. Ogma could see trees shifting in the banks of fog behind them. Off to her right the sky darkened, a patch of stars in an otherwise day-lit sky.

She's following.

Ogma lowered herself the rest of the way to the stream, swinging to the bank.

"Okay!" she called up to the tower, chiming her bells. The cistern barrel started a slow descent. Ogma slipped the pouch out of her collar again and took out the twinned charm.

I hope this works. She held the charm out in front of her, looking for any change in the fog. It shifted as it always did, but she saw no sign that it might be pulling the caravan closer to her. *Melial didn't say you had to do something with them, did she?* Ogma scanned her memory. *No, she just said the fog brings twinned charms together.*

Ogma hoped and the barrel descended.

"You got it?" Kit called down from the platform above.

Ogma sighed, scanning the tree line. *Nothing.* She looked up. The barrel had stopped a few feet above her.

"A little lower!" The barrel dropped a bit further, and Ogma leaned out over the river, guiding it to a deeper spot. It dipped into the water and the river pulled against the winch as it filled.

"All set!" Ogma rang her bells up to Kit. She heard a mechanical *clunk* from above and the barrel started its return journey.

Ogma turned back to the trees and the distant fog, looking for any flash of brightly-colored wagon paint in the undergrowth. She remembered the splintered wagon in the road. *What if they never got away from Faceless?*

She buried that thought deep.

"All right! I'm pulling you up next," Kit called down.

"Just a moment!" Ogma called up. She held the charm out to the fog so that she could look through the small hole in the stone. Through that slender aperture, the fog riled and the landscape shifted, but still she saw no wagon.

She felt a tug on her tether. "All right! Pull me up!"

Ogma slipped the charm back around her neck and tried to contain her disappointment as the winch team pulled her up. *She said they don't always work,* she berated herself. *Maybe if the fog gets closer.*

The journey back up to the platform was less pleasant than the journey down. Disappointment robbed her of the sensation of flying, and instead she just felt the straps of the harness digging into her thighs. She was glad to finally clamber back onto the platform.

"Nicely done." Kit clapped her on the back. "That worked a treat. I'm sure they'll put you on the tethers after this."

Ogma nodded but didn't return his smile. She spent the rest of the afternoon preoccupied.

That afternoon, she sat with the winch team for her meal. Grace directed the food line with an iron ladle, and most of the children were too tired to do anything but eat. Still, there were a few genuine smiles as some sat with their friends and complained together about the day's labor.

Two girls about Ogma's age, one dark and one fair, approached the table.

"May we sit with you?" They seemed to be asking Ogma, so she nodded, and scooted over on the bench. They sat next to her for a moment eating their stew in pleasant silence. Then the blonde one giggled. Realization dawned on Ogma.

"Billie? Clara?"

The two burst out laughing. Grace hushed them but they ignored her.

"Took you a minute, didn't it?"

"We spotted you right away."

"It's true, isn't it?" Billie touched Ogma's shoulder as if hardly able to believe she was there. "You haven't changed a bit. It's been *ages*."

The two girls had still been small enough for Ogma to carry them over her shoulder when she'd seen them last. She nodded mutely.

Clara leaned in to give her a hug. "I'm glad we recognized you. You look just the same! I remember the others. Daniel, Brigid..."

"Daniel used to brush our hair."

Ogma gave a watery smile. "Mine too. He called me little grub."

"Ha! I remember that. But their faces are fuzzy..."

"Is Wheeler here?" Ogma hardly dared hope.

Clara and Billie's faces fell.

"No... he's not here."

"So he was lost. Like me." Ogma swallowed a lump in her throat. *But if he's aged like them... too old. He was* already *too old.* She put her head in her hands.

The table fell quiet for a moment. Kit and the others were respectfully silent. They too had friends they'd lost.

Ogma shook away visions of phantom claws reaching for Wheeler's throat. *I can't. I just can't think about that right now.* She gathered her courage to ask another question she wasn't sure she wanted the answer to. "Grace said something. She didn't like how I was scrubbing the dishes—"

The two girls snorted at that.

"She said, 'Remember Cole.'"

Clara and Billie sobered.

"Remember Cole." As soon as Ogma said it, Kit and the others repeated it in a somber chorus.

Ogma grasped the girls' hands. "What does that mean? Are they talking about our Cole? Ambrose said he *was* here." Cole had been such a sober child. He always took the watch so seriously.

Billie looked at her hands, and then up at Ogma. "Most of the children here don't remember, even though they say the words."

"How could they?" Clara put in. "*I* barely remember. It weren't long after we were taken."

Billie nodded. "There weren't no spindlers then. Just the wagons. We lived in an old quarry. That's where the blots took us."

"They chained us up!" Clara added, indignantly, "Shackled us to this wall outside the cave."

"Cole wouldn't have it. He kept fighting 'em and fighting 'em till finally the blots got fed up."

Ogma swallowed a knot in her throat. "What happened?"

The two girls looked at each other and lowered their voices. "Most of 'em here don't remember this, but there's a *king* blot."

Clara shook her head. "I don't think he *is* a blot. I think I saw him once just inside the cave. I could see his hands. I think he's a person."

"Well whoever he is—back in the quarry days, if you misbehaved, they'd take you to the cave." She shivered. "They'd leave you in the dark, and then... *something*... would whisper to you in the dark. Whisper and whisper til you begged to be let out. Begged to be good."

That's the one, Ogma told herself. *That's who I have to find. The one who stole the name of the shadow in the desert.*

"After that you got straight to work and didn't make any trouble."

"Except Cole. He must have been in ten times. He kept trying to escape. Kept telling us we should fight. Then the last time he went in..."

"He never came out again."

The girls fell silent. Kit and the others were listening open-mouthed.

"Hard to remember he was actually one of us. It's just a story we tell now. To make the little ones behave, y'know?"

"'Remember Cole?'" Billie shook her finger. "'If you keep that up, you'll wind up just like him.'" She sniffed and wiped her eyes. "We were so young when it happened. Seeing you—it makes it real again."

"I hate this place," Clara said.

"Hush."

"I do! Sometimes I think I don't, but I really do. I *hate* it."

"Shh. You don't want the blots hearing that kind of talk."

Clara quieted. Billie had more to say, but she whispered it like gossip. "Old king blot—he has them all wrapped around his finger. They're like puppets to him. After Cole disappeared, he made 'em build the spindlers."

"He's here, I think," Clara said. "In the third tower. None of us go there, just the blots."

"Almost none of us," Billie corrected. "Ambrose has been. He won't talk about it though."

As if summoned, Ambrose appeared at the doorway, flanked by two of the blots. The girls' faces fell. "Oh no... is it time already?"

A rash of whispers whipped around the room and then fell silent. The veteran children looked grim, the new ones puzzled.

"Listen carefully, everyone. You've all done very well. You new lot have learned quickly and the rest of you have done good teaching. The blots are pleased."

He doesn't sound very happy about it.

Ambrose cleared his throat. "That means you're done learning. We'll be doing a tower trade. Winch and larder teams, split the food and water. The rest of you—I've had your nominations for those to go."

There were groans around the room, and dishes clattered as the children stood up.

Ogma whispered in Billie's ear. "What does he mean, 'those to go'?"

"Normally a tower trade just means we send over half the food and water we've gathered to the other spindler," Billie explained. "But this time, some of us or some of the new ones will go with them to live in the other tower."

"It happens every time they take a new village," Clara continued. "They train the children here, and then they split us up and send us over."

"I wish they wouldn't do it. Ambrose tries his best, but the blots won't let him keep us together. They want to split the villages so no one tries to escape."

Clara snorted. "Not that we *could* escape. Where would we go?"

"It's always hardest on the new ones. At least if we go, we might see some old friends again. They'll just be separated. More strangers."

Ogma wanted to ask a dozen more questions, but people were bustling all around them: a cacophony of frantic activity. Ogma found herself swept up by Kit and the others from winch duty.

"Come on. You're good with tethers, you should watch this part." Kit led Tera, Connor, and Loll careening through the hallways and up the ladders, dodging other children carrying sacks of food and other supplies to be transferred over. Ogma struggled to keep up. They were going higher up the platforms than Ogma had yet been.

At an upper landing, Kit paused and they caught their breath. He looked to Ogma again. "If you wind up working tethers, you might have to do this someday."

He opened a hatch and they emerged on a wooden catwalk that ringed the outside of the spindler. The towers settled to a halt on level ground, and Ogma could see other children flanked by looming blots on the corresponding catwalk across the way. On the far platform, someone was swinging a weight on the end of a rope. They released and the rope sailed towards their railing, falling too early and clattering on the wooden boards of the spindler body below them.

The other crew wound the rope back in and tried again. This time the weighted rope sailed cleanly over the gap.

"Careful now!" Kit warned. Ogma stepped back as the heavy hook clattered to the boards. One of the tether team on this spindler scooped it up and hooked it to a complex-looking winch mounted to the rail. After threading it through the wheels of the device, Loll began turning a crank which first tightened the slack in the rope line, and then began pulling the rope across the gap in a continuous loop.

Across the way, someone attached a hanger to the rope, and a simple bridge of wooden slats was winched across the gap between the two towers. Ambrose emerged from one of the hatches and started directing the children across the gap. He demonstrated how to walk out onto the bridge with one hand on the rope. It swayed beneath him, but truthfully, compared to the swaying of the spindlers themselves, it didn't look that bad.

The children in line to cross didn't seem to think so. They clung to each other with frightened faces, knuckles white on the ropes. A young boy had dropped to all fours on the platform and thrown up his lunch.

An older girl with three small ones hanging onto her belt was the first to cross. Others followed, some clinging to the rope, some walking across more confidently. Most of those being sent over were new children from Tallstone—probably half of those who had been captured. But a few veterans crossed as well.

One girl turned back halfway, tears running down her cheeks. "Ambrose—can't I stay?"

One of the blots growled.

Ambrose stepped out onto the platform. Ogma could see the girl pleading with him. He held out his hands in sympathy, but gestured back at the blot behind him.

The slap echoed off the walls of the tower. The girl balled her hands into fists as Ambrose nursed his cheek, and then turned on her heel and stalked across the bridge. Ambrose's shoulders fell.

I can't watch this. Face hot with anger and shame, Ogma fled along the catwalk towards the other side of the tower. Kit started to follow, but Connor held him back. Ogma was thankful. She wanted to be alone.

How can it be so wrong? How can they live like this? She

thought of Clara and Billie laughing at the dinner table. *How can they laugh in a place like this?*

The rear balcony of the tower was utterly deserted. Ogma sat on the planks, feet dangling, and watched the stars come out and begin to dance. The moon's blue sister was high in the sky, though she herself was hidden.

For that matter, how'd we ever laugh at home? Skinned knees and soggy patrols. Fog phantoms every night. She hugged her knees. *Even if we aged off the wall before something worse happened, half of us always had to leave.*

She sat disconsolately in the cold and tried to tune out the quiet sobs of children who were being separated from their friends. *Is this so different?* She didn't blame Ambrose; it was clear that he didn't have much choice. He was trying to keep the blots from having their way by force.

It is. It is different. The towns were hard too, but this... we were stolen for this.

Ogma blinked and rubbed her eyes. *What was that—?*

She jolted out of her reverie as her mind finally realized what her eyes were seeing. She bolted to her feet, scanning the dark.

Where was it? A flash of light in the dark had caught her eye. *Please let it be real...*

The fog was drifting in lazy coils around the trees. It seemed to grow bolder in the dark, drifting closer to where the towers held still. Ogma gripped the rail tightly in both hands, eyes straining in the gloom.

Nothing.

Wait, I wonder if—

Ogma fumbled in her pockets. She pulled out the glass firefly, and the stone on the cord. She cupped the firefly in her hand, willing it to life. It began to glow.

Ogma chewed her lip. *Now maybe...* She held the stone on

the cord to eye level and held the firefly charm out in front of her. Through the aperture in the stone, she could see the charm in the foreground, and the trees behind.

She panned slowly across the landscape. The firefly flickered and brightened.

Yes! Ogma could see fireflies in the woods beyond. They winked in and out, traveling in a line on the edge of the fog bank. The landscape shifted.

Ogma scanned the trees. There was a small silver flash.

There! Near that redwood. A branch with rich red-brown bark dipped—*Wait! That's Melial!* The Shepherd waved up at her, silver charms glinting in the moonlight.

Ogma's heart soared. *It worked! They found me!* She wanted to shout her joy into the night. Melial was pointing. Ogma followed the line of her arms and saw a brighter green and yellow glow. *That's a firefly lantern—one of the wagons!*

Barely restraining herself, Ogma chimed her bells as loudly as she dared and held up her hands.

Just wait. I'll—please just wait.

Ogma turned and ran for one of the hatches. She dashed inside and barreled down the stairs. The interior of the tower was dark. Most of the lamps had been extinguished while the children and the blots were above.

Ogma's footfalls sounded like thunder in her ears in the darkened hallways. She careened around a corner and bounced off an inky black shape. She fell sprawling to the floorboards. *Oh no—not now!* She tried to scramble away but two pairs of hands pinned her arms, pulling her around. A third face loomed over her in the dark.

"Regal!" It was her friends. "Mane. Rump. Are you all right?"

The puppeteers nodded.

"Where have you been?"

They covered their faces with their hands.

"Hiding, of course. You've got to come with me! Melial's here. I've found the caravan!" The puppeteers nodded excitedly and clambered after her as she turned and ran for the stairs. She leapt down the rungs from level to level until she'd reached the bottom platform.

The cage. It was in its usual place, set into the opening that made up the main hatch. *We'll have to move it.* Ogma scrambled for the ropes and hooks of the large interior winch. She heard the beast mutter as she clattered the hooks against the cage.

Oh please be quiet.

She looked up and saw the puppeteers standing rigidly by the stairs. They were staring at the cage.

"Can you help me?"

She found the crank mechanism and began winding. At the top of the winch's arc, she had to jump in the air and put all her weight on it, even with the pulleys. Impossibly slowly, the cage rose through the floor. Ogma went to the bars to try and swing the cage aside. She pushed with as much weight as she dared that close to the edge. As the cage swung, the beast inside wailed a sobbing chorus.

Mane and Rump fell across Ogma's feet, weeping with their fingertips down their faces. Regal stood perfectly still. Anger came off the puppeteer's noble form in shimmering waves.

"I'm sorry. These were your friends, weren't they?"

Regal nodded. The furious puppeteer reached into her belt pouch and raised a mask to her face. A jagged grimace tore the lower half of the mask, thorns curled around the corners of the eye sockets. Though the furious mask was not directed at her, Ogma couldn't help but step back.

"Maybe the Caravaners can help. Please, will you help me move it?"

After a moment, Regal inclined her head and came to Ogma's side to help her pull. As they exposed the hatch below, the cold night air made her shiver.

Please still be there, please still be there. Ogma ran to the smaller winch with the tether line and tossed the harness down through the hatch. She held the tether with both hands and waited.

The moment stretched, and just as she was ready to scream with impatience, she felt two hard jerks on the line.

"Yes!" She said it aloud and clapped a hand over her mouth. The beast in the cage grumbled, turning over in its sleep. She ran to the smaller winch arm and began winding.

They've found me. We can do this. We can do this.

Slowly, the winch pulled up the leather cord, and Ogma could hear a faint tinkling of silver charms as Melial's branches crested over the edge of the hatch. As soon as she pulled herself over, Ogma ran into her arms.

"You found me! You're here!"

Melial chuckled softly. "That we did, little one." Ogma didn't mind so much when Melial said it. "Now let's get out of here. I've never seen anything like this, but it's not safe."

Ogma stepped back and shook her head.

"We can't. My friends are here! From my village. These are the ones who took them."

"So you found them, then. Good for you, child! But we'll have to be careful. Sneaking them out won't be easy—"

"You don't understand! We have to rescue all of them." Ogma unhitched Melial from the harness and tossed it back down the hole. "Even the blots—the puppeteers! There are other puppeteers here, only they've been... *changed.*"

Melial let out an angry breath, but there was pity and regret in her eyes. "Ogma..."

"I have a plan. I found something." Ogma hesitated. "In the desert."

"The desert?" The fear was plain in Melial's voice. She knelt and took Ogma by the shoulders. "Are you all right, child? Are you whole?"

Ogma looked away. "I'm fine."

Two hard jerks came on the tether, and Ogma began winding.

"We got out." Behind her, emerging from the hatch was a girl with tousled hair and a boyish grin that Ogma had not expected to see.

"Rora?"

Rora's grin widened as she pulled herself over the edge of the platform and tackled Ogma with a bruising hug.

"But how?" Tears stung Ogma's eyes.

"It's a long story. The old man is here too. And Dunkirk." Rora stepped back to shrug off the harness. Her eyes glittered as well.

Ogma's vision swam. It was too much.

Melial put one arm around Ogma's shoulder. "We'll hear you out. The puppeteers and I can help the others up. Go talk."

Ogma nodded mutely and led Rora into the same pantry that the hooded children had been herded into. She sat down heavily on a crate.

"How? Just... how?"

Rora took a deep breath. "The old man. His name is Somerset, by the way. He told me." Rora paused, apparently as stunned by the old man's speech as anything else that had happened to her. "He led the way; followed these... stones. Half-buried out in the fog." She shook her head as if she hardly believed it herself.

"The sleeping stones. The markers. That's a Caravaner thing—how'd he know?"

"He traveled with them for a while, I guess." Rora worried her lip. "We thought it was the Caravaners who took you. Or I did, at least. He seemed sure he could find them. Well anyway, we followed those stones until—no, I'm telling this all backwards."

"What made him think he could find us?"

"We had these." Rora pulled a handful of iridescent blue fragments from her pockets.

"After the attack, the old man—Somerset—he got agitated. He wanted to go after you. We thought he was crazy. Dunkirk was right there with him though. The crazy old fool rifled through all our things—practically tore apart the watchtower—until we found these." She held up one of the fragments. "Bowen had some in his bunk."

"Those were from Dunkirk's armor."

"Exactly! And the Caravaners had the rest of it, right? Somerset seemed to think it would help us find them. Maybe find you."

Ogma spoke slowly, the shape of the idea coming into focus. "It must work like the twinned charms."

Rora gave her a blank look.

Ogma pulled the small stone from her pocket and handed it to Rora.

"That's how the caravan found me. It's a twinned stone. There's another like it from the same river, and they've both got a hole through the center. The fog likes to put twinned things together. The pieces of Dunkirk's armor... I'm not sure there's anything like it anywhere else. Maybe the fog tried to put them back together."

Rora shook her head. "I'm not sure it did. That was the problem. Instead of finding you, they led us to—I think it was a battlefield." Rora wrinkled her brow. "Dunkirk recognized it. He, um... he started crying. And digging in the dirt. He kept

saying these names, over and over. His fellow soldiers, I think."
"

Ogma shook her head.

"Anyway... after he... afterwards, he wouldn't talk about it. And we thought we were lost for good."

Ogma let out a breath. "I know that feeling."

"That's when the old man started following those stones. The markers I guess. He found one buried in the dirt nearby, and he seemed to think it gave us a chance. It seemed like the fog was just taking us anywhere, but—"

"And the fog didn't touch him? That really was him, in Wheeler's story? It was true?"

She remembered the strange treasures she'd seen in the old man's chest when he bargained with Nod. "It was. He's immune."

They both contemplated that in silence for a moment.

"Where was I? Right—the stones. So we kept walking and everything kept changing, and frankly I have no idea where we were going, but we kept finding more stones." Rora took a breath. "And then we found one of the wagons. The harts were dragging it through the trees. Dunkirk had to use his running charm or we'd never have caught them."

"I'm glad you found them."

Rora nodded. "Too bad there was no one inside. But we heard the crashing in the trees then. And voices. We followed them until we found the other wagon. It was smashed to bits. And—and—"

"Faceless. You found Faceless."

Rora closed her eyes and nodded.

"When he saw the wagon—*that's* when Somerset looked scared. We'd been out in the fog for days and I'd never seen him scared before." She fell quiet again.

"What happened?"

Rora smoothed her hands against her knees. "Son stayed with us while the others led that *thing* away.. He's pretty friendly for a shadow. Nod and the others circled back. They—they didn't all make it."

"Oh no... who-?"

Rora's jaw worked silently. "I—I don't think I can talk about it."

Ogma shook her head and patted Rora's hand. "Then don't. What happened after?"

"We only just missed you! Melial said you had a charm that should bring you to us, but it wasn't working. We tried for days."

"I was somewhere the fog couldn't reach."

Silence fell and Rora stared grimly into space.

Ogma reached out and took her hand. "I'm glad you came. Is Effie with you?"

Rora shook her head ruefully. "She tricked me, y'know. As soon as the old man and Dunkirk had the mad idea to go after you, she knew I'd want to go." She paused and looked at her hands. "But after you disappeared and so many of the others were taken... there weren't many left who were old enough to manage the wall."

"How did she convince you to go?"

Rora chuckled. "She didn't. As soon as Dunkirk explained what they were going to do, she insisted that they needed help, and volunteered herself. She knew I wouldn't let her do something so stupid."

Ogma smirked wryly. "So you insisted on going instead."

Rora blushed.

Ogma haltingly asked the last question she still needed. She knew how many children had been taken by the puppeteers, but not how many had been saved. "Who made it back?"

"Brigid is there. She was injured pretty badly in the attack, but they didn't even try to take her. She was on the mend when we left. And Eric had gone to cover your part of the west. He's pretty reliable."

"Effie's reliable too."

Rora snorted at that.

"In her own way. Anyone else?"

Rora shook her head. "They took Cole, I think. I hope he's here." Ogma winced, but let Rora continue. "Bowen managed to stay out of sight. He's been taking care of the little ones."

Ogma was quiet a moment. "Daniel didn't make it, did he?"

Rora picked up Ogma's hand and squeezed it. "No, he didn't."

Rora's face blurred as Ogma's eyes filled with tears. The girls wept together, mourning their friend.

Once the tears slowed, Ogma dried her eyes. "Emma?"

Rora sighed. "She made it back. That tether of yours was a good trick. We got all of them back inside. But Emma's still—she got hit pretty hard. She still needs some help with... just about everything." Rora hastened to offer hope. "At least she did when we left. It was only a few days after, though, and Bowen was doing a good job taking care of her. Maybe she's better now."

"I hope so." Ogma was still heartbroken remembering the vicious head wound that had left her hardly able to stand on her own. *It feels so long ago.*

Rora picked up her story. "By the time I figured out that Effie had tricked me into thinking I was protecting her—"

"Giving you the excuse to go," Ogma cut in.

"—we were already deep in the fog." Rora studied her hands in her lap. Her shoulders started to shake. "I wonder if I'll see her again..."

Ogma put an arm around her. "I know you will."

"Ha." Rora shrugged Ogma off and wiped her eyes. "How do you know?"

Ogma held up the twinned charm again. "You two belong together."

Rora smiled through her tears. "Maybe you're right."

Ogma gave Rora another hug, and then stood on the wooden platform.

"Come on, we have work to do."

Ogma and Rora stepped into the lantern light where Melial waited. Old Man Somerset stood there, dressed in tattered clothes. He held the bird's skull under one arm. Dunkirk was wearing the beetle shell breastplate. The shattered hole in the abdomen was a sobering reminder of its fragility. Ogma looked to Melial. "The others?"

Melial shook her head. "Nod was hurt. He's in the wagon with Tramet and Son."

"Semane?"

Melial looked stricken. Ogma remembered her dream: black nails tangled in long hair as Faceless turned its new head towards her.

"Oh no." Ogma covered her face.

"It's not... as bad as you might think."

"How can it not be?"

Melial shook her head. "There's a chance she can be saved. Her shape. She's a doll. Doll's can be put back together."

Ogma's eyes widened, but before she could ask another question, the platform lurched below them. The spindlers were moving again, which meant the tower trade was complete, and children and blots would soon be filtering back down. "There's no time to explain. Nod will follow below, but if we're going to do something, we should do it soon."

"Rora was able to tell me who made it back to the village. So the children who were kidnapped are"—she counted them off on her fingers—"Mae, Billie, Ambrose, Cauly, Isak, Clara, and Cole." She stumbled over the last name.

"And the ones lost in the fog were you and Wheeler." Rora put in quietly.

Ogma nodded grimly. Her throat tightened. She still couldn't let herself think about Wheeler.

Ogma steadied herself. "The truth is, our village was lucky. They didn't have these machines when they attacked us and they didn't burn our village. I've talked to some of the others, and they usually take nearly every child in the village."

Ogma let that sink in for a moment. She could see that everyone understood the doom that meant for the villagers who were left defenseless against the fog.

"I've found Billie, Ambrose, and Clara, but that's all so far. Ambrose says Isak is in the second tower. He's seen him sometimes and they can hear each other's bells—so the others should be there as well." She paused.

"What is it?" Dunkirk asked softly.

"Cole. He was here, but he's... not anymore. I don't know what happened. They gave him to the fog maybe or..." Ogma had to turn her face away from the tears on Rora's cheeks. "There's one more thing." Ogma took a steadying breath, not sure how to convey it. "Ambrose and the others... they're older. Eight seasons or so older than they were when the attack happened. They've been here a long time."

Rora looked up in shock. The old man was shaking his head. Dunkirk spoke first.

"I don't think I understand." The soft buzz of the translation charm hummed behind his words. "Maybe this"—he pointed to his throat—"isn't working? You say he's older?"

"Yes. He's older than I am now. And Billie and Clara have grown, too. They're just about my age."

"But how is that possible?" Rora looked from Ogma to the others.

Melial was whispering to the old man in Caravaner tongue.

"I think I know," Dunkirk's voice hummed. He nodded to himself, and then looked up at them. "It is what happened to me. It should have been obvious, right?" he half-chuckled, but his voice cracked. "When you found me, I couldn't speak your language. I had no bells until Brigid gave me these." He reached into his shirt and pulled out a leather thong with three small bells. They rang a diminished chord. "I had no idea what this fog could do. Everyone I knew..." He looked at the floor and took a breath. His voice descended to a whisper. "My brothers and sisters—they're gone. Hundreds of *years* gone."

The word *years* was unfamiliar to Ogma's ears, but in the hum of the language charm, it sounded something like 'seasons' or 'harvests.'

"I'm sorry," Ogma said, breaking the brooding silence that stretched on after Dunkirk's revelation. "But you're right. When our village was attacked, there were only a dozen puppeteers, and they just had wagons. It must have taken them seasons to build these."

She gestured at the rocking wooden platform of the spindler that they rode.

"The fog must have taken them back. Only eight seasons or so"—she glanced again at Dunkirk in sympathy—"but where we've been traveling for weeks, all the others—they've been growing up."

Rora shook her head, panic in her voice. "Ogma—how do we know they went back?"

The horrible possibility crept up Ogma's spine before she recognized it.

"What if we went forward?"

Ogma sat heavily against one of the pantry crates. "I—I don't know."

Melial spoke up, the charms in her branches tinkling softly. "I do not think you are the ones who moved. Even for the fog, this is not normal." She looked piercingly at Dunkirk. "You were the first sign of it. The first one out of time. I think this strange fog follows you."

The old man was shaking his head. He turned to Melial and began speaking in heated Caravaner tongue. Melial inclined her head.

"Or perhaps not. But still, something has happened. We have traveled the fog for generations. Nights are nights, and days are days." She cut the air with her hand. "We are not unstuck in time."

"Look—whether we moved or they did, whether we can get back home or not—we still have to do something. Not just our friends. Not just the other children. Even the blots." Ogma's voice was firmer now.

Melial spoke up. "All right, but how? What's your plan?"

This was the part Ogma was dreading. "I made a deal."

Dunkirk cocked an eyebrow. Rora looked puzzled.

"In the desert," Melial said flatly. It wasn't a question.

Ogma nodded. She waited for a reprimand, but Melial fumed silently.

Old Man Somerset clucked his tongue. "Who with?"

Melial answered for her. "Third-to-last. You *know* who she was, Ogma?"

"I think so. She was their mother. Of the puppeteers, I mean."

"She was a wizard," Melial said sharply. "One of the strongest at the end of the war. It took the Blue Wizard and the Forgotten both to bring her down. They stole the sun from her, and her people became like night."

"Her name was stolen, too," Ogma put in, firmly. "Or she lost it. It was how she controlled them, and after she'd forgotten, they were free. Someone found it. He's using it to control them again. To twist them. Eventually he turns them into this."

She rattled the canvas-covered cage, and the beast inside wailed in many voices. Inky black hands reached between the bars, pleading. Mane and Rump turned away, quaking, but Regal stared unflinching in her war mask.

"And you agreed to get it back for her?" Melial guessed.

Ogma looked at her feet. "Yes. In return for letting my friends and I go."

Melial shook her head, "Ogma— you can't trust—"

"I made her swear." Ogma met Melial's eyes firmly. "On her *name.*"

Melial's protest died in her throat. She took Ogma by the shoulders to search her face.

"Do you know how dangerous that was? How dangerous it still is if you cannot fulfill your oath?" Melial voice softened. "How do you plan to do it?"

Ogma took a deep breath. "The towers are puppeteer made. Well... blot made, anyway. Mane and Rump should be able to drive one. With you all, maybe we can drive the others too."

Melial nodded slowly. "But only until they catch us. There's too many to fight if the 'king blot' still has his hold."

"We don't need long. I'll distract him." She tried to say it with confidence. Her voice sounded steadier than she felt. "You just get these towers turned around."

"But where are we going?"

Ogma met Melial's eyes. "Never let the desert pass you by."

Ogma stood on the catwalk, wondering how in the world her friends had bought her plan. *Are we really going to do this?*

Sneaking back through the spindler without anyone noticing the new passengers had taken seasons off her life, she was sure. *Now we're about to do something really stupid.*

Dunkirk stood next to her, shrugging his shoulders as the beetle wings on his back flickered and buzzed to life. Rump and Regal stood against the wall of the platform. With the tower lurching and swaying as it strode forward, she couldn't blame them.

Between the rush of cold air and the clunking of the spindler mechanism, it was hard to hear anything. Dunkirk cocked his head towards her and raised an eyebrow, as if to say, 'Well this was *your* idea.'

Don't remind me.

Ogma jutted her chin forward and went to stand at the very lip of the platform. Dunkirk cut the wind as he took his place behind her. He reached under her arms and hugged her tightly to his chest.

"Ready?" His breath and the strange buzzing of his translation charm tickled her ear. She nodded once. He stamped a two-beat cadence with his right foot and snapped the fingers of his left hand.

No turning back.

The buzz of the beetle wings filled the air. They plummeted from the platform. Ogma closed her eyes. She felt her feet dangle as Dunkirk's wings strained against gravity. She could hear them humming. Seconds later, she felt wooden boards beneath her feet as she fell against the walls of the second tower.

She opened her eyes and looked back. She caught a flash of Dunkirk's grin as he jumped—and then he was away, flitting back to the other tower to carry over Rump and then Regal.

Ogma picked her way around the exterior of the tower until she could see her goal: the last of the spindlers—the one with the windmill on its back. She watched the fog billow in front of it as the stars danced overhead. The blue moon was just setting behind it, and the blades cast stark shadows that played across the ground in the still light. It felt like forever, but a moment later, Regal and Dunkirk were at her side.

"Rump made it?"

Regal nodded.

"Good." Ogma turned to Dunkirk. "Can you make this one? It's further out."

Dunkirk was studying the shape. "It's shorter." He peered over the lip. "And the walkway is lower." He nodded to himself. "We'll make it."

"Can you make it back? Rump will need you here."

"I'm not going with you?"

"No you're not!" Ogma was ready to tear her hair out; she'd gone over this part of the plan with him at least a dozen times. She noticed his eyes twinkling. She jabbed him in the chest with one finger. "Be serious. This tower's the biggest risk. Rump can't do it by himself. Can you make it back?"

Dunkirk sobered. "I can. Without the weight"—the translator charm buzzed—"without carrying anyone, I can go higher."

"Good enough. Let's go."

Dunkirk picked her up beneath the arms again and leapt from the catwalk.

If anything, the second trip was worse than the first. The tower loomed in front of them as the cold wind cut through Ogma's clothing. They were dropping fast... *too fast.*

"Dunkirk!"

"I see it! I see it!"

She could feel the buzzing of the beetle wings in her teeth. The wind whipped around them as they picked up speed. *Not fast enough.* They were going to miss the walkway.

Ogma stretched her arms out—

They hit the side of the tower at a bruising speed and nearly bounced off. She clung with both hands onto the wooden planks. She could feel splinters beneath her fingernails as Dunkirk hung from her waist, the beetle wings still humming, holding just enough of his weight to keep them from falling. The spindler tilted forward in its gait, and Ogma felt the wooden shingles under her feet. She clambered over the lip and Dunkirk pulled himself up with her.

"That was too close." Ogma sucked her injured fingers.

Dunkirk said nothing, but the wings on his armored back fluttered.

"Still think you can make it back?"

He looked at the tower they'd just come from. It seemed much higher as it stalked behind them. He turned and looked up the side of the windmill. He found a handhold and started climbing.

I guess that works. Ogma watched him ascend. He was still a poor climber. About two thirds of the way from the top, he turned and leapt off the tower. His wings sputtered and Ogma sucked in her breath as he dropped fifteen feet in an instant, but then they kicked back to life and he flitted to the other tower. *He's too low.* He hit the shingles below the catwalk and clung to the spindler's side. With short bursts from his wings, he flitted up from handhold to handhold in fits and starts.

Finally, he pulled himself back onto the platform and picked up Regal. *She's lighter than I am. They should make it.* Dunkirk's wings behaved this time and they managed to land on the walkway.

"See? Not so hard."

Ogma glared at him.

He touched two fingers to his brow in a cocky salute. "Good luck."

"You too."

He started his climb up the back of the windmill.

Ogma turned to Regal. "Now to get inside."

They circled the tower, looking for an unguarded hatchway. Ogma didn't expect to find any other children here, but there might be any number of the corrupted puppeteers. Finally, they found a hatch. It was unlocked.

"If we're attacked..."

Regal simply stared at Ogma from behind the war mask.

Right. If you're attacked, you'll be all set. Now, me on the other hand... Ogma took a breath and opened the door.

It was dark inside and empty. The chamber was small. It seemed to be another pantry. Gears clacked inside the mechanism and pulled the thick ropes which operated the spindler's legs. There was a ladder with a hatch leading downward into the body of the spindler, and a spiral staircase that led upward into the windmill.

"Which one do you figure goes to the controls?"

Regal pointed to the ladder leading down.

"Then I guess I'm going this way." Ogma jerked her head towards the staircase. She gave Regal a hug before they separated. "Let's save our friends."

Sneaking up the spiral staircase, Ogma felt alone and exposed. Somewhere below her, Regal would be fighting for control of the spindler, and behind her, the others fought for their own towers. *But I have a promise to keep.*

The staircase ended on a landing with a ladder that led to a hatch in the middle of the ceiling. *Probably just one big room.* There would be nowhere to hide when she emerged.

She found herself with one hand on the rungs of the ladder, unable to go higher. Tears came to her eyes. Not because she was afraid, or because of everything that had happened—not even because of Daniel or Cole—but because the person responsible was just through that hatch.

She felt the tower lurch as it began a wide turn.

I'm just standing here while Regal is fighting. She's doing her part. Ogma blinked back her tears and forced herself up the ladder.

She opened the hatch into a room that was just as exposed as she had feared. Yet, apart from that, it was nothing like what she expected. It was bare except for iron-clad fireplaces set along both walls. The floorboards were set in a herringbone pattern and pointing toward a raised dais. On the dais stood an imposing wooden chair, with claw feet and a tall back with spines that rose from the crown and shoulders.

Ogma approached the dais warily. The light cast by the fireplaces behind her flickered and went dim. She whirled. Dark figures stepped from the shadows beside the grates. They cast long shadows that fell across the floor, meeting on the chair.

At first Ogma thought it was the darkness that made their features hard to see, but as her eyes adjusted and the shapes became no clearer, she realized they were blots.

Or... She looked more closely. These still looked more like puppeteers. They were stretched and thin, and they stood before the hearths with heads bowed. Something about them was not quite like those who roamed the other spindlers.

They're shackled. Each one bore an iron band around one ankle, connected to a chain.

Ogma felt something flicker behind her. Her hackles rose, and she turned slowly towards the chair. With a strange detachment, she remembered the word for it from an old story. *Throne. It's called a throne.* And it was no longer empty.

The long shadows each puppeteer cast across the throne had solidified and merged. A taller shade sat easily there, the shadow of a haughty crown above its temple.

It beckoned Ogma closer.

Raising her chin defiantly, Ogma strode to the base of the dais.

"Let my friends go." Her voice was steady and carried through the room.

The shadow king fell back in its chair, flickering at the edges.

What's happening? Ogma looked back at the shackled puppeteers. They quailed.

A deep, throaty laugh filled the throne room, echoing through the whole of the tower until Ogma had to cover her ears. The shackled puppeteers cowered, their hands clapped to the sides of their heads.

"Why are you doing this? You're hurting them!"

The king's laughter stopped, and it leaned forward in its chair. "No." The voice shivered the walls. "I am hurting *no one.*"

"Yes you are! The puppeteers *hate* you. You change them! Can't you see you're hurting them?" She gestured at the shaking shapes shackled to the fireplaces.

"Puppeteers?" It spat the word with contempt. "They are shadows! *I* am the puppeteer."

"But you're a shadow, too!" The king fell silent. Ogma pressed further.

"What about the children? They're afraid. They want to go home!"

"They are *not* afraid!" The shadow king's fist crashed down on the arm of the chair, and the dais shook. "They *are* home. Here, they are safe. Here, I protect them."

Ogma felt tears in her eyes and blinked them away angrily.

"No you don't! You hurt them. Daniel died." The image of the boy's broken body came unbidden. Ogma choked back a sob.

"Daniel?" The shadow-voice quavered. There was an absent confusion in its tone. "Who's Daniel?"

Ogma remembered little Emma's dazed expression and the ugly lump on her temple.

"How many of them have you hurt like Emma? How many of them died?"

"Em-Emma?" The voice still shook the halls, but there was a crack in it. "I never hurt Emma." The voice hardened again. "No one is taken by the fog. Here we are safe."

"No. They're taken by *you* instead."

The shadow king rose to its feet and bellowed. "Better me than the fog! They protect me!" The voice was sullen and defensive.

Ogma looked up sharply. "Don't you mean *you* protect *them*? That's what you said before."

"That is what I say *now! I protect them from the fog!*" The shadow king paused, visibly controlling its anger. The voice softened, and the shape sat back in the throne, throwing a knee casually over one arm.

"I will protect you also," the voice promised. "You need not fear the fog."

"But you didn't." Hot tears fell from Ogma's cheeks. Her hands clenched. "You've already been to my village. You took my friends, and you killed Daniel, and you hurt Emma... and..." The sobs became too much. Ogma had to stop to breathe, but the shadow king recoiled, as if her words were hurting it.

"You beat Wheeler. You were hurting him over and over... and then the fog came. He was so afraid of it..."

The shadow stood. "I hurt no one."

"What about Cole?" Ogma spat. "Do you *remember* him? He was my friend." The shadow king shrank back, retreating behind the throne. Ogma was so angry that no trace of fear was left in her heart. She gripped her bells tightly in one hand. She could almost hear the chimes of her friends.

She chimed her own melancholy chord softly. "You let it take me."

The words struck the shadow like a blow. The voice broke. "I didn't want this. Ogma, please..."

Her head snapped up. "How do you know my name?"

The shape was silent. The room darkened, and Ogma took a step forward, eyeing the shadow suspiciously. It flickered in the dark.

"This is my place!" The shadow surged upwards, towering almost to the ceiling. It reached out its hands and twisted the air. On either side of her, the puppeteers' bodies melted and flowed like water, their fingers lengthening into talons and brutal spines emerging from their backs.

"Stop! You're hurting them!"

But the shadow king didn't, and the puppeteers shuddered and fell to the floor.

One by one, they stood and their hollow sockets locked onto Ogma's face. They stepped forward jerkily, each limb dragged as if on a string. Ogma backed away until the dais left her nowhere else to go.

The blots stalked forward. She turned.

"How do you know my name?" Strong arms grasped her like bands of iron, pulling her back from the throne. "No! You have to stop this! Let me go!"

"Give her to the fog," the voice growled. Ogma kicked and bit at the puppeteers, but they dragged her towards the hatch in the floor. She was nearly there when a shape burst up from the ladder.

"Regal! It's not safe—run!"

The small puppeteer, no taller than Ogma herself, clambered out of the hatch, and drew herself up. When she raised her head, the gruesome mask which covered her face bared its teeth in the firelight. The puppeteers holding Ogma recoiled, slackening their grip on her arms.

"What's this?" The shadow king's voice was surprised, and then quickly became silken and soft again. "A new puppet to play with?"

Ogma could see the shadow king's hands on the far wall as it raised its arms. *Wait. That's... it can't be.* The fingers twisted and with them, Regal twisted in pain. Shadows danced on the wall behind her and Regal's features changed. Her arms became wings, then chicken feet, then hooves. She fell to the ground as her body changed from shape to shape. Ice crawled up Ogma's spine.

This is wrong. I know this.

Ogma finally understood. "Wheeler—no!"

Everything stopped. Regal became herself again, lying on the floor. Ogma turned. The shadows flickered and disappeared. A thin, haggard man with a dirty beard stood on the dais, tears streaming down his face. He stared at Ogma with wild eyes.

"It *is* you." He stumbled down the dais steps. He spoke in his own voice now, not the voice of the shadow king.

Ogma felt the tears on her cheeks echoing his own.

His voice broke. "You found me."

The puppeteers surged forward in wordless anger, straining at the end of their chains. The haggard man—the shadow king—*Wheeler*—cowered. He put one hand to his chest and there was a dull clatter—a muffled note. The other hand twisted into a claw, reaching for the raging puppeteers. They twisted back and recoiled.

"Stop hurting them!" Ogma shouted.

Wheeler looked up at her, expression wild, his hold on the shadows forgotten. "I—I didn't want to—"

Surging with anger, the shackled puppeteers lunged. Their chains jerked them back, but one stretched its arm sickeningly far and grabbed Wheeler by the ankle. They pulled him from the dais, his head striking the corner with a *crack*.

Blow after blow rained down from those inky black arms, hard as iron bands.

"No! Please stop."

Ogma saw him again—the young Wheeler, the one she remembered—being beaten by the dark shapes outside the walls so she could try to save the others. Before the fog took them all away.

They ignored her. The blows kept falling. Ogma threw herself at their backs, but the twisted shapes were too strong for her to overcome.

Regal waded in to the fray, war mask grimacing, trying to pull them away from Wheeler. The mask gave her a terrible strength, and she threw two of them aside before one of them gathered up its chains and swung, knocking her back against the wall. The mask clattered to the floor.

Regal picked herself up slowly. She was trembling and yet still held a quiet dignity. She clambered up onto the dais and stood on the throne. Opening the pouch at her belt, she took out her crown, placing it carefully on her head.

They don't see you! They don't care.

Blow after blow crushed Wheeler's body.

Please, make them stop.

Silence filled the room. A silence so loud and resonant that Ogma couldn't move, or think, or even breathe. The puppeteers froze, heads turning as one towards the throne. Ogma tore her eyes from Wheeler's crumpled form.

Regal lowered a wooden horn from her lips. Slowly, the silent note faded.

The shackled puppeteers advanced on the throne, dragging their chains behind them.

Ogma's heart was in her throat.

As one, the puppeteers fell to their knees before the throne. Their twisted shapes began to soften.

Ogma exhaled and ran to Wheeler's side. He was unconscious, but breathing.

"How could you?" She put a hand to his cheek, feeling the wiry tangle of his unkempt beard. There were lines under his eyes. His face was hollow. *He's so much older. How can he be so old?*

But she knew how. The others were older, too, but the fog hadn't taken him with the wagons. It took him in the open, all alone. *He was the oldest. He should have been off the wall already. I should have taken over when he asked. I should have let him rest.*

Ogma could picture him wandering in the fog, as lost as she had been, but so much more afraid. *He knew he was getting too old.* She could see him wandering, day after day, each day wondering when the fog would be able to touch him. When it would send a phantom to tear him apart.

Beneath the lines and the bruises and the split lip, she could see a memory of the boy beneath.

She rocked back and forth with his head in her lap. "I don't understand." She wept, tears falling on his face. "How could it be you? How could it?" She found the leather cord around his neck, and pulled out the clear tenor bell, battered and dented. Her tears left streaks in the grime. She tried to ring it, but it clattered hollowly.

What happened to you? She turned the bell over in her hands. Wheeler had replaced the clapper with something else.

A small piece of wire was wound around something made of glass.

Understanding struck Ogma like a thunderbolt.

"There'd been a boy once. He took something."

HE HAS MY NAME—THE ONE THEY TOOK FROM ME. HE WAS AS LOST AS YOU ARE. OUT OF TIME AND OUT OF PLACE.

"The phylactery," she breathed. "It was you. You stole it from the caravan."

She suddenly remembered the plan—*her* plan. "Oh no. No! Where are we? How far have the towers gone?"

Ogma searched frantically for some way to get outside.

A doorway behind the throne opened to a small cloister. A sour smell filled the room and it was cluttered with dirty clothes. *This is where he slept?* Ogma strode to the opposite wall and flung wide the two shuttered doors. She felt cool air pulling at her clothes as one of the windmill blades turned in front of the balcony, blocking out the stars. Ogma raced to the balcony rail and looked out.

Black sand glittered below the tower, stretching out to the horizon.

"No. No, no, no..."

Regal arrived at Ogma's elbow.

"We have to turn around! Tell them to turn around."

Regal cocked her head quizzically, the crown slipping down her temple.

"I know this was the plan! It's *my* plan! It was a bad plan! We can't let her have him—he's not—he's not... who I thought."

Regal studied her face.

She has no reason to pity him. Ogma had no words. *She shouldn't forgive him—I shouldn't—but I can't let this happen to him. Not this.*

Finally Regal nodded, touching Ogma on the cheek. She turned and ran for the control room.

"Come on... come on..." Ogma urged her on and turned back to the balcony. As before, the stars were hard points of light, still and cold. They were reflected beneath an absent horizon by the glittering grains of sand.

Wait. A black spot grew in the distance. *No—not now.*

Stars sparkled and winked out as the dark shape grew.

The tower lurched and began to turn. She could see the other towers behind her, and even Nod's wagon, paint chipped and wood cracked, struggling over the dunes behind them. They were at least a mile from the edge of the sand. Ogma cupped her hands around her mouth.

"Turn around! Go back! We have to go back!"

A shape emerged from the tower. "Ogma! Is that you?"

"Isak!" Later she would have time to be overjoyed at seeing him. Right now, she just needed him to get the tower turned around. "Yes! It's me! Go back! Tell them to go back!"

"What?" A wind was rising. Grains of black sand stung Ogma's eyes.

"Go back!" The wind caught her words and carried them away.

It howled, sand swirling. Ogma looked up. The stars above her winked out as a dark wave crested over the tower.

The world went black. Ogma could neither see her hands in front of her face nor feel the boards of the tower below her. She groped in darkness.

She felt cool water lapping around her ankles. And then the world faded back into view. She was standing on the mesa. Stars glittered above, reflected in the black water below.

Ogma looked to her right. Wheeler was there, dazed, eyes unfocused.

Ogma looked to her left. Dunkirk and the old man were there, standing beside the caravan wagon, bright colors turned to gray under the night sky. Melial stood in the foot box and Nod sat beside her, one arm in a sling. *That's right, he was hurt.* She wondered vaguely if Tramet and Son were inside.

How WELL YOU'VE DONE, MY CHILD. The voice grew in ripples on the pool.

Ogma looked before her and saw the shadow against the stars.

AND HOW I WORRIED THAT YOU MIGHT ABANDON YOUR POOR MOTHER.

Dark, child-sized silhouettes gathered where the stars met the pool.

AND YOU BROUGHT ME NOT ONLY MY NAME, BUT THE ONE WHO STOLE IT.

Wheeler was staring vaguely at the stars, muttering to himself.

The voice turned its attention to the caravan. IT HAS BEEN LONG SINCE SHEPHERDS VENTURED HERE. AND NEVER HAVE THEY BROUGHT MY CHILDREN WITH THEM.

Nod spoke and Ogma could hear the effort it took—the formless pressure bearing down on all of them. "We come peacefully in fulfillment of a bargain."

IT WAS NOT YOUR BARGAIN TO FULFILL, the voice rebuked. Ogma felt the attention flick over to her and then back.

BUT YOU KNOW YOUR COURTESIES, AND THUS YOU MAY STAY.

Nod inclined his head respectfully but did not speak again.

The gaze turned to Somerset and Dunkirk beside him. OLD CHILD, I NAME YOU. YOU ARE NOT WELCOME. AND TO

BRING A SOLDIER OF MY ENEMY HERE? THAT IS NOT WISE, WHATEVER ARMOR HE MAY WEAR.

Dunkirk stiffened, but Somerset held him back with one arm.

Ogma felt the gaze of the dark shape return to her.

SO MANY GIFTS FOR YOUR MOTHER, the voice purred. YOU EVEN BROUGHT MY CHILDREN BACK TO ME! YOU ARE A GOOD CHILD. I ACCEPT YOUR GIFTS, AND IN REWARD YOU MAY COME STAY WITH ME.

The voice filled Ogma's mind. It was hard to think. Hard to remember where she'd just been. She wanted to acquiesce, to join her mother, to live here in the pool.

"No," Ogma barely managed to whisper it, but the word spread across the pool. "We had a bargain."

IT WAS A POOR BARGAIN. The voice rumbled. YOU BROUGHT MANY GIFTS. YOU COULD HAVE MORE. YOU COULD STAY. The words smothered all doubt.

Yes, that's what I want. I want to st—

"No." Ogma said it more firmly this time. She felt the pressure in her mind easing somewhat. "I hold you to our bargain. You swore that me and anyone I called friend would go free. Even your children!"

She could feel the voice gathering its strength. Darkness blotted out the stars and wind lashed the pool.

"You swore on your name!" Ogma shouted into the gale.

The shadow howled in impotent fury.

FINE! THEN I WILL HAVE WHAT IS **MINE**.

The darkness gathered around Wheeler. He shook his head, muttering under his breath. A faint glow appeared at his collar. The phial drifted from beneath his shirt, pulling the bell with it on the end of its tether. Wheeler stumbled forward as it tugged at his neck. He raised a hand to his collar.

"No... it's mine." He muttered the words feverishly.

It is *not* yours, **thief**. The phial jerked forward, leather cord snapping. Wheeler fell to his knees.

"Don't hurt him!" The phial froze in the air above the pool, ripples radiating out beneath it. "Take your name but *please*, I call him friend as well."

No. No, clever girl. That is too far. The thief is mine. He stole from me—it is my **right**.

Ogma covered her ears, but the voice thundered in her head.

Wheeler's eyes snapped to the phial glittering in the air before him, and he surged to his feet. "No! It's mine!"

He splashed through the pool. In an instant, a dozen child shadows sprang up around him, tearing his sleeves, tripping him by his ankles. His face twisted in a snarl, and he laced his fingers together. The child shadows flickered and recoiled.

He leapt for the phylactery.

The formless shadow that was Third-to-Last swelled and thundered. An inhuman roar filled Ogma's mind—and Wheeler's hands closed on the phial. Before anyone could move or think—before even She could act—he brought his hands to his mouth.

The sound of glass breaking between his teeth filled the pool. Ogma shuddered, but couldn't look away. He swallowed and choked—coughing wetly. At last, he straightened and spat into the pool. Red stars danced at his feet.

Thief! Insolent thief! the voice raged. Small ripples crested into waves that caught Ogma's knees and knocked her down.

Tricksters! Ogma felt the full force of Her hatred. You are **not** a good child. Ogma cowered, and the dark water began to rise.

I will take you all for this! The voice began to laugh, a terrible sound that even the stars shrank away from. And for

NOTHING, YOU BETRAY ME. FOR NOTHING! THE NAME IS IN HIM STILL. I FEEL IT IN HIS MIND!

Wheeler coughed again and thick droplets splashed into the pool. He wove on his feet and took an uncertain step forward.

Ogma couldn't move—couldn't speak. She tried to climb to her feet, but the water climbed with her—to her waist, to her chest. It scratched like sand against her skin. She could see the others sinking fast, trying to keep their heads above the lapping dunes.

Still Wheeler walked forward, captive under the shadow's gaze. For him, the water came no higher than his ankles.

Please no, not after all this. As the water closed over Ogma's head, she felt sand filling her nose and mouth.

Somehow she could still see—see Wheeler reach out for the dark shape—see it lean down to embrace him—

See the shadow that stood in his place once SHE touched him.

Ogma closed her eyes, unable to breathe, unable to cry.

"Stop this," Melial's voice pealed faintly, like a distant bell. "Your bargain is filled. You have the name."

All at once, Ogma stood again in shallow water. She gasped for breath.

Dunkirk doubled over coughing, and the old man was clutching his chest. Melial held a small silver charm in hand, which glowed faintly, reflecting an echo of the moon in the pool below.

THE BARGAIN WAS BETRAYED. YOU ARE FORFEIT.

"No. The bargain was for the name, and you have the name now."

Ogma spoke through a mouth still dry with sand. "You said it yourself," she sobbed. "You took him. You have the name after all. You have to let us go."

The voice considered.

Ogma's shoulders fell. She hardly cared if SHE accepted the bargain or not. She just wanted this to be over.

"Are you not fair?"

The voice growled. **I AM**. WE HOLD THE BARGAIN FILLED. YOU MAY GO.

The wind began to rise, and Ogma felt black sand stinging her cheek.

"Wait!"

The voice rumbled warningly. I'LL HAVE NO MORE OF YOUR **CONDITIONS**, CHILD.

"Please. When you have the name from him—or if he forgets—please, will you let him go?"

The voice was silent and the stars began to dim as the sand swirled around the pool.

Ogma heard Nod speaking slowly and deliberately, as he always did. "It would be just, Old Mother. It is the bargain you agreed: to let her and her friends go once you have the name. She calls him friend."

ONCE WE HAVE THE NAME—**AND** HE HAS FORGOTTEN IT.

"You are merciful," Nod replied.

Ogma's vision went dark once more.

Ogma found herself on an obsidian dune. The sun was rising over the fog to the east, dancing on the horizon. But here, on the edge of the desert, unmoving stars still stood above.

Ogma looked to her left. There was the single, battered caravan. Melial stood in the footbox next to Nod, Dunkirk and Somerset beside it.

Ogma looked to her right. Wheeler was gone.

The spindlers loomed over them. She could hear the faint

sounds of the children calling to each other in confusion. She heard bells chiming.

Ogma watched the sunrise.

Nod touched her shoulder. She hadn't heard him approach. She put her hand over his taloned fingers. Dunkirk stood beside him.

"I couldn't save him."

Nod squeezed her shoulder gently. "You might yet. She may still release him."

"She'll change him—he won't be the same."

Dunkirk spoke softly. "He'd already changed."

Ogma bowed her head.

"I—I'm sorry. I know he was your friend. He might have been mine, if I'd known him better."

"At least here the fog can't find him. He was so afraid." She turned to Nod. "Why do we get more scared when we get older?"

Footsteps pounded the sand behind them. Ogma glanced back to see Rora running up the dunes. She pulled up breathlessly.

"What happened? All the inky, blobby things—the blots?— they just gave up." She grabbed her knees and panted. "Is it over?"

"It is," Ogma said quietly.

"What do we do now?"

Ogma looked up at the nearest spindler, the windmill on its back turning lazily, and then out at the shifting landscape on the horizon.

"We sail the fog."

THANK YOU

I hope you enjoyed Ogma's story. If you'd like to support my work, please visit **aspenthornpress.com** to sign up for my newsletter, find information on upcoming releases, buy special editions or other merchandise, and more.

As an independent author, my community of readers is my most precious resource. I'd love to hear from you through any of the channels listed on my website, and I'd love for you to share my work with your friends.

All the best,
T.H. Lehnen

About the Author

T.H. Lehnen is an author who believes that young adult and children's literature is simply more honest about the magic in the world. Under Aspen & Thorn Press, he writes young adult fantasy for children who are old souls, and old souls who are children at heart.

He lives with his family in Portland, OR, and studied creative writing, philosophy, and English literature at Reed college. When he is not writing, he is tinkering with machines mechanical and digital (though he has yet to figure out how to fit a sports car through a wardrobe).

Learn more at: **aspenthornpress.com**

goodreads.com/thlehnen

patreon.com/thlehnen

instagram.com/thlehnen

tiktok.com/@fogandfireflies

facebook.com/thlehnen

x.com/thlehnen

amazon.com/author/thlehnen

youtube.com/thlehnen

bookbub.com/authors/t-h-lehnen

linkedin.com/in/hestenet

Printed in the USA
CPSIA information can be obtained
at www.ICGtesting.com
JSHW021144030324
58379JS00003B/5